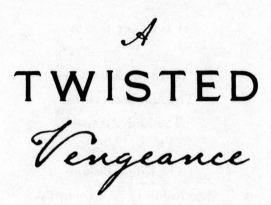

A

TWISTED

Vengeance

*The **Owen Archer** Mysteries*
The Apothecary Rose
The Lady Chapel
The Nun's Tale
The King's Bishop
The Riddle of St. Leonard's
A Gift of Sanctuary
A Spy for the Redeemer
The Cross-legged Knight
The Guilt of Innocents
A Vigil of Spies

*The **Margaret Kerr** Mysteries*
A Trust Betrayed
The Fire in the Flint
A Cruel Courtship

Historical Novels (as **Emma Campion**)
The King's Mistress
A Triple Knot

A TWISTED Vengeance

A Kate Clifford Mystery

CANDACE ROBB

PEGASUS CRIME

NEW YORK LONDON

A TWISTED VENGEANCE

Pegasus Books Ltd.
148 W. 37th Street, 13th Floor
New York, NY 10018

First Pegasus Books cloth edition May 2017

Interior design by Maria Fernandez

Library of Congress Cataloging-in-Publication Data is available.

ISBN: 978-1-68177-452-7

10 9 8 7 6 5 4 3 2 1

Printed in the United States of America
Distributed by W. W. Norton & Company

For mothers and daughters

A Twisted Vengeance

GLOSSARY

⸺◦◦◦⸺

BEGUINES: a community of women leading lives of religious devotion who, unlike those who entered convents, were not bound by permanent vows; they dedicated themselves to chastity and charity and worked largely among the poor and the sick, usually in urban settings.

FACTOR: in business, one who is trusted to transact business as an agent, deputy, or representative of a merchant/trader.

KELPIE: a shape-changing aquatic spirit of Scottish legend. Its name may derive from the Scottish Gaelic words "cailpeach" or "colpach," meaning heifer or colt. Kelpies are said to haunt rivers and streams, usually in the shape of a horse. The sound of a kelpie's tail entering the water is said to resemble that of thunder.

LADY ALTAR: an altar dedicated to and holding a statue of the Blessed Virgin Mary.

LOLLARDS: beginning in 14th century England, those inspired by the teachings of John Wycliffe, essentially stating that the Catholic church had been corrupted by temporal matters, and urging a return to the simpler values of living a life in imitation of Christ; by the 15th century the term "lollard" was a synonym for "heretic" in England.

MARTHA HOUSE: a term derived from Bible story of Lazarus and his two sisters, Martha (active) and Mary (contemplative); one of the many terms used throughout Europe to indicate a household of lay religious women dedicated to serving the community.

MAISON DIEU: hospital.

SEMPSTER: an early form of the word "seamstress."

Family Relationships

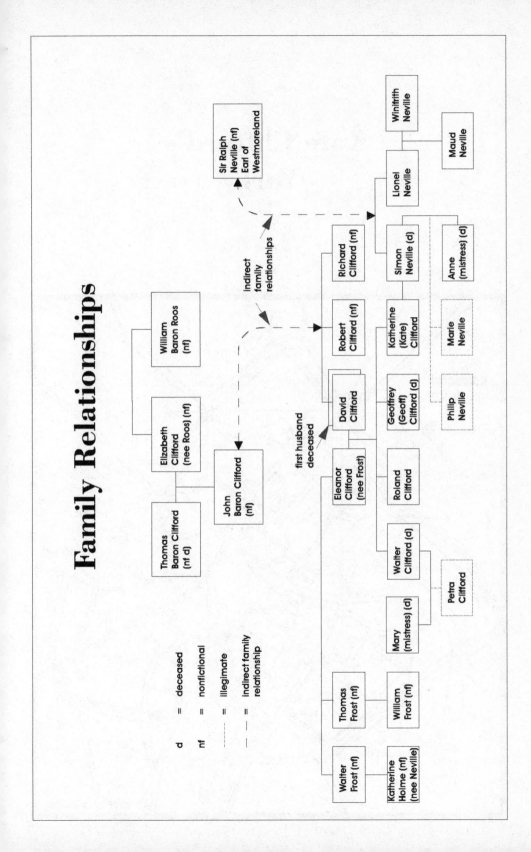

Kate Clifford's York

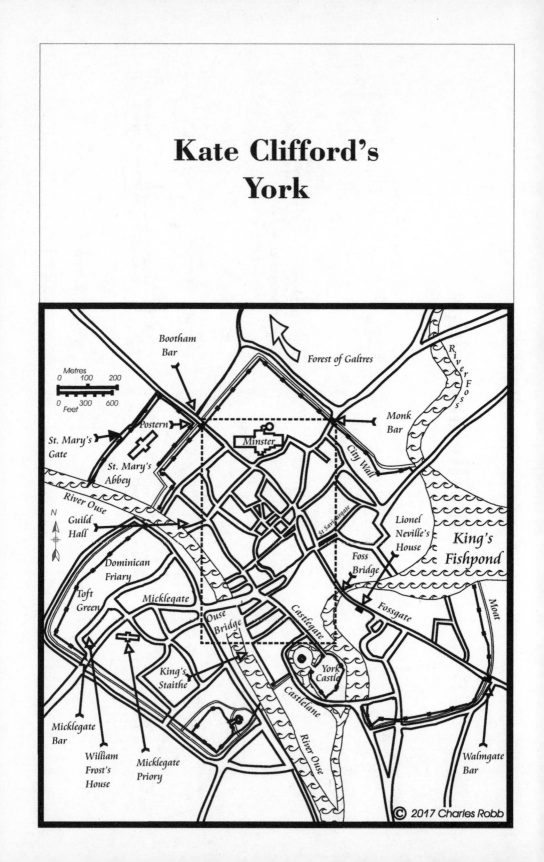

York Minster

Lop Lane

High Petergate

Blake Street

Stonegate

Low Petergate

Swinegate

Goodramgate

Girdlergate

Davygate

Coffiergate

Shambles

Hosier Lane

Fossgate

Lionel
Neville's
House

William
Frost's
House

Ousegate

Coppergate

Nessgate

Castlegate

Thursgail

Hertergate

Franciscan
Priory

York
Castle

1 Masons' Lodge
2 Chapter House
3 Deanery
4 Sir Alan's House
5 Kate's Guesthouse
6 York Tavern
7 Richard Clifford's Gift
8 Hugh Grantham's House
9 The Bedern
10 Hawise's House
11 John Paris's House
12 The Martha House
13 Thomas Holme's House
14 Kate Clifford's House
15 Holme's Gardens
16 Maison Dieu
17 St. Mary's Church
18 Merchants' Hall

Angels are bright still, though the brightest fell.
Though all things foul would wear the brows of grace,
Yet Grace must still look so.
　　　　—William Shakespeare, *Macbeth* IV, 3, 22–24

The fall is so deep, she is so rightly fallen, that the soul cannot fill herself from such an abyss.

—Marguerite Porete

PROLOGUE

York, second week in July, 1399

The terror of the dream never abated. She opened her eyes in the dark prison of her childhood bedchamber. Heard his ragged breathing, smelled his breath—cloying sweetness of wine, rancid stench of bile—as he leaned down, reaching for her, whispering of his need, his hunger. She opened her mouth to scream, but she was mute. She struggled to push him away, but her arms were limp, heavy, dead to her.

Why do you not strike him down, my Lord? How can you abide such abomination, my Savior? Are you not my Savior? Is he right, that I deserve this?

It is a dream, only a dream, now, tonight, it is truly only a dream, he is dead, he can no longer hurt me, it is a dream, wake up wake up wake up.

She sat up, panting, her shift clinging to her sweat-soaked body. A noise. Someone moving about on the other side of her door, in the kitchen. Outside her window it was the soft gray of a midsummer night. Who would be moving about the kitchen in the middle of the night? Why had Dame Eleanor lodged her here, across the garden from her sisters, all alone? But they did not know she was alone. They thought Nan, the serving maid, would be here. Perhaps it was only Nan she heard, returning early.

He had sworn that he would find her, rise from the grave and take her, that they were bound for eternity. Whoever it was, they were at the door. The dagger. She slipped it from beneath her pillow. The door creaked open. Not Nan—much too tall for Nan. A man's breath, a man's smell. He took a step in. She leapt from the bed, throwing herself on him, forcing him to fall backward into the kitchen. Stabbing him, stabbing, stabbing. Not speaking. *Never speak. Never make a noise. He will kill me if I wake the others.*

"God have mercy. Have mercy!" he wheezed.

She stopped. This voice was soft. Frightened. *God forgive me. It is not him. Not Father.*

She dropped her dagger in the doorway as she backed into her room. Heart pounding, fighting the fear and confusion clouding her mind, she dressed, stumbling in her haste. She must think what to do. Berend. He was strong and kind. He would help her. She would go through the gate to Dame Katherine's kitchen and wake Berend.

She retrieved her dagger. Bloody. Slippery. Wiped it on her skirt. Tucked it in her girdle. Stepped to the door, lifting her skirts to step over his body. But there was no body. *God help me!*

A hand over her mouth. He spun her round and clutched her so tightly she felt his blood flowing, soaking the back of her gown, the warmth of it. She gagged on the sickly sweet smell of it, like her father's wine-breath. He dragged her outside into the garden. The great wolfhounds began to bark. Salvation? She struggled, but he did not lose his grip; even when he stumbled he grasped her so tightly she could not breathe. Her feet skimmed the grass, the packed mud of the alley. *I am dying.*

A jolt. She was pulled free, falling forward.

"Run to the church." It was the soldier who watched all night from the street. More than a soldier, a guardian angel. He kicked the wounded man in the stomach.

She curled over herself, gasping for breath.

"Get up. Run to the church. Do not stop. Do not look back." He nudged her, gently. "Run!" Suddenly there were more men. They rushed at her savior.

She rose and ran, her breath a searing knife in her throat and chest, but she ran, ran for her life. She heard the men attacking the soldier, bone against flesh against bone. Surely an angel could not suffer mortal wounds. But she would pray for him. To the church across Castlegate. Door locked. Stumbling round to the side, where the sisters entered. Footsteps coming her way. She fled, and there it was, the door, opening, the candle by the lady altar. She crumpled to the floor, the cool tiles. She stretched out upon them, bloodied, cursed, saved.

1

IN THE NIGHT

———❧❧❧———

Yet again Kate was undone by her mother's biting tongue. A gift of fresh berry tarts was received with delight by her mother's three companions, but Eleanor Clifford responded with a tirade about Kate's lack of religious fervor. A month earlier, the three beguines would have looked confused at Dame Eleanor's odd response to such an offering from her daughter, but apparently they had grown accustomed to this peculiar aspect of their benefactor's behavior and simply removed themselves to the other side of the hall. Their movement did nothing to disrupt Eleanor from her recitation of opportunities for spiritual advancement ignored by her errant daughter—joining their morning prayer, attending daily mass, saying the rosary and evening prayers before the lady altar in the hall, encouraging her wards to join her in all these activities.

"Yours is a singularly ungodly life, Katherine," she concluded.

A strange lecture from the mother who had raised Kate to view with skepticism all those who wore their spiritual beliefs like a badge and who had never encouraged such activities in their home. Growing up in the border country of Northumberland, Kate had been taught to rely on her kin, her wits, and her knowledge of the countryside rather than prayers. "Prayers are for spineless cowards and addle-pated sophists," Eleanor had told her children time and again. Their remote parish shared a priest with several other clusters of farms and manors so that they heard mass infrequently, and, when they did, the cleric's rambling sermons occasioned much eye-rolling and giggling among the children, while the adults sat with heads bowed in slumber.

So Kate might be forgiven for questioning the sincerity of her mother's newfound piety. She was not the only person perplexed by Eleanor's return to York in the company of three beguines, or poor sisters, with whom she intended to found a Martha House. It had caused a stir in her cousin William Frost's household and more widely among Kate's fellow merchants and guild members. All wanted to know what catastrophe had left Eleanor widowed, pious, and fleeing from Strasbourg.

"Well? What of that?" Eleanor loudly demanded.

Glancing up at her mother's flushed face enclosed in the incongruous wimple, Kate could do nothing but shrug, having stopped listening early in her mother's tirade. After all, she'd heard it all before.

Growling, Eleanor took Kate by the shoulders and shook her. A mistake.

Kate's father had trained her to defend herself, and she had spent her years since his death perfecting her martial skills. In one sweeping motion she caught her mother's hands and used them to push her so that she lost her balance and stumbled backward against a—fortunately—heavy table.

Sisters Clara, Brigida, and Dina rushed to Eleanor's aid, helping her to a chair.

Knowing there was nothing she could say or do to make peace in the moment, Kate turned to leave.

But Eleanor was not finished. "What will the children you claim to hold so dear think when they learn their guardian is a bawd? Have you thought of that?"

Kate had established her guesthouse on Petergate before she added two wards and a niece to her household. The fees wealthy merchants and the occasional noble or cleric paid for a discreet night with their mistresses had been necessary to pay off her late husband Simon Neville's debts and provide for the masses he had requested for his soul. By the time Simon's children by a prostitute in Calais had been brought to Kate upon their mother's death, the household servants were already in the habit of discretion. Indeed, her clients paid for secrecy. However, worldly-wise Marie and Phillip had ferreted out the nature of the guesthouse, their own mother having been the mistress of many married men. The first thing Phillip, a boy of eleven, had said in Kate's presence was a matter-of-fact explanation of what her brother-in-law Lionel had intended in Calais: *He meant to comfort Maman and fill her with another baby she could not feed.* Too late to shelter them. Pray God her mother never discovered how much they knew. But how had *Eleanor* learned of it?

"And who is to tell them? You, Mother? Is that what your sudden obeisance to the Church has taught you—to slander your daughter? To undo all my work in healing three children who have already lost so much?" God in heaven, Kate had said it aloud. She had vowed to remain silent, to refuse her mother's bait.

"Your life is a shambles, Katherine." With every word, Eleanor sought to undermine all that Kate had accomplished. Why? Why would a mother abuse her daughter in such wise?

"I am leaving you now," Kate said, stepping through the door and out into the night.

At least she did not include me in the attack, her dead twin whispered in her mind.

Yes, at least that, Geoff.

Eleanor had brought Kate to York shortly after Geoff's death in the hope that distance would sever the powerful link between the twins that remained strong even in death. She did not understand that, as twins, Kate and Geoff shared souls, life force. There could be no sundering. Her twin's spirit lived within Kate, and she feared the bond between mother and child, though not nearly so strong as that between twins, might allow Eleanor to sense his presence. Apparently not. Or at least, not this night. A mercy.

Her mother's tumble did not prevent her from pursuit. "You are a young widow whose husband left you mired in debt and burdened with his two bastards, and yet you have turned away all the prominent men who have asked for your hand," Eleanor proclaimed from the doorway.

Kate knew she should keep walking. In such a mood, her mother could hear nothing. But the word *bastards*. If Marie and Phillip learned she spoke of them that way . . . "I have asked you not to call them that, Mother," Kate threw back over her shoulder.

"It is only the truth."

Kate paused, turned to shake her head at the gray-robed, white-wimpled taunter in the doorway. "You do not say that of your grandchild Petra, though it is equally true of her."

Eleanor took a step across the threshold. "If you care for the three of them as you claim, you have a duty to remarry. Yet look at you, bone buttons instead of silver, your hair untidy, skimping on the cloth in your skirts—you are revealing your penurious situation, frightening off future suitors."

"A duty to remarry?" Kate stepped closer so that all the neighborhood might not hear. "Were you not listening when I explained Simon's will? I lose the business if I remarry."

"You will not need it."

"No? After all my unpleasant discoveries about Simon, I trust no man."

"You have a duty to those children—"

"As did you to me. Yet you betrothed me to Simon Neville without a care as to his true circumstances. Or did you know of his profligate ways? Perhaps you knew he had a mistress with children in Calais. But you were so eager to be rid of me that you handed me over to the first man who showed an interest."

"The marriage was to protect you."

"Protect me? I was barely fifteen, Mother. My parents should have protected me. I was grieving for my twin brother. And my brother Roland. Did you ever stop to think of my feelings?"

"How can you say such things to me?" Eleanor raised a hand to slap Kate.

Kate blocked her, turned, and hurried away through the hedgerow gate, cursing herself for again being caught up in the fray.

⸻❦⸻

Of course Kate was aware of her delicate situation. It kept her awake at night, it curdled her food. When Simon had died over two years earlier she discovered that he had left enormous debts and a will that left her in control of his business only until such time as she remarried, when it would go to his brother, Lionel. And then, almost a year to the day of Simon's death, Lionel appeared on her doorstep with the unpleasant surprise of the recently orphaned Marie and Phillip. Swallowing her pride and hurt, Kate had taken them in, determined to love and care for them as her own.

For more than a year she had worked hard to care for her wards while using all her wits to accrue wealth at a speed sufficient to appease her creditors with frequent payments, while quietly setting enough aside that she would someday have the means to choose whether or not to marry, according to her own desire. Once she had set aside sufficient funds in her own name, she would sell off the assets of Simon's business, pay the remainder of the debts, and hand Lionel his brother's business, with pleasure.

And then, in late winter last, a tragedy of her mother's making brought Petra, the daughter of Kate's eldest brother, into the household. The child had been orphaned by Eleanor's careless rekindling of an old feud that had earlier cost the lives of two of her sons. That winter her last son died as well as three others, strangers, and, if it had not been for Petra's help, Kate's ward Phillip would have been murdered as well.

Her niece was a dear child for whom the city was even more alien than it had been for Kate six years earlier. But however much Kate welcomed her, Petra's arrival upset the fragile balance of the household; now Marie and Phillip needed to be reassured that with her niece's arrival, a blood relative, they were no less cherished than before. Indeed, Marie's rivalry with Petra had hastened her brother's decision to lodge in the home of Hugh Grantham, a master mason at the minster stoneyard under whom he was apprenticed. Though Phillip was realizing his dream with the apprenticeship, Kate worried that he had felt pushed out betimes.

On the heels of the tragedy, Eleanor Clifford herself arrived unexpectedly in York, announcing that she meant to establish a Martha House in the city with three beguines who accompanied her from Strasbourg. Newly widowed, for a second time, Eleanor gave no explanation for her hasty departure from Strasbourg on the death of Ulrich Smit. To say that Kate did not welcome Eleanor's return was an understatement.

And now her mother had moved into a house just across the hedgerow.

As Kate shut the gate behind her, her kitchen door opened and her Irish wolfhounds rushed out to greet her. Lille butted Kate's hand, wanting her ears rubbed. Ghent leaned his warm bulk against Kate, lifting his head so she might scratch his throat. Here she was welcome, loved, treasured.

"Did they enjoy the tarts?" Her cook, Berend, had followed the hounds from the kitchen, his powerful, battle-scarred bulk a reassuring presence.

Kate gave each hound one more round before she straightened. "The sisters blessed you for them, but Mother took the offering as an opportunity to lecture me on my lack of piety."

Berend chuckled. "A riddle. How is a fruit tart like a penance? I should hope it would be received as a blessing."

"*You* are a blessing, Berend. And no doubt Mother is now happily partaking of one of your berry tarts with the beguines. Who can resist them?"

"Perhaps. But I doubt she is any merrier than you are," he said.

"She is troubled, I know. And that is the cause of this vexing behavior. But why she will not confide in me—why she instead attacks me, despite choosing to live so close . . ."

"God tests you."

Kate heard the smile in Berend's voice. He was her cook, and so much more. Confidant and confessor, Berend was the person she most trusted. He was bemused by the contradiction in her sense of responsibility for her mother's welfare despite their contentious relationship.

"I tell myself she chose the only house that was offered to her. It is as simple as that," Kate said.

The tenant of the house, Agnes Dell, a recent widow, had offered to transfer her lease to Eleanor if she would accept her as a sister, or beguine. It was a house of modest size, smaller than Kate's. With Eleanor's maidservant and Agnes's maidservant Nan, who now assisted the four sisters, it was crowded, though not intolerably so. Many large families lived in less space. It had not been an unreasonable choice.

"She will come round," said Berend.

"By then she may have difficulty picking over the rubble of my future." Kate told him about her mother's threat to inform the children she ran a discreet brothel.

"She is too late to shock Phillip and Marie. They already know the nature of your guests."

"But Petra."

"Your niece is more worldly-wise than her grandmother. She would not flinch."

Berend was right; her mother's words held no danger unless she took them to heart. "I should go in. See how Petra is feeling."

"I've not noticed her hurrying past to the privy this evening as she did last night."

"So her stomach is on the mend. That is a blessing. Sleep well."

Kate called to the hounds to follow her into the hall for the night.

⚬⚬⚬

She woke to the deep-throated barks of her wolfhounds. Kate sat up, listening for running footsteps, her father or one of her brothers calling the warning—Attack! The Scots!

But it was her manservant Matt she heard addressing the hounds down below in the hall, his voice rising in questions. She was in York. She was not on the borders, she was in the city of York, her cage, her home. Her brothers and her father, all dead. Her mother—this was not the time to think of her.

The hounds continued barking. They would not be silenced. Did Matt recognize the tone, that these were not about a passing dog or a demand to be let out, but warnings? *Danger.*

That was real. The danger. It might be York, not the borders, but it was still a place of danger. Especially now.

Kate threw off the light covers, grateful it was summer and her feet would not meet an icy floor.

"Dame Katherine?" her niece, Petra, called from outside Kate's door. She and Marie slept in opposite ends of the solar to keep the peace, with Kate's chamber in between. The girls were as different as night and day, but Kate hoped that, in time, they might grow close.

"Come in, come in. I've heard them. I'm dressing." Kate was fumbling with the bone buttons on her gown.

The girl, a seven-year-old version of her aunt, all wiry dark hair and tall for her age, began to enter but paused, tilting her head to listen as the door opened down below and the hounds' warning barks subtly changed. "Jennet," Petra whispered. Kate's maidservant and, like Berend, fiercely loyal and ever ready to defend the household. "They think she's come to let them out to search."

"Stay up here, in the solar, you and Marie, until I return." Kate finished her preparations by concealing her knife beneath her belt, then she kissed Petra's forehead and hurried down to the hall.

Her mother was not the only threat to the peace of York. Henry of Lancaster's return from exile was why Matt slept down below now, not out in the smaller house across the yard, on the street—to assist Kate in protecting her niece and ward. Duke Henry was believed to have landed just northeast of them, on the coast of the North Sea. A royal messenger had arrived in the city several days ago with orders from Edmund, Duke of York, to hold the city against Duke Henry. The sixty knights and esquires and hundred archers who had been readying for a march to Ware were now to defend the city. The city sheriffs were paying out money for carpenters, plasterers, and masons to repair the defenses. That Henry had chosen to return almost as soon as King Richard himself landed in Ireland in the company of most of the military might of the realm meant to Kate that Duke Henry was here to wrest the crown from his cousin, the anointed but not-so-beloved king of England. Blood would be shed before their feud was resolved, and she doubted that both would survive.

No one in York slept easy at present. In times of war, civic law and order suffered. She had learned that all too well in her childhood on the border with Scotland. And York, the great city of the north, a wealthy city of merchants, seat of the second most powerful archbishop in the land, one who might be persuaded to support the Lancastrian army—Duke Henry might find it an irresistible first stage in his coup.

Armed men had been passing through the four gates of the city for a week or more. Strangers. Each of them lusting for a fight. Had one of them found a combatant in the night? Is that what had set Lille and Ghent to this insistent barking? Or did the hounds sense an intruder on the property? Had a siege begun? Or was it merely her mother, marching through the hedgerow to resume her tirade? For once, that was Kate's hope. But the hounds knew Dame Eleanor; they would not be so alarmed were it her.

As Kate reached the hall Lille and Ghent rushed up to her, leads in mouths. She smiled at Matt's whimsical training. While she bent to attach the leads, the dogs nuzzled her, their rough gray fur warm with their agitation, Ghent gazing up with his soulful eyes, seeking reassurance. Lille danced sideways, her eyes a little wild.

Jennet and Matt began talking at once.

Kate straightened up and raised a hand, silencing them. "Jennet first."

"I noticed nothing out of place in the yard or the garden." Jennet wore a man's linen shirt over leggings, easily donned. "But Lille and Ghent will be far better judges of that."

"Matt?"

"They rose up as one. I first noticed their heads up, on the alert even before they stood and began to bark. Ghent sidled over to see that I was awake, but he kept his watch on the garden door. I've never seen one of them behave so." Kate had taught Matt since spring to work with Lille and Ghent. Young, eager to prove himself of use, Matt had learned quickly.

"Arm yourself and stay in here," said Kate. "Petra is awake and knows to keep Marie up above. Come, then." She gave a gentle tug on the hounds' leads and led them out into the night garden. Softly, "Lille, Ghent!" She signaled them to track—silently.

Her eyes were still adjusting to the dark as the hounds led her straight toward the hedgerow separating her garden from that behind the house on Hertergate that her mother had leased. *Dear Lord, no, not Mother*, she prayed.

A futile prayer, Kate's twin said in her mind, his presence a sure sign of danger.

I know, Geoff, I know. Trouble shimmered in the air about their mother. *But of our family, I have only Mother and Petra. I mean to keep them safe.*

Petra I understand, but you know better with Mother. And after yesterday's attack? No thanks for a peace offering?

Kate shrugged him off.

As the dogs continued on to the shut hedge gate, Kate signaled a halt so she might listen. Lille and Ghent sat, heads high, scenting forward to sense what might be across the way.

There was no light in her mother's house, or the kitchen nearer the hedgerow. With seven women in residence, if anything were wrong, surely one would light a lamp. They would be moving about, calling out to each other. But all was still. Whatever had disturbed Lille and Ghent, Kate saw no sign of anything amiss.

Bending to the hounds, Kate whispered that she understood, the scent was still there, but all was now quiet. She led them away from the hedge and around her own property—the house, the smaller building out on the road, back to her kitchen, the small lodging and the garden shed behind it. When she was satisfied that no one lurked in the shadows, she joined Berend, who stood in the kitchen doorway, barefoot.

"Lille and Ghent are keen to cross through to your mother's house." He spoke quietly, as if they might be overheard.

It was true. They sat at her feet on alert, ears pricked, eyes trained on the gate. "I see no disturbance over there," she whispered. "If someone came to harm in the night, one of them would hear and wake the others. We would see lamps lit, movement. But there is nothing." She looked back toward the latched gate. "I pray my irritation with Mother does not cloud my judgment."

"With the influx of armed men to defend the city, we can expect strangers wandering about, folk following the army, hoping for work," said Berend. "They must find their own lodgings, food. Some help themselves." He spoke from experience, years in the field, some as a soldier, the latter years as an assassin for hire.

Kate knew he was right about the situation in the city. She watched him now as he walked over to the gate in the hedgerow. Jennet joined him there, peering into the dark, her long braid swinging as she moved her head back and forth, apparently listening. Taking a deep breath, Kate followed, Lille and Ghent moving to surround and protect her.

The hounds were formidable in size—though Kate was a tall woman, the tops of their heads reached her shoulders, and the three moved as one, alert to one another's slightest shift in direction of speed, divining each other's intentions. Berend once told Kate, "Often I cannot detect how the hounds see your hand signals—they suddenly change direction, or halt, and I've seen nothing, nor have I noticed them watching you." Kate took pride in that. And comfort. Her father's master of hounds had praised the twins for their connection with the hounds. He had teased her father, asking how far back in family history a Clifford had wed a shape-shifter.

A few feet from the closed gate, Lille and Ghent halted and pricked their ears. Kate rested her hands on their backs, signaling them to hold still. Light footsteps. Stealthy, pausing, hurrying on, pausing, coming from Hertergate down the alley beside the Martha House. Kate considered moving back out of sight, the brightening predawn light both a gift and a threat. No, best to hold steady. The footsteps continued toward them. She felt the hounds' muscles tense, noticed Jennet slightly shifting, reaching for the latch, poised to move quickly through the gate. Berend touched Kate's arm, as if to steady her.

From round the corner of the Martha House a woman appeared. By her slight limp Kate recognized Agnes's maidservant, Nan, a young woman whose colorful clothing was a topic of dissent in Eleanor's household. Her mistress had chosen to take vows of humility and chastity, but not Nan. Kate wondered what she had been doing moving about the sleeping city. The young woman paused, glanced down, lifted her skirts, and shook one foot, as if she had stepped in a puddle. But it had not rained for days.

Lille growled.

More slowly now, her steps more furtive, Nan moved through the garden to the kitchen. She paused at the door of the small detached structure, looking back toward the alley, as if checking whether someone followed, then stepped inside. Without opening the door. Why had the door been open? A moment of silence, then Nan pushed open a shutter, moved away. Kate heard the soft sound of a poker stirring the embers. Now a lamp glowed. So a servant's day began.

Kate eased a little, but the hounds did not.

"Shall I just go peek?" Jennet whispered.

Kate nodded. "The hounds are still on alert."

Jennet was halfway to the kitchen door when Nan appeared in the garden, holding a lantern. "Sister Dina? God be thanked, I was so worried when I saw—Oh, Jennet. I hoped you were—" Her voice quavered with emotion. "Something has happened. Sister Dina is not in her room and there is blood!"

Jennet placed a hand on Nan's shoulder as if to steady her. "Start from the beginning. What did you see in the alley?"

Back at the gate, Berend leaned close to Kate to whisper, "Do you see Nan's shoes in the lantern light?"

She glanced down. "They are wet," she said.

"Though it has not rained in days."

"No, it has not." Kate moved through the gate with Lille and Ghent. "Shine the lantern down on your shoes, Nan." She offered her arm for support.

Someone called down from a solar window. "Is there trouble?"

"Is Sister Dina up there?" Jennet called back.

Murmurings, the sound of movement.

"God help me, I thought it was water," Nan whispered, covering her mouth as she lifted a foot, saw the blood.

"You did not smell it?"

Nan shook her head. "I do now."

Kate nodded, then left her, letting Lille and Ghent lead her out to the alleyway, where they stopped by a pool of blood that was beginning to soak into the earth. Ears back, the hounds growled at the strong scent, then wanted to track on, but Kate led them back to the kitchen, where Jennet now held the lantern aloft. Bloodstains pocked the rush-strewn floor, especially vivid where the rushes had been scuffed away. Jennet shone the lantern round—a bloody handprint on a small door to the side. Lille and Ghent strained at their leashes.

"Sister Dina's bedchamber," Nan whimpered.

There were several more bloody prints on the inside of the outer door.

"What is it, Katherine? Why are you here with the hounds?" Dame Eleanor demanded as she approached across the small garden.

Seeing to your latest disaster, Kate thought. But this was not the time for grudges. "Lille and Ghent sensed trouble. Then Nan cried out. There is blood in the kitchen—on the floor, the walls, the doors, and pooled in the alleyway." Kate stepped back to let her mother see, Jennet holding the light down toward the floor.

"God help us." Dame Eleanor turned to Nan. "Where is Sister Dina?"

Nan ducked her head. "I know not, mistress."

"Come with me," said Kate, taking the lantern from Jennet, nodding to Nan to follow her into Dina's bedchamber. She shone the light on the small space. No blood on the floor. But smears on the bed. "Look round. Is anything missing?"

"Gown, hose, shoes," said Eleanor, who had come in behind them. "How is it that you did not raise the alarm at once, Nan? Where were you when all this was happening?" She stood with hands on hips, chin forward, eyes steely. Despite her new, modest garb—white wimple and veil, soft gray gown: she had several, well cut of the finest wool and silk, her household keys hanging from a simple leather girdle—Eleanor still impressed one as the lady of the manor ready to call down her armed servants to fend off an attack. Always quick to blame.

Nan shook her head with a small cry and scuttled from the room to the garden. Kate nudged her mother aside and followed.

The widow, Agnes, had her arms round Nan and was rubbing her back as one might do to calm a sobbing child. Agnes was a short but substantial woman, half as wide as she was tall, with upper arms as big as hams. She stuck out her heavy chin as if defying Eleanor to say her nay.

"She has just returned from her nightly vigil at her mother's bed, is that not so, Nan?"

A sniffle, a nod.

"Nightly vigil?" Eleanor looked to Sisters Clara and Brigida, who stood in the garden halfway between the house and the kitchen, holding hands, looking unsure where they should be. "Did you know of this, either of you?"

Sister Clara, plain, competent, the guiding spirit of the house, said, "No. I should have been informed." Sister Brigida, bold-featured, tall, a brilliant scholar, seemed diminished by the early waking, the confusion of the scene. She simply shook her head.

"And have you left the kitchen door unlocked when you depart each night?" Kate asked the maidservant.

"Well of course she does," Agnes snapped. "She does not hold the keys, Dame Eleanor does."

Kate looked to her mother, who visibly trembled with righteous indignation.

"I don't understand," said Eleanor. "I lock the house and the kitchen every night. It is the rule in a Martha House. Have you found a way to unlock it, Nan?" By now Agnes and Nan stood apart. When Agnes began to answer, Eleanor snapped, "Be quiet. Let the truant answer."

"I know how to prop the door open so that it is not noticeable but the lock is useless," said Nan.

Eleanor took a deep breath. "Sister Agnes, I—"

"You might deal with that later," Kate said quietly to her mother as she turned to address Dina's two companions. "Brigida, Clara, have you seen Dina this night? Did you hear anything?"

"I heard nothing, nor have I seen her since we parted at the end of evening prayers," said Sister Clara in her Bavarian accent.

Sister Brigida shook her head. "Nor I. May God be watching over her." Her accent was softer than Clara's, more French, like that of Kate's wards, Marie and Phillip.

Both women crossed themselves. Dame Eleanor did as well.

"Agnes? Did you hear or see anything?" Kate asked.

"Nothing." She was a bit breathless, but then so were they all.

Kate took her at her word. For now. "What was Dina's room used for in the past?" she asked.

"Boarders, I screened it off for boarders," said Agnes. "But I've had none since autumn. Or course there will be no more, as it is now a Martha House." So very breathless, and her eyes scanning the garden as if looking for something.

"Come into the kitchen," said Kate. The woman bowed her head and followed. "Do you notice anything missing?"

"No, but perhaps in daylight . . ."

Sweat shone on the woman's face. It could be many things—concern for Sister Dina, remorse for keeping Nan's nighttime absences a secret, fear for her own safety. Agnes might even regret offering the house to Eleanor. She would not be the first to realize too late the risk involved in participating in Eleanor's schemes.

Kate stepped into the bedchamber, pulled off the bloody sheet, and wadded it up in her hand. Back in the kitchen she nodded to Jennet. "Stay with them. Berend and I will take Lille and Ghent, see whether they are able to track Sister Dina." She led the hounds out into the garden.

Matt, pacing by the hedgerow gate, called out, "What is it? What has happened?"

Kate shook her head. "No time now. Protect the children."

He nodded and turned back to the house.

Berend joined her as she let Lille and Ghent smell the sheet. "Track."

She had little need to command them. They were already following a scent, noses down. They returned to the pool of blood in the alley, a dark stain in the pale, predawn light. A pause as they reached Hertergate—glancing to the right, toward the King's Staithe, then to the left, toward Castlegate. The scent moved in both directions? The hounds chose the staithe, snuffling their way down the street, onto the dock area, lost the scent at the water. No, no, now they picked it up a bit upriver, along the staithe, then lost it again in the incoming tide. On a gamble, she led them up to Ousegate. They snuffled around, lifting their heads, lowering them, then sat. Nothing strong enough to warrant tracking.

Berend was still standing at the edge of the water. He pointed to a small boat on the opposite bank. Shrugged. They returned to Hertergate, silent, thoughtful. She knew that he knew the memories called up by the blood, and a young woman she cared for gone missing. Her friend Maud, long ago . . .

"We will find her, Dame Katherine."

"I pray we find her alive, Berend. So much blood."

"May God watch over her."

Mother, Mother, what have you done?

And she will find a way to blame you for all the ill that comes of this, Geoff whispered in her mind.

—◦◦◦—

Eleanor had expected trouble from the silly maidservant. But not of this sort. Considering Nan's bright clothes and roaming smiles, she had anticipated a lover sneaking in, or Nan sneaking out. She felt betrayed, a too-familiar experience and one that she would not tolerate. She would have her man Griffin investigate the story of a dying mother. As Katherine and her implausible cook withdrew with the dogs, Eleanor resumed her challenge to Agnes and her maidservant.

"Was Sister Dina aware you were not here at night, Nan?" Eleanor asked, not troubling to soften her tone.

Agnes and Nan had settled on a bench in the garden, arms round each other, looking frightened.

"So much blood," Agnes whispered. "Who is to protect us?"

Coddled city women with no backbone. "I will send for my man Griffin," said Eleanor. She should not have agreed to the sisters' injunction against men on the property. "Now answer my question, Nan. Was Sister Dina aware of your absence at night?"

"We did not speak of it, mistress." The minx kept her eyes downcast. Oh, yes, *now* she played humble.

"Did it not occur to you that you were exposing her to danger?"

"No."

Agnes sniffed and pushed out her ample bosom as if to impress upon Eleanor the weight of her words. "We never had trouble here."

"That is no excuse." And what precisely would she call trouble, Eleanor wondered, when she kept a maidservant like Nan. She bit back a threat to let Nan go. Too soon. First she would have Griffin find out just where the young fool had been. "For the short term, Griffin will sleep in the kitchen, and Nan will take her rest with my maidservant."

"On a pallet at the foot of your bed?" Agnes huffed. "And what of Nan's mother? Who will sit with her at night while the children sleep?"

Eleanor had not considered that. "We shall discuss that later. Sister Dina's welfare is our first concern." As it should be theirs. But both seemed entirely wrapped up in their own self-protection. Eleanor glanced at her daughter's maidservant, Jennet. She was such an odd young creature, freckle-faced and petite with a walk and a manner of speaking far more like a young lad. "Might I trouble you to summon my man Griffin? I want him to search for Dina."

Jennet nodded. "As soon as I repair this lock."

"It is broken?" Eleanor went to look.

"As Nan said, it is stuck, not broken." The young woman took out a small metal tool and fussed with the latch. "There." She stepped back with a look of satisfaction.

Eleanor thanked her.

"Let us withdraw to the hall and kneel in prayer for Sister Dina's safety," said Sister Clara, stepping out of the kitchen and into her role as senior sister. Sister Brigida followed, head bowed, hands folded in prayer.

"I suppose you must leave the door unlocked for Griffin," Eleanor said to Jennet.

"You need not worry, Dame Eleanor. This tool will allow me to let him in. Shall I tell him to await you in the kitchen?"

"You are able—" Eleanor stopped. "You will find Griffin in—"

"I know where he bides, Dame Eleanor."

"How—" She stopped herself again. "Bless you, Jennet. Yes, ask him to wait here in the kitchen."

So the young woman might enter the house whenever she pleased. And knew where Griffin was staying. Eleanor had chided her daughter for her choice in servants, but they certainly seemed to earn their keep and provided her with a sense of safety. She said a prayer of thanks for the help of Katherine and her servants as she followed Clara and the others into the hall, though her gratitude was tempered by a worry that they would discover more than she would wish brought to light. A dilemma.

As Eleanor knelt, the enormity of Sister Dina's disappearance blotted out all other concerns. *Merciful Mother, protect gentle Dina, guide her to a safe haven where we might find her and bring her home to be comforted.*

⤙◈⤚

As Kate and Berend neared the Martha House, someone hurried down Hertergate toward them.

"One of the sisters from the *maison dieu*," said Kate. She handed him the dogs' leads and went to meet the woman.

"Magistra Matilda sent me." Matilda was the mother superior of the poor sisters who tended the sick in the *maison dieu* attached to the parish church across Castlegate. The three beguines had lodged there while Dame

Eleanor was away for a time in the spring. "Sister Dina is in the church, lying before the altar, and . . . there is blood on her gown." The woman crossed herself. "Magistra Matilda says come quickly."

Out on Castlegate a few folk were stirring, though so early in the morning they did not pause to chat, focused on going about their business, opening shops, stoking fires, delivering goods for the day's work. The sister led Kate and Berend to the side door of the church, offering to watch the dogs. "My father raised hounds. I miss them." Lille and Ghent sniffed her outstretched hand, then her face, and sat obediently as Kate handed her the leashes. The woman's little cry of delight as Lille nuzzled her hand convinced Kate. Berend was holding open the door.

Kate stepped over the threshold, pausing a few paces in, blinded by the dimness after the early morning sun. Across the church, a figure in gray knelt on a prie-dieu before the lady altar. As the door swung shut behind Berend, the figure straightened, turning toward them. Magistra Matilda. She gestured toward a prostrate figure on the ground before the altar. Gray gown, white veil. Slender. Sister Dina. Kate approached as quietly as possible, lowering herself to her knees beside the woman, placing a hand on her upper back.

"Sister Dina, praise God that you are here. Safe. Your sisters have been so worried."

At first Dina did not move, not even a twitch, and Kate feared the worst, though there was no evidence of blood pooling beneath her. She sat back on her heels and waited. The prie-dieu creaked as Magistra Matilda rose. Tucking the paternoster beads up her sleeve, she approached, but stopped as Sister Dina drew in her arms and tried to push herself up. She wobbled. Fearing she might fall back on her face, Kate reached out to support her. But Dina went limp in her arms. Kate glanced back toward Berend, nodding.

Berend came forward, and, bending to the slight woman, gently lifted her up in his arms.

Magistra Matilda rushed over with a cry of distress. "What if she wakes and sees him? If it was a man who attacked her . . . Forgive me, my good man, but you look . . ."

Scarred, missing an ear, several fingers, and with a muscular build, Berend was intimidating, Kate was well aware of that. She found it useful. "I need him. And Dina is in a faint, Sister. She is unaware of us. Carry her back to my home, Berend."

"No. The *maison dieu* is closer," said Magistra Matilda. "Let us nurse her."

Kate looked at Berend, who nodded his approval. "Bless you, Sister. It might be best that Dina not wake in the house in which she experienced whatever frightened her so."

As Berend carried Sister Dina into the light he paused, gazing down at the woman's gown. Kate saw it now, blood on her right sleeve and across her torso. Hers? Or someone else's? They would soon know.

2

A BLOODIED ANGEL

Kate had sent a servant from the *maison dieu* to let her mother and the others at the Martha House know where Sister Dina was, and that she was safe. Dame Eleanor and Sister Brigida had just arrived when Magistra Matilda beckoned for Kate to come see for herself that Dina had suffered bruises and a small scrape, but nothing to account for all the blood on her gown.

"Dina, did you injure someone in defending yourself?" Kate asked softly.

Though awake, Sister Dina stared off at the ceiling, mute and unmoving.

Perhaps Sister Brigida might have more success—she had been Dina's good friend in Strasbourg. Kate asked her to try. She did, but to no avail. Dina would speak when she was ready. Kate was content that she bide there for now, until she was herself once more and could tell them whether she could bear to return to the Martha House.

"What of her shift?" Kate asked Matilda. "Was there blood on the shift she wore beneath her gown?" She would have worn only that if awakened by an intruder.

The sister gestured to the pile of clothes. Beneath the gown Kate found the shift, encrusted with blood. So it had been quite soaked. Kate ached with grief for the woman's ordeal.

"Yes, it is a horror to consider what gentle Dina suffered in the night," Matilda whispered. "A child already so haunted, so frightened. May God watch over her." The sister crossed herself.

"God expects *us* to watch over her, Magistra Matilda. Her life is in our hands."

"I understand, Dame Katherine. You may rest easy."

No one might rest easy. Especially now, as the city prepared for war. But Kate simply thanked the sister, letting Brigida be the one to stress to Matilda that either she or Sister Clara, or Dame Eleanor, should be summoned the moment Dina seemed ready and able to speak. "Send for one of us at once."

Magistra Matilda bristled. "Do you not trust us to care for Sister Dina?"

Brigida asked her forgiveness; she was merely worried for her dear friend. "You know how timid she is, how she jumps at loud noises or sudden movements. I did not mean to imply a lack of confidence or trust, just that she may need to see a more familiar face. We are most grateful for your kindness."

On that warmer note, the four of them withdrew. As they stepped out of the *maison dieu*, Kate was glad to see how peacefully Lille and Ghent sat with the sister who had watched them. She handed over the hounds' leads, and all six crossed Castlegate together, separating at the hedgerow gate. Dame Eleanor, who had been quiet all the while, even now deferred to Brigida, who thanked Kate and Berend for taking Dina to safety. Eleanor merely nodded to them, then continued on through the gate.

"I do not understand your mother," Berend said as they watched them depart.

"You are not the first to say that, nor will you be the last. Perhaps she is irked that *we* found Dina." They turned toward the kitchen. "Before we are set upon with questions, I would have your thoughts, Berend. What do you think happened?"

"Are you asking whether this might be the work of soldiers?" He shook his head at her nod. "Knowing so little, I cannot say."

No longer able to hold back the emotion she had choked down, Kate sank onto the bench beneath the kitchen eaves, letting the tears come. Lille and Ghent settled at her feet.

Berend crouched between them. "You think of Maud?" Kate's dearest childhood friend, who had been raped and brutally murdered.

"And the shattering of the sisters' beautiful, trusting calm. I took comfort in the peace of their presence. I saw another way to live." Without fear, without constant vigilance. "But it was an illusion." She blotted her eyes with her sleeve as Marie's voice rose inside. "The girls must not see me this way. Go in. And take Lille and Ghent. I will compose myself and join you in a moment."

"Of course." Berend straightened with a grunt. "God help me, I grow too old for such a posture, eh?"

She leaned her head back against the wall and mirrored his gentle smile, watching him as he rubbed his own eyes with his three-fingered hand, then motioned to the hounds to follow him. Strong, steadfast Berend. He never failed her. He opened the door now, laughing at something Marie said in her most imperious tone, throwing it back with a silly comment rewarded by both girls dissolving in laughter.

Bless him, with a simple gesture he eased her back into her own household. All were well, happy, and mostly at peace. Mostly. Marie, a delicately beautiful child, had arrived in York grieving her parents and feeling betrayed by all her kin. In the course of a year and a half she had begun to thaw, but her temper still flared at perceived slights or disappointments. At times she reminded Kate of her own mother.

Hunger and thirst roused Kate. She ordered her thoughts, then rose and followed Berend inside.

All the household was gathered in the kitchen—Jennet, Matt, Marie, Petra, Berend, Lille and Ghent. Though it was just past dawn, the tension of the past hours had brought them all fully awake. The bread Berend had left to rise during the night had been baked. Marie's work. Kate thanked her, ruffling her curly hair. The child pretended irritation.

"Matt helped. He feared I would burn myself." Marie sighed and rolled her eyes. Forced to grow up too quickly in her mother's house in Calais, cooking for the household, Marie took pride in helping Berend.

"Have you saved me some bread?" Kate asked, sliding onto the bench beside Berend.

Marie handed her a warm loaf. Berend poured her a bowl of ale, then returned to his own pieces of bread, slathering them with butter and cheese and eating them quickly, washing them down with good ale. Pulling her small loaf apart, Kate asked him to tell the others what they had discovered. Matt and Jennet both sat up, eager to hear it.

When Berend had told all he knew, Jennet added what she had learned about the lock on the kitchen. "And then Sister Clara shepherded them all to the hall to pray." Jennet shook her head. "There is a time for prayer and a time for action."

"I could not agree more," said Kate. "Anything else?"

"I went to Griffin's lodgings, told him he was needed. His landlady was not cordial about the early hour." Jennet helped herself to more ale.

"So there it is." Kate nodded to Berend, Matt, and Jennet. "I want to hear your thoughts."

"Sister Dina rarely leaves the house," said Matt. "I cannot think she has drawn attention to herself. So this was not an attack aimed at her."

"But people are doubtless gossiping about Dame Eleanor's beguines," said Jennet. "They will be known to be young women, and with all the soldiers crowding the city . . ."

"Sister Dina has difficulty understanding us. Or being understood. Though I am beginning to catch much of what she says, it is a struggle," said Matt. "Might she have misunderstood someone looking for help?"

"In her bedchamber in a private garden before dawn?" Jennet snorted. Matt blushed. Marie giggled.

"Berend says many of the men are left to find their own beds. He's warned us not to go out after dark unattended," said Petra. "Maybe Matt is right."

"My niece the peace weaver," Kate whispered.

But she did wonder. It was true that Dina's speech sounded to all of them like a mixture of languages, but Brigida, Clara, and Eleanor were able to converse with her. Her efforts to learn to speak to the people of York were improving, and now it seemed more a matter of being so timid that Dina chose to go nowhere, see no one, without having one of the others with her. Fortunately she was a skilled sempster, so as her reputation spread, the work came to her.

"Why did Dina not cry out?" Kate wondered aloud. "How is it that she fled rather than calling out for help? Why did Nan not tell the others about her mother? Is caring for the ill not within their calling? Why did my mother assign that room to Dina? I have so many questions."

She sighed as everyone turned toward her. "I know that I swore before all of you that I would not be swept up in my mother's Martha House scheme. But I have come to have great affection for all three sisters, and none of them, especially Sister Dina, should suffer for my mother's poor judgment."

"I will see what I might learn about Agnes and her maidservant, and whether Nan *is* caring for an ailing mother. If not, what she's doing," said Jennet.

Kate nodded. "I need to see Griselde and Clement at the guesthouse today. I will ask what they know of Agnes and her boarders, and what her late husband did on his long journeys. They keep their ears open about such things."

"Will Sister Brigida take us to Master Frost's house for our lesson today?" Marie asked. Brigida, who had been schooled for a time in a convent in Paris, was tutoring Hazel Frost, the daughter of Kate's cousin William, as well as Petra and Marie. They assembled at the Frost house because Hazel was often too unwell to move about in the city. Marie, born in Calais, spoke French, but not the elegant Parisian French that Brigida was teaching the others, so she had insisted on being included.

"Until we know what happened, and whether our households are safe, you will stay close to home," said Kate. "If Sister Brigida is willing to tutor you and Petra this morning, she may do so in the hall. But you will respect her decision about whether or not she wishes to do so." She looked pointedly at Marie. "Is that clear?"

Marie nodded and pushed aside her bread to lay her head down on her folded arms. Petra whispered, "Clear," and went to sit by Ghent, resting her hand on his back. He sighed and sank lower into rest.

Kate smiled at Petra and smoothed Marie's hair. "Bless you," she whispered, before turning back to Berend and the others. "I want to know who frightened Dina last night," she said, as if the interruption had not happened. "It might have been quite innocent. Soldiers spilling out of the taverns drunk, brawling . . . One *might* have lost his way."

"Except that he was so quiet," said Jennet.

Kate agreed.

"You mentioned a boat," said Matt. "Someone bleeding so badly, would they be able to row?"

"So he had an accomplice." Berend nodded.

It seemed likely to Kate as well. "Whoever it was," she said, "they might pose a further danger to the sisters, or to some other household in the city. We need to know."

"We might talk to the knights who are now your tenants on High Petergate," said Berend.

Kate owned a pair of properties on High Petergate, near the minster, two houses side by side. One she operated as a guesthouse, managed by her late husband's former factor, Clement, and his wife, Griselde. The other house had been empty for a while and was now leased to a knight, Sir Alan Bennet, who was sharing it with some of the other well-to-do knights arriving in the city.

"They will be watching for any trouble that might suggest Duke Henry has spies in the city," Berend continued. "They will have men watching the rivers and the gates. They might have seen or heard something last night."

Kate disliked the current use of the house, but the enterprising knight who had leased it to accommodate his fellows, at a fee, of course, had laid down a handsome deposit against damage and assured her that he would say nothing to anyone of the comings and goings next door at her guesthouse. The truth was, with Edmund of York's call to arms, the house would have been requisitioned had she not made her own, undoubtedly more lucrative, arrangement, and perhaps the guesthouse as well, robbing her of income and the worthies of York of a venue for distraction from their mounting anxiety. "You're quite right, Berend. I will pay them a call."

"Or if Brigida comes for the little ones, I might do it myself," he said. "The men might be more likely to talk to me."

"Or they will be too busy recruiting you," said Jennet.

Berend was laughingly assuring them that was not his purpose when out the window Kate saw Thomas Holme, her neighbor and business partner, come out of his house, glance toward hers, then hasten down the adjoining alley toward Castlegate. He had dressed with care, in the sort of attire he wore as alderman, or for guild events.

Guild events. "I almost forgot the guild meeting called for this morning." Collecting Jennet, Kate hastened across the garden to the hall and up to her bedchamber to dress for the occasion.

It bothered her that Thomas had glanced this way but hurried on. It was their custom to walk to the guildhall on Fossgate together. More cause for unease on a morning when Kate's world was tumbling down around her.

―⁓⊛⁓―

"I shall go directly from the meeting to High Petergate." Kate cursed as they discovered a tear in the hem of the dress she wished to wear.

"Quickly mended." Jennet helped her step out of the gown so she might work on it.

"We know so little about any of this. My mother and her cursed secretiveness."

"She is skilled in dancing far from the point," Jennet muttered as she worked.

"They say that mothers and daughters are always in conflict. Did you and your mother agree?"

"I never knew her."

Kate felt herself blush. Jennet had been abandoned as an infant. "Forgive me."

"It was an honest mistake, on a morning when you have much on your mind, Dame Katherine. Ready." She held the gown up for inspection.

"You are a wonder."

A pleased shrug as Jennet helped her with the small silver buttons. "Your mother would approve of this one."

"She would find some fault with it, you can be sure."

Jennet stepped back with a satisfied nod. "It should not take long to discover whether or not Nan has been sitting with an ailing mother. What else might I do while you are at the meeting?"

Kate thought while Jennet brushed out the tangles in her hair. "It would be good to know with whom Dina has had contact. Who has brought sewing to her. Women sometimes forget that a sempster has ears, or, in Dina's case, knowing her troubles with our speech, they might have spoken freely in her presence thinking she would not understand. Too freely. About something that must not be repeated."

"Do you think it likely a customer sent a man to silence a sempster?"

"Now that I hear it in your words, no. But we cannot dismiss any ideas, however unlikely. I want to know the names of her clients."

"I will snoop," Jennet agreed. "Though we might already know the answers to many of our questions if only you and Dame Eleanor were able to talk."

"We would, I know. But life is never so simple."

"No." Jennet finished tucking Kate's hair into a silver crispinette and gave her an encouraging hug. "We *will* find out what happened in that room last night. And Dame Eleanor need never know it was us. Her man Griffin can take all the credit."

"That would require our working together—Griffin and our household."

"It would make sense, would it not?"

"Of what use is he? He knows York little more than do the sisters."

"Not entirely true," said Jennet. "It is said he has family both in the city and a day's ride from here. He was away visiting them in the countryside for almost a week. Just returned. And he has explored the city."

"You have been following him?"

Jennet grinned. "Asking about him, that is all."

Kate was very curious about the man. As Ulrich Smit's retainer, he must know something of her mother's experiences in Strasbourg. And he might know, or at least guess, why she left in such haste upon Ulrich's death. "You have a point. Family in York, you say? But he sounds Welsh."

"I know nothing more."

"I will talk to him at the first opportunity. How will you approach Nan's mother?"

"I shall take her a gift of Berend's bread."

"You are inspired! Who would not be grateful for that?"

Jennet stepped back. "Dressed!"

Kate spun round. "Am I all that a merchant of York must be?"

"That and more." Jennet smiled.

Rushing down the steps and out into the garden, Kate almost collided with Sister Brigida. The beguine gave a startled cry, then apologized for lurking so close to the door. Kate had glimpsed a frown on Brigida's expressive face before she had cried out and stepped aside.

"Has something happened?" she asked.

Brigida's pale eyes lit up with a warm smile. "No, Dame Katherine. Sister Clara has set Sister Agnes and Nan to work on cleaning the blood from Sister Dina's room and the kitchen, and Dame Eleanor is resting. I thought the best use of my time would be to distract Marie and Petra."

Kate thanked her. "I told them they will take their lessons here in my house until we feel certain the danger is over. Will that suit you?"

"Of course."

The relief on the faces of Jennet and Berend said it all. They wished to head out into the city and learn what they might about the intruder. Now they were free to do so. Matt would stay to watch the property.

"I think it best you know that Sister Dina sleeps with a dagger under her pillow," said Brigida. "But I did not see it in the room as Sister Agnes and Nan began to clean it."

"A dagger?" Berend looked surprised.

"An elegant one. We have never talked about it. She did not offer a story or a reason, and I did not feel it my place to ask. But I fear—"

Kate kissed Brigida's cheek. "Bless you for telling us this. It is a help."

3

A CITY ON THE EDGE

———❧❧———

The master began the guild meeting with a reading of the orders from Edmund of Langley, Duke of York, who was governing the realm on behalf of his nephew King Richard, while he was away on the Irish campaign. There was much repetition of "for the common good" and an emphasis on the importance of the city of York in the north. An influx of knights and armed men was not to anyone's liking, yet their presence and the fortification of the walls provided a sense of control in such troubled times, so the merchants in the hall were largely quiet during the reading. But Lille and Ghent, sitting at Kate's feet, stayed alert, sensing tension in the hall. And, though Kate realized the events of the morning had heightened her feeling of impending danger, the widespread frowns, guarded glances at neighbors, and postures gave witness to the growing agitation in the room. Once the clerk had read the orders, the guild master invited suggestions as to how the guild might support the defense efforts.

Kate had purposely taken a seat beside her neighbor Thomas Holme at the very end of a row of current and former aldermen. More unusual behavior—his custom was to sit toward the front of the room and never with this group. She might have been worried that she'd somehow offended him, but he'd greeted her with courtesy, asking about the barking of the dogs in the night. She'd hoped that he might have noticed something, but he had not.

"Poor Sister Dina," he said. "I am glad that she sought safety at our parish church. I am not surprised that Magistra Matilda has stepped forward to help. As I told you, she grew fond of Dina in the short time the sisters lived at the *maison dieu*. Matilda fussed over the young woman, seeing how she jumped at every noise and avoided attention." Thomas had founded the *maison dieu* beside the parish church on Castlegate years ago, and it had been at his generous invitation that the sisters had resided there for a brief time after arriving in York.

"I wish I knew whether Dina has cause to be so wary, or whether it is simply her nature," said Kate.

"That was one of Magistra Matilda's concerns," said Thomas. "She asked whether Dame Eleanor knew the backgrounds of the three women, whether she had ensured they were appropriately devout or simply escaping unhappy or unsatisfying lives. Or worse."

"Why worse?"

"It is *her* nature. Magistra Matilda is a formidable interrogator when considering a fresh recruit. She suspects that your mother simply stepped into one of the beguine communities, clapped her hands, and asked if anyone would like to accompany her to York."

Though it was an apt depiction of her mother's tendency to make hasty, careless decisions, Kate said, "It is my understanding that the sisters had undergone careful scrutiny in order to be accepted in their beguinage in Strasbourg."

"To be sure. But Magistra Matilda does not approve of beguines. She has heard that the sisters might leave at any time to marry, and that some are permitted to return after having children—apostates in Magistra Matilda's opinion. You recall how she insisted that Sister Brigida be accompanied by one of the other sisters when escorting your wards

to the Frost household for lessons. Her lay order observes stricter rules."
He shrugged. "I believe her dislike of beguines arises from her dislike of
anything never encountered in York."

"Sister Clara says Matilda referred to them as the Saxon Lollards."

Thomas gave a surprised laugh. "I've no doubt."

"They follow the teachings of Meister Eckhart, I am told." A Dominican
scholar and philosopher who had taught in Strasbourg. "From what I
have heard, his interpretation of Christ's message lacks the darkness and
asceticism of Magistra Matilda's religion."

"If they shared that with Magistra Matilda, it is no wonder she did not
trust their devotion. Eckhart was denounced as a heretic."

"I rather like what I've heard."

"Never say that in the presence of Magistra Matilda." He shook his
head. "So what did Sister Dina have to say about her ordeal?"

"Nothing. Whatever happened, it has silenced her." For the moment.
Kate prayed that might be only temporary.

Each in the crowd seemed to have their own purpose in attending—to
share unease about the growing military presence, to gossip, to complain.
One guild member after another stood to recite stories of ships sighted in
the mists along the coast of the North Sea and gangs of armed men on
the roads, all heading north. There were those who believed Ravenspur
had been the obvious landing place. No, no, more likely Bridlington.
Ravenspur had no quay, the town had been largely abandoned as the sea
encroached on the land. It must be Bridlington. More came round to that
conclusion as their fellows listed the salient amenities: no castle to guard
it, a quay at which to disembark and unload, and a town in which horses
and men might find food and shelter as they awaited their exiled leader's
arrival from France.

"Dull-pated asses. Ravenspur or Bridlington, Bridlington or Ravenspur,"
Thomas Holme muttered. "What matters is he's landed in the north and
he's"—a glance at Kate, a cough—"too close to allow us to remain neutral.
We know his ships paused at Cromer in Norfolk to take on supplies and
more men. That is what we know."

They knew now. There had been rumors of a landing in the southeast,
at Pevensey, Sussex. Edmund, Duke of York, had gone to its defense only

to discover there was no need, and that some of Henry's ships had instead landed at Cromer, a Lancastrian estate in Norfolk, to take on supplies. The Lancastrian supporters had cleverly spread a misleading rumor.

Someone reported rumors that soldiers were heading west from Bridlington. Down the row, someone whispered, "Knaresborough. They have heard?"

Knaresborough. Had Henry of Lancaster already come so far inland? Kate was paying close attention to who spoke up, who kept a guarded silence, ordering them in her mind as to who was likely to side with King Richard or Henry of Lancaster—for that was the other matter stealing into the sharing, whether the city was wise to side with the king. "The king has not been so friendly of late." That sent a ripple of consent down the row. Were the worthies of York secretly supporting the duke rather than the king?

All were agreed about *who* had landed, and most seemed quite certain as to Henry of Lancaster's intention. Even before the arrival of the royal messenger, no one had doubted that he had come to claim the Lancastrian inheritance that his cousin, King Richard, had declared forfeit. The orders from Edmund of Langley, Duke of York, to raise troops and make repairs to the city defenses in preparation for war had merely verified the rumors.

"But Edmund of Langley is fond of his nephew Henry. If it comes to choosing sides . . ." Thomas Graa muttered with a shake of his head. Kate was glad of his low, easily distinguished voice. One of the wealthiest merchants in York, Graa knew the royal family, and his opinion mattered in the city. He had served the city as mayor, councilman, and, most recently, chamberlain, as well as representing York as a member of Parliament.

The guild master attempted to move on from what he clearly considered unnecessary chatter, reminding the guild members that he'd summoned them in order to discuss tactics for defense. Regardless of whether or not one welcomed Henry of Lancaster's return, civil war was bad news for merchants, dangerous for both land and sea commerce, potentially destroying long-held trade agreements, indeed all manner of treaties. If the conflict resolved quickly, it would be a mere inconvenience. But it was anyone's guess how King Richard would respond, his changeable moods and emotional outbursts impossible to predict. Experience had taught them to step warily with the king's representatives. Many in the crowd would find any slowdown in trade particularly difficult to endure because of heavy fines levied on select guild members in recent years; King Richard's tax collectors coyly referred to them as loans, but they were plainly punitive measures for those merchants targeted for their support of the barons critical of the king. Considering the circumstances, Kate regarded the king's recent levies as poorly timed now that he needed the support of the realm against the returning exile.

The meeting dragged on, everyone with any opinion whatsoever determined to have his say. Though they had begun in the cool of early morning, the sun had now risen over the rooftops and the hall grew hot enough to ripen the crowd, who had dressed to impress rather than accommodate the July heat. They grew restless and querulous. Kate herself fought drowsiness, her mind wandering back to the morning's events and her ever-growing list of questions.

"Nonsense," Holme muttered, pulling Kate's mind back to the guildhall.

One of the younger guild members was defending his theory that King Richard had not actually set sail for Ireland but was using the story to lure Henry of Lancaster into a trap. His pronouncement was greeted by shrugs, shakes of the head, raised brows, whispers. A few wondered aloud whether "the lad had lost his wits."

Kate considered the idea. It would be a clever move. Subtle. Too subtle for the king? The consensus seemed to be that King Richard did not listen to others, that he was far too confident, believing that God protected the anointed sovereign from all who would challenge his right to rule.

Was that Duke Henry's intention? To remove his cousin and be crowned King Henry in his stead? If anyone might succeed in such an effort, it would be him. The Lancastrian inheritance, when added to his wealth as Duke of Hereford, would make him the most powerful baron by far—that is, if he could wrest those lands and coffers back from the hands of the king's favorites. It all depended on how many stewards and retainers had shifted their loyalty from Lancaster to the king.

The present discussion predictably fell apart as soon as the guild master broached the subject of actively helping to arm and defend the city. Few members of the merchant guild had ever ridden to war, and their experience with weaponry was limited to hunting or defending themselves in dark alleyways. Kate occasionally joined them on St. George's Field to practice at the butts and knew how few of their arrows ever hit the mark. The city's defense was quickly deemed the business of the sheriffs and the knights and esquires already summoned, and the discussion dissolved into a despairing account of how many able bodies the king had taken with him to Ireland—or wherever he lay in wait for his cousin. And the influx of armed strangers into the city, men no one might personally vouch for. If they caused trouble, to whom did the citizens take their complaint?

"It is our misfortune that Duke Henry's power lies in the north," Thomas Holme grumbled as he and Kate stepped out into the bright July morning. "We will bear the brunt of this, while our London colleagues will hardly be inconvenienced."

Kate agreed and silently cursed her luck. She was so close to digging out from beneath Simon's heavy debts—a few more shiploads of precious spices, added to a lease agreement her cousin William Frost was negotiating for her on the family property she had inherited in Northumberland, and she would be clear of that burden. But if her ships were seized, or if William's lawyer met trouble on the road north and failed to complete the negotiations, the liberation she so yearned for would be delayed.

"There are rumors that Duke Henry is already in Knaresborough, and he's making promises that only a king has the power to keep. What of that?" a man said to his companion as he passed. His companion hushed him.

Knaresborough again. "Have you heard that rumor, Thomas?" When he feigned confusion, she repeated what she'd just overheard.

"Juicy gossip, that is all it is. Meant to impress his companion."

That is not how it had seemed in the guildhall when his companions had whispered among themselves at mention of Knaresborough. "Perhaps it is time to move our business south, eh?" she teased, patting Thomas's arm. She took care to appear confident and at ease, even with her partners. Few knew the enormity of the debt she'd discovered on Simon's death, and she meant to keep it secret.

"Trading through London, eh? I pray it does not come to that."

She tried a different tactic. Thomas had a troubled history with King Richard; a member of Parliament when it moved against the king years ago, he had been pardoned, yet the king retaliated still with fines and the searching of Thomas's ships. "We might all be better off to welcome Duke Henry, truth be told."

Thomas grunted. "I might agree but that I fear what fate would befall our king if Duke Henry takes the crown. I do not wish him dead, merely chastised. A near victory that frightens him into a more reasonable sovereignty. Ah, look—in the shade of the tree outside the gate." He motioned with his head. "Your knight awaits you, Katherine."

Just a trick to change the subject? She shaded her eyes against the glare of the mid-morning sun. No, it was true, Sir Elric stood just outside the gate, his eyes on the departing throng. Sir Elric was captain of the company of retainers stationed at Sheriff Hutton Castle, one of the properties of Ralph Neville, Earl of Westmoreland. It lay north of York in the Forest of Galtres; the earl used it as a base from which to keep an eye on York and the temper of the citizens. The earl had set Sir Elric on Kate for two reasons—to engage her as a spy among the York merchants, and to retrieve certain letters he believed to be in her possession, letters incriminating him as supporting both King Richard and Henry of Lancaster, a double deceit. Ralph Neville called on her as kin—he was the patriarch of her late husband's family. Regarding the spying, she obliged him, though only so far, careful what she shared about her fellow merchants. But as for the letters, she had never admitted to possessing them. A lie of omission. They had fallen into her possession as a result of his treasonous manipulations, and should he ever dare threaten her or her family, she would use them to ruin him. "My knight. Hardly!"

Thomas chuckled. "My wife envies you his attentions. She tells me that not only is Sir Elric most pleasing to the eye, but as he is one of Ralph Neville's favorite retainers, he will go far—even farther if the Earl of Westmoreland chooses the right side in this conflict. And as you are the widow of a Neville . . ."

"God's blood, she has played out the wooing all the way to my becoming a lady?" Kate laughed. "She would be disappointed to hear our conversations. We are swordsmen on the field, dancing round each other, waiting to see who attacks first. A mutual distrust."

"I've no doubt. But she believes the king holds court like Arthur of old, and that every knight is noble and pure." He bent over to stroke Ghent's proud head. Thomas had a great affection for the wolfhounds. But at the moment the petting was a ruse to lean close and whisper, "Look how Sir Elric studies the crowd. I pray he is not after information about your trading partners. Or your customers." Thomas was a regular client at Kate's guesthouse on High Petergate.

"You need not worry on either count." Sir Elric knew how she used the house when it was not occupied by important visitors to the minster, but he had no interest in exposing either Kate or her clients. The wealthy lovers of York were safe with him. Or so he said. So far. "But why he stands there, waiting, I cannot guess."

"Perhaps he wishes to ask you about the knights Sir Alan Bennet is gathering in your house on High Petergate? Or your mother's sudden return from Strasbourg?"

"I pray it is neither."

Thomas seemed deaf to her distress. "Considering what we have just discussed in the hall, who could fault him? How do we know that Sir Alan is not bringing in comrades hostile to King Richard?"

Would Elric care about that? Kate wondered. She believed his lord to be ready to support Duke Henry. Thomas, too, truth be told. And the cronies with whom he had chosen to sit at the meeting, all current or former aldermen of York as well as past mayors. She wondered about the current mayor.

"No one is to be trusted, or so it seems to me," Thomas continued, chattering on as if relieving a pent-up need to express himself. "And we've no idea whether Duke Henry had connections in Strasbourg, but as you recall the king's men searched all ships known to be carrying cargo from that fair city. Sir Elric might wonder whether your mother is here on Duke Henry's behalf."

If that were so, Elric would likely consider Dame Eleanor an ally. But he had given no sign of that. "Nonsense," said Kate, pretending a confidence she lacked. For she still had no idea why her mother was in York. When she'd departed the city six years earlier to begin life anew in Strasbourg with her second husband, Ulrich Smit, Eleanor had sworn never to return, that she was finished with the land of her birth. That, too, had been done in haste—Kate's father, David, was only a few months buried. But seeing them together, Kate had guessed that her mother and Ulrich had been lovers a long while. He'd been one of her father's trading partners and a frequent guest in their home in Northumberland, on the border with Scotland. When Eleanor returned in April, a widow once more, her plans had been made in such haste that she arrived before the letter announcing her return. Again, her husband was only a few months buried. A pattern, and one that raised questions in everyone's minds.

Eleanor had brushed off all Kate's questions about her hasty return, saying she had been inspired to found a beguine house, or Martha House, to serve the poor, the ill, and educate young women in York. No matter that there were already a number of small houses serving the poor and ill in York, as well as grammar schools that accepted girls; Eleanor claimed that the beguine houses of Strasbourg were a step above what York offered, both for the women and the community. Her mother had no talent for diplomacy. But she was exceptionally skilled at evading questions.

Though Kate assured Thomas that he had nothing to fear from Sir Elric, she did not trust the knight. And she very much dreaded his appearance at this particular moment. His men watched her home, as if Elric knew not to trust that she kept him informed of all she knew. What might he make of last night's misadventure? How might he twist it to further his earl's interests? "Might I be of use concerning Sister Dina?" Thomas asked. "Perhaps speak with Magistra Matilda about what she might know?"

"Bless you. She would be more willing to speak with you, her benefactor, than she is with me."

"Dame Katherine, Master Thomas." Sir Elric joined Kate and her partner as they passed through the gate.

"Good day to you, Sir Elric, Katherine." Thomas Holme nodded to each in turn. He leaned over to scratch the hounds once more behind their ears, then strode away down the street, hastening to join Thomas Graa and, to Kate's surprise, her cousin William Frost, who had not attended the meeting. How she would love to follow, see where they were headed. The council chambers on Ouse Bridge? Something appeared to be brewing among the ruling elite of York. But they would notice her trailing them no doubt, and lead her astray. And, of course, she now had Sir Elric in tow.

—◦◦◦—

"The hounds are accustomed to him," Sir Elric noted.

"They are grateful for the run of Thomas's river gardens." Kate laughed at the knight's expression. "Never underestimate the intelligence of a wolfhound."

"I will remember that, Dame Katherine."

"You would be wise to do so."

"Such grim faces exiting the guildhall. Is there trouble?"

"Just the small matter of the Duke of York's orders to hold the city against Henry of Lancaster. The effect this turmoil will have on trade. The influx of armed strangers into the city. By the saints, the exile's return affects us all." She softened her irritated response with a quick, false smile. "You waited patiently for us to adjourn. Your mission must be important?"

"You are right, of course. Duke Henry's movements are uppermost in all our minds. In truth, I was curious about this meeting."

"I applaud your honesty. And now you know all. Forgive me, but I must be off—I was to meet with Griselde and Clement this morning, and this meeting went on so long. I despaired at the long-windedness of my fellows. It takes a great deal of hot air to dance around responsibility for the city's safety."

"Might I walk with you?"

She hesitated, distrusting his intent. He had searched her room for the incriminating letters when her family was in crisis, and she hated him for that. But it was a mark of her ambivalence about him, a grudging respect, that she did not think it at all likely that last night's intruder was one of his men. And he might be useful. She might learn something more about Knaresborough and Duke Henry's movements. "Of course."

She snapped her fingers at Lille and Ghent, who had settled in the shade at her feet.

As the four set off up Fossgate, a group of soldiers made way for them. There were more and more of Elric's kind on the streets, swords and daggers bristling. The people of York already had enough of them, drinking, brawling, crowding the city, many encamped on Toft Green across the river, beside the Dominican friary.

Across the river. Kate thought about the small boat Berend had noticed, left on the bank just opposite the staithe.

Another group of soldiers veered to the left of Lille.

"I am glad you go about with the wolfhounds," said Elric. "A man would be a fool to bother a woman flanked by them."

She smiled to herself. "They are good companions." And for the fools, she had a dagger and, occasionally, a small battle-axe concealed in her skirts. She overheard one of the men as he glanced back, "War hounds. Should be handed over to those defending the city."

Elric stopped, turned, called out to the man to watch himself.

"Do not antagonize them," Kate hissed. She tightened her hold on the leads and hurried on. Another worry, though she could not quite imagine how anyone would take Lille and Ghent by surprise. They were too well-trained and experienced. Still, she would tell the household of the man's comments so they knew to be on their guard.

"Has the duke come to claim his Lancastrian inheritance, or the crown?" she asked to distract herself when Elric fell in beside her again.

"In truth, I would not be so bold as to try to fathom his purpose," he said.

Sensing Lille's discomfort with the knight's nearness, Kate stroked her to reassure her.

"Dame Katherine," an acquaintance called, stepping past a group of soldiers slowly walking past Kate, eyeing the hounds. "How glad you must be to have your mother returned to York after her journey north. With soldiers on the road, you must have worried for her." Her mother had traveled to Northumberland to meet with the steward of the family estate and hold a formal requiem for her son Walter, Kate's eldest brother, Petra's father. Kate had told no one of her mother's journey, yet everyone in the city seemed to know of it. He turned a knowing glance at the armed men, then leaned close to say, "Your knight watches over you, I see." And they all noticed the knight who shadowed Kate as well.

She followed his gaze and saw Sir Elric had his hand on the hilt of his sword. Like Thomas's wife, this man would have the two of them wed within hours. *A widow with three wards, surely she would happily give her hand to such a fine knight.*

"Yes, I am most grateful for Dame Eleanor's safe return," she said. "As for Sir Elric, I cannot guess what is in his mind, for clearly you had already come to my assistance."

The compliment quieted the gossip in the man, and he moved on, no doubt shaping the tale of his heroism for his friends at the tavern.

She noticed how people greeted *her*, but hurried on without returning Elric's nods. It was no wonder. In the cause of holding York for King Richard, the citizens bore the strain of hosting an unruly lot. The sheriffs could not very well challenge the soldiers on carrying arms in the city when they were there to defend it. She cursed both the king and his belligerent cousin for bringing such danger to these shores. Ahead, another small clutch of soldiers gathered round two young women who were prettily gesturing about something. How lighthearted they seemed, so free of all cares, though both were older than Kate had been when she married Simon. She could not recall ever feeling so free. From childhood she had been taught to be vigilant, ever ready for trouble. She wondered what it must be like to be them.

"Were you ever so unguarded?" Elric asked, startling her. He was regarding her with interest.

"Growing up on the border? No. Never." She shrugged and changed the topic. "Are your men part of the force defending York for the king?"

"My earl's interests are farther north. Raby."

"Not Knaresborough?" she teased, immediately regretting it for fear he would take her tone as flirtatious.

But he walked on in silence.

Near the Shambles, the dogs grew restive, the stench of the butcher shops a fascination. She often indulged Lille and Ghent with a detour. It was rare that one of the butchers did not offer them a treat. But on this summer morning the odor was too unpleasant, moving her to take a perfumed cloth from her scrip and hold it to her nose.

Still Elric said nothing. What had been his purpose in joining her? His men might have witnessed whatever happened to Dina. Then why did he not mention it? Might he be spying on her for someone else?

As they passed into Colliergate, he bent to retrieve a package dropped by a young woman who was all giggles and smiles and gushing gratitude. No wonder—he was a handsome man, broad-shouldered, with a face that might be beautiful were it not a mirror for his self-delight. But perhaps most enticing on first meeting was a sense of coiled danger that had at first excited Kate, but now, with familiarity, worried her. He knew so much about her—her brother-in-law Lionel would have shared with him the content of Simon's will and the extent of his debts; he could so easily ruin her. Still, if her life had been different, she might have been the one flirting with him for the thrill of catching his eye, inspiring a smile. He bowed to the woman, who blushed prettily as she bobbed her head at Elric, then Kate, and hurried on.

"Do you envy the city bred—pampered, protected, growing up so innocent of the shadows?" Elric asked.

Now twice he had read her mind. "I prefer to face life with my eyes wide open."

He grinned. "I like that about you."

She laughed to hide her confusion. They moved on.

Kate wished she knew where his spies in the city lodged. Watching her house as they did on their rounds, one of them might have seen someone stealing about the area in the early morning, might provide some clue as to who had intruded, and why. For it was quite likely that Sister Dina would be unable to identify the intruder—in the dark, in her fear, knowing so few people in York.

Unless someone had followed the group from Strasbourg? Kate shook that thought away.

The street had narrowed into Low Petergate, and the traffic thickened. Up ahead Kate noticed Drusilla Seaton approaching, a confidante, a widow who frequented the guesthouse with Kate's cousin William Frost. Eyeing Sir Elric with apparent amusement, the widow Seaton nodded to him as she greeted Kate with a kiss and a hug, whispering, "Is anything amiss that you are in the company of Westmoreland's creature? Shall I fetch Berend? I saw him calling on the knights in your lease on High Petergate."

That was good to know. Kate smiled and assured her that they merely happened to be walking in the same direction.

"I trust you attended the guild meeting? Was anything decided?" The widow fanned herself with an embroidered cloth that perfumed the air with lavender while she stole glances at Elric.

"In their wisdom, the merchants chose to leave the defense of the city in the hands of the knights and their men. Or perhaps they simply could not bear sitting in that stifling hall one more moment," said Kate.

"No surprises then. Ah me." Drusilla nodded to Sir Elric, scratched Lille's ear, then Ghent's, and strolled off.

"I feared this would come to pass," Kate said, "that Henry would take advantage of the king's ill-advised departure for Ireland with his army. Either way, to claim the duchy of Lancaster as his inheritance or the crown of England, the duke is inciting civil war. We will all suffer."

"You will be safe within the walls of the city," Elric assured her.

"The Duke of York is not so sanguine about our safety."

Elric paused just before the crossing with Stonegate, clearing his throat. "I believe the threat of a siege is past. For now."

"Then it is true Duke Henry is already in Knaresborough?"

"Please, Katherine, take no risks. And keep the wolfhounds with you at all times."

That comes from the heart, her twin whispered in her mind. *Beware. Quiet, Geoff.*

She met Elric's gaze for a moment, seeing in his eyes more warmth than usual. Far more warmth. "Have you spoken with your men this morning? The ones who watch my house at night?"

"No. I came straight to the guildhall. Why? Was there trouble?"

Was that a slight flinch? She could not be sure. "One of the beguines . . . It must have been a bad dream."

He bowed to her.

"Have a care, Elric."

He reached out as she began to move on, a strong grip on her arm. "About the letters . . ."

She laughed with relief. Back to their usual tussle.

But he was not laughing. "It is life or death now."

"It is immaterial now," she said. Lille growled. Kate hushed her with a touch. "Your warning me means that you're about to ride north in the earl's company. I assume to welcome Henry and offer him your support. A letter, letters—it means nothing now. By the earl's actions shall he be judged." *Not by evidence that he'd spied on both sides*, she added silently.

He met her comments with a blank stare.

She shook off his hand and crossed Stonegate into High Petergate. He followed. She paused in front of the guesthouse. "I do not wish you harm, Elric. I will tell no one what I have guessed. Good day to you, and Godspeed."

"I am not departing York quite yet," he said quietly, turning on his heels and striding off toward Bootham Bar.

Kate bent to slip the leads out of the hounds' collars, letting them precede her to the door of the guesthouse. She looked forward to some ale—it had been quite a day, and it was not yet noon.

⟶✺⟵

In the heat of late morning Dame Eleanor commended Nan and Sister Agnes on their work in the kitchen and adjoining bedchamber. The pooled blood had been mopped up and the stains covered with rushes, Dina's bedding changed, the stained linen tidily folded in readiness for the laundrywoman.

"Go back to the house. Lie down and rest awhile," Eleanor suggested.

She opened the shutters and the door in the kitchen, and sat just outside the entrance spinning and keeping watch, while the heat soaked up the dampness from the scrubbing.

When Sister Clara's gentle shake wakened her, Eleanor silently berated herself for falling asleep. Anyone might have strolled right past her and into the kitchen or the house across the garden. "Is aught amiss?" she asked, gazing up at the comfortable bulk of the beguine. She could never tell what went on behind Clara's calm façade, her soft brown eyes gazing on the world with benevolence. Was she worried? Angry? Bored? Who could tell?

"Were you in the room when Nan and Sister Agnes changed the bedding?" Clara asked with a note of worry. Ah, but she had less control over her voice.

"No. But I found no fault with their work."

"*Mein Gott.*" It was as close to a cry of concern as Eleanor had ever heard from Clara. "Did you move Sister Dina's dagger? Perhaps you

43

did not wish them to see it? I cannot find it. I've searched the room, the kitchen."

"A dagger? Sister Dina keeps a dagger in her bedchamber?" Dame Eleanor set aside her work and rose. "What is a beguine doing with a weapon?"

"Protecting herself. She slept with it beneath her pillow. I might have thought it merely ornamental, a keepsake, but the blade is long and sharp. Holy Mary Mother of God. Sister Dina carries a burden of such fear. I've asked Nan whether she or Sister Agnes moved the dagger, but she swears they took nothing away."

Remembering the blood, and that it was not Dina's, Eleanor crossed herself and prayed for guidance as she followed Clara into the small bedchamber. *Merciful Mother, it is clear that I do not know Sister Dina at all, yet I felt called to her way of life, drawn by the grace I beheld in her. Was I wrong? Did I mistake grace for cunning?* The bedchamber was sparsely furnished, and such a small space it offered little opportunity to hide an ornate dagger. Dina's traveling chest was in Sisters Brigida's and Clara's bedchamber. They had insisted that she not take it out to the kitchen. "It is gone, then." Eleanor wrinkled her nose at the damp smell.

"Perhaps Sister Dina dropped it when she ran. I imagine she ran." As Clara raised her head she dashed away tears. "Now Sister Dina's terrible burden might never be purged from her heart."

Eleanor drew Clara into her arms, shushing her as she had done her children when they were distraught.

"What happened here last night?" Clara sobbed. "What happened to gentle Dina?"

"Hush, now, hush," Eleanor spoke softly. Though her head was abuzz, she stayed quiet, letting Clara work through her grief for her friend. Only when, with one last sob, Clara pulled away and dabbed her eyes did Eleanor lay out her plan to have Griffin sleep in the kitchen until they felt safe.

Clara gave an emphatic nod. "Bless you, Dame Eleanor. He is a reassuring presence. It seems I was hasty insisting that no men bide on this property."

It gave Eleanor, who had advised against the ban, no pleasure to be proved correct in such wise. "Perhaps you might search for the dagger between here and the church," she said. "Take along my maidservant. I think it best we go nowhere without a companion for the nonce."

"Of course," said Clara. "Yes. As we did in Strasbourg. Yes, that would be best." The beguine moved toward the doorway as if in a dream, almost stepping on the feet of Agnes's servant, Nan, as she entered the kitchen. "Oh, Nan! Are you rested?"

A little nod. "Master Lionel Neville is in the hall, Dame Eleanor, and asked to speak with you."

The loathsome Lionel. God help us. Katherine's late husband's younger brother was greedy, grasping, scheming, and but half the man his brother was—or Katherine, for that matter. "What does he want?"

"He is concerned about a rumor that there was trouble here last night."

He is, is he? "Offer him some ale. Nothing better. If he asks, say, sweetly, 'Poor sisters,' and smile. You know how." *You smile at all the men.*

"Yes, mistress."

As Nan turned to do as she was bid, Sister Clara called out, "Wait. Tell Sister Agnes I wish to speak with her."

Nan glanced back. "But what about—"

"Now," Sister Clara ordered in such a voice Nan skittered away.

Eleanor raised a brow in silent query.

"I see that his visit worries you, Dame Eleanor. If we have brought trouble to you or your daughter, I would know at once. I pray you, question her. You must know what this is about." Her face brightened with a surprising smile. "I confess, Nan tests me. I offer up my aggravation for the benefit of all souls."

"Dame Eleanor? Sister Clara?" Agnes stood in the doorway, her face shiny with sweat on her forehead and upper lip. The day *had* grown warm, and she had been scrubbing, though from the creases in her gown it was clear she had indeed been resting awhile.

"Lionel Neville is taking his ease in the hall," said Eleanor. "I state the obvious. You know this. You have perhaps exchanged some pleasantries as you passed through in coming here?"

"I did wish him a good morning and ask his business."

"His answer?"

"That he had come to speak with you about the trouble here last night."

"I wonder why he is so solicitous?" Why would Lionel Neville's ears prick up at news of this particular dwelling? Eleanor searched her memory for what she had heard about him. He lived for the day that Katherine remarried so that he might take possession of his brother's business, but what had that—? Ah, he was known as a niggardly landlord. "Unless he is concerned about possible damage to his property?"

A crease of her sweaty brow. My, my, how the white wimple and veil accentuated Agnes's high color.

"His property, Dame Eleanor? I don't understand."

"Don't lie to me, Agnes. Am I correct in guessing that he owns this house? Why else would he be so concerned about what happened last night?"

Agnes gave the subtlest of nods, as if hoping she might be obedient without incriminating herself. "He is a kind man."

Eleanor gave a bitter laugh. "Lionel Neville kind? There is not a soul in York who would count him so. You have no talent for lying, Agnes. You were wise to choose silence instead." The woman's face had turned an unhealthy crimson. "Oh, for pity's sake, you cannot be surprised by my disappointment. Had you thought I would be pleased to know he owned this house you would have told me."

"I meant to tell you, I did. But he asked that I say nothing. He said that the best gifts are those we give without any wish for recognition. It matters only that God knows, it is enough. So I thought . . . I did not think you would be angry."

"Had you any sense in that head of yours you would understand why I am. Lionel Neville is—no, I waste my breath."

God help her, she had rushed right into Lionel Neville's trap. That business with his brother's will. The man would do anything to push Katherine into the arms of a suitor, always spying on her, looking for an opportunity to trip her up. Or so said young Petra, and Eleanor had learned to trust her granddaughter's confidences. Eleanor closed her eyes and took a breath. Katherine would never believe she had not known she was leasing the house from Lionel. Nor would she forgive. All Eleanor's hopes of reconciliation dashed by her own heedless haste.

"I will go to him," she said.

"Shall I come, Dame Eleanor?" asked Clara.

"No. Take my servant Rose and look for the dagger. No, take Sister Agnes. She could use some fresh air. And, Agnes, as this is not your house, I am at liberty to cast you out. If there is anything more I should know, it is best to tell me now."

Tears welled in the woman's eyes as she reached out in supplication. "Dame Eleanor, I beseech you . . ."

"Obey her and you've nothing to fear," Sister Clara said.

Agnes shook her head. "There is nothing more."

"Good." Sister Clara took the woman by the arm. "Come, we have work to do." With a nod to Eleanor, Clara led Agnes out into the garden.

Squaring her shoulders, Eleanor swept out of the bedchamber, through the kitchen, and across the garden, not pausing until she'd taken a few steps into the hall. Lionel had not yet noticed her. Well dressed and tall, Lionel Neville might have been handsome had he possessed any admirable qualities. But there was a pinched quality to his face and a guardedness in his bearing that suggested petulance and defensiveness—quite accurate signs, which might be considered advance warning to those who must endure his presence. At the moment he was leaning toward the altar as if assessing the value of the embroidered cloth, the statues, crucifix, and candle holders.

"Lovely, isn't it?" she said.

He straightened abruptly. "Dame Eleanor. I did not hear you enter."

"I noticed. We are a quiet household." She bestowed on him her most gracious smile and suggested they sit by the window, where there was a slight breeze. "A gift on such a warm day." Fussing with her skirt, she schooled herself to silence on the matter of the house. She would consult with Katherine before confronting him about it. "You wished to speak to me?"

"I came out of concern for your welfare and that of your household of women. There is talk of an incident here last night? One of your poor sisters attacked?"

"Attacked? Oh, dear me, no. No, Master Lionel. Oh dear, how shall I put it. Sister Dina had a dreadful dream, and paired with . . ." She glanced away as she cleared her throat. ". . . her monthly courses . . ." A shrug. "I fear she is excitable in that way."

He had colored slightly and now averted his eyes in embarrassment. "I am sorry for her suffering, but relieved to hear the cause, that there was no assault or intrusion." He rose. "I pray you, Dame Eleanor, if there is ever anything you might need, be assured you have a friend in me."

And why would I be such a fool as to believe that? Eleanor growled inwardly. But she smiled as she rose to escort him to the door. "You are most kind. At present Sister Dina is being cared for by the poor sisters at the *maison dieu*. I trust there will be no more trouble."

As Lionel ducked out the door and strode round to the alleyway, he glanced back at her with a frown. Wondering whether he had been deceived? Eleanor smiled and nodded to him, then closed the door.

4

RUMORS

———⁓⦵⦵⁓———

Frustrated by how little he had learned from the knights, Berend was about to take his leave when Sir Alan's squire entered from the alleyway and sidled over to the knight, speaking softly, but not softly enough. People took Berend's lost ear as a sign he was deaf. But he plainly heard the squire say, "Westmoreland's man, Sir Elric, has just passed, headed toward Bootham Bar." The knight nodded, dismissing his man.

"You take an interest in Westmoreland's men?" asked Berend. He smiled at Sir Alan's surprise.

The knight flashed an angry look at his squire, then composed himself. "I am curious why he is still here and not on the coast—or Knaresborough, if the current rumor is to be believed—with the earl, welcoming Henry of Lancaster."

"You are so certain Ralph Neville will choose that side?"

"The Earl of Westmoreland married a Lancaster, did he not? For what other purpose than to cast his lot with that powerful house?"

What indeed. Berend noticed the knight peering at him, as if reconsidering.

"I forgot for a moment that your mistress is a Neville by marriage," said Sir Alan. "Perhaps Dame Katherine has heard otherwise?"

Berend did not believe for a moment that the knight had forgotten the connection. "Not to my knowledge," he said as he rose. "It grows late and I would not wish to outstay my welcome. We will talk again." He bowed and departed.

Out on the street Berend hastened toward Bootham Bar, reaching it in time to catch a glimpse of Sir Elric just passing through the gate. He noticed how Elric tilted his hat over his face as he passed a party of knights and foot soldiers arriving on the other end. Cautious about being seen here? But of course he would be aware that those loyal to the king would wonder about the Earl of Westmoreland for the reason Sir Alan stated—married to a Lancaster . . . Berend followed, surprised when Elric turned down toward the gates of the Benedictine abbey of St. Mary's. Now what might he want there?

A group of clerics and two peddlers with a wagon provided the cover Berend needed to draw close to the knight as he reached the abbey gate, close enough to hear his request for directions to the abbot's house and the infirmary.

Seeking permission to visit a wounded colleague? Berend nodded to himself, rubbing his scarred ear.

—◦⊙◦—

The guesthouse hall benefited in such weather from several windows on each alley, allowing for a refreshing breeze. Kate sat with her back to one of the windows and closed her eyes for a moment while Goodwife Griselde led Lille and Ghent out to the kitchen for water. The heat and the events of the morning had already wearied Kate, and it was not yet midday. She meant to quiet her mind, but it kept jumping to Elric, that moment of warmth, and warning.

"I've cold meats, bread, cheese, and ale," Griselde announced as she returned to the hall. Kate nodded, eyes still closed, listening as the housekeeper's husband, Clement, entered from the kitchen, his limp giving him away. She smiled to hear yet a third member of the procession. Berend—she would know his tread anywhere. Solid, sure. When they were assembled round the small table, Kate opened her eyes and sat up, brushing a stray curl back behind her ear.

Griselde rose to help, tucking the curl into the crispinette. "When you arrived you looked as if your morning had been full and troubling, Mistress Clifford. I thought to give you a few moments to rest. I am glad to see you already more at ease."

Would that she were. Kate patted the woman's hand in thanks. "Our day began far too early." She nodded to Berend. "So much to tell. I don't quite know where to begin."

"As ever, at the beginning. The hounds sounding the alarm," said Berend.

"That is how it began," said Kate.

"I am eager to hear of what happened," said Griselde as she settled across the table. "Jennet asked me to tell you what she learned about Nan's mother. I invited her to wait for you, but she was in such haste." A shake of her head. "On the subject of Nan I've plenty to say. And about her mistress, Agnes Dell."

Kate remembered Griselde's dismay at the news that Eleanor had chosen Agnes Dell's house as her Martha House, how she'd sniffed at the news that Agnes meant to bide with them as a sister. She had predicted it would be but a brief partnership. Kate had refrained from comment, asked for no explanation, in truth told Griselde she wanted to hear no more. Her mother had judged it a mutually beneficial arrangement. She might make of that what she would. She did not need to share her suspicion that her mother's pretense at piety served a temporary need to conceal her true reason for fleeing to York.

"Perhaps you might start with your news," Kate said, now regretting how she had silenced the woman, wondering what she might have prevented had she known more.

Griselde settled back with her bowl of ale in hand. "Jennet said to say that Nan's mother, Hawise, has long been ill. She sleeps through most of her days, attended by the four children who have not yet left to go into service. All too young for such responsibility, if you ask me," Griselde huffed. "That was me, not Jennet. It is true that Nan comes at night, but the children seemed to be keeping some secret about that—frightened eyes, pokes in the ribs. Nan has a reputation on the street for being easy, loving the men, that is what Jennet heard. So she intends to explore some of the rumors further, see whether Nan visits her mother alone. As for Agnes Dell, I've told you that Dame Eleanor did her beguines no favors in moving in with that lot. I should know, Agnes had been here often enough with her husband's employer, your neighbor John Paris, both before and after she was widowed."

"John Paris's Agnes? That I did not know."

"I tried to tell you, Mistress Clifford. But you did not wish to hear what I knew of Agnes Dell."

"I remember. My anger clouded my judgment."

Griselde pressed Kate's hand. "Dame Eleanor has caused you trouble and great sorrow, I know, Mistress Clifford. You will be glad to hear that since Agnes took up with your mother's beguines she has not been here."

"At least that."

"Do not blame yourself," said Berend. "We know now, when we most need to know, eh?" His expression was caring, without judgment.

Kate relaxed a little. "What else do you know about Agnes, Griselde?"

"She was no better than her servant Nan, so they say. There was much gossip about Agnes and her boarders."

"Her boarders? Did Jennet say that?"

"Jennet said nothing about Agnes."

"So Agnes came here with John Paris while she was taking in boarders—boarders who also may have been lovers?" Berend asked.

"So they say." Griselde seemed hesitant now. "Though it is only gossip. I have no personal knowledge of the woman, except as a guest here."

"Might John Paris have arranged the boarders? Might Paris have threatened Agnes—and possibly her husband—if she did not oblige?" Kate looked around the table. "What do we know of her husband's death?"

Clement and Griselde shook their heads.

"He died at sea, or while away," said Berend. "There might be something there."

"So what have Agnes and Nan done that you are asking about them?" asked Griselde.

What had they done? What had Kate done in neglecting to look into the household before her mother moved in? Not that she could have deterred Eleanor.

Fortified by an occasional pause for ale, Kate proceeded to sketch out the events since the dogs woke her in the night. It was important that Griselde and Clement knew the situation. They were her representatives here in the guesthouse, and oversaw what they could in Kate's other property next door, the house leased by Sir Alan Bennet and his gathering of knights. "What did you learn?" Kate asked, turning to Berend.

"The knights gave no sign that they'd heard of the morning's event. In that, as in everything, they were too closemouthed for my taste. They did express surprise about the response to the defense of York. Weaker than they had expected, according to Sir Alan."

"York is splitting at the seams with armed men," Griselde said. "How many more did they expect? And where, I ask, did they think to stuff them?"

Kate told them of her suspicion regarding the current and former aldermen, and the rumor about Knaresborough, especially the comment that Duke Henry was making promises only a king might carry out.

Clement nodded. "He is promising taxation only in times of emergency, that is what I heard in the tavern."

"Sir Alan's men also mentioned Knaresborough," said Berend.

They were all silent for a moment, pondering the significance of all that had been spoken. How much blood would be shed, would Lancaster punish all those who supported their anointed king, what fate did he intend for King Richard, if deposed? Kate shivered.

"I do not know for whom to pray," said Clement, "King Richard or Duke Henry?"

"Pray for us, husband," said Griselde.

Berend nodded. "It is the small folk who suffer, it is always so. The farmers whose crops are trampled and burned, the foot soldiers who fall beneath the knights' destriers, the merchants who cannot use the roads while the armies roam freely . . ."

"As Mistress Clifford said, the guild knows there is trouble ahead," said Griselde. "Look at us. Already the presence of too-curious knights next door has frightened off some of our best customers."

"Is that true?" asked Kate. It was the first she had heard of it.

"It is indeed," said Griselde. "Your cousin William Frost and the widow Seaton are choosing discretion while Sir Alan holds court next door. And Dame Catherine and her Stefan."

Thomas Holme's wife. "But not Thomas?"

"No. He and his Mary are not so easily frightened."

"God give me patience." Kate closed her eyes and took a deep breath. Less income to apply to Simon's debts and memorial masses. People would notice if she neglected the latter. "Drusilla Seaton said nothing about this when we met on the street just now." She hoped it was simply because of Sir Elric's presence, nothing more, not distrust.

"I still believe you were right in accepting Sir Alan's offer," said Berend. "It might have been far worse had you been ordered by the mayor and aldermen to open your house to the armed men. At least Sir Alan is paying you generously and keeping the house in knightly hands."

Kate knew he was right, but the loss of income was a setback she had hoped to avoid. Sir Alan's rent was temporary. If the hiatus inspired Drusilla and William to separate for good . . . *God forgive my selfishness,* she silently prayed. Aloud she asked Berend what else he had learned from Sir Alan and his guests.

"We will want to watch them. They were far too ill at ease about my visit, though they seemed not to have heard about last night's events."

"Before we stray too far afield, we should consider just what happened last night," said Kate. "Nan went out, leaving the kitchen unlocked. According to her, she has done so for a while. Someone entered by that door and found Dina in her bedroom. Did someone know about the unlocked door? Had Nan done this before it was a Martha House, when there were boarders? Who were the boarders?"

"John Paris once mentioned in passing that Leonard Dell—that would be Agnes's late husband—had far more pleasure of his maid-servant Nan than he did of his wife. He grinned at that—of course he would, being the one who did have pleasure of the man's wife, the bloody . . ." Clement shifted uncomfortably as a tremor ran through his body.

Griselde pressed his hand and poured him more ale. He lifted the bowl with both hands, the contents splashing round but never spilling. Griselde knew just how much to fill it. Clement's tremors were more frequent of late. Kate had noticed several while they reviewed the accounts earlier in the week. She knew better than to ask whether they were tiring him.

"It seems I need to get to know John Paris better," she said. "Do you know him well, Clement?"

He shook his head. "I doubt I know any more than you, Mistress Clifford." The words came out slightly slurred and Clement reddened. Kate's heart ached for him.

"So the knights next door were of no help?" Griselde asked, drawing attention away from her husband's discomfort.

"They *did* ask whether I knew any of the monks of St. Mary's Abbey. At first I thought they were confused, as I'd said I live in the parish of St. Mary's Castlegate. But they asked about monks, no mistaking. Odd on the same morning that Sir Elric makes a visit to the abbey."

Kate sat up. "When?"

"I've just come from following him to the gate. He asked the gatekeeper for directions to the abbot's house and the infirmary."

So that was where he had been headed. The abbey infirmary. Had one of his men been injured? Had he lied about not having spoken to his men? When Berend poured himself more ale and seemed to slip into his own thoughts, Kate asked, with some urgency, "You did say the infirmary?" Berend nodded. "And do you know any of the monks?"

"When I first came to York I had a swelling in my scarred ear. Or what was once an ear. I was told that Brother Henry, the infirmarian, might be able to help. I had not expected such an elder. He was in ill health at the time but assured me that the sub-infirmarian, Brother Martin, was in fact far more skilled in such wounds than he was. So, yes, I know the monks in the infirmary."

"I should think those in the infirmary know all that happens in an abbey," said Kate, excited. "Do you think Brother Martin will talk to us?"

"It has been years since I spoke with him. But we parted friends. I returned a few times for the unguent, but once he was confident my ear was healing he sent me to the apothecary in St. Helen's Square, assuring me that she would know exactly what I needed. So I've had no cause to return."

"Until now," said Kate. "Bless you, Berend. He might have some answers for us. Go to him. See if he will talk."

⁕⁕⁕

Sister Clara returned to the hall empty-handed, the dagger still missing. "I saw Master Lionel depart," she said as she sank onto a bench with a sigh. "Might I ask what you told him?"

Eleanor crossed herself. "I lied to him. It seemed my only recourse. I could think of nothing else."

Clara nodded. "I might well have done the same. I propose that Sister Brigida and I ask to join Sister Dina in the *maison dieu*, vowing to obey the rules of the house while we reside there, and that you return to William Frost's residence until this is resolved. By taking such actions we will prove to Dame Katherine our sincere regret for our error in trusting Agnes Dell."

"The error was mine, Sister Clara. You should not suffer for it. Their rules would deprive you of your work outside the sister house, your means of support." Not to mention that the thought of returning to bide under Isabella Gisburne Frost's roof nauseated Eleanor. She despised the woman—a mutual dislike. Though if it would appease Katherine, it bore consideration. Despite what Katherine thought, Eleanor still hoped to find a way to make peace with her daughter. She was all she had left. "What of Sister Agnes? Do we simply abandon her? What if she is sincere in wishing to embrace the life of a beguine?"

Bowing her head, Clara seemed absorbed in folding her hands one way, then the other on her lap. Just as Eleanor began to wonder whether a response was forthcoming, Clara sighed. "In truth, I cannot find it in my heart to trust Agnes now—or consider her a sister. If she does sincerely wish to embrace the life of poverty, chastity, and obedience, she has many small houses from which to choose in York. It need not be ours."

Though Eleanor felt much the same, she found it jarring from a woman devoted to spreading word of God's all-abiding love. "And where am I to find another house for us?" Eleanor wondered, startled to hear her own voice. "Forgive me, I did not mean to burden you with my concerns. This is not your difficulty to resolve."

"We work together, Dame Eleanor. It is *our* problem." Clara looked round the hall, her eyes resting on the lady altar they had furnished so lovingly. "Our Blessed Mother shall show us the way."

A dangerously foolish philosophy, Eleanor thought, but kept her counsel. "Before we say anything to Agnes, I propose that you and I consult with my daughter and my man Griffin. I would have their thoughts on abandoning Agnes."

A simple bow. "I am happy to take that precaution. Is that the correct word?"

"Your grasp of the language is nothing short of remarkable, Sister Clara."

Meanwhile, Eleanor thought she might do well to have a word with God. She feared that this hindrance was a sign that he rejected her avenue of atonement for betraying her husband David, the father of her children, with Ulrich. But why had God not stopped her earlier? In Strasbourg? On the journey to York?

She excused herself and knelt on a cushion before the altar. After a few Hail Marys, she silently asked, *If you did not wish me to do this, my Lord, why did you not give me a sign before I plucked these good women from their home in Strasbourg? Punish me, not them, I pray you.* She bowed her head and waited. A sharp pain in her right knee jolted her upright. As she shifted on her cushion she felt a flush of warmth and her mind cleared. This was merely a test, a trial, all part of the path. *I hear you, my Lord. I will go softly, with care.*

As she rose, crossing herself, she was surprised to find Sister Clara still perched on the edge of her chair.

A gentle smile. "You are reassured, Dame Eleanor?"

"I am, Sister Clara. I will send for Katherine and Griffin."

"He is already here, in the kitchen. You sent for him earlier?"

"Ah. So I did." Eleanor shook out her skirts. "So. Time to face my daughter."

—◦◦◦◦—

Kate and Griselde were up on the landing outside the guest bedchambers shaking out the cushions when they heard Lille and Ghent barking a welcome down in the yard. Jennet stood by them, looking up, shading her eyes.

Kate called down to her. "Have you news?"

"Not from me. I believe Dame Eleanor has something to tell you. She says she needs to speak with you. A matter of some urgency, she said."

"That does not bode well," Griselde muttered.

"No. No, it does not." Kate turned away, thinking. "I did want to stay until Berend returned from the abbey. And to help you with this."

"Oh, do not stay on my account, mistress. I do not have so much work at present that I cannot shake out the cushions in good time. We've only one room occupied tonight. No one is here tomorrow night. I can manage. I will send Berend straight to you when he returns."

Kate nodded. "I would rather stay, but if I linger I will begin to spin a web of horrific possibilities regarding Mother's 'matter of some urgency.' I did hope to find something that might keep me busy in the alley so that I might chance to overhear what my knightly tenants discuss next door."

"I could give Seth such a task," Griselde suggested. Young Seth Fletcher assisted Griselde and Clement with the more strenuous tasks.

"I'd not thought of Seth. Where is he today?"

"Have you not heard the hammering? He is repairing the garden shed. He loves to keep busy, that young man. A blessing he is."

"Good. Try to find him some quiet task in the alleyway so that he might hear conversations."

Griselde plucked the cushion from Kate's hands. "I will, mistress. And you will send word with anything we should know?"

"I'll send Matt to you this evening. You will hear all. For now, I'll have Jennet give Seth some training in discreet spying."

—◦◦◦◦—

Discovering the postern gate of St. Mary's Abbey locked, Berend cursed at the need to go the long way once more, out Bootham Bar and round to the main gate of the abbey. The Bootham gatekeepers were busy with merchants and more of the armed men coming to the defense of the city. It seemed that today's fresh influx traveled in smaller groups than they had at the beginning, and he eyed them with unease, certain that some were mercenaries and killers for hire, as he had been at one time. He was not concerned with the ones in livery—they were easily brought to heel by their lords if they caused trouble. It was the ones with no obvious badge of belonging that caused a tingling in his scarred ear. These might as easily be spies for Lancaster disguised as men ready to defend the city for the king; or, perhaps worse, solely interested in plunder and blood sport.

As he passed through the stone enclosure and felt the sun on his head, he caught a movement out of the corner of his eye. In a moment, four men had drawn daggers and were dancing round each other. No livery. No way to know who had started the altercation, or why. But it was just the sort of fight that could grow into a bloody tragedy—one that a spy might use to undermine confidence in the city's defenses.

By the time the gatekeeper shouted for help, Berend was in the middle of the fray, tossing one of the dagger-wielding bullies out of the tight circle. Already three more had joined the tussle.

"At your side. You go right, I'll go left," said a man in livery, sword drawn, and Berend nodded, drawing his dagger and moving as suggested. Two more joined them, and soon the fighters were sitting on the side of the road guarded by four swordsmen in the livery of Edmund, Duke of York. A fifth, the one who had spoken to Berend, slapped him on the back, thanking him.

"We could use you."

"So you could. But I've left that life behind."

"You were quick to act just now."

"I don't like trouble in my city."

The man squinted in the sunlight. "I've seen you before. With the lady of the wolfhounds."

Berend did not like the knowing tone in the man's voice. "So you have. She, too, dislikes trouble in our city."

"Your wife?"

"My employer."

"Ah. I can see why you choose to stay." A leer. "Those are war dogs."

"They are. And trained from birth to attack anyone they sense a threat to her or anyone in her household." Not trusting himself to control his rising irritation, Berend nodded to the man and headed down toward the abbey gate.

The man was right about Lille and Ghent. Irish wolfhounds were excellent war dogs—he'd fought alongside some. But he'd never encountered any so well trained as they were. In truth, he had never encountered anyone like Katherine Clifford. He had been in York but a few days when he noticed her moving through the city with her gray sentinels. Intrigued, he'd asked about her. A Clifford, people told him, married to a Neville, connected to the Frosts and Gisburnes—no one to toy with.

So he had been surprised in the best way when she had approached him at the market, sauntering over to him as folk gave way for the imposing dogs. "You are rumored to be a good cook. Is it true? Are you looking for work?"

"I am," he'd said. His parents had owned a tavern. He'd worked in the kitchen until running away to be a soldier.

"I need a cook. Are you interested?"

He would have laughed at her proposal but that he'd heard on the street how she had caught Jennet in the act of stealing the pewter plates in her hall as the family slept, and had hired her that very night, as her maidservant. An assassin turned cook, he would feel quite at home.

"I can think of no household in which I'd rather serve."

She'd smiled then, a genuine smile, her eyes warm. "So Jennet was right. She wagered you would agree. Come, Berend, help me shop for dinner. My husband likes spicy food."

God's grace was with him that day. He would do anything for her. Anything. Even break the vow he'd made when he walked away from his previous profession. If she ever needed an assassin . . . But she would never ask that of him. She would do what needed to be done herself.

He was keenly aware of how Dame Katherine would fascinate the warriors arriving in York. Though few were as battle-scarred as Berend, he saw himself in them, himself and all with whom he'd fought. He noticed them watching the three of them, the tall, enigmatic woman with the gray giants flanking her. They imagined in her a woman who would understand their hunger for strength and beauty in a violent world, a woman who could admire their feats in arms, comprehend their stories, what the victories and defeats meant to them. And Dame Katherine would. She did. Berend was grateful for that. He was not worried about her ability to defend herself; he had all confidence in her. But the other women—weak, unarmed, frightened women such as Sister Dina—these were the women for whom he feared. As did Dame Katherine.

As he stepped through the abbey gate, Berend felt a surge of relief. For a moment he forgot his mission and said a prayer of gratitude that there was such a place so near the city, a haven of peace, a sanctuary in which he might lay down his burden of worry. Brothers and servants moved about their chores in silence, their pace much slower than out in the city, as if they had all the time in the world. Berend slowed his own steps, and as he made his way to the infirmary he allowed his gaze to rest gently on the elegant buildings and the lovingly tended gardens. One could forget for a moment the gathering of armed men to defend the city, the sense of imminent danger. He had missed his visits to Brother Martin. The apothecary had indeed provided the same unguent, but her shop was no refuge from his cares.

He rapped gently on the door of the infirmary, drawing his mind back to his purpose. Today the abbey was more than a retreat from the world; it was a source of information. Here he hoped he might discover whose blood stained Sister Dina's gown.

A dark-eyed, chubby novice opened the infirmary door.

"I have come to speak with Brother Martin."

The novice gazed up at Berend in startled silence for a moment, then seemed to hear his request. "Oh. I pray you forgive me. It is not every day I discover a stranger at the door."

And today, at least two? Berend wondered.

"Brother Martin is in the herb garden. Is he expecting you?"

"No. But he will remember me." Berend slipped off his simple felt hat and tilted his head to display the scar where once was an ear. "That it has healed so well is thanks to his skill."

A slight frown and a subtle drawing back suggested the novice was not sure he would consider it healed. But he quickly recovered, and, bowing, said, "I will escort you, Master . . . ?"

"Berend."

Another bow, and the novice stepped out the door, shutting it behind him, and led Berend round the building.

He smelled the herbs before he saw the garden—spicy, sweet, aromatic. And now he beheld the serene order of the beds, heard the murmur of bees and other winged gardeners. Eden. Paradise.

A black-robed form bent over a hedge of lavender.

"Brother Martin?"

The figure straightened, pushing back a wide-brimmed hat that had half fallen over his eyes. "Yes, Andrew, what—Oh, Master Berend." He came forward, brushing off his gloves, then removing one to take Berend's hand. "What a pleasure to see you. It has been so long. How is the ear?" His cheer seemed forced.

"Healed, as far as is possible, thanks to your care, Brother Martin."

"I hear that you are now a cook. Are you here to beg some unusual herbs?"

"I would not say nay to anything you might offer. What dishes I might concoct with such variety! But I've come on less sanguine business."

"An illness in the household?"

"No, God be thanked. Might we sit somewhere quiet? Here in the garden, if you please." Berend gestured toward a bench shaded by an old linden.

A little shrug, a nod to young Andrew and a gesture releasing him to return to the infirmary. "A moment in the shade would be welcome, Master Berend."

"Just Berend. I am no man's master."

A surprised laugh. "You sounded like my father just then." As the monk settled on the bench he removed his hat and pushed back imaginary hair—he had so little hair he'd scant need for a tonsure. An old habit then, from before he'd taken vows. Berend tried to imagine what he might have looked like in youth. Thin, long-limbed, and, judging by his brows and lashes, fair-haired. He would have been a comely lad, even-featured, with large, expressive eyes. Eyes that now returned his gaze with a wariness they'd not held when they last met.

"I will not trifle with you by circling round my purpose, Brother. One of the Earl of Westmoreland's knights, Sir Elric, came to the abbey this morning asking to be directed to the abbot's lodgings and the infirmary."

A shrug. "Many come to the gate, for blessings, in hope of healing." The monk coolly met his gaze. "Abbot Thomas rarely sends them on to me. You touched him. That is why he welcomed you when you first came to York, your quest for absolution, redemption. Have you found it in service to Dean Richard's niece?"

Clever how he diverted the questions to Berend himself. And well informed. "I am on the path, as is my purpose in coming to you. A young woman was accosted by an intruder in Dame Eleanor Clifford's house of poor sisters last night. I have cause to think the young woman, Sister Dina, might have injured her attacker. I wondered whether he had found his way here."

"A poor sister was accosted?"

Choosing his words with a care to accuracy yet a sense of the horror of Sister Dina's ordeal and her frightened silence, Berend took the monk through the events of the night and early morning. "My employer, Katherine Clifford, is determined to find out what happened. I ask in the hope that Sir Elric possibly heard something of the incident from one of his men in the city?"

"May God watch over Sister Dina," Brother Martin whispered, crossing himself. "And all in her household." The monk sat for a moment, folding his hands in his lap—work-roughened hands, despite the gloves he had tucked in his rope girdle.

Berend tried to quiet his own mind, allow anything to arise that pointed to something he might have missed in the telling. "I understand that I am casting a wide net," he added quietly.

A little smile as Brother Martin shifted on the bench, facing Berend. "I am not a stranger to the investigation of a crime. My father—foster father—"

"He who was master to no man?"

A nod. "I sometimes assisted him in solving crimes in the city. So my mind has gone straight down that disused path, calling up questions so that I might sort them. It seems you have many unanswered questions. Why choose to come to me? The city is filled with armed men at present. Strangers."

"With such a background you will understand why I must consider all avenues that might help resolve this as soon as possible. Before someone else is threatened. Did Sir Elric come to you? Is an injured man lying in your infirmary? One of his men?"

"Perhaps if you spoke to my abbot, you—" The monk paused as the novice Andrew came round the corner of the infirmary in some haste.

"Brother Henry says you must come at once, Brother Martin." Andrew glanced at Berend, bit his lip, looked down, bowed, and made a hurried retreat.

Brother Martin crossed himself and rose with a deep sigh.

"I can return," Berend said.

"Go with God," Brother Martin murmured as he tucked his hands up his sleeves and hurried after the novice.

5

REMORSE

———— ~ᗡᘐᗭ~ ————

After their long rest in the guesthouse kitchen, Lille and Ghent fairly trotted alongside Kate, happily sniffing at passersby, far calmer than earlier in the day. Kate, on the other hand, forced herself to the brisk pace in an attempt to combat the creeping weariness of early afternoon in high summer. The air felt thick, heavy, and her shoulders ached with the tensions of the day, yet she felt restless. Some time at the archery butt, or practicing with her battle-axe, that is what she needed.

Lille's rumbling growl caught her attention.

Danger! Geoff shouted in Kate's mind.

As Kate drew her dagger, she and the hounds turned as one, startling two armed men who were much too close. One carried a rope. Kate pointed the dagger at one, then the other, and warned them that she was about to order the dogs to attack. The men backed away, disappearing down an alleyway. Her mother's man, Griffin, appearing from nowhere, chased after them, but he returned in a moment, shaking his head.

"I've lost them."

Kate considered the Welshman, who had spent years in the Holy Roman Empire, judging by his accent. Crusading? As a mercenary? Just as she'd not bothered to investigate Agnes Dell, she'd ignored Griffin.

Ghent stepped between them, ready to protect Kate.

Holding up his empty hands, Griffin had the good sense to take a few steps back. "My mistake, Dame Katherine. I thought you might need assistance."

"You see me through Dame Eleanor's eyes." Kate rubbed the hounds' ears, caught up their leads, and turned to continue on her way, more disturbed by the encounter than she wished Griffin to guess, but also oddly satisfied, all weariness gone. "What is your business on Coney Street?"

"Searching for you. Dame Eleanor said it was urgent."

"She sent you as well as Jennet?"

"Patience is not her virtue?"

"No, it is not. Jennet did not know what the urgent matter might be. Do you?"

"No."

God help her. What had her mother done now? Noticing with annoyance that Griffin kept pace slightly behind her, she motioned for him to walk beside Ghent. "He shakes off his response to danger faster than his sister," she said when he hesitated.

He did as she wished. "Berend is right, you've a rare connection with your hounds."

So he'd been discussing her with Berend?

Interesting, Geoff said in her head. *But I wouldn't hold it against him.*

We'll see, Geoff. We'll see.

They fell into easy laughter over the strangers' apparent ignorance.

"He thought they would submit to his attempt to catch them with a rope?" Kate laughed.

"A plot conceived over one too many tankards of ale, I would guess," said Griffin.

As they approached Kate's house, Lille and Ghent pricked their ears. Across Castlegate, two men stood guard at the *maison dieu*. Kate changed direction, crossing toward them. "Sister Dina is there," she said in answer to Griffin's questioning expression.

"Did you order a guard?" he asked.

She shook her head, recognizing the two men. "Sir Elric's." His visit to the abbey and now this—it was clear that Elric had known about the intruder all along. Devious man, she was right not to trust him. "I will step inside, have a word with Magistra Matilda."

"But Dame Eleanor . . ."

"I shall try her patience a while longer. This cannot wait."

Griffin nodded. "I'm glad to wait with the hounds."

Surprised by the offer, Kate held out her hand for his, then guided him to touch Lille's back, then Ghent's. She bent to rub their ears. "Be easy with him," she whispered. "I won't be long." She greeted Elric's men, who stood aside to allow her in. "Did you or your comrades witness anything last night?"

The men bowed to her but did not speak. Which suggested the answer was yes. But nothing more. Elric had trained them well.

In the dimness of the sisters' hall, Kate was greeted by a servant who knew her, knew who she wished to see.

"Come this way, I pray you, Mistress Clifford." She led Kate into a small room off the hall, warmed with a brazier even on this summer afternoon. Magistra Matilda sat at the side of a small cot, watching Sister Dina sleep. A crucifix on the wall, a small table beside the cot, a shuttered window. Bare essentials.

"Any change?" Kate asked.

"At last she sleeps a healing sleep," said Matilda. "For a long while she lay watching the ceiling and moving her lips, but no sound, no sound." She shook her head. "What terror does she revisit?"

"I have been too incurious about the beguines my mother collected."

"She is not your responsibility, surely?"

"When did the Earl of Westmoreland's men take up the guard here?"

Matilda shook her head. "I knew nothing of it until one of the sisters returned in tears, fearing that we were being put out of our house so that the soldiers might lodge here. The men say they were ordered to ensure Sister Dina's safety until her attacker is found. I demanded to see their captain."

Elric knew everything, damn him. "And have you spoken to him?"

"Not yet." Her veil trembled with indignation. "But I have sent word to the sheriffs."

Unhappy news. "Did your message mention the intruder last night?"

"Only that there was one. And I am concerned that the Earl of Westmoreland has overstepped his bounds." A sniff of irritation.

Not as bad as Kate had feared, but still . . . Once the sheriffs knew of the intruder the story would spread quickly throughout York. Any scandal touching her was bad for business—lenders and customers became uneasy. And with all the soldiers, it was no time to stand out. "Had you mentioned an intruder to anyone before Sir Elric's men arrived?"

"Do you accuse me—"

"No." Kate raised her hands in surrender. "But I cannot understand how the knight knew to put guards here, can you?"

"I have said nothing to anyone outside this house. And I ordered all in my charge to say nothing."

"Then someone else knows and told Sir Elric," said Kate. She bowed to Matilda, thanked her for watching over Dina.

"I will send for you if there is any change," Matilda assured her. "Or if the sheriff sends someone."

Perhaps Berend's visit to the abbey might reveal what Elric knew, what his night watch had witnessed. If not, Kate must think of a way to confront the knight without seeming to confront him.

Outside, the sun beat down. She was glad to see that Griffin had found a shady spot beneath a tree to rest with the hounds. As she approached, he rose with a fluidity that impressed her.

"How is Sister Dina?" he asked.

"Sleeping peacefully." Kate smiled as Lille and Ghent joined them, nudging her hands for ear rubs. As she obliged them, she thanked Griffin for watching them.

"To be honest, it felt as if they were keeping me polite company," he said.

Kate waited until they crossed into Hertergate to ask Griffin why her mother had sent him and not a servant to fetch her.

"Dame Eleanor grew anxious that Jennet might not have stressed the urgency of her summons. I set off to find you."

A stroke of luck that he'd found her, then. "But you know nothing of what happened that she's so keen to see me?"

"To see both of us. Devil if I know. Except that she had an unexpected visitor—Lionel Neville."

That sent a shiver down Kate's sweat-dampened back. "God help me. If Dame Eleanor and Lionel are in league—"

"No, no, I did not mean that. I assure you, she dislikes him as much as you do."

"So she has told you all about us?"

"To be honest, I heard it on the street."

Of course. Their bad blood would make good gossip. "I take no comfort in your empty assurance. She has not as much cause to dislike him as I do." She led Lille and Ghent down the side of the Martha House and into the garden, finding a shady spot for them beneath the kitchen eaves. "A bowl of water?" she asked Griffin.

He fetched it from the kitchen without hesitation, and proffered a small plate of cold meats. "Not so rich as what they deserve."

"But welcome for now." She smiled, a peace offering.

"Dame Eleanor awaits us—" Griffin gestured not to the main house but the kitchen.

"In here?" As she stepped into the kitchen, Kate wrinkled her nose at the warring scents of damp earth and lye.

"The intruder bled enough to weaken a man," Griffin noted.

"Yet he managed to elude us."

Kate paused in the doorway to the small bedchamber, nodding to her mother, who had been sitting on the bed, hands folded. Now Eleanor rose and came to kiss Kate on the cheek. A surprising gesture.

"Bless you for finding her, Griffin."

"She was already on her way, Dame Eleanor. I merely accompanied her from Coney Street." He said no more.

Placing a cool hand on Kate's arm, Eleanor leaned close to request that they adjourn to her house. "I would as lief not be overheard."

Kate glanced around. It was only the three of them. What did her mother fear? "Of course. Berend is out, so the kitchen should be quiet. I have some information for you as well." She noticed shadows beneath her mother's eyes, and a subtle bowing of her shoulders. "What did Lionel want?"

"At your house, daughter. Griffin, come along."

The Welshman grinned good-naturedly and followed.

Kate called to Lille and Ghent as she moved through the garden to the gate in the hedgerow. In her own kitchen, Matt was piling wood and coals by the hearth. Changing her plan, Kate told Matt they'd be in the hall.

"But Sister Brigida and the girls . . ."

"The weather is so fine, they might enjoy taking their lessons out in the garden. Bring ale and some food to us, then wander down to the staithes, chat with the workers. Perhaps someone's talking about trouble there in the early morning."

Matt's expression brightened. Kate knew he missed the bustle of High Petergate, where he'd supported Griselde and Clement.

Sister Brigida and her pupils greeted Kate's idea with delight, the girls hurrying from the hall clutching their wax tablets and giggling as they attempted to express their happiness in elegant Parisian. Brigida followed at an only slightly more sedate pace, whispering to Kate, "They are such joys."

In the ensuing silence, Griffin settled on a bench between the two windows. Taking off his felt hat, he leaned back and sighed with pleasure as the cross-draft ruffled his coppery curls.

Eleanor had been drawn to the vertical loom directly beneath the east window, touching the bright threads. "You've done some work on it."

"Petra and I. It reminds her of happy times with Old Mapes, the healer who raised her." Kate's niece had quickly adapted to the sounds and rhythms of her household. The loss of a father she'd never known, and the two who had brought her up, still burdened her with sorrow, but as she discovered her deep similarities with Kate, and was shown over and over again by all in the household—even Marie, in her own way—that she was loved and appreciated, she found the strength to hold that sorrow. "We both take great pleasure in the time together." Kate felt herself bracing for the much-remembered criticisms: *You are all thumbs. Your color pairings are no better than if a blind girl chose them. Do you call that a pattern?*

But Eleanor merely nodded, settling in one of the high-back chairs. "As we worked the loom when you were learning. Do you remember the songs?"

Kate exhaled. "I do." It was a bittersweet memory, conjuring scenes of her brothers crowding into the hall with the dogs and cats, threatening to topple the tall loom. All dead now, all three brothers. Though Geoff, her twin, lived on in spirit, it was not the same, would never be the same.

Matt's arrival with ale and food drew Kate out of her sudden melancholy—his smile was a grace, always able to warm her heart.

"I will be away now." He hummed a jaunty tune as he strode from the hall.

Griffin bestirred himself, pouring some ale, slicing some cheese to balance on a chunk of bread.

"Some woman will be most fortunate in that young man," said Eleanor. "Or have you claimed Matt for yourself, Daughter? I saw how you brightened with his arrival."

Eleanor, with her startlingly green eyes and winning ways—when she chose to use them—had always charmed men into caring for her and dancing to her tune. Her husbands, sons, nephews, cousins, brothers, neighbors—the males had all been hearts to conquer and shape to her advantage.

Kate chose to ignore her comment about Matt. "So. Lionel paid you a visit?"

Eleanor's teasing smile vanished with a sigh, and she bowed her head. "That odious creature. He pretended concern about our welfare, having heard about an intruder." She fussed with a sleeve. Was that a tear rolling down her cheek? "But Agnes lied to us, you see. The house was not her gift to give. It belongs to Lionel Neville."

"God in heaven," Kate whispered. He must be praying for a scandal in the Martha House, something to ruin her good name by association.

Eleanor leaned toward Kate, reaching for her hand, pressing it with both of hers. Yes, there were tears spilling down her face. "I am so sorry, Katherine. I didn't know—I never imagined—I was in such haste. It is my fault. I am to blame. How can you forgive me?"

Kate touched her mother's cheek with the back of her hand and shook her head at the impossibility of what her mother had uttered. Never had she heard those words from her mother: *sorry, my fault, I am to blame.* Months earlier, when she had confronted Eleanor with the horror she had unleashed by carelessly advising Walter, Kate's eldest brother, to reach out to an old enemy, stirring the flames of an anger that would not be slaked until both men were dead and Petra was an orphan, her mother had refused to take responsibility, much less express remorse. She had even tried to lay the blame on Kate and her brothers. Yet now here she sat, clutching Kate's hand, asking forgiveness.

Was she entirely to blame? Kate might have discovered Lionel's name on the property had she taken the trouble, had she not washed her hands of her mother because of the guilt she would not own. She, Jennet, and Berend investigated the holdings of all with whom Kate did business. It was her own fault for neglecting to do so with Agnes Dell.

But it was no time for pointing fingers. For Dina's sake, indeed for all their sakes, Kate needed to discover what had happened in the house Eleanor had leased, whether any or all of them were in danger.

"Do you say nothing to me, Katherine?"

Kate placed her free hand over her mother's. "Forget about blame, Mother. Tell me all that you know. That is how we will discover what happened, whether it was a random encounter or something more sinister."

"Do you think the rest of us are in danger?" Griffin asked.

Kate glanced over at him. "That is what we need to find out." She patted her mother's hand and offered her a cup of ale. "Wet your throat, then tell me all. From the beginning. What made you suspect Agnes had not been honest with you?"

She listened closely as Eleanor recounted Nan's announcement that Lionel was in the hall, her obvious discomfort and reluctance to fetch Agnes, Agnes's consequent blubbering, and the conversation with Lionel, the lie about what had happened with Dina.

"A story perfect for Lionel," said Kate. "Certain to dissuade him from asking further questions. You were inspired, Mother. Have you informed Magistra Matilda of this version of this morning's events? This must be our story going forward."

"With everyone?"

Kate thought about Sir Elric, his men, Thomas Holme, Griselde and Clement, the monk at the abbey infirmary. And what had Berend told Sir Alan and his guests?

"No, it is Lionel's special tale. With anyone else, say that you do not wish to talk about it. Though if you are pushed . . ." It would not be that simple. Kate threw up her hands. "How can I advise you when I do not know what happened? For now it is best to say as little as possible."

Eleanor gently cupped Kate's face in her hands, then released it with a tearful smile. "I promise to keep my own counsel, except with you. Now. As to what we do about the house—" She explained Sister Clara's proposal and her own insistence that they consult Kate before making any changes or saying anything to Agnes and Nan.

Kate caught herself glancing over at Griffin as she might Berend or Jennet to gauge their reaction. The breeze had dried his hair, now a coppery mass of curls that gave him an angelic appearance.

"Let me discuss this with Berend and Jennet," said Kate. "Until we come to a decision, say nothing, Mother."

"Agnes will ask," said Eleanor.

"Advise her to pray. Is that not what she joined with your sisters to learn, how to live all her life as a prayer? Suggest she find a work that is pleasing to God, helpful to the community." Agnes Dell. What was her story? What was her part in this? "What do you know of Agnes? What reason did she give for her offer of the house and her wish to be a beguine?"

Eleanor tilted her head back with a sigh, leaning against the high back of the chair. "What exactly did she say?" she said softly. "She spoke of her grief over her husband's death, and at sea. With no body to clean, dress, bury with blessings and prayers for his soul, she feels robbed of the farewell. She seeks solace, grace, a life devoted to good works. As you say, it is time she found good, honest work through which she might gain grace for herself and her husband's soul. May God grant them that."

Was her mother still referring to Agnes and her late husband, or herself and Ulrich? Kate glanced over at Lille and Ghent. The two slept, Ghent's head resting on Lille's back. She rose and helped herself to some cheese and bread. Griffin joined Kate at the table, his back to Eleanor.

"In truth, I asked Agnes very little," Eleanor said as she rose to join them. Peering into Kate's eyes, she demanded, "What do you know, Katherine? I sense there is much you are not telling me."

Kate's hands itched for the release a session with her bow and a quiver of arrows would bring. "I know far less than I would like, and what little I know is confusing. I need to be quiet now and think. Go to the *maison dieu*, tell Magistra Matilda what you told Lionel. And then quietly go about the rest of your day as if nothing were changed. We can consult further when we know more."

Eleanor lifted a hand. "The *maison dieu* reminded me—Dina sleeps with a dagger beneath her pillow."

"I know."

"You do? Did she—?"

"Sister Brigida told me."

Eleanor had returned to the loom, running her hands over the threads. "Well, the dagger is missing. Agnes and Clara searched for it between the house and the church, thinking Dina may have dropped it as she fled to sanctuary, but they found nothing."

Sanctuary. An interesting choice of word. "What does Dina fear so much that she would resort to such ends as sleeping with a dagger at the ready?" Kate asked.

Eleanor still fingered the threads. "I wish I knew. I do not believe either Sister Clara or Sister Brigida know."

"Most unfortunate," Griffin said quietly.

Kate glanced at him. "Will you sleep in Dina's bedchamber tonight?"

"I will."

"And I will send Sister Agnes to sit with Nan's mother," said Eleanor.

"Why Agnes and not Nan?" Kate asked.

"Punishment. For both of them."

"But Mother . . ."

Save your battles, Kate. This one isn't worth it, Geoff said in her mind.

I don't know. Mother's judgment . . .

Allow her this small act.

Of spite, Geoff. Pray God this does not end badly. We don't know if we can trust Agnes.

Kate shook her head at her mother's puzzled frown. "No matter."

"You said Simon had this loom made for you?" Eleanor asked. "I should like one for the Martha House—when I feel certain I have one."

It was one of Kate's most treasured gifts from her late husband. "When the time comes, I will introduce you to the man who fashioned this for me."

"I pray that it comes to pass."

Another unexpected response from her mother. In the past she would have expressed anger at those who stood in the way of her dream. Kate walked Eleanor to the street-side door. "Sit with Sister Dina awhile, Mother. Perhaps, seeing you there, she might confide something—"

Eleanor nodded. "I will pray for her trust." Kissing Kate on the cheek once again, she departed.

Kate watched her walk through the yard and past the small house on the street. She was an elegant woman, her mother, proud, vain, stubborn. But there was something new, a softening, a sadness. A troubling thought—was her mother using the news about Lionel to mask distress over something else? Something to do with Sister Dina?

Turning from the door, Kate watched Griffin finish what was left of the cheese and bread. She needed to find a way to draw him out, learn what he knew about her mother's life with Ulrich Smit.

"You are patient with Mother," she said.

What was it about his eyes when he smiled? They seemed to dance. "She obliged me by trusting me above the others in Ulrich's household."

"Others? Ulrich had more than one retainer in Strasbourg?"

"He did. Though he called us factors." The grin broadened.

"What does a merchant need with several retainers?"

"Surely you saw a few of them when he stayed in your father's house in Northumberland? He always traveled with two or more. You don't remember them?"

"I remember he came with others, but I never took note of them. I understand why he traveled with them. But once he was back in Strasbourg, what was the need? Did he continue to travel after he wed Mother?"

Griffin ran a calloused hand through his hair. "It is not my place to speak of Ulrich Smit and Dame Eleanor."

"She has requested your silence?"

"Not in so many words."

He reached up as if to rake his hair once more. She caught his hand, turned it palm up, studied the calluses.

"You're an archer."

"I am Welsh."

She glanced up, caught his grin, and laughed. "So you are. Do you have your bow and quiver with you?"

"At my lodgings."

"Bring them back with you when you fetch your things."

"Is that an invitation? I've hesitated to ask if I might join you at practice. I would enjoy that."

His hand grew warm in hers. A nice hand. Dry. Strong. She let it go and thanked him again for not mentioning the men who had followed her on the street. "You might do something for me," she said, shifting the topic.

"Yes?"

"The Earl of Westmoreland's men at the *maison dieu*. They will be relieved at some point."

"I have seen them often, here and elsewhere in the city."

"I would like to know where the two lodge."

He bowed. "I will follow them when they are relieved." Opening the door, he glanced back. "Does this mean you trust me?"

"We shall see."

He nodded and took his leave.

Time to clear her head. From the cupboard near the hearth she plucked her bow and a quiver of arrows. Taking it as a signal, Lille and Ghent rose and shook themselves. Together they went out into the garden.

—◦◦◦◦—

Sister Dina's was a small, stuffy room despite a shutter being slightly ajar. Eleanor opened it wide for a moment, appreciating the pleasant prospect, Thomas Holme's gardens tumbling down the slope to the river Foss. But the summer afternoon offered little breeze, certainly not enough to risk the danger of inviting access. Though the window was high in the wall, a determined intruder might easily climb with the help of the vine growing up the side of the building and drop into the room. Eleanor remembered a time when Ulrich . . . She shook her head against the unwelcome memory and closed the shutters. Sir Elric's men guarded the *maison dieu*. Sister

Dina was safe here. But once she woke, Eleanor would insist she return to the Martha House. And then what would Sir Elric's guards do? She smiled to think what her daughter might say about their presence across the hedgerow. There was something between Katherine and their captain, she could see it.

Eleanor shifted the high-backed chair in such wise that Sister Dina might see her and recognize her on waking, and close enough that she might hear her prayer. Settling, she drew out her paternoster, shaking out the silver and pearl beads. Bowing her head, she began a silent prayer to calm her thoughts, draw her heart to the place from which she might reach out to Sister Dina, touch her suffering with her own. In the background, sisters quietly called to one another in the hall as they went about their duties, a cart rattled past on Castlegate, a dog barked; not her daughter's great beasts. Katherine—had Eleanor any hope of regaining her trust? She had taken the news more calmly than Eleanor had expected . . . She shook herself. It was not the time for those thoughts.

Softly she began to say Hail Marys aloud, watching Sister Dina's sharp-featured face for a sign of awareness. After two or three rounds, the beguine's eyelids flickered, but nothing more.

"Blessed Mary, Mother of God, pray for me, a sinner, that I might make amends," Eleanor murmured. "I see now that I have been a willful, heedless creature. When Ulrich died and I learned—But I do not need to tell you what I learned, our all-seeing Mother. When I understood the depth of his betrayal, and my part in it, I prayed for a sign of how I might redeem myself, how I might atone for my sins. You brought me Sister Dina, a beguine, a sempster fitting me for my mourning clothes, a woman radiating such comforting grace that I begged her to tell me how she came to be so. Sweetly she shared with me the words of Meister Eckhart, his sermons of love, compassion, the light within, the Mother's grace. 'Love is nothing else in itself than God.' As long as I love, I am on the right path." Remembering herself, Eleanor glanced behind her to check that she was not overheard by anyone but Dina. It would not do to speak of Meister Eckhart in Magistra Matilda's hearing. Eleanor did not need a rumor spreading that her beguines were heretics.

She bent close to Dina, looking for a sign that she heard, remembered. Sister Dina had consoled Eleanor and given her hope when she had resigned herself to damnation, certain there was no path to redemption. Did she remember? Did she regret her kindness? Dina gave no sign. Eleanor spoke a few more Hail Marys, then prayed for the beguine, prayed for forgiveness for drawing her away from the safety of Strasbourg. "May God smite me for plucking this good woman from her home and putting her in harm's way."

Sister Dina's eyes flickered.

"Do you wake?" Eleanor gently lay a hand on hers. "It is Dame Eleanor. You are safe, my dear. Magistra Matilda has brought you to this quiet room where you may rest."

Dina's eyelids flickered, opened. She turned her hand to grasp Eleanor's. A firm grip, too firm, tightening, tightening. A look of horror. A quavering thread of voice. "He came for me. He said he would, but I did not believe. No grave can hold him. He will not rest. Cannot rest."

"Heavenly Mother," Eleanor gasped, dropping her beads to squeeze Dina's wrist until she released the hand.

But the young woman now clawed at Eleanor's face. She cried out for help. Two sisters rushed into the room.

"Hold her arms. Gently, but firmly," Eleanor gasped, sitting back to catch her breath.

"He will not rest!" Dina shrieked.

Magistra Matilda came striding in and slapped Dina's cheek. The young woman gasped. "Release her arms," Matilda ordered.

The sisters obeyed, backing away.

Dina crossed her arms, pressing them close to her, as she stared from face to face.

"You said he came for you, Sister Dina. Who?" Eleanor asked in a voice she hoped was soothing. "Who frightened you?"

The young woman turned her head away from all of them. "Shamed," she whispered to the wall. "Shamed. Bloodied. Cursed."

Magistra Matilda lay a hand on Eleanor's shoulder. "Perhaps we should let her rest in quiet, Dame Eleanor."

"He made me commit a terrible sin. I have murdered a man," Dina moaned.

"We do not know that, Sister Dina." Matilda spoke with authority.

But Dina had experienced the attack, not Matilda. Eleanor did not want the magistra confusing Dina, making her question what she remembered of the attack. "Now she is awake, I want to bring her back to my Martha House," she said.

"Is that wise? To take her back there? After all, that is where she—"

"Not out in the kitchen, of course, but up in the solar, where she will be with her sisters."

"Of course I have no authority over you, but I urge you to leave her here. There are many of us to watch over her."

Too many ears. Too many mouths. No. Eleanor could not allow that. Nor could she abide this arrogant magistra much longer. "I have decided."

6

THE NIGHT WATCH

———⟡———

At dusk the two households sat in the coolness of the garden. Catching her breath after practicing at the butt she'd set up behind the kitchen, Kate stood for a moment at the corner of the building, watching as Sister Clara and Sister Brigida walked into the garden arm in arm, Clara struggling a little to keep up with Brigida's long stride. Kate quietly thanked Berend, who stood in the kitchen doorway. It was he who had proposed to feed both households a good meal to end the upsetting day. The two sisters had at first declined the invitation to dine in the garden, feeling they should stay up in the solar with Sister Dina—Berend and Griffin had carried her back to the Martha House earlier, and she was now settled in the room she would share with her sister beguines. Dame Eleanor had argued the wisdom of nourishment and good rest, assuring Clara and Brigida that her own maidservant, Rose, could be trusted to care for Dina for a little while. Kate had seconded her mother, having watched Rose gently arranging Dina's pillows and covers, placing water within easy reach. Clearly, the two sisters had at last agreed.

Nan sat off to one side casting wounded glances toward Eleanor and anxious glances toward the gate in the hedgerow, as if she was expecting someone. Sister Agnes had already gone to sit the evening with Nan's ailing mother, so she had no cause to worry on Hawise's account. Did she dread more trouble? A visitor? Matt kindly tried to engage Nan in conversation, but he was met with silence. Glancing at Kate with a shrug, he abandoned his effort and settled himself near the girls.

At Kate's request, Griffin had taken his food into Eleanor's hall, where he could watch Elric's guards at their post in front of the Martha House and follow them when they moved on. Satisfied that everyone was in their place, Kate eased herself down onto the bench beneath the kitchen eaves.

"Better now?" Berend asked as he handed her a bowl of ale and motioned to a serving of stew and bread sitting on the bench beside her.

"My shoulders ache with a good ache, and I am otherwise much restored." She smiled as Lille and Ghent rose from where they had sat beside Berend and resettled at her feet. All was well. For the moment. Though clearly everyone was tensed for trouble.

Marie and Petra managed to lighten the mood for a moment with a song Sister Brigida had taught them earlier, and then Marie regaled them with the wonders of Hazel Frost's wardrobe, the colorful embroidered cushions piled on her bed, and ribbons of every hue for her pretty brown hair. Petra groaned and crawled over to sit by the hounds.

Eleanor, unusually quiet and withdrawn, picked at her food and occasionally pressed a cloth soaked in rosemary to the welts on her cheek. Kate felt a twinge of remorse for urging her mother to visit Sister Dina, though she was grateful for her efforts. At least Dina had responded. She was not completely lost in the past.

Shamed, bloodied, cursed. No grave can hold him. He came for me. Whatever had happened, for Dina it was a repeat of something in the past. Kate wondered whether they would ever make any sense of her account. And for all their efforts, they knew little that pointed to an explanation for the intruder.

While she ate, Kate turned over in her mind all that had happened since she'd awakened to the hounds' barks. She kept returning to Elric's silence regarding Dina's ordeal despite having already set guards to watch over her—or to ensure that she did not escape. In either case, he had chosen to lie to her, to say nothing of what he knew, or suspected. Something of import. Why else assign two men to such specific duty when Elric's chief mission was to spy on the soldiers crowding the city? The other bothersome item was the incident with the hounds.

She had taken a break from her archery practice when she heard Matt, Jennet, and Berend talking in the kitchen. After listening to their frustrating investigations she told them of her mother's experience with Dina and the foiled attempt to catch Lille and Ghent.

"You say you thought they were soldiers hoping to impress their superior with war dogs," said Jennet. "So they wore livery?"

"No. I saw none."

"Then why soldiers?" Jennet persisted.

"From their bearing," said Kate, "and their clothes—fine but made for ease of movement."

Berend mentioned his encounter just beyond Bootham Bar, the comments about the dogs. "I've worried someone would try to command you to loan them Lille and Ghent."

"If so, they have little understanding of the loyalty of trained wolfhounds," said Kate.

"And I'd wager they'd not encountered a woman warrior before," said Matt. "Not of Dame Katherine's skill and courage."

"Still," said Berend, "we should pay heed to anyone eyeing Lille and Ghent with too much interest when we're about."

"What if they were not after the grand hounds for war dogs?" Jennet said in the tone of one trying out an idea. "What if their aim was to quiet them tonight?"

"A bold, desperate act," said Berend. "Are you thinking whoever it was will return?"

"Sister Dina caught someone who wanted something at that house," said Jennet. "Now someone might mean to finish what last night's intruder meant to do."

"But what did they want?" asked Kate. "Or who?"

No one had come up with an answer to that. Who were those men? Was Jennet right, that they had hoped to silence Lille and Ghent so they might finish the task they had bungled last night?

As the light faded in the garden, the diners grew quiet. Kate imagined they were all wondering whether the intruder would return.

Berend rose and stretched out his arms, shook out his legs. "I must see to my evening chores before drowsiness overcomes me."

Kate told Marie and Petra to go up to bed. "You woke early. It has been a long day. Jennet will come with you. And Matt will be down in the hall." Though they dragged their feet, the two obeyed, which was unusual for Marie, as was her silence for most of the evening. She seemed to understand that it was not a night to defy Kate.

In the kitchen, bowls and spoons clattered softly in the tub of water Berend bent over. Kate stepped in, shutting the door behind her.

Berend paused, still stooped over the tub, studying her. "You told the girls that Jennet would join them soon, and Matt would be in the hall. What of you? Where are you sleeping tonight?"

"You listen too closely." Kate smiled. "If Griffin has gone off to follow Elric's men, I thought to sit in the doorway of the hall at the Martha House so that I can watch both the house and the kitchen until he returns."

Berend paused, regarding her with a frown. "You will, of course, be armed."

"Always."

"And then he will take your place in the doorway?" Berend shook his head. "The sisters might object."

"We shall see." Kate fully expected that she would be sleeping in her mother's hall. She would tell him that when the time came. He worried about her, despite his claim to be confident in her ability to defend herself.

As I do, Geoff said in her mind.

As he would a comrade-in-arms. I do understand.

"What about Lille and Ghent?" said Berend. "Why not take them with you?"

"Sister Clara fears them. And, truth be told, I would rather they were in the main house, protecting the girls."

"I will be listening."

"I depend on that. Geoff, too, will be alert."

"A ghost sharing the watch." Berend shook his head. "Only you."

Out in the summer night Kate paused, gazing up at the stars.

I wonder what it means that he is able to sense my presence?

I don't know, Geoff. Now quiet. We are on watch.

She moved through the hedgerow gate with care in the darkening evening, peering into the shadows, checking the kitchen and Dina's—now Griffin's—small room. All was peaceful. Across the garden she picked up a three-legged milking stool, idly wondering if the garden had once been home to a goat or a cow. Or perhaps the stool was someone else's castoff, gratefully reused. She placed it in the doorway and sat to begin her watch. From the hall came the soft murmur of the sisters and her mother at their evening prayers. Their voices were tense, their prayers halting. Then Sister Brigida began to read a meditation on the Mother's love, and how that love was God, was the source of all creation, and held all in natural grace. Sin was but a forgetting. A soul need only remember, and return to love. After the reading, the voices rose again in prayer, calm now, strengthened by the remembering.

Kate might envy them the solace they drew from their devotions if they also took steps toward learning to defend themselves. She had never witnessed a heavenly avenger appearing to protect the pious, despite all their orisons.

After a while, Griffin strolled into the yard. Kate stepped out but left the hall door ajar so that she might hear the women's voices. She drew Griffin just inside the kitchen so that they would not disturb them.

"Well?" she asked. "Did you find Elric's men?"

A nod. "Two of their comrades relieved them. I followed the two now off the watch to Toft Green."

"They are camping with the other soldiers?"

"I think not. They were asking about, looking for three men who might have returned in the early hours this past morning, one of them bleeding from the neck and the stomach."

"They know so much?" *Damn Elric and his silence. What is his part in this?* She stared out at the starry night. "So Dina's intruder was a soldier?"

Griffin shrugged. "They were not greeted warmly, and were soon in a brawl. I chose to leave. But I will be watching here tonight."

"Three. And soldiers. I wonder whether we met two of them today, hoping to silence Lille and Ghent so they might return and complete their mission?"

"I wondered that as well. I did not spy the ones we'd encountered, but the camp is crowded and I saw but a small part of it."

"I should sleep in my mother's hall tonight. If three come calling, you'll need help."

"Why not have Jennet stand watch in the hall?"

"She is already abed."

"Berend?"

"He will be listening for trouble, never fear." She went to collect what she would need for the night.

⚬⚬⚬

Back in her own kitchen, Kate shared a bowl of ale with Berend while she told him Griffin's news.

"Soldiers. I knew there would be trouble. Why would they think your mother's kitchen worth robbing, if that's what they were about?" Berend scratched his scarred ear as he stretched out his legs. "And Sir Elric's men—did they witness it? Why would he not tell you?" He cursed under his breath.

"That worries me. But it's clear we need to do our own sleuthing." She told him her plan.

"Sleeping in your mother's hall?" Berend shook his head. "Send Jennet."

Griffin, too, thought of Jennet rather than Matt. They both underestimated him. "Jennet went to bed a while ago."

"She will wake when you go up. Send her."

"Why? Are you thinking she might like Griffin?"

"Is he sleeping in the hall as well?"

They laughed, dispelling some of the tension.

"No, the kitchen," said Kate.

Still grinning, Berend shrugged. "I will not argue."

Kate grew serious. "You've discussed me with Griffin."

"I've warned him. In case he thought he might dissemble with you. I thought to keep the peace between our two houses."

"Ah." She was leaning back with her eyes closed but could hear the grin in his voice.

They were quiet awhile. A moment's respite.

"How did Sir Alan discover you had a house to lease?" Berend suddenly asked.

"My uncle sent him to me." Richard Clifford was dean of York Minster as well as King Richard's Lord Privy Seal. He also happened to be one of the few people Kate had come to trust implicitly. She prayed he had not misled her. But when the king he served was in danger, might he not choose to protect him, even if it meant betraying her? "I don't recall his telling me how Sir Alan happened to approach him." She sat forward, curious about the change of topic. "Why?"

Berend raised his uneven brows and shrugged. "I do not mean to question Dean Richard's integrity, but it might be worth asking him about Sir Alan. What do the knight and his men know of all this? We know they have spies moving about the city. Yet they behaved as if they knew nothing, could offer nothing."

"Except to ask you about the abbey."

"A question for me, yes. So, your uncle the dean?"

"I cannot expect him to put my welfare before that of the king he serves, or his archbishop." Archbishop Scrope's loyalties were the subject of much conjecture in the city. His mentor was the former archbishop, Thomas Arundel, now one of Henry of Lancaster's closest advisors. On the other hand, King Richard and his court had attended Scrope's enthronement as Bishop of Lichfield shortly before he was promoted to Archbishop of York. He was an enigma. "I will go to the deanery in the morning. No matter his purpose, I trust my uncle will tell me what he can once I tell him what has happened this day."

"I pray he does not disappoint you."

"As he did Mother?" Dame Eleanor had asked the dean to be the confessor for her beguines. Richard had declined, saying that his time was not his own, as he could never predict when he would be summoned to Westminster. Eleanor had felt snubbed; she believed that he wished to distance himself from the foreign sisters. Kate thought it more likely he was wary of becoming too involved in her mother's scheme.

"He is fond of you. I pray he knows something of use."

Kate closed her eyes for a moment, thinking, appreciating the peace of Berend's kitchen, a place of sanctuary. His presence made it so.

"Perhaps he might speak to the abbot of St. Mary's on my behalf, asking that the infirmarian talk to us." She opened her eyes and sat up before she grew too comfortable and abandoned her plan.

Berend nodded. "That would be helpful. We need something. I see no clear direction, and that worries me."

"I know. We're grasping at anything and everything." She tried to mask a yawn, but it escaped her. "If only I could corner Elric and demand that he tell me all he knows."

Berend grinned. "Sic the hounds on him?"

"Why not?" Her laugh lacked mirth.

He sighed. "We need sleep. Perhaps we will see more clearly in the morning."

Kate rubbed her eyes, flexed her shoulders and arms. "I need a month in the countryside with my bow, a horse, and the dogs."

"I am sorry Duke Henry prevents you from such refuge." Berend shifted, drinking down the dregs in their bowl. "What make you of Griffin?" he asked. There was an edge to his voice. "Do you think he might be of use to us?"

"He was helpful today," she said. "But I wonder how it is that he managed to appear just as he might be useful. He was sent by Mother, but he came from the wrong direction."

Berend shook his head. "I don't think he's fool enough to toy with us. But he has his secrets."

"As do you," Kate said softly, rubbing Berend's shoulder affectionately. She rose with reluctance, wishing she might stay. But she should be in her mother's hall. Stepping out into the garden she turned, feeling Berend's presence in the doorway. They smiled to each other.

He is a good friend.

He is, Geoff. I trust him with my life.

⎯⎯◦⊙◦⎯⎯

Across the hedgerow, up in the solar, Eleanor lay in bed, rubbing a salve into the scratches on her face. Her tears had washed away what she had earlier applied and the salt burned on the open wounds.

Why do you forsake me, my Lord? Why do you reject my offering? Am I not sufficiently humbled? Is my Martha House an abomination to you? How may I serve you? How may I make amends? Is there no path of grace for me?

She had so wanted the peace she'd found in the company of the beguines. To forgive. To forget. To begin again. Perhaps that had been too selfish. The blame she saw in Katherine's eyes was fair. Eleanor *was* to blame for Walter's death, her last surviving son, her eldest. Encouraging him to seek out his child, Petra, never thinking how that might reignite all the hate between her family and that of Petra's dead mother, the Cavertons. She would do anything to take back that letter. Too much blood had been spilt between the Cavertons and the Cliffords for the families to ever come together in peace. Their enmity had long ago gone beyond that between the Scots and the English, the border raids. For Eleanor Petra was both a precious gift and a painful reminder of Katherine's childhood, of her three sons—all killed by the Cavertons, and of her husband, whom she had betrayed. *The pain is too much, Holy Mother. It comes out in angry words.*

And now she might lose the house in which the beguines had begun to make their home. How brave and selfless Sister Clara was, to suggest returning to the *maison dieu*, living for the nonce under Magistra Matilda's rules, which meant, among other changes, that they might be forbidden to work for pay, depending only upon the largess of Thomas Holme and other benefactors. They would lose income, their independence further from reach than ever.

I pray for grace, my Lord. Am I so unworthy of your gift? Why does everything I touch turn to ashes?

Or is your quarrel with my beguines and their message of love, compassion, finding you within themselves? Is it possible you forsake them? That those who condemn the beguines for their message of love as arrogance speak for you?

She could not believe that. Would not believe that. Did not God say, "I am the light of the world, and whoever follows me will no longer walk in the dark, and he will find and have the light of life"? Surely the gospels did not lie.

Breathing slowly and deeply, Eleanor tried to quiet her mind. She'd begun to drift off when she heard two sounds, one here in the room, one down in the hall. In the near darkness, one of the women rose from the pallets near her door, stumbling with a soft thud. A muttered curse. Nan. Rose never cursed. And someone was down below in the hall, Eleanor was certain of it. Griffin? He would enter only if he had cause, to follow an intruder. Eleanor lay still, moving her attention back and forth between the near sounds of Nan dressing and the far sounds of someone moving about in the hall. What to do? Let Nan discover the intruder? Or was she expecting him? Eleanor held her breath, waiting for Nan to step through the doorway. Then she would follow.

The wait was agony, her heart pounding, hands and feet going so cold they ached, but she dared not move. She wanted to catch Nan in the act. She was certain now, Nan had risen almost at once when the door opened down below. She must have been lying awake, alert, waiting. For whom? Eleanor meant to find out. Perhaps this was why she could not sleep, this was God's will, that she was awake to discover Nan's betrayal.

No, she was judging before she knew the truth. *Quiet, Eleanor, empty yourself.* She closed her eyes for a moment, breathed.

The door creaked open. The leather hinges were old, dry, causing the wooden door to rub against the doorway. Someone had lit a candle or lamp down below, and Eleanor could just make out Nan's outline in the doorway.

When the maidservant was out of sight, Eleanor rose, rubbing her hands and stepping from foot to foot to bring life back to them, listening at the open door. Rose stirred. Eleanor whispered that it was nothing.

Down below, Nan called softly, "Robin? Is that you?"

"No, Nan. Not Robin."

Katherine. It was Katherine down below. *God bless her.* Eleanor rose, threw on a light mantle, and slipped out to the landing.

--⚬✦⚬--

Though Kate would have preferred the dark, she was too unfamiliar with her mother's hall to move about blindly, so she'd brought a lantern from home, opening the shutter just enough to find a sheltered spot and settle.

She was about to close the shutter when the floorboards creaked directly overhead. Stealthy movements. Someone dressing? She held her breath, waiting. A door groaned open. Bare feet on the creaky steps.

"Robin? Is that you?" Nan's voice.

Rising from her corner, Kate shone her light on the young woman.

"No, Nan. Not Robin."

The young woman gasped. "I—I thought—" Nan's fair hair hung loose round her shoulders. She carried shoes in her hands, and a scarf.

Kate took her firmly by the arm and guided her out through the starlit garden to the kitchen. For Griffin's benefit. He should hear what Nan had to say for herself. She indicated a bench near the door. "Sit down. Now. You thought what? Was it this Robin who frightened Sister Dina? Were you expecting him to return tonight? To finish what he'd begun?"

"No. No, I . . ." Nan began to cry. "I fear something terrible has happened to him."

Griffin stepped out from the small bedchamber, shielding his eyes from the sudden light. "Who is Robin?"

"Tell us all, Nan. All of it," said Kate. "Who is he? Where does he lodge?"

Nan drew her scarf round her. "I don't know. I've no idea where he lives. He comes to Mother's house. Always there. So that I can keep watch while my brothers and sisters sleep up above." Kate glanced up at the doorway, where her mother now stood. "He is gentle with me."

"Oh, no doubt," Eleanor muttered.

"Peace, Mother," said Kate. The brash young maidservant from the Martha House had crumpled before her eyes—the yearning in her voice, the trembling hand clutching the scarf. "Where did you meet him?" she asked.

"At market. He said he noticed me. Couldn't stop thinking about me." Tears welled up. "He said I was a bright bauble of a woman and I inspired him to mend his ways."

"Was it he who came last night?"

Nan shook her head. "I don't know. He did not come to me last night. I waited at home—my mother's house. Waited and waited."

Kate found a pitcher of water and filled a wooden bowl for Nan, handing it to her as she settled beside her. "Drink. Calm yourself."

Sniffs.

"You betrayed us," said Dame Eleanor.

"No!"

Griffin offered Eleanor a chair, but she shook her head.

Sitting beside Nan, Kate asked gently, "You said 'mend his ways.' What are his sins?"

"Naught but that he wants me. I cannot think what an honest, hard-working man would want with me." She plucked at her colorful skirt, touched the comb in her hair. "He has the coin for these pretty things, but where he earns it, and how, he will never say. 'What you don't know cannot harm you, eh, my Nan?' he says."

So he is a thief, thought Kate. *What might he think worth stealing in the kitchen of a Martha House?* "What did you tell him about the Martha House, Nan? Why would he be in the kitchen?"

A hurt expression. "Do you think I sent him here? Why would I do such a thing?"

"I mean no such thing, Nan. I merely wonder whether you might have mentioned something of value in the house, and he might have bragged of the fine establishment in which his lady worked, eh?"

Nan shook her head. But she would not look at Kate. Was that significant?

"He might be hurt," Nan whimpered. "Sister Dina was bloody, they say. And her dagger is missing."

"That is true," said Kate. "And we must find him so that he can receive proper care. What might he have been after here in the kitchen?"

"The key," Nan whispered.

"To what?"

"The main house. Dame Agnes hid it here. I might have said . . . I might have said so many things. I love him. I wanted him to know what fine, *holy* women employ me. I am trusted. I can be trusted. Only that's not true. Not true!" She covered her face with her hands and sobbed.

Eleanor stepped forward with a hand up. Kate knew that look, that posture. She meant to slap Nan to stop her crying.

"Mother, if you touch her, you will have no more help from me," Kate said.

The hand hovered. Then Eleanor dropped it to her side. "It still stinks of blood in here."

Nan's sobs grew louder.

"God have mercy," Eleanor whispered. "It is best I leave you to your work." She withdrew.

Kate watched her mother cross the garden and step into the hall, closing the door behind her. The set of her shoulders, her bowed head, bespoke defeat.

With a sigh, she looked up at Griffin, who leaned against the wall. "What now?"

"Go to the hall, get some rest," he said. "Nan can sleep out here in my bed, where I can guard her. I'll sleep beneath the stars. I've done it often enough. Helps me think."

He was right. There was nothing more to do in the middle of the night. Kate helped Nan to the small chamber, then dragged herself back to the hall.

7

A VIOLENT END

———◦⟨∾⟩◦———

An angry challenge, a man's frightened cry. Kate sat up in the dark, confused for a moment, the hall so dark, the bed so hard. Had it been a dream? Someone softly snored up above. Her mother. She had forgotten her mother's snore.

"Halt!" a man shouted out on the street.

This was no dream. She thought she heard the pounding rhythm of people running. Not so near as Hertergate. Castlegate, more likely. Was it the night watch? Or Griffin?

Rising and slipping on her shoes, Kate felt her way across the hall to the garden door. Opening it, she paused a moment, listening. Men's voices, quieter now. She stepped out into the garden. The blankets near the kitchen door had been tossed aside, as if Griffin had risen in a hurry. She went round the side of the house, moving with caution down the alleyway as she drew her knife from her skirt. Out on Hertergate she spied Griffin coming toward her, assisting someone who limped badly, a lantern dangling from his hand. In the distance, muffled voices again, then silence. The injured one tried to pull away at the sound of the voices, his lantern swinging wildly, lighting up shrubbery, the warehouse on the corner, himself. It was Severen, one of the night watchmen. Griffin said something to him and shook his head. They continued on toward her.

"Bloody-minded bas—" Severen cut off his curse as he noticed Kate standing in front of the Martha House. "Beg pardon for waking you, Mistress Clifford."

She shielded her eyes from the light now aimed at her, inspiring Severen to mutter another apology as she relieved him of the lantern and turned to guide the two men back down the alleyway to the kitchen. Once inside, Griffin settled the injured man in a chair.

Nan stumbled out of her chamber, wrapped in a blanket, rubbing her eyes. "What is it? What has happened?"

"Severen was wounded in a scuffle with a group of drunk soldiers," said Griffin.

"Soldiers, pah," growled the watchman. "Cutthroat villains, more like. No livery that I could see. Here to cause trouble, they are. I say if they have no captain here to watch over them, let them camp outside the gates. They want access to the city for drinking and whoring and thieving, naught more."

While Severen talked, Nan gently removed his hat and brushed the hair from his high forehead, revealing a long gash that bled profusely. She fetched water and a cloth and began to clean it as Griffin asked about the men.

"One of them was far drunker than the rest. They dragged him along." Severen winced and waved Nan away. But she stood her ground, giving him the eye. He surrendered, sitting back and closing his eyes. "When I called out, they dropped him," he said. "He lay there as they came at me. Three men, reeking of ale, such cursing as to please the devil himself. Before I had a chance to draw my dagger I was slashed, punched in the belly and kicked in the—" He winced again, this time from the memory, Kate guessed. But he smiled wanly and patted Nan's hand as she wrapped a cloth round his head. Not so badly injured. "I finally dropped my lantern to draw my dagger, but they were gone on down Castlegate. Disappeared down the gardens, I think, going down along the bank of the Foss, trying to stay clear of the other watchmen, I'd wager."

"Did they gather up the one lying on the ground?" Kate asked.

"Not right away," said Griffin. "He's right about the gardens. While I was helping Severen I saw several men dragging something off the road and down into Holme's property."

"I saw none of that. My head was splitting by then." Severen followed Nan with his eyes as she took away the bowl of bloody water, pouring it out in the garden.

"I should have gone after them," Griffin whispered, as if to himself.

Kate did not disagree, but she was chasing another thought. She drew him to one side. "Did you notice how Nan took over the care of Severen, and his ease with her touch, how he patted her hand? Yes, he winced at the pain, but he understood that look she gave him and gave way to her."

Griffin watched Nan return, check her work on Severen's head, and bend close to whisper something in his ear.

"Lovers?" he said.

"Perhaps not now, but they've been intimate," said Kate. "I've wondered about her courage in walking to her mother's house and back in the dark. And she's apparently been unchallenged by the night watch. Could Severen be her escort?"

"Ah. Because Robin *would* have been challenged. If you are right, I wonder what he might know about this Robin?"

Kate nodded. "See what you can learn. I'm taking Lille and Ghent down through Thomas Holme's gardens for a look round."

"Just you and the hounds?"

"Matt will wake when I fetch them. I'll take him along."

"I have not yet earned your trust?"

"I've trained Matt to handle Lille and Ghent should I need him. You are still needed to guard here, remember? Now you've Severen *and* Nan."

"Of course." He caught her hand as she turned to leave. "Take Severen's lantern. He will not be going out again tonight."

He was right. Slumped in the chair, the watchman already slept. Kate took the lantern and stepped out into the mild summer night. Crossing through the hedgerow, she paused, listening. Was that a splash she heard?

No, she was too far from the river. Her mind played tricks on her, the shadows secretive, mysterious. Shadows. The sky was lightening. She shuttered the lantern and could see the outline of the house before her. Whatever she found, there would be no more sleep tonight.

Lille and Ghent were at the door, ready for her, Matt standing behind them, rubbing his eyes.

"Has the intruder returned?" he asked.

"No. Trouble out on the street. They injured Severen the watchman, then headed down the gardens to the Foss. One of the men was either very drunk or injured. I want to see if they left him behind. I just need one item." She slipped out of her shoes and padded up to the solar.

Jennet stood at the top of the landing, holding out the leather-sheathed axe. "The girls are tucked up in your bed. I heard you down below and retrieved this as quietly as I might, thinking you might need more than a dagger."

Kate thanked her. "Keep them safe. I'm taking Matt and the dogs to the gardens."

The four slipped from the house, down the alleyway, and crossed Castlegate. Kate opened the lantern shutter as they moved down into the gardens, Lille and Ghent leading. In the silence before the dawn their descent sounded loud in her ears and she glanced around, realizing how vulnerable they were with the light, the noise. But the hounds showed no sign of alarm, focused on moving down the hill. Matt limped more than usual as he kept up with them, though it had been months since an accident that had hobbled him for a while. The dogs led them to a tree with broken branches dangling, the ground churned up beneath.

"It looks as if something was dragged across that flower bed and over the rosebush," said Matt. Easing himself down by the bush he teased a piece of cloth from the thorns, holding it up to Kate.

"Not something, but someone," she said softly.

Now they dropped farther down toward the water, the hounds watchful, pausing now and then to sniff the air before returning their noses to the ground. Kate brushed against flowers and shrubs, releasing their scents. Thorns caught at her skirts. A root almost brought Matt down, but she reached out in time to steady him. Down, down they wound, the smells less sweet as they neared the water. In the quiet before the city awoke she could hear subtle interruptions in the Foss's current, flotsam and jetsam thumping against the bank, eddies gurgling. Suddenly the dogs halted, standing alert, on guard.

She touched Lille's head, Ghent's, and they moved aside to flank her for protection. She handed Matt the lantern. He crouched down, shining it on a body. The man lay on his stomach, his arms outstretched, not crumpled beneath him—he'd not had time to break his fall. Drunk? Or already dead? Kate smelled nothing until she crouched beside Matt, then she caught the scents of urine, shit, ale—and blood, but faintly.

"God help us," said Matt. "The intruder?"

"Let us roll him over and see."

"I can manage." Matt set the lantern aside, crab-walked uphill from the body, grabbed hold of the shoulder and hip closest to him, and began to roll the man, but stopped with a gasp as the head moved unnaturally. He looked to Kate, visibly sickened. "Neck's broken."

"I can help," she said. "Go gently." She held the head so that it moved with the body as Matt eased the man down on his back.

"Sorry. I'm not hardened to this yet."

"Pray you never are."

He sat back on his heels and wiped his forehead, then turned and emptied his stomach.

Kate shone the lantern on the dead man's battered face. "Hans," she whispered. One of the menservants her mother brought from Strasbourg. As the beguines were accustomed to having no men on the premises, the two menservants had gone to work for Thomas Holme for most of the spring and summer. She crossed herself, saying a silent prayer for his soul.

She had seen bodies more badly beaten, but, as with Matt, she hoped she never found it easy to witness such suffering. Hans's nose had been broken, the blood crusting his face, and beneath that, bruises discolored the flesh. She lifted his hands, examining his fingers. A few split knuckles. He'd fought back. Whoever had done this might wear the scars. Another broken nose? A blackened eye?

"A brawl," Kate whispered to herself, thinking of what Griffin had seen at the camp on Toft Green, and later what Severen had described. But Hans had impressed her as a gentle man.

"To the death," Matt said. His breathing was easier.

"So many soldiers in the city," said Kate. "Any one of them might have the strength. They are all hungering for blood." Thinking of Griffin's description of the men dragging the body off Castlegate and into the gardens, she added, "I pray Severen can provide some description." But why here? In the garden? Mere chance that he fell on the street above it?

Matt lifted the man's tunic and shirt. "I see no sign of a wound that would have bloodied Sister Dina," he said. "Shall I check his arms and legs?"

"That can wait until later, when he is stripped and washed, prepared for burial."

Kate gave Lille and Ghent the order to track. They led her down to the water, sniffed along the bank, then sat, looking out over the water. She remembered the splash she thought she'd heard.

Matt was close behind, clearly preferring not to be left alone with the corpse. She understood. "Thomas Holme should know at once. Go to him. Ask him to send a servant to the sheriff. He may want to return with you to watch the body. If not, ask if Hans's friend Werner is there, and bring him back to wait with you."

Matt nodded and headed up the hill.

Leading the dogs back to Griffin and Severen, she found Griffin curled up beneath his blankets, seemingly asleep. Severen still snored on the bench in the kitchen. And Nan? The door to her bedchamber swung wide. No Nan. Kate slipped back into the hall to check whether the maidservant was there. There was enough light coming through the chinks in the shutters to see her mother kneeling on a prie-dieu before the lady altar.

She glanced up. "Katherine?"

"Have you seen Nan?"

"Was she not sleeping out in the kitchen?"

"She was, but not now."

Nan had slipped through their fingers. Griffin's fingers. And Severen's. The two of them were worthless. Cursing under her breath, Kate started for the door.

"What is it?" her mother asked. "What is wrong?"

"Finish your morning prayers, Mother." There would be time enough to tell her of Hans's death.

Out in the garden, Kate kicked Griffin's feet to wake him. How could the man sleep through such a night?

He grumbled as he sat up, then cursed to realize he had fallen asleep on watch.

"Cursing does not undo it," she said.

He scrambled to his feet. "Did you find something?"

"A body in the gardens. Near the riverbank. Hans."

"God have mercy. Murdered?"

"Neck snapped. But he'd been beaten before that. He reeked of ale. A drunken man with a strange accent accosted by carousing soldiers? Would that you had gone after the men." Kate turned away from him, finding his pathetic expression annoying. "I haven't the heart to tell Dame Eleanor until after her morning prayers."

"Hans." Griffin spoke the man's name, then went quiet.

Kate glanced back, saw him cross himself and whisper a prayer, then rake a hand through his bright hair and call a curse down on himself. Had he any training as a guard?

"Why did I help Severen instead of chasing after the men? I might have saved him."

Despite the pain evident in Griffin's voice, Kate could not be bothered masking her own regret in trusting him. Hans was a good man. He'd deserved better. "Why indeed?"

"You've every right to take that tone with me. Did you see any trace of them?"

"Lille and Ghent lost the scent at the river."

"The men swam away?"

"Unless they had it planned and set a boat down there for their escape."

"I cannot—Why did I choose to help the watchman? But I did not recognize . . . I would not have left Hans lying there. I might have saved him. Dunderhead!" He kicked the tree.

"Petulant and pointless," Kate muttered. "It *is* possible Hans was already dead."

"He might not have been dealt the final blow, his neck not yet broken. I want to see him."

"Go. Matt should be there. And maybe Thomas Holme and one of the sheriffs' sergeants. But what did Severen tell you?"

He paced away from her, shaking his head, muttering to himself.

"You can curse yourself later. Tell me what you learned."

Deep breath, one last muttered curse. Then he faced her. "You were right to suspect he was helping Nan move through the city at night when he had the watch. But he believed she was caring for her mother. He swears he knew nothing of a lover."

"Does he know what sort of man Robin is?"

Griffin shook his head. "I didn't ask. I thought we would ask Nan—"

"Nan is gone."

"What? I failed with her as well? Bloody worthless—" He turned on his heels, storming into the kitchen, cursing at Severen.

The injured watchman stumbled out holding his crotch, blinking at the soft dawn light.

"Go piss over there." Kate pointed to the midden as she handed him his lantern, then called to Lille and Ghent and went to lean against the hedgerow gate, struggling to set aside the emotions that clouded her thoughts.

Breathing deep, she trained her gaze up into the arching branches of the plane tree, its broad trunk almost touching the wall of the kitchen. It provided refreshing, dappled shade on summer days. Kate imagined Agnes Dell standing in the garden, dreaming of raising a brood of children who would tumble about beneath the strong limbs of this great tree. She wondered whether Agnes had been happy with Leonard Dell, what had driven her to become John Paris's mistress. Perhaps the lack of children, perhaps loneliness with Leonard so often away. On his death, had Agnes been disappointed to discover her husband's secrets, as had Kate? She straightened as Griffin stepped out from the kitchen.

Shoulders hunched, his face pale, the man looked beaten. "You must think me the greatest fool."

Perhaps not the greatest, she thought, but he'd certainly no mind for guard duty. What had Ulrich seen in him? "Your mistake was lying down and covering yourself. I doubt Nan will come to harm. It's dawn, and she seems to know the watchmen. Go now, see the body. Severen can take himself home."

Once both men were gone, Kate returned to the kitchen, pouring water from a pitcher into a wide bowl, setting it on a bench for the hounds. She availed herself of a small bowl of ale from the jug in the cupboard, taking a seat on the bench Severen had vacated. She sat there a long while, going over all that had happened, searching for a pattern. Nan and Robin—who was he? Might the two be connected with Hans, and the unliveried soldiers encamped at Toft Green? She sat there long enough that she witnessed the three beguines depart for morning mass across Castlegate and Rose come out to the kitchen to fetch ale for her mistress.

"Shall I fold up your blankets, Dame Katherine?"

"Yes. If you would put them by the door, I will fetch them later."

Kate almost rose to follow her back to the main house. This might be the time to prepare her mother, tell her about Hans before the sheriffs' sergeants came sniffing around. *If* they could be bothered. Too often they simply called for the coroner to record the death and let it be. A servant, with no family in York, who would care? But she did not go to her mother. Instead she sat a while longer, until she heard Berend moving about in the garden across the hedge. She was about to go break her fast with him when she noticed Lille and Ghent sitting up, ears pricked. Now she heard it—voices in the alleyway, men's voices. Signaling the dogs to stay and be still, Kate moved back into the shadows where she might watch undetected, knife at the ready.

Two Dominican friars stepped into the garden, one, slightly stooped, keeping a grip on the other's forearm. As they moved closer, the white gowns beneath their black mantles caught the light, as did the milkiness of the stooped one's eyes. Aged, dependent on the younger to guide his steps. Kate did not know them, but the younger knew which entrance to use, moving straight to the hall door. He rapped on it, waited, then rapped again. Rose greeted them respectfully, explaining that the sisters were at mass and her mistress was just dressing.

"We come unannounced, I know," said the elder friar, "but Dame Eleanor will wish to see us."

The maidservant bowed them in.

Two friars, unannounced. Dominicans. Their friary stood beside Toft Green, near the crowded military encampment. They might know something of use. Kate was deciding whether to follow them into the hall and introduce herself when Sister Brigida came down the alleyway.

"*Benedicite*," she called out to someone invisible to Kate who must be standing at the hedgerow gate. "Clara and Dina stayed to talk with Magistra Matilda after morning mass, but I excused myself as soon as I might do so without offending the good woman. Are the girls ready for their lessons?"

"They have just tumbled into the kitchen," Jennet responded. "You need not have hurried."

Kate replenished the hounds' empty water bowl and stepped out into the garden, joining the two at the gate.

Jennet caught something in Kate's expression with one glance, giving her a questioning look. Kate shook her head. *Not now.*

Turning back to the beguine, Jennet asked her if she'd had a difficult night. Brigida looked far from rested.

"You can see that?" A weary smile. "Sister Dina did not rest easy, so neither did we. Clara and I took turns getting some rest while the other was there to whisper soothing words when Dina wakened, frightened. She is plagued with remorse for injuring the intruder. She cannot accept that she had little choice." A yawn. "We had managed to calm her when a brawl broke out on the street. I heard you out there, Dame Katherine. I pray no one was hurt."

"You are right about the brawl," said Kate. "Are you certain you wish to tutor the girls today?"

"Bless you, yes. Nothing I say or do serves to calm Sister Dina for long, and I grow impatient with myself. I wish to care for the ill, the poor, the troubled, yet I cannot even comfort my sister. So it is good to have a purpose outside the house today."

"You might want to wait until the others return, so that you might all meet the friars who have called on Dame Eleanor."

Brigida tilted her head, looking puzzled. "Friars?"

"A pair of Dominicans. They await my mother in the hall. Apparently they were not expected, but assured Rose they would be welcomed."

Brigida smiled. "I should think that is good news. In Strasbourg we were guided by members of the Dominican friary near our house. A friar might be a comfort to Dina."

"Have you learned any more from her about that night?" Kate asked.

"No. Clara and I were so glad she wished to attend mass this morning we did not pry. We thought to let her speak about it in her own time."

"We might not have the leisure of such patience," Kate said. "The brawl on the street did end in violence. And death." She told them about finding Hans's body, and what Severen had witnessed.

"Hans, gentle Hans." Brigida's voice broke. "God have mercy." She bowed her head in a silent prayer.

"Matt is alone with the body?" Jennet asked.

"Griffin is there. And soon the sheriff. Possibly Thomas Holme. And Werner. I thought he would wish to be there."

"Poor Werner," said Brigida. "He misses Strasbourg. Hans was his last link to it. Werner seemed most at ease in his company. Does Dame Eleanor know?"

"Not yet. I will tell her after the Dominicans depart," said Kate. "I know I can trust you not to speak of this to anyone. Watch the girls closely today." She told them about Nan waking, thinking Kate was her lover Robin sneaking in, how she had helped with Severen, then disappeared.

"The nights caring for her ailing mother were a lovers' tryst." Jennet nodded. "That explains much. Was he at her mother's house on the night of the intruder?"

Brigida looked from one to the other as Kate shook her head. "Do you think it was him? That Dina surprised Nan's lover coming into the kitchen?"

"Nan said that it was the one night he had not appeared at her mother's house," said Kate. "But it is dangerous to judge when we know so little. I am hoping she fled to her house. I need to talk to Berend before the sheriffs' man arrives, ask him to go see if Nan is there."

Kate paused a moment, observing the men arriving for work in the small warehouse that sat on the corner of Hertergate and Castlegate. The warehouse was managed by John Paris, the employer of Agnes's late husband, Leonard. He lived across the alley from the Martha House, and, as Kate had learned yesterday, at one time entertained Agnes in the guesthouse. "But first, I'd like to know whether there is a night watchman in the warehouse." She lifted a hand in greeting to one of the men and strolled over to the adjoining yard to talk to him.

—◦◦◦—

Eleanor stood on the landing, observing the unexpected visitors. The two black-mantled friars stood before the small altar that held a statue of the Blessed Mother, which she and the beguines had dressed in colorful silks, the table draped with an altar cloth embroidered with motifs from the life of the mother of Christ. Offerings from the sisters lay at the Virgin's feet—delicate shells, stones, and other precious objects. Framed by the painted walls, the altar was the colorful center—indeed, the heart—of the hall. The friars' dark mantles and white robes looked out of place before it.

One of them was elderly, large but stooped, the other a stocky young man. The elder picked at the offerings on the altar with clawlike hands speckled with age spots, pursing his lips, drawing his wrinkles downward. *Sour old man*, Eleanor thought. Who was he to disapprove their sincere devotion? She cleared her throat and descended the steps.

As the subject of her distaste turned toward her, she saw that his eyes were milky with age and wondered whether he could even see the items he'd handled. How had he known they were there? His companion? The other was young, barely past his novitiate, Eleanor guessed, with a cherubic face marred by a dark red birthmark that splashed his left cheek and forehead. He leaned close now to whisper something in his elder's ear. Yes, that was his role, he was his master's guide. And just as lacking in courtesy.

The elder smiled on Eleanor, bowing and offering a blessing. "*Benedicite*, Mistress Smit." One might almost doubt that he was blind, he aimed his sightless gaze so naturally. She guessed he had not always been blind.

"Mistress Clifford. Smit is such an ugly name. But I prefer Dame Eleanor."

"My pardons, Dame Eleanor. I am Friar Adam, of the Dominican house of St. Mary Magdalene. I am answering your call for a cleric to guide your poor sisters."

She gave him a slight bow, though only his companion could see it. Answering her call, was he? She had made no public request. *Not so hasty, you ill-tempered friar.* She cleared her throat. "Beguines, not poor sisters. They go out into the world and earn their keep as well as caring for the people of the city. Welcome to my Martha House, Friar Adam, and . . . ?" She gazed pointedly at the younger man.

"This is Friar Walter—my eyes, as it were," said Adam.

"And Friar Walter." She nodded to the young man. "You are his eyes and he is your mouth?" She chuckled. "Be easy, I pray you. We all walk the path of love, as revealed by the teachings of Christ, our Savior. Love is a happy virtue."

"Beguines." Friar Adam sniffed. "You would do well to remember His Holiness Pope Clement condemned them as heretics."

It was Eleanor's turn to sniff. This sneering, sniveling toad of a friar would not do for her Martha House. But she must extend the sisters the courtesy of allowing them to meet him and come to their own decision. She was confident they would see his closed mind and follow her in deeming him unsuitable. "Sisters Clara, Brigida, and Dina do not presume to preach but confine themselves to good works. I should like them to meet you. Unfortunately you have arrived as they are attending mass at St. Mary's. Might I offer you refreshments while you wait?" She signaled to Rose to fetch a tray.

"You are most kind, Dame Eleanor." No longer smiling, Friar Adam pressed a hand to his heart. "May God bring peace to this household."

"I have found immense peace in the company of the beguines. While we wait, I might ask your advice in bringing a new sister into the household."

"This would be Agnes Dell?"

"You are quite knowledgeable about us, considering none of this information comes from me. I believe you owe me the courtesy of telling me how you came to know so much—that I sought a confessor for the house, and that Agnes Dell had asked to join the sisters."

"I have the honor of being Dame Isabella Frost's confessor."

"Dame Isabella. Yes. I see." *Oh dear me, of course, how did I not guess?* This officious creature would appeal to that tiresome woman. Eleanor folded her hands. "And Agnes Dell?"

"This was her home, was it not?"

"It was indeed, though how you would know that I cannot fathom. No matter. Now you are here, I will of course do you the courtesy of an interview. Let me see . . ."

She studied the disagreeable pair. The old friar's face had gone briefly crimson—the subtle insult of a test was not lost on him. But he quickly recovered, bowing to her.

"How *would* you advise us to bring Agnes Dell into the fold?" she asked. The overbearing were so easy to bait.

Adam produced a smile meant to be beneficent, but the milky eyes lacked expression and the man's breath was sour. "First, you should have her speak with me, tell me why she chose to make such a change."

"And what would you seek in her answer? A spiritual yearning?"

"It is for her to say. If her answer was satisfactory, I would instruct the sisters to ensure that one of them accompany Dame Agnes at all times for the next few months. After our weekly meetings they would tell me all that they observed as she goes about her day. In confidence, of course."

Of course. You would not want Agnes to know what the sisters said behind her back, you miserable . . . Eleanor breathed deeply. "Yes? Go on, I pray you."

"In such wise, we might arrive at the best advice for the woman going forward."

The woman. Poor Agnes, to be the subject of such scrutiny. Under such treatment she would come to question her decision, regardless of whether or not her vocation was deemed sincere. Eleanor felt Walter watching her closely. She turned her gaze on the youth, staring him down until he averted his eyes, making a great study of his hands. Neither of the friars reflected the same warmth as the beguines. She wondered who had observed *them*, judged *them* fit for God's work.

Admittedly, she and the sisters all agreed that the life of a beguine might not be what Agnes had expected, and as for any potential sister, they had advised Agnes to look into her heart for the next few months and ask God's guidance in her decision. It was also customary that sisters go forth in pairs. But to spy on the woman and tattle to their confessor, especially this cold creature who was overdue for his grave—Eleanor saw no love and compassion in such an instruction. Her smile to Friar Adam was more a baring of teeth.

"Your daughter, Mistress Neville—" he began.

"Clifford. But you may refer to her as Dame Katherine."

"Dame Katherine." He bowed. "She is a singular woman. I have heard disturbing tales about her and the men in her household."

Eleanor bristled. Friar Adam was nothing more than a common gossip. "My daughter has taken in three orphans and given them a good, loving home. In such times as these, with soldiers setting up camp in Toft Green—so close to your abbey, Friar Adam, you must be aware of them—I count my daughter wise and responsible to have men in the household who can defend the children, as well as herself, a young widow. Do you take offense at such precaution?"

Adam's smile was stiff as Walter took the cup of wine Rose proffered his master and placed it in his hand. "My mistake, Dame Eleanor. The arrangement as you describe it is most admirable. Though, as she is a widow, a great temptation to the men in her household."

Ah, me, poor clerics, how they fear their bodies. Eleanor merely smiled, stubbornly saying nothing, though her mind conjured delicious retorts about where weak men go to hide. Walter leaned close to his master and whispered in his ear, no doubt describing her smile. Fit to burst, Eleanor was about to excuse herself and cross Castlegate to fetch the sisters when the beguines appeared at the garden door. God be thanked. Before the introductions could be made, Eleanor herded them back out to the garden with a vague excuse to the friars and assurances that they would not be long.

"Dame Eleanor, I do not wish to be discourteous, but the good friars, we wish to meet them," said Sister Clara, her round, usually placid face reddened with the perceived slight to the holy men.

"Good friars they are not, which you will discern once you speak with them," said Eleanor. She gave them a brief account of Adam's sour and judgmental opinions.

"*Mon Dieu*," murmured Brigida.

"How unfortunate," said Clara.

Sister Dina, her face flushed with health once more, gave Eleanor a hug. "Bless you for warning us. I had thought to confess to him."

How Eleanor would love to overhear such a confession. What did Dina remember of her ordeal? But the Dominicans must hear nothing of that night. "I feared as much. Say nothing. Tell them nothing. They believe they already know all, so they will hardly notice." Eleanor kissed Dina's cheek, nodded to Clara and Brigida. "We can and will do much better. Now go, send them off with all courtesy."

Before turning toward the door, Brigida touched Eleanor's arm. "Dame Katherine has something to tell you." The three swept into the hall, shutting the door behind them.

Eleanor smiled to herself as she imagined Friar Adam's surprise when he was shown the door.

Gazing out at the garden, she discovered an interesting tableau—Katherine and Griffin with their heads together, talking earnestly, the great wolfhounds lounging in the kitchen doorway. She approached them.

⸻◦⊙◦⸻

Kate had watched with interest as her mother swept the sisters back out into the garden with that scheming look of hers. But Griffin had interrupted her attempt to listen in. Irked, she was glad to see her mother approaching.

"Such a tiring pair," Eleanor said as she reached Kate and Griffin. "Dominicans. Always preaching."

"But you have asked them to guide your Martha House?" Kate asked, confused.

"Oh, no, they seem to have chosen me. Or, rather, Isabella Frost prompted Friar Adam to do so."

Kate felt her jaw tightening. What was Isabella's interest in this?

"I have warned the sisters," Eleanor went on. "They know to send them off with all courtesy. York is full of holy men eager to guide impressionable young women. We will find someone suitable anon." The excitement in her mother's voice belied her weary sigh. "You are York's Mary Magdalene to him, by the way, Katherine. I defended you sharply. But now I wonder—as she is the saint to whom their friary is dedicated, perhaps I misunderstood."

Ignoring her mother's attempts at humor—Kate was in no mood—she brought it back to the point that troubled her. "Isabella Frost," she said. A meddler and a gossip, her cousin's wife had bowed to her husband's insistence that they host Eleanor and her beguines when they first arrived in York, but she had made no secret of her distrust and disapproval. The intolerable situation had inspired Eleanor's hasty acceptance of Agnes Dell's offer. "It bodes ill that she should take such an interest."

"I did wonder." Only now did Eleanor look closely at Kate and her companion. "Brigida said you wished to speak with me. What is it? What has happened? Is it Nan?"

Kate touched her mother's arm.

Eleanor winced. "Nothing good follows such a gesture. Tell me, Daughter."

"Nan is gone," said Kate. "I trust she has simply joined Dame Agnes at her mother's house. But there is harder news. Hans is dead. Murdered."

Eleanor gasped, shaking her head and looking to Griffin, but he was moving off toward the kitchen, his back to her.

They knew something, Kate realized. She took her mother's arm and escorted her after Griffin.

"For once could you not have tamed your unruly hair before you stepped out?" Eleanor blurted.

"My hair is the least of our concerns," Kate said, hating herself for reaching up to tuck a stray lock behind her ear.

Eleanor sank down on the bench to which Kate had led her, leaning her head against the cool wall in the kitchen. "No, no, that is not what I had intended to say. Forgive me," she whispered.

In times of stress she was a cornered cat, hissing and slashing. Accustomed to the behavior, Kate waited quietly as her mother composed herself. As a child, Kate had taken the criticisms to heart, despite her father's reassurances that her mother did not mean what she said when she lashed out. He tried to teach her that patient silence afforded the best outcome. Her brothers all learned it. But not Kate; she'd winced at each insult. Still did.

"Hans. Dear Hans," Eleanor's voice broke. She bowed her head.

Sitting beside her, Kate took her mother's hand. "I am sorry to deliver such sad news."

He had been Eleanor's favorite of Ulrich's household staff. She had assured Thomas Holme that he would not be sorry for employing Hans, that he was efficient, cheerful, energetic, quick, and always willing to assist others to ensure that all was as it should be. Eleanor had known him for years—indeed, Hans claimed he remembered Kate from when she and Geoffrey were first learning to walk, when he and Werner accompanied Ulrich Smit on the journeys that brought him through Northumberland. For her part, Kate only vaguely remembered a group of men accompanying Ulrich. Her grief rose from a more recent affection for the man.

Eleanor raised her head, dabbing her eyes with a cloth she slipped from inside her sleeve. "How did he die? Where?" She listened quietly to Kate's description of Hans's injuries, where he had been found. "Heaven help us," she whispered, nodding to Griffin as he handed her a cup of water.

"Boiled, Dame Eleanor, as you like it," he said.

Kate wondered what had led to her mother's new whim. Suddenly she could not abide the taste of water unless it was boiled, strained, then stored in a cool place with a cloth over the top. Or was Kate too quick to deem it a whim—might her mother fear someone might poison her?

Eleanor drank. Breathed. "Werner. Does he know?"

"He is with Hans," said Kate.

"Yes. Of course he should be. I do not know Werner as well as I did Hans. He is so quiet. I agreed to his offer to accompany us because of his strength. When he traveled with Ulrich he served as a retainer, but at home in Strasbourg he served as a gardener and groom. Not as clever or personable as Hans. Dear Hans. To die so horribly, so far from home." She glanced up. "Forgive me for going on like this. I cannot imagine—you have described his wounds, but how? Where was he when attacked?"

When Griffin described the brawl on the street, Eleanor frowned in disbelief. "Hans reeked of ale? I never knew him to take a drop."

"According to Werner, Hans has of late been sneaking out after all are abed," said Griffin, "spending his nights in the taverns. His work has suffered. Thomas Holme meant to speak with you about him."

"Merciful Mother. Why did Holme wait so long? And you, Griffin, why did you not tell me?"

"I heard of it only this morning. All I knew of Hans and Werner is that they were both tolerable traveling companions, neither drank too much in my company, both kept themselves tidy, caused no trouble. In Strasbourg I had little need to befriend the household servants."

"God help me, I meant to do good bringing them here, accepting Agnes's offer. Ashes. Ashes." Eleanor had gone quite pale, and she seemed more frightened than grieving. She kept trying to catch Griffin's eye, but he kept his gaze averted.

Kate thought it might be best to separate them, try to speak with them individually.

"Do you need food, Mother? Or to lie down? There is a bed a few steps away."

Eleanor waved her on. "I am stronger than you give me credit for. Send Werner to me. I wish to speak with him." She took a deep breath. "There is much to do. I am responsible for a household. Should I tell the sisters?"

Kate told her that Brigida already knew.

"No. It is my place. You should have left it to me."

"The sheriff or his sergeant will be here soon, and all the city will know," said Kate.

"Ah. Of course. I shall tell the others when the friars depart. What a cursed morning. We must consider what the news of Hans's murder will do to Dina, already so burdened. I cannot guess. Perhaps I should wait to tell Dina and Clara."

"The sheriff might send someone to question all of you, Mother. It is best that Dina and Clara hear it from you first. Tell them, then go about your day. Griffin will be here to protect you. And Berend is close." Kate saw her mother's wounded expression at her impatient tone.

"I will tell them." Eleanor rose and walked out into the garden.

Kate followed. "Mother—"

"We will pray for you. Go. Find the answer to this nightmare before we suffer more loss."

As Kate opened the hedgerow gate, she overheard her mother telling Griffin to talk to Werner, find out whether Hans might have said anything in his cups. Damn her. Did she think this was a game? Kate turned round and retraced her steps.

"Is there something that I should know?"

Eleanor looked at Kate, aghast. "That was not meant for your ears. I raised you to keep your own counsel and let others keep theirs."

Fighting to hold her temper in check, Kate took her mother's hands, looking into the eyes that would not settle on hers. "What do you fear Hans might have divulged?"

An impatient sigh. "I should think it obvious. Household servants know all sorts of intimate details."

Her mother's hands were cold, but her face was flushed and damp. She was frightened. Very frightened. Kate fought the urge to berate her mother—*What are you thinking? Do you realize the danger?* "Of course." Kissing her mother's cheek, Kate took her leave.

8

SHERIFFS AND ARCHBISHOPS

———— ❦ ————

"Maddening woman! How can I help her if she will not confide in me?"

"I am glad that the children are in the main house doing their lessons with Sister Brigida," Berend said, calmly closing the kitchen door behind Kate. He leaned against it, arms folded. "Jennet told me of Hans's death and Nan's disappearance. Would I be correct in guessing that Dame Eleanor is the maddening woman, and that she still will not confide in you?"

"How could you know?" Kate could not help but smile at his teasing eyes.

Sitting down near the window, she welcomed Lille and Ghent to settle at her feet. "Bless you," she whispered, rubbing their ears. She saw that Berend had been chopping meat and vegetables for a stew. Wonderfully ordinary work.

He handed her a bowl of ale. "What of the friars?"

She had forgotten them. "They have been sent away. Unsuitable. But I cannot help but wonder about their appearance. They say Isabella Frost suggested they come. But is it possible they came here, today, because of Griffin's presence on Toft Green last night? Or for the same reason that Elric's men went there, something related to the intruder in the Martha House?"

Berend frowned, considering. "Their abbey does overlook the green. And if they are ministering to the soldiers, they might hear much. So what are you thinking?"

"I wish I knew. It's all a jumble." She smiled as Ghent responded to her tone by resting his great, grizzly head on her lap, gazing up with soulful eyes. "Griffin puzzles me. I begin to trust him, then he fails to follow the men out on the street and loses Nan. As Ulrich's retainer, surely he was trained to consider priorities. Which makes me wonder whether his are the same as ours. And Mother seemed distracted, as if the news of Hans's death—" Kate shook her head.

"You wonder whether Dame Eleanor and Griffin have a secret purpose here?"

"Yes." She told him what she had just overheard. "She has been secretive about so many things. How did Ulrich die? Why did she leave Strasbourg? Do we know all the reasons why Griffin is in her company? Answers would help me set aside my suspicions."

"Or prove you are wise in not trusting either Dame Eleanor or Griffin."

Distrust her mother. Put so bluntly, it unsettled Kate, not because it was unimaginable but because she could not imagine the reverse. "Precisely. And if Hans was part of whatever they might be hiding, might Werner be as well?"

"All questions we must answer, eh?" Berend shook his head as Kate bent to remove her shoes. "You have no time for that. Your uncle's secretary, Alf, was here. You are summoned to the deanery. His Grace the archbishop has just arrived in York. He is with your uncle and wants to talk to you."

"The archbishop? Why?" Kate knew him only slightly—a few dinners, brief conversations.

"Alf did not say."

If he would not say, he had not been told. "Am I cursed?" For a moment, Kate forgot to breathe.

Berend touched her shoulder. "Shall I go to Nan's mother's house? Ease our minds that she is there, and safe?"

"I would be grateful. Meet me at the deanery when you are finished. If I've already been dismissed, Helen will know where I've gone." Her uncle's housekeeper, Helen, was a strong ally. As was her uncle, usually. And Alf.

Lille rose to look out the doorway. Ghent followed.

"One of the sheriffs' sergeants approaches," said Berend. "It's Selby. Good. He is happiest when reassured that all is taken care of, eh?"

A small gift in the midst of trouble. The sergeant was accompanied by Thomas Holme, Matt, and Werner.

"Would you like me to talk to them?" Berend asked.

"A generous offer, but no, I must see this through." Kate was about to step out the doorway when she remembered one more thing Berend should know. "I spoke with the man who sleeps in John Paris's warehouse on the corner. He heard and saw nothing the past two nights. But it's no wonder—he is very deaf. I had to shout to make myself understood."

Berend nodded. "John Paris cares only that there is a body by the door. Will you mention the intruder in the Martha House to Selby?"

Kate reminded him that Magistra Matilda had already told the sheriffs of it when complaining about Elric's men. "I will let Selby mention it, and then deal with him."

"He has a fear of dogs, as I recall." Berend grinned.

"So he does!"

Kate signaled Lille and Ghent to accompany her as she stepped out into the yard. "Master Selby, Thomas, I trust you are here about Hans."

Selby took a few steps backward, tucking his hands behind him. "As you are the finder, we require your silver to ensure that you will stay in the city while we have need of your witness, Mistress Clifford." It was the law, the money to be held by the coroner.

"Ah. I will fetch it. If you give me a moment . . ." She made as if to hand the leads to Selby, who blanched.

"No," said Thomas Holme, stepping between them. "I will see to the fee. He was my servant."

Selby shook his head. "My good man, the finder pays the fee."

"And I said I would see to it," said Thomas.

Kate touched her partner's arm, thanking him. And she thanked Selby for seeing to this himself rather than sending one of his constables.

Selby shifted feet, no doubt questioning the wisdom of his choice. "As this is the second incident in as many days . . ." His attention was on Lille, who sniffed the air in his direction. "I understand that the Earl of Westmoreland's men were set to guard Magistra Matilda's *maison dieu* while a Sister Dina, from Dame Eleanor's house, was being cared for. After an intruder—"

"A drunk, yes. He stumbled into Dame Eleanor's kitchen, frightening Sister Dina." Kate kept her voice level, no excitement. "I cannot guess what he thought to gain—the sisters have few possessions. Perhaps the statue of the Blessed Virgin?" She shook her head. "I suspect he sought a warm, dry place to sleep off the ale. I am more concerned about Hans's murder and the watchman's injury. You have talked to Severen? It is he who tussled with the men. Indeed, his description of Hans, lying lifeless on the street, would suggest he was the one from whom you should collect the silver. It was Severen who was the finder." Smiling, she touched Lille's head, signaling her to be still. "And now, if you will pardon me, I have been summoned to the minster by His Grace the archbishop."

"Archbishop Scrope? Of course, of course. One does not keep His Grace waiting," said Selby, bowing to her and shuffling off down toward Castlegate. Without the fee.

Kate drew Thomas aside to ask whether he had learned anything of interest from Magistra Matilda.

"Nothing you had not already heard. I do begin to wonder whether she is right to distrust Dame Eleanor's beguines."

"You blame the victims? And who is to blame for the murder of your servant?"

"I wish I had never hired Hans and Werner, truth be told. Though they both work hard, my wife could not abide being near Hans after one of his nights out drinking. She said she could smell the ale from across the hall."

"And Werner?"

"He is a cipher to me, though a hard worker, I admit."

Kate did not pursue the argument. She knew Thomas had a good heart. He would think better of all this in a few days. She excused herself and hurried to the hall to tidy her hair and shake out her gown.

⚬❧⚬

Kate fought to regain some sense of peace as she let Lille and Ghent lead the way from the more open spaces on Castlegate, where the birdsong and the sounds of the river soothed the mind, into the crowded streets of the city center. But the city was a hellhole in summer, hardly a place that might lift her spirits. The heat and the river damp coaxed out all the noxious odors of the trades and the crush of people and animals. She lifted her skirts and wished she had remembered a cloth soaked in lavender to hold up to her nose. But it rarely worked to have Lille's and Ghent's leads in one hand, and today she was grateful for their presence to either side, steering the flow of people well away from her.

As she was crossing Ousegate she was hailed by a familiar voice, and turned to find Agnes Dell approaching. Lille and Ghent sniffed in her direction but knew not to get too close—Agnes was skittish around them. The woman looked wretched, hollow-eyed and drained, her borrowed gray gown wrinkled and so tight around her ample breasts and upper arms that Kate could imagine the woman's discomfort. Dina had hemmed up one of Clara's gowns for her, but Agnes was much rounder than her benefactor.

"I cannot go back to Dame Hawise's house, Dame Katherine," Agnes began as she reached Kate. "I pray you, speak with Dame Eleanor, tell her that Nan is far better seeing to her mother than I am. And she seems to want to be there. She came back to the house this morning, asking whether her man had appeared—he has not—and fretting over the children. And she told me about Hans." She crossed herself, breathing hard.

So Nan still expected Robin to appear.

The crowd of people flowing to and from the shops and offices on Ouse Bridge parted around them with curious glances.

"I was on my way to the minster deanery," said Kate. "Where are you going? Home?"

"To the minster to pray for Nan's wretched mother. And for Hans."

"Why there?"

"I want my prayers to be heard. Such a great holy place—I prayed there for my Leonard's soul."

Agnes's reply silenced all argument. "Then walk with me," said Kate. "We will be less noticeable than we are standing here, eh?" She signaled to Lille and Ghent to continue up Coney Street as Agnes fell into step beside her.

"Did you know that Jocasta Sharp sends food to Dame Hawise and the children each day?" said Agnes. "She is a good woman, much like the beguines in her work but that she is married."

"Dame Jocasta is a very fine woman." Kate admired her friend, a wealthy woman who had made it her mission to care for the city's poor. Jocasta carried out her work with the enthusiastic support of those she had assisted in the past. "Agnes, you say that Nan should have the care of her mother, yet surely she went into service for you in order to support her family. What do you propose?"

"That Nan do her duty. I have released her from our service."

"So harsh, Agnes?" The woman opened her mouth to protest, but Kate ignored her. "In any case, that decision was not yours to make."

"We can find another maidservant. She is not happy with the beguines."

"And you, Agnes. Are you?"

"Do you doubt me? Did I not obey Dame Eleanor and sit with Nan's mother, listening to Dame Hawise wheezing and sighing and complaining all through the night? I invited her to pray with me, explained to her the joy of the beguines' faith, but she cares nothing for that. And the children are wild, the house filthy. I yearn to be back with the others, Dame Katherine."

"So you released Nan from Dame Eleanor's service for your own comfort."

A little gasp. "I—no! Nan is unhappy. Would you speak with Dame Eleanor?"

"I will, but I cannot promise she will hear me."

Agnes thanked her. For what, Kate did not know. She was not greatly inclined to help the woman at the moment.

"Do you know anything of Nan's lover, Robin?" Kate asked.

"Now that she's confessed who he is, yes. He was one of John Paris's warehousemen. When he worked during the day he was one of several of the men who would come to my house for dinner midday. John considered it part of Leonard's duties, though my husband was often away, so, in truth, it was my duty. It also went toward the rent on our house. As for Robin, when he was promoted to the night watch at the warehouse, he betrayed John's trust, consorting with thieves, and John let him go, though he kindly did not hand him over to the sheriff."

"Why not?"

"I never asked. I have not seen Robin in a long while. Of course he would avoid being seen on Hertergate. Nan did not tell me it was Robin she met at Hawise's. I trust she knew I would warn her away from him. He knew the house, Dame Katherine. No wonder he knew where to search for the key. I am that angry—I told Nan that even if she were happy, she is no longer welcome in any household in which I reside."

She seemed quite certain that Robin was the intruder. Kate wanted proof. "Do you feel Nan shares the blame for his act?"

"She admitted to me how she bragged about all the lovely things in the Martha House. What things? I have seen nothing of great value. Though it is said that Dame Eleanor has some grand gowns in her chest, and jewels, Nan should not have seen them."

As they parted in the minster yard, Kate encouraged Agnes to speak to Dame Eleanor herself. "You must convince her that you are sincere in desiring a life of prayer and work, a life without a man, Agnes."

"Why would you doubt it?"

"I know that you and John Paris were guests in my house on High Petergate."

Agnes blushed and averted her eyes, uncertain what to do with her hands of a sudden. "That was—I feel only shame for that."

Kate watched the woman cross the yard to the minster, broad shoulders hunched, head bowed. The brief encounter had changed Kate's impression of the woman. "Go in peace," she whispered. There was a story to her relationship with John Paris. But that was a conversation for another time.

Dean Richard's housekeeper, Helen, greeted Kate at the deanery door with a little frown.

"Oh, my dear, I have heard about the troubles at your mother's Martha House. I am so sorry."

"Bless you, Helen." As Kate stepped into the hall she noticed enticing smells from the kitchen—cinnamon, butter, fresh-baked pies. "My uncle and the archbishop are expecting me."

"They are, to be sure." Helen reached down to rub Lille's and Ghent's ears and whisper a promise of ham bones. "I am about to take Dean Richard and His Grace the archbishop some refreshments in the parlor. Go ahead in." She paused, touching Kate's arm. "Your uncle did not like that His Grace wished you summoned here."

"Why?"

"When Scrope requested the meeting, his stated purpose was to discuss the defense of York. He wishes to be seen as doing all he can to support it."

"Against his mentor's prodigy, Henry of Lancaster?"

"I know, it seems to go against his natural inclination, but as Archbishop of York his fealty is to the anointed king."

"What has that to do with me?"

"That? Nothing. Richard Scrope arrived this morning with a different matter on his mind, rumors about the events at your mother's house."

"God help us."

"Yes. In truth, both men are quite disturbed by Dame Eleanor's ambition to establish a beguinage, as they are calling it, in York. This is one issue on which they are quite agreed. You are forewarned."

"But why summon me? Why not Mother?"

"Your uncle and your mother? Have they ever conversed without argument?"

No indeed. But then, who did escape argument with her mother? "Is that why he declined to act as spiritual guide for her Martha House?"

"As I said, it is more. He disapproves the beguinage. And—well, I do wonder what Dame Eleanor has done that so alienated him. In the past he has regarded her with mild irritation. But this—your uncle is rarely so sharp. I am doing my best to ignore him."

"All this because Mother chose to found a Martha House?"

"Truth be told, I doubt he could tell us the cause. Men's feelings are as mysterious to them as they are to us. Now go, before they hear us and think we are conspiring against them."

"Is that the mood?"

"That is my sense of it."

"Do they know I found a body on the riverbank this morning?"

A nod. "The sheriffs' men can go nowhere without gossips following on their heels. His Grace brought word of it. How awful for you, my dear. Your mother's servant. Did you know him well?"

"No, not well. Hans moved to Thomas Holme's household after accompanying Mother on her recent journey to Northumberland."

"Ah. But he did arrive in Dame Eleanor's company. More cause for distrust, you see. Poor man. May Hans rest in God's grace." Helen crossed herself, then patted Kate's shoulder. "Go on. I will settle Lille and Ghent in the kitchen, then come serve the three of you." She clucked to the dogs and herded them off to the kitchen, shutting the door behind her.

Outside her uncle's parlor Kate paused, gathering her calm like a protective cloak. She reminded herself to take time to think about a question before answering it, to offer nothing beyond a simple answer, then wait for more questions. Nodding to herself, she lifted her hand to knock, but paused. Helen's comment about their suspicions that the women were conspiring against them gave her an idea. What if she conspired *with* them, bargaining a fair exchange, favor for favor? The air felt slightly lighter, her mood brighter. Fear fell away, allowing space for cunning. Smiling to herself, Kate knocked, then entered.

Lamplight played along the rich colors in the tapestries, and on the cushions spread around the chamber. The shutters of the one window were flung wide, inviting the air from the shaded garden into the chamber. But not enough. Her uncle's forehead glistened with sweat as he rose to welcome her, gesturing toward a chair that had been placed so that both he and the archbishop could observe her. Richard Scrope inclined his head to her respectful greeting and asked whether her beautiful hounds had accompanied her.

"They have, Your Grace, and are now enjoying the hospitality of Helen's kitchen."

She took her seat, fussing for a moment with her sleeves while composing herself. It was most appropriate that the archbishop had not risen; he was the power in the room. Even so, she took it as an ill omen of the outcome of this bargaining session, that the two Richards held themselves so stiffly. She felt herself following suit, perched at the edge of her chair, resenting the atmosphere in the room. If either of them had just hours earlier stumbled upon the body of a man beaten to death, they would not subject themselves to such a meeting.

"Now then," said Helen from the threshold as she held open the door for a young clerk to set a tray on the table near the dean. A pie heaped with spiced fruits and custard, bread, butter, cheese, bowls, goblets, and a servant holding a flagon of wine and pitcher of water, ready to serve.

Though Helen was almost as skilled in the kitchen as Berend, Kate had no stomach for food at the moment. She did accept a goblet of wine, unwatered, the better to dull her irritation.

Her uncle and the archbishop each accepted a slice of pie, tasting it with apparent pleasure. But as soon as Helen and her helpers withdrew, they put aside their bowls.

Dean Richard leaned toward Kate, his brows pulled together in a concerned frown. His gray eyes softened for a moment. "My dear Katherine, is it true that you came upon a murdered man on your walk this morning? One of Dame Eleanor's servants from Strasbourg?"

"It is, Uncle."

"May God calm your troubled heart."

"It was a disturbing beginning to my day."

"What do you know about this man?"

"No more than you do, I imagine, Uncle. He was most recently employed in the household of my neighbor, Thomas Holme. Why do you ask?"

The archbishop made a little sound.

Her uncle's frown deepened, his dark brows pulling together. "We are merely concerned."

Clearly it was more than that. "You are most kind."

"And what of the beguine who sleeps with a dagger, whose gown and shift were stiff with someone else's blood?" asked the archbishop.

"Forgive me, Your Grace, but I do not understand what it is you wish to know."

"What do you know of Sister Dina?" her uncle asked in a quiet voice.

"She is a skilled needle woman. Mother hired her to make her mourning robes in Strasbourg, and she was impressed by her compassion and quiet wisdom. I know little more."

"I heard that she became agitated while Dame Eleanor was sitting with her at the *maison dieu*," said Scrope.

Magistra Matilda must be quite the tittle-tattle. "Your Grace, I humbly suggest that you continue this conversation with Dame Eleanor. She is the one who knows her servants and the beguines whom she brought with her from Strasbourg."

Scrope nodded, sat back in his chair, elbows on the arms, hands steepled. "What do you know of beguines?"

"They are dedicated to God and good works, celibate, and, rather than bringing large dowries to convents, they work to support themselves— which means the life is available to women of lesser means. Other than their work outside the Martha House, I see little difference between them and the poor sisters of York."

"Pope Clement condemned them," said her uncle, picking up his goblet, sipping his wine. "And the Holy Fathers who have followed him have concurred."

"I am fond of the three sisters. I see much good in them, no harm. They do not preach, as did Marguerite Porete."

"How do you come to know about the heretic Porete?"

Kate had stepped in it now. Brigida had told her of Marguerite. "I cannot recall. Perhaps you, Uncle?"

The dean frowned, shook his head. "Not I. Dame Eleanor, no doubt." She saw what Helen meant—he spoke her mother's name as if it were a curse.

Archbishop Scrope leaned forward. "You say you see no harm in them. Even Sister Dina, with her dagger beneath her pillow?" He held Kate's gaze, as if eager to hear her rebuttal.

"A woman must often defend her virtue and her life against those who would force themselves on her, Your Grace. I assume she suffered some terrible experience in the past, a terror she has not yet forgotten. How could I condemn her for finding comfort in a form of protection? We do not as yet know what the intruder was after, or what he had done to Sister Dina. Which brings me to my proposal."

Her uncle shook his head in warning, but the archbishop sat back and sipped his wine, gesturing to her to continue.

"In exchange for introductions and information, I will keep you apprised of my investigation into the intruder and Hans's murder."

"You have agreed to assist Dame Eleanor in this?" His Grace asked.

"I have chosen to do so." Kate glanced at her uncle, who scowled into his cup. She had never seen him like this. "Kin help kin."

His eyes, when he lifted them to hers, were most unfriendly, his strong jaw, usually expressing a comforting air of command, jutted forward, as if challenging her. "Cliffords do, but Frosts? That would be news indeed." He snorted. "You would be best to remember how much trouble your cousin William and your mother, both Frosts, have brought you. How much sorrow."

She could not deny that. But neither could she reconcile this angry man with the uncle who had supported and comforted her during those troubles. His voice was sharp, his tone challenging. What did he know? "Do you mean to warn me, Uncle?"

"I do."

The archbishop cleared his throat. "I will leave that to the two of you to discuss. You speak of introductions, Dame Katherine. To whom?"

Kate was relieved to break away from her uncle's scowl. "Abbot Thomas of St. Mary's and Prior Norbert of the blackfriars, to begin." She explained her interest—Sir Elric's visit to the abbey, the infirmarian's caution, the brawl at Toft Green so near the Dominican friary, Friar Adam's subsequent visit to the Martha House.

Richard Clifford muttered something that sounded very much like a curse when she mentioned the blind friar and his assistant. "Friar Adam. Why did Dame Eleanor send for him?" he growled.

"It is puzzling," said Scrope. "It would be far more convenient to approach the Franciscans. Their friary is so close to her house."

"Friar Adam had no invitation. He came of his own accord," said Kate. "Hence my interest. He heard of their need for a confessor from Isabella Gisburne Frost. He claims to be her confessor."

"Frosts," the dean muttered.

"Isabella is far more Gisburne than Frost, Uncle."

The archbishop chuckled. "She speaks my own thoughts, Richard. Isabella Gisburne is her father's daughter through and through, God help her." He turned back to Kate. "And the information you require?"

"My usual sources have become secretive when I most need to understand who is fighting for what."

"Your usual sources being your influential guests on High Petergate?" asked the archbishop.

Kate appreciated Scrope's blunt question. She had long guessed he knew the nature of the local patrons of her guesthouse. "Yes, and my fellow guild members. I sensed a great deal of conflict in the aldermen and their friends at the guild meeting yesterday."

"Ah, the meeting at the merchants' hall, yes. What was the purpose, might I ask?"

"The guild master read out the orders from the Duke of York, listened to members' concerns, and then made a modest attempt to organize help toward those here to defend the city against Henry of Lancaster. The ease with which he withdrew the proposal was telling. All the while he watched the row of aldermen. I know, I sat at the end of it."

"With your partner, Thomas Holme?" asked the dean.

She nodded.

"And has he become secretive as well?" the archbishop asked.

He had. And perhaps not only because of the political conflict but also because he regretted hiring Hans and Werner.

They are challenging you, Kate, Geoff whispered in her head. *Even our uncle, who has been your ally in the past.*

No one trusts anyone at present, Geoff. Now quiet. I must be sharp.

Kate remained silent.

"And was your cousin William Frost in attendance?" asked the archbishop.

Pointed questions might mean they knew something. "He is not a guild member, Your Grace," she said. "Do you ask because of his wife's connection to Friar Adam?"

It was her uncle who responded to the question. "Two violent incidents connected to Dame Eleanor's household—past or present—in as many nights, Katherine. And, coming in the midst of the threat to the peace of the realm, my inclination is to suspect everything, everyone. It is all one dangerous knot, and we must tease out the threads, discover how they are intertwined."

"I do not *know* that both incidents are connected, Uncle. The city is teeming with restless soldiers. That is why I need information."

"You spoke of conflict among the merchants, Dame Katherine." Scrope nodded to the dean. "We have been discussing that very issue, have we not, Richard? It is time to share what we have heard."

The dean frowned at the archbishop as if questioning his judgment, but Scrope merely motioned for him to speak.

The dean cleared his throat. "William Frost and his colleagues have sent a messenger to Duke Henry at Knaresborough carrying a sum of money to assist him in his efforts to reclaim his inheritance." Her uncle's face was now a study in quiet. Kate guessed that he was as yet unsure with whom his own loyalty lay. "In their message they said nothing of Henry's shifting intention—to take the crown from his cousin and place it on his own noble head. But such have been the reports."

"The promises he is making only a king has the power to fulfill," she said.

Scrope sat up. "You heard that at the meeting?"

"I did, Your Grace."

"Hm. Yes, it does appear that he has been persuaded by the Lancastrian forces to reach higher than he had set out to do."

"Or than he had dared admit even to himself," the dean said softly. "It appears that we've no need to fortify the city. The Lancastrian army is headed westward."

God be thanked! Her mood lifted. For a moment. "Who will tell the men gathered on Toft Green, hungry for a fight?" Kate asked. Which reminded her of the question she'd meant to ask her uncle. "Sir Alan Bennet. How did he approach you about leasing my house, Uncle?" He'd asked about the abbey, had his men watching Elric.

"How?" He bowed his head as if to hide his reaction, allow himself a moment to craft his response. A shrug, a slight frown. "I told you. He asked about lodgings, I thought of your empty house for lease. Why? Is he unsatisfactory?"

"I am not sure. What do you know about him?"

"I know little, to be honest. A mutual friend provided him with a letter of introduction. Staunch king's man. Should I have a word with him?"

Kate shook her head. "No. I hoped for some further background, that is all. Duke Henry's heightened ambition—is it more than gossip? How are people receiving it?"

"I do not believe it is widely known yet," said the dean. "But Frost's friends sitting together at the meeting today, and joining him afterwards— that would suggest they fear the word has spread."

"How did you know that William joined Holme and the others?" Kate asked.

The archbishop smiled. "You miss nothing, Dame Katherine. My secretary passed them near the council offices on Ouse Bridge."

So they had moved on to a meeting of the council. Kate stared at the floor, digesting all she had heard, wondering whether Hans died because he worked for Thomas Holme, one of her cousin's associates, not because he had come to York in her mother's party. But why had Isabella sent Friar Adam sniffing around her mother's household?

Scrope was nodding and speaking. Kate forced herself back to the room. "We have an agreement. In exchange, you will provide an account to us of all you learn concerning the events in your mother's and your neighbor's household."

Your neighbors to either side . . . Geoff whispered.

I know.

"What do you know of your mother's late husband, Ulrich Smit?" her uncle asked.

Kate stared at him for a moment, the question was so unexpected. "Ulrich? Very little, except what he told us when he was our guest in Northumberland. Mother has said nothing about him since her return."

"Where are her loyalties—with the king or with the duke?" asked the archbishop.

Ulrich. Hans. The beguines. Something they brought with them? Or her mother brought with her? Something connected to the conflict between the royal cousins? Now that was a nasty thought, though Kate could not imagine what the connection might be. "We have not spoken of it, Your Grace."

"If you should have such a conversation, I wish to hear about it," said Scrope, softening the demand with a warm smile. "Forgive me. I hear myself lacking all courtesy. That is not my intention."

Kate inclined her head toward him in acceptance of his odd apology.

"I do not know how long I will be in York," he continued. "So we must rely on trusted messengers. Who shall be our go-between here, Clifford? Your secretary, Alf?"

"Alf? Your Grace, I keep him quite busy . . ."

"I will provide the deanery with any news," said Kate. "I leave it to the dean to pass it on to you. Will that suffice, Your Grace? Uncle?"

The archbishop nodded. Her uncle looked relieved, calmer now. Kate rose to help herself to some pie. As she ate, she listened to the two men discuss the leanings of the Dominican Prior of St. Mary Magdalene and the Benedictine Abbot of St. Mary's. Prior Norbert had been known to criticize King Richard in his sermons, whereas Abbot Thomas had little to say about the crown or court but was devoted to the archbishop "for some small favors I had it in my power to confer, to the good of the abbey and the poor of the city." St. Mary's was one of several abbeys and friaries in the city that fed the poor.

"I should like to speak with Abbot Thomas as soon as may be," said Kate. "Prior Norbert as well."

"I shall summon my man from the kitchen and have him write an introduction while we talk," said Scrope.

The dean rose and opened the door, speaking quietly to the clerk who sat at the ready. When he returned, he was grinning. "I am enjoying the image of Dame Eleanor rounding on Friar Adam, while he sniffs and chuffs."

"The situation does not incline me to smile," said Scrope. "Adam is a dangerous one for Dame Eleanor and her beguines. He is of the opinion that Meister Eckhart, the theologian whom the beguines revere, was as much a heretic as their own Marguerite Porete. That Eckhart was a fellow Dominican makes it all the more personal for him. Does he mean to condemn them, make an example of them? In a city armed for war? No, I do not like this at all."

If publicly condemned, they would be shunned, unable to support themselves. Kate could well imagine the rumors that might arise in a city already awash in suspicion. How would her mother cope with such a crisis? "I know nothing about the teachers the sisters from Strasbourg revere," she said. "If I might ask, Your Grace, why would you assume my mother's companions claim Eckhart and Porete as their teachers? Did Magistra Matilda tell you this? She certainly did not share it with me, nor did any of the others."

"We are merely pointing to a possible danger, Katherine," the dean said with a warning look.

"If we are to work together, we must be honest with each other, hold nothing back that might be of use," said Kate. "I need to know who else is providing you with information so that I know who else is interested in what has happened." The archbishop seemed to be giving her argument some thought when someone knocked, then entered. Scrope's clerk. "I hope to speak of this later," Kate said.

"I am afraid I must soon be away. Your choice is the letters or more conversation," said the archbishop.

Kate considered. "The letters, thank you, Your Grace."

She sat back to finish the remarkable pie and attempted to engage her uncle with news of the children.

But he rose and began to fuss with a pile of documents on a table by the window, and Kate lapsed into hurt silence.

—◦✌◦—

In the kitchen, Kate found Berend had come to meet her, as agreed. It was a peaceful scene, Berend kneading dough, his arms dusted in flour, while Helen stirred chopped vegetables into a large pot, and Lille and Ghent slept near a door opened onto the garden. The two cooks were discussing various herbs and spices that might improve the broth. When Kate cleared her throat, Helen glanced up with a worried expression.

"You are unscathed?"

"At moments I did not recognize my own uncle, but I found an ally in His Grace." Kate held up two scrolled letters bearing the seal of the

Archbishop of York. "He has written to both Abbot Thomas and Prior Norbert telling them to cooperate with me."

"What did you give them in exchange?" asked Berend, wiping his hands and arms.

"I will keep them both informed of what we learn as we proceed."

Berend nodded. "Seems fair enough."

Helen was beaming. "You have prevailed, dear Katherine. I am so relieved."

As they walked to the abbey to speak to Abbot Thomas, Kate told Berend all that she had learned. "My uncle knows so little about Sir Alan. Why would he send him to me?"

"As I said before, you might have done much worse. What most troubles me is the prospect of all those soldiers told to pack up and leave with nothing to show for their time here."

Kate heard the concern in his voice and crossed herself. "Aye. We will do much praying before it is over, I fear. But what to make of my uncle's comments about the Frost family? They were never fond. He clearly felt his youngest brother might have made a better marriage. But I've never heard him speak so harshly about Mother, indeed all the Frost family and those in her company."

They grew quiet as they approached Bootham Bar. Kate sensed that Berend was on high alert, watching all who looked their way. When for the third time he'd stepped in her path as if to take an arrow for her, she demanded to know what trouble he anticipated. He reminded her of the men who had followed her, speaking of her war dogs.

"I've seen no soldiers arriving," she noted, though gently, moved by his concern.

They were through the gate now, and turning toward the abbey.

Berend paused to look back, studying the crowd. "An ordinary market day, it would seem. Perhaps word has gotten round that the threat of a siege is past? Let's pray the soldiers choose to move north and west, following the duke. Friend or foe, where he is, there will the battle be."

9

THIEVES AND MONSTERS

———⟨∘⟨ତ⟩∘⟩———

Having read the letter, Abbot Thomas glanced up at Kate. "I am advised to give you my complete cooperation." He did not hesitate but told the novice to fetch Brother Martin from the infirmary. "Forgive our earlier silence, Dame Katherine, but in such times . . ."

"Of course," said Kate.

The abbot bent down to offer Lille and Ghent his hand for inspection.

"Such noble creatures, and courteous. So finely trained." He shook his head as if in wonder, his round face lit by a smile of pure joy. "Bless you for bringing them. They are a benediction in a troubling day."

Kate took the comment as a sign he wished to say more. Perhaps about the presence of two of Sir Elric's men outside the gates? "I pray your troubles are not connected to the injured man in your infirmary."

First Lille, then Ghent sniffed the abbot's hand and approved his touch. He took a moment to stroke their heads, then sat back with a sigh, closing his eyes for a moment. "Our troubles are insignificant. Your prayers are better spent on a peaceful solution to the kingdom's developing crisis. I

CANDACE ROBB

cannot help but think that our patient's suffering is connected to that. There is madness in the air. The soldiers, all the weaponry . . ."

Kate could not argue with that.

Abbot Thomas suddenly turned an ear toward the door. "Brother Martin is here. I will let him explain."

Berend rose as a tall, fair monk ambled into the room, solemnly bowing to all of them, pausing over the dogs seated between Kate and the abbot. "Mistress Clifford's magnificent wolfhounds." He glanced at Kate. "May I touch them?"

"After they have taken your measure, Brother Martin. Too soon and they will not be at ease."

He bowed to her and took his seat between Berend and the abbot. "Master?"

Thomas handed him the archbishop's letter. Kate watched as the monk read. He did so quickly, moving his lips, but silent, then sat back with a frown. "I wish you had brought this yesterday, Berend. It might have avoided much pain on the part of the man in the infirmary."

Kate breathed out, grateful to hear that the man was still there. "There has been trouble?" she asked.

"His friends returned for him in the early evening, saying their captain wished him taken to Sheriff Hutton Castle to be tended by their leech. I protested. Earlier, when I cleaned the pus from the man's wound, the bleeding had resumed. I had covered it in a paste of comfrey leaf that staunched the flow and gave him some ease, but any movement would disturb it. Of equal concern was his fever, and the chills that required a fire in the brazier and—well, Berend is welcome to come see how we have managed to cover him but keep the weight of the blankets off his wound. Poor man. Kevin is his name. I suspect you already know that he belongs to a group of Westmoreland's men stationed in the city."

Kate nodded. Kevin. He was always polite when she encountered him on the street. A cut above the rest, in her mind. "I am sorry to hear it is him," she said. "So his comrades came for him?"

"Yes. They were determined to move him." Brother Martin passed a hand over his eyes. "One of them coaxed Kevin in his delirium to attempt to stand, and the wail of anguish startled the comrade so that he let go."

The monk's face creased in remembrance of the scene. "God be thanked that the strength I gained from training long ago as an archer did not fail me. I caught him and eased him back onto the bed. He clung to me, begging me to keep him here."

"His comrades complied?"

"Not happily. But I believe their affection for him won out over their fear of their captain's anger. They withdrew but warned me that I would receive another visit from him."

"Sir Elric."

A bow. "He had come earlier in the day—" Martin glanced at his abbot. "It is more appropriate that Master Thomas tell you."

The abbot cleared his throat. "Sir Elric, Westmoreland's man"—a disapproving twist of his full upper lip—"commanded silence on the matter of Brother Martin's patient. I am pleased that His Grace's letter relieves me of that order." A little smile. "It galled me to support the captain of that traitor to our good King Richard."

"Why would he request your silence?"

"They are soldiers. Spies, more like, sneaking about the city watching the soldiers mustering in support of King Richard. I presumed Sir Elric considers his men vulnerable, liable to be attacked. With Kevin so weak, helpless . . ." The expressive brows rose. "I assured him that although St. Mary's Abbey is not officially a sanctuary, most Christians put aside their weapons on abbey grounds, and thus Kevin is safer here than out in the city. But my argument did not convince him."

"And he did not give you the courtesy of an explanation? Why no one must know Kevin was here? Why he wished to remove him?" Kate asked.

"No, he did not. He said that he would continue to check on his man, and move him as soon as possible."

"We noticed at least two of his men standing guard outside the abbey gates and wondered why," said Kate. "I will inform the archbishop of Sir Elric's behavior."

Abbot Thomas shook his head. "There is no need. When they appeared I sent a message to His Grace at once."

Kate did not like that. "His Grace knew all of it? Elric's threat? The men involved? The extent of Kevin's injuries?"

A nod. "I assumed that is why he provided you with this introduction and instructed me to tell you all. That you will arrange our protection." He glanced from Kate to Berend. "I see I was mistaken."

"I will think how we might help," said Kate. She turned back to Brother Martin. "How was Kevin injured? Has he told you anything?"

A nod. "I regret I said nothing when Berend was here earlier, but as Abbot Thomas explained . . ." He shrugged. "Kevin thinks he was stabbed by the man who had dragged the sister out of the Martha House. It might have begun as a small wound, but he fought with his attacker and was then kicked and punched by some others. How he managed to cross the city to the lodgings of his comrades . . ." Martin shook his head.

"We find the strength to save ourselves," Berend said softly.

Martin studied Berend's face, glanced at his hand. "Ah, of course you would know."

"I am glad to hear he is able to speak," said Kate.

"Now and then. And he talks in his fever dreams. He worries about the sister. His comrades had assured him that she is recovered." He glanced up, smiled at Kate's nod. "I listen, hoping to learn something that might help me heal him."

"How is Kevin now?" Kate asked.

Brother Martin rose. "Poor enough that I feel I must return. Berend is welcome to sit with him a little while." He bowed to Kate. "Some of my brethren are in the infirmary, else I would welcome you as well."

"I trust Berend to be my eyes and ears, Brother Martin. And now, before you depart, Lille and Ghent would be honored to make your acquaintance." She signaled the hounds to rise and approach the infirmarian.

He touched their heads, then crouched to meet them eye to eye. "A pair of your cousins once saved my life. They leapt on my assailants without hesitation, bringing them down so that my father and I might—" He glanced up, as if remembering himself. Thanked Kate, rubbed Lille's and Ghent's ears, and excused himself, holding the door open for Berend.

As the two men left the room, Thomas chuckled. "It is ever so with brothers who take the tonsure after full lives out in the world. Forever half-wild, their memories confound them."

Kate liked Brother Martin. So did Lille and Ghent, who stood gazing at the door for a few moments before resettling.

⁓◦◦⁓

"Forgive me for my hasty departure yesterday," said Brother Martin.

Berend appreciated the apology. "You had your orders. Do you think Kevin will live?"

"It is in God's hands," said the monk, smiling down at his sandaled feet as they walked along a garden path that connected the abbot's house with the infirmary.

"You smile?"

"I hear my teacher's voice when I say such a thing in this garden. For it was here that Brother Wulfstan walked with me when my heart was heavy."

"You were fortunate to have such a guide."

"I was. I would have taken his name when I took the cloth, but it came to me that I should take the name of the man who saved my life—the first time." A little laugh. "A pirate and a knave, and one of my dearest friends."

Berend was quiet, letting the monk enjoy his memory, inhaling the fragrance of the garden, clearing his mind so that he might give Dame Katherine as much detail as possible. After what she had learned at the deanery, he deemed it even more important that he keep his eyes and mind open. Nothing might be as it seemed. Nothing.

In the infirmary, a screen gave Kevin some privacy and kept the heat of the brazier in his corner, though on the other side of his bed a window let in heat of a different sort. Flushed and sweating, the man lay beneath a tent of blankets. He lay so still, his breathing so shallow, that Brother Martin leaned down to listen and to feel the breath on his cheek. Nodded.

"He is still with us."

An elderly monk sat beside the bed, nodding over his prayer beads. Martin lay his hand on his elder's shoulder and leaned down to say in a soft voice, "Brother Henry, you are relieved."

A sputter, a confused glance at Berend, some alarm, then awareness. "Ah. Good, Martin. I fear I am of little use in this heat."

135

"No matter. If Kevin had thrashed or called out, you would have awakened." Martin assisted the elderly monk in rising.

"God go with you," Henry murmured as he shuffled past Berend.

Martin lifted the covers to show how they protected the wound. Hazel wands had been fashioned into an arch over the man's torso so that the blankets warmed but did not touch him. Blood seeped through the bandage that covered Kevin's stomach. The man stirred, muttered something unintelligble. His eyelids flickered.

"Might he speak to me?" Berend asked.

"You are welcome to sit here awhile, see if he fully wakes."

Berend moved the chair directly beneath the opened window, for the screened area was so warm and he did not wish to miss a chance to talk to Kevin by falling asleep; he'd had little sleep the previous night. This man had fought the intruder, might have recognized him or those who'd spirited him away. From his position Berend could see past the screen to a table at which Brother Martin worked, mixing herbs, writing notes in a journal. His motions were easy, assured. Berend wondered about the monk's life before the monastery. Trained as an archer, he had said, yet when Berend had first come for healing, Brother Martin had told him he'd been an apothecary out in the world. He was tall, broad-shouldered. What would move Berend to leave the world and enter a monastery?

"Berend?" Kevin blinked, licked his lips.

"Yes." It was a good sign, that he could so quickly recall a name.

"The sisters on Hertergate—they are safe?"

"Yes."

"My comrades. I asked them to protect them."

"Ah, that is why they keep watch. But there is no need, Kevin. We are taking care of them, and Dame Eleanor's retainer, Griffin, is sleeping in the kitchen."

Brother Martin joined them, apologizing for the interruption. "But Kevin will be thirsty, am I right?" He looked at the man, who licked his lips again but held up his hand to wait.

"I have tried to remember more. The man who dragged the sister from the house," said Kevin. "We fought. He stabbed me. Then others came. Kicked me, pulled me away from him. Soldiers. From Toft Green. They knew him. Called him Robin. Said they knew he would be trouble. They took him away." He closed his eyes, breathing hard. "I didn't understand. Why take him?"

So it *was* Robin. Berend lay a hand on his hand. "Enough for now. More than enough—this is helpful, Kevin, bless you. Unless you can give me names of any of the soldiers who took him away?"

"Seen them."

"At Toft Green?"

"Yes. Sent my comrades to find them. Tents near priory. Tall man with one leg cooks for them."

The one-legged cook Berend had noticed recently at the market. "I have seen him. One last question. Do you know Dame Eleanor's servant, Hans, who worked for Thomas Holme this summer?"

A blink.

"He was murdered last night. His neck broken. Does Robin have such strength?"

"Hans murdered? Why? No. Not Robin."

"I don't know why. Did you ever see those soldiers talking to him?"

"No." A shuddering breath. Kevin closed his eyes.

Berend stood back. "Enough. I am most grateful."

The infirmarian helped Kevin sip from the cup he had filled with his herbal concoction. "This will dull the pain while I change your bandage and repack the wound," he told his patient.

The man winced. A memory of pain. Berend offered to help, but Martin assured him there was no need.

"Go. Find the men who have caused so much sorrow. May God watch over you."

--᪥᪥᪥--

Midday, Kate's household chose to take their main meal out in the garden, beneath the shade of the lindens. The sisters and Eleanor's servant had prepared a cold repast for all, though they chose to eat separately, in their hall. Kate was grateful Berend was relieved of the duty. She smiled down at Petra, who lounged against her, smoothing her curly raven hair, so familiar, so like her own. Kate dropped her hand as she noticed Marie observing them from where she sat beside Jennet. Jealously watching. Yearning. The child ached for a love that was already offered; she could not see it. What she knew was that Petra was Kate's niece; she envied their blood bond. Needlessly.

Kate patted the bench beside her, but Marie looked away. Such a beautiful child. There was truly nothing of the Neville family in their looks, yet their mother had named Simon the father of Marie and Phillip, and Lionel Neville had sworn it was true. She suspected that Lionel, hoping the knowledge of his brother's infidelity would break her, might have exaggerated the certainty of the claim. But though she sometimes had her doubts, she had never regretted taking them in. They had enriched her life, and she loved them both as much as Petra.

The rest of the household, including Griffin, sat at a second table a few feet away. All eyes were on Kate and Berend, who had returned from the abbey deep in excited conversation. Though Kate had been tempted to tell Jennet everything at once—this was what they had hoped for, confirmation that Nan's Robin was the intruder—she had disciplined herself to wait until all were present. Now she nodded to Berend.

"I have spoken to Sir Elric's man who lies wounded in the abbey infirmary." Berend recounted what he had learned from Kevin.

When he was finished, everyone began to talk at once, and Kate found herself clapping her hands for order. "One at a time, I pray you. All your thoughts are welcome. Jennet? You have been seeking information about Robin."

Jennet nodded. Summer had brought out the freckles that ran across her cheeks and nose, making her seem even younger than usual. But she was no naïve youth, and Kate pitied anyone who mistook her for one. "I've learned that he is known across the city as a thief for hire."

Berend leaned forward. "For hire, you say? No ordinary thief, then?"

"As with an assassin for hire, such a thief is caught between the devil and the temptation," said Jennet, "never satisfied, never at rest. He is not his own man. We must find his employer." As soon as she had spoken, Jennet covered her mouth, blushing. "Forgive me, Berend. I did not mean to imply . . ."

He shook his head. "You are right. It needed to be said."

Kate turned to Griffin. "Did Mother manage to send the Dominicans away, as she planned?"

He glanced up from his food, nodded. "They left not long after you did. The sisters were quiet as they prepared food in the kitchen. Took it back to the hall. All in silence. I was loath to speak. I thought they might be praying for Hans. So I know nothing new." He shrugged, drank down his ale, poured more.

Jennet fidgeted, a sign that she was annoyed with Griffin. "Did you notice anything about the men who had Hans?" she asked him.

"Only that there were three of them. I was seeing to Severen."

"He was not so injured that you would have risked his life by following the men," said Jennet.

"I did not know they were about to murder Hans, did I?"

"You saw someone dropped on the road, apparently lifeless."

"I thought him just one of the soldiers, falling down drunk. Do you imagine I don't blame myself for my mistake?"

Shrugging, Jennet took the jug of ale. After filling Matt's, Berend's, and her own bowl, she set the jug out of Griffin's reach. Berend looked to Kate to intercede. He was right. There was no benefit to antagonizing Griffin. She motioned to Berend to change the topic. Petra had rested her head in Kate's lap and fallen asleep. She preferred not to wake her.

"So we know that Kevin came upon Robin dragging Sister Dina down the alley, and as he freed her he was accosted by a group of soldiers from Toft Green," said Berend.

"Who know Robin," Matt added.

"Perhaps as a thief for hire," said Jennet.

"Nan should be told that the intruder was Robin," said Griffin. "She should be warned he might seek her help."

"You think he was able to break away from the soldiers?" Berend asked.

Griffin shrugged. "Anything might happen. We owe it to her to warn her."

"Unless she set him on us," said Jennet. "Thieves often band together in support. And to protect one another."

Berend nodded to Griffin. "Pay attention. Jennet was once one of them."

Marie whispered something to Jennet, who whispered something back. The child nodded solemnly.

Jennet continued. "They find allies in the servants of the households they are watching. The unhappy ones are the easiest to befriend. And Nan certainly seems to have given her heart to Robin. How do we know what she might do for him?"

Griffin raked a hand through his hair and wiped his forehead with his sleeve, the shade evidently not cool enough for him. "Do you think that is likely with Nan?" asked Griffin. "Was she so dissatisfied?"

"Nan's home is dark, mean, crowded," said Jennet. "You see how much she loves color, pretty baubles. Easy to woo when almost any life would be brighter than what she has."

"Dame Eleanor's house is comfortable," said Berend. "And Nan had another sharing the duties. The sisters as well. They all appear to take their turn in household tasks."

"That might be true," said Griffin, "but I understand Nan's discomfort. Dame Eleanor distrusts her, watches her, never has a good word for her. No wonder the woman ran off every night into the arms of a man who promised to take her away from her misery, gave her pretty trinkets."

"Stolen baubles," said Jennet. "Possibly provided to him for the purpose."

"So you think that Nan told Robin about something worth taking from Dame Eleanor's house?" Griffin wiped his forehead with his sleeve again. "But what? We brought so little with us. Each of the women had a trunk. One trunk each, and not very large, except for Dame Eleanor's. But that is said to be filled with gowns, should she change her mind about the life of a beguine. She said she had little room for anything but clothing."

"Jewels take little room," Jennet noted.

So do documents, Kate thought.

"I was told to protect the women, not the trunks. And I've not seen Dame Eleanor wear anything of significant value—nothing I would think Nan would boast about to Robin." Griffin finished off his bowl, set it aside. "Though Werner did make a point of staying with the baggage at all times."

"Perhaps one of us needs to talk to Werner," said Berend. "And Nan. Who has her trust?"

"Agnes Dell," said Griffin. "But do we trust her?"

"Nan has sought me out now and then," said Jennet. "I might talk with her." She glanced at Kate, who nodded.

Griffin offered to talk to Werner.

"Let us give Werner the day to grieve," Kate said softly. "Then we can choose who should talk to him. We have already learned much."

It was true. Berend had spoken to Werner earlier. Apparently Thomas Holme had discovered Hans was good with numbers—he had worked in Ulrich's office as well as serving in the household—and had set him the task of helping with the household accounts. Considering what Kate had learned about the money Thomas and his coterie, including her cousin, had sent to Duke Henry, she and Berend wondered whether Hans could have been approached by spies for the king.

"I will be glad to talk to him if that suits you," said Griffin. "I am more at ease with Werner than I was with Hans—my soldierly ways disturbed him." When Berend raised a brow, Griffin added, "Women in the taverns." A shrug. "None of the servants had taken vows, but Hans seemed to feel we were on a sacred mission and should behave as befit clerics."

Jennet gave a little snort. "Like the vicars choral at the bawdy houses round the Bedern?"

"And yet Hans had recently turned to drinking," Kate noted. "Something had changed him."

"I cannot reconcile that with the man I knew. I thought his lack of curiosity kept him innocent," said Griffin. "Poor man, to die unshriven." He crossed himself.

"From what you say, he had no sins to confess," Berend said softly. He had often told Kate that God accounted for those who died sudden, violent deaths—he was sure of it, else he could not have borne his days soldiering. So many rotted on the battlefields awaiting a priest's blessing. Surely God did not condemn all those souls.

"Had someone rescued him, we might have found out why he had turned to drink," Jennet muttered, glaring at Griffin.

But the man seemed oblivious to her anger, reaching over to pet Lille and Ghent, then stretching farther to grasp the jug.

⁓❧⁓

Sister Dina took the cup of brandywine with trembling hands. "May the Mother show me the way, guide me in my speech," she whispered, sipping the wine as if it were the communion offering.

Kate and Dina sat near the window of her mother's bedchamber. They had been offered the choice seats, two high-backed, cushioned chairs facing each other, so that they might look out on the view of York Castle, the Franciscan friary, the river, the sweet summer afternoon. And it afforded them a slight breeze as the solar warmed beneath the sun-hammered roof. Kate had suggested they gather in the garden, where they might sit in the breezy shade of the great plane tree. Lille and Ghent could alert them to anyone approaching. But Dina had chosen this enclosed space, and so the five women had climbed the steps to the solar in communal silence. Brigida and Clara sat with Eleanor on her bed. All, including Kate, no doubt, gave face to their dread, Dina looking as if she wished it were over. For this would be no happy telling.

Still, Kate was grateful to be included, and that the sisters had been encouraged by Dina's growing strength and restored spirit to coax her out of her silence. Sister Brigida had come to Kate in the garden bearing the news that the reading during the midday meal, wisely chosen and read by Sister Clara, paired with the terrible news of Hans's murder, had convinced Sister Dina that those present deserved to hear all she remembered, and had inspired her to trust that they would receive her tale with compassion, not judgment.

"May something I remember help find the man who took Hans from us," Dina said, "and help me begin to make amends for my own part in the tragedy." She bowed her head and made the sign of the cross.

"You are innocent," Eleanor whispered.

Dina lifted her head, shook it once. "I have caused great harm." She shivered, despite the warmth of the day.

"The brandywine will soothe you," Kate said.

Dina took a sip, coughed, took another, sat back with a little sigh. "You are kind, Dame Katherine. I fear—He is dead?" She added something in German to Sister Brigida, who explained to Kate, "The one whom she stabbed in the gut."

"We have not found him," said Kate. "But Berend spoke to the one who helped you. Kevin."

She understood that without need for Brigida, and asked, "How is Kevin?"

"Wounded. He is being cared for by the infirmarian at St. Mary's Abbey." Kate paused as Brigida explained. "He asked after you. He's asked his comrades to protect you and all the 'good sisters.'"

"God bless him."

"I pray you, tell me what you remember," said Kate. "Just speak in your own tongue. Sister Brigida will tell me what you are saying."

Another shiver ran through the woman. She set aside the brandywine and turned her gaze to the window as she began to speak, and Brigida to translate.

"I was suddenly awake, aware that someone was in the kitchen. It was still too dark for it to be Nan. But I'm not certain that I thought so clearly at that moment. I feared it was happening again. That he'd come back." Brigida shook her head at Kate's frown. She did not know of whom Dina spoke. "I reached for the dagger beneath my pillow. Listened. Prayed that he would not be aware of me in the room. I heard noises. Perhaps someone searching through the pots and the bins. And then he was at my door, pressing the latch, slowly opening the door." Dina's hands traced the motion. "So frightened." Her eyes were huge in her face. "He was in the room. He was in the room." Shaking her head. "I threw myself at him. We toppled, slid through the doorway into the kitchen. And I was stabbing him, stabbing him." She jabbed the air, tears streaming down her pale cheeks. "In my fear—" She shook her head. "I thought he was my father returned. He said he would. He swore he would. And I remembered what I had to do. Never speak, never make a noise, he would kill me if I woke the others." Her gaze was unfocused, frightened, her voice but a whisper. "But I did not need to say a word. My dagger said it all. You will not hurt me again. You will not!" She sobbed, her hand in the air, clutching the imaginary dagger. "He lay there, clutching the dagger's haft. He groaned. He said something. I don't know. I don't know. God forgive me. This was not my father. It was not his voice. Soft. So soft, this voice. Fear. Pain." She covered her face with her hands, breathing shallowly.

Kate touched her hand, offered her the cup of brandywine. After a few moments, Dina took it, sipped while gazing out the window, and her breathing steadied. Kate sensed the three on the bed holding their breaths. No one stirred. Dina took another sip, then set the cup aside, her hand trembling.

"I went back into my room and dressed. I would go to your house for help." She looked Kate in the eyes, nodding. "I would seek out Berend, who sleeps in your kitchen. He would make it right. But the man—how he had the strength—he caught me as I stepped out of my room. Covered my mouth. Carried me out into the garden, round to the alley. He stumbled once, twice, but held me ever tighter—so tight I could not breathe—and kept going. How did he have the strength?" She searched Kate's face as if thinking to find an answer writ on it.

"I don't know," Kate whispered. "Are you certain he was the same man as the one you stabbed?"

Dina frowned down at her hands, as if considering whether she might be mistaken, but then nodded. "It was him. His blood soaked my gown." A pause. Kate heard dogs barking out on the street. Dina held up a finger as if to say, *Listen!* "Your dogs began to bark. Like that! And then the soldier who watches, he came out of the darkness and grabbed my—the one dragging me. He made him let go of me. All this time, no screams, no screams. I could not make a sound, even when I tried." With a trembling hand she rubbed an eye. "The soldier told me to run to the church. 'Do not stop. Do not look back.' I did what he said." A shrug. "I woke in the *maison dieu.*" Tears streamed down Dina's cheeks. "He ruined me. Bloodied, cursed, dirty. And now I have taken a life because of the fear he burned into my soul."

"Your father?" Kate asked softly.

Dina leaned toward Kate, grasping her hands. "Pray you not to judge me." She looked at the others. "I was but a child. So young. I did not know why he was hurting me and saying he loved me, that I was his angel." A sob. "He knew me until I became a woman. Then he sent me away." She bowed down over her hands.

"You are no sinner," Clara whispered.

"You are safe in our love," said Brigida, looking to Clara and Eleanor, who nodded.

Eleanor began to assure Dina that they would not send her away, but Kate interrupted her. She felt ill and angry at the monster who had raped his daughter, then turned her out when she became fertile and might quicken, exposing his terrible sin. "I see you as a strong, courageous, unblemished woman," she said, nodding to Brigida to translate. Her voice broke as she did so.

Dina reached for Kate's hands, pressed them, looked up at the three on the bed. "I still cannot forgive him."

Eleanor shook her head.

"Your heart will know when you are able to do so," Sister Clara said in the gentlest of voices. "Drink some more brandywine. You have lived through it all over again. Warm yourself."

As Dina sipped at the wine, Kate asked, "Forgive me, but I must ask, would you know the man in the kitchen if you saw him again?"

"It was dark. But maybe his voice?"

"Do you know where your dagger is?"

Dina shook her head. "I did not see it after I"—a breath—"stabbed him." She crossed herself.

Kate wondered about the dagger—who had given it to Dina, whether she had ever thought to use it on her father—but she had no right to ask. "I am grateful to you, Sister Dina. Rest now. I will not disturb you further."

"May God bless you and bring you peace." Hands pressed together in prayer, Dina bowed to Kate.

The sorrow and the beauty that was Dina moved her. Kate mirrored the gesture, her heart too full for words.

Eleanor offered her bed, but Dina preferred to return to the chamber she now shared with Brigida and Clara, who assisted her out the door.

When the sisters had departed, Kate and Eleanor sat for a while, facing out the window, deep in their separate sorrows, blind to the summer day. The voices of the three women in the adjoining chamber rose and fell.

Outside, Petra laughed her deep-throated laugh, Marie screeched with delight, drawing Kate out of her thoughts. The innocence of children. An innocence taken from Dina.

Eleanor had taken Dina's chair and now stared out the window with the same stricken expression she had worn as they'd prepared the torn bodies of Kate's brother Roland and her twin, Geoffrey. It would not do. This was not the way to find Robin and Hans's murderer.

"Did Sister Dina think Friar Adam an acceptable confessor?" Kate asked.

Eleanor started at the sound of Kate's voice. "Ah me, I lost myself for a while. Dina and Adam?" She shook her head. "None of the sisters cared for him. His is not the gentle faith of the Dominican friars they knew in Strasbourg. They felt he had condemned them before he ever met them."

"What did he say that gave that impression?"

"I might have influenced them with my warning, but his chilly gaze and impatient manner proved my point. He prodded the sisters with questions that had little to do with such an interview."

"Such as?"

"He asked whether they could read, which puzzled them, for they have yet to encounter a beguine who does not read, write, and know her numbers. Many of them teach. Perhaps he asked Sister Dina because she is a sempster, but Sister Brigida?"

"What else?"

"What books they had read, whether any member of the household owned any, and something about golden idols. God help us, does he think them pagans?"

"Or does he want to know whether they own something worth stealing? Or that would brand them as heretics?" Kate said it more to herself than as a response.

But Eleanor heard. "Heretics. I had not thought—But the other makes no sense. Friars take a vow of poverty, do they not? Do you think they might be thieves?" She glanced at the door, uneasy. Because she had not thought of that? Or because there was something of value in the house that Eleanor realized she must guard? The books? Perhaps Marguerite Porete's work?

Kate had not considered the possible value of the books from which the sisters read at meals. They were brought out for the event, then put away. Books were certainly items of worth, especially those that were adorned with colorful images. She had not looked at the pages.

Or Friar Adam wanted to know whether the books preached interpretations of the Bible and God's message of which the Church did not approve.

"Did any of the sisters tell him about the books?" Kate asked.

"Sister Clara says they did not admit to the books, as his attitude toward their revered teachers troubled them. They feared he might confiscate them." Eleanor's worry had given way to indignation. "We would see about that."

Kate bowed her head to hide her smile at the image of her mother confronting Friar Adam should he try to walk away with anything at all.

Unaware of her daughter's amusement, Eleanor continued. "Sister Clara assures me they did not need to lie, they simply asked whether it is his experience—or expectation—that poor sisters bring such valuable items as dowries, suggesting that he confused them with nuns. She explained that beguines do not bring dowries, they support themselves by working in the community." Eleanor chuckled. "Sister Clara claims difficulty with our language, but there is more subtlety in her speech than most people I know."

"It is good to hear you laugh."

"And to see you smile." But Eleanor's momentary cheer faded with a sigh. "My dear Dina. I did not know what she suffered, the burden she carries."

"What did he say about golden idols?"

Eleanor shook her head. "Clara did not tell me his precise words. But it troubled them, all three of them. Of course it did. Heretics? Pagans? As if he was searching for the most damning accusation. God help us. I expected better of York, though I do not know why. So many are stuck in the mire of the old ways. I blame Isabella Frost for this."

Kate reached out for her mother's hand, drawing her attention back to the present. "Friar Adam's sudden appearance is troubling. You know that Griffin followed Sir Elric's men to the camp on Toft Green?" Eleanor nodded.

Kate deemed it time to inform her mother of all that Berend had learned from Kevin.

As she recounted it, Geoff whispered in her head, *It is the connection. Perhaps Friar Adam has Robin in the priory infirmary.*

You might be right. But quiet now, Geoff. Mother might sense your presence. I do not want more of her lectures about letting you go.

"So Sir Elric's men are not our enemies but our allies," Eleanor noted with a small smile.

"Matchmaking again, Mother? You should know better by now," Kate warned, but she was relieved that her mother's preoccupation with having a knight for a son-in-law drowned out any tingle she might have sensed from Geoff's presence. "You mistake the man for the man he serves. Kevin, who lies wounded in the abbey infirmary, is our ally, it seems, but I would not be too quick in extending that to Sir Elric or the other men."

Eleanor wagged her head, unconvinced. "I will send Griffin to the priory with a message for Friar Adam, informing him that we have found another spiritual guide," Eleanor said. "But who? Would Richard Clifford reconsider? As Dean of York Minster, your uncle has power in the city. He might fend off any trouble from the Dominicans."

Kate was shaking her head. If her mother only knew how impossible that was! "He will not reconsider. If we have any trouble with Friar Adam or Prior Norbert, I will bring it to the attention of His Grace the archbishop." She told her mother about their alliance.

"My. You do know how to bargain with the mighty." Eleanor shook her head at Kate, her expression one of wonder. Leaning over, Eleanor adjusted the sleeve on Kate's gown, tugging it down over her wrist, then reached for her hand, studying her fingernails. "I do wish you would pay more attention to your appearance."

"I am not a child for you to poke and prod and correct." Kate withdrew her hand.

Eleanor raised her eyebrows as if to say that was debatable.

Kate regretted her outburst. She'd hoped that her mother's compassion for Sister Dina might inspire her to be more forthcoming about whatever frightened her. Taking a deep breath, she apologized, taking heart as her mother patted her hand. Perhaps it was an opening. "Is it possible that the intruder and Hans's murder are connected through Ulrich?" Kate asked quietly. "Might someone suspect you carry something of his, something Hans might know about, that is valuable? Value of any sort—information, gold?"

Lips pinched, eyes pressed shut, knuckles white as she clutched the arms of her chair, Eleanor was a study in unease. "You are determined to lay the blame at my feet."

"That was not my intent. It is a question that arises naturally out of the facts. And as I know nothing of what happened to Ulrich, what brought you back here in such haste, I ask in the hope that you will confide in me. Help me, Mother, before someone else comes to harm."

Silence. Tears stood at the corners of Eleanor's eyes, and her breathing was ragged.

"Mother?" Kate said softly, laying a hand on one of Eleanor's.

A rustle of silk. Eleanor caught her breath, opened her eyes, blinking in the light from the window. "What about a Franciscan friar? The friary is close, just over there." She gestured to the right, toward the river.

Silently cursing at her mother's continuing secrecy, Kate bit back a retort and just nodded. "My friend Jocasta Sharp might be willing to speak with her spiritual counselor there, ask him to recommend someone."

"Jocasta Sharp. You have mentioned her before. You respect her."

Eleanor's voice trembled. Whatever Kate's questions had conjured had brought up strong emotions. How she yearned to ask more. But the change in topic was her mother's way of slamming the door on further discussion. Perhaps if Kate kept her talking, another opportunity might arise.

"Yes, I respect and admire Jocasta," said Kate. "Much as the beguines, she has answered a call to help the neglected members of the community. She does it in such wise that she wins their affection and loyalty. They will do anything for her. According to Agnes, Jocasta has been seeing that Nan's mother and the children have a good meal each day. Perhaps . . ." She heard someone leaving the bedchamber next door. As Brigida appeared, Kate asked after Dina.

"I believe she will sleep," said Brigida. She sank down on the bed, drawing a piece of linen from her sleeve with which she dried her sweaty forehead. "How is it that we were all so blind? Our families were friends. I knew her father when I was small. I never guessed. Everyone treated him as if he were the best of men."

"Of course he knew the enormity of his sin," said Eleanor. "You heard Dina, he frightened her into silence. And anyone who guessed would be threatened as well, you can be certain. I imagine he presented himself to the world as a most honorable man with a horror of sin."

Kate watched her mother's face, the pinched mouth as she paused—she described someone she'd known. But of course—hypocrites were legion.

Brigida stared down at her hands. "The apostle John said that God is love, and anyone who lives in love lives in God, and God lives in him. Yet God permits such sins against children, in whom he dwells. Nor does he strike down such a monster as Dina's father. I do not understand." She looked up at Eleanor. "Friar Adam cannot hear Dina's true confession, nor could I ever confide in him. He—We all felt judged. For my part, I did not sense God dwelling within him, though I know that he must. The apostle John—" She broke off, eyes closed, shaking her head.

"Would you consider a Franciscan friar?" Kate asked. "The friary is so close, and I know someone who would commend you to them. Her confessor is a grayfriar and a kind, gentle soul. I have met him."

Sister Brigida nodded. "Thank you. I will ask the others, but I believe they will all be grateful. Agnes had suggested the grayfriars."

"What of Agnes?" asked Kate. "Is she to bide with you?"

"For the nonce. As we would with anyone new to the house, we will watch her, guide her, and, in time, we will know whether or not she is suited to this life. It would help to have a confessor who is a guide, not a judge."

Eleanor had sniffed when Brigida said Agnes would bide with them for the present, but she'd held her tongue. Now she shifted, her gray silk gown rustling.

"You do not agree, Dame Eleanor?"

"I cannot trust the woman."

"What has she done that you cannot forgive?" Brigida asked.

"She hid the truth of who owns this house. What else might she be hiding?"

"Have you never held something back for fear that you might be shunned? Denounced? Might lose everything?"

Kate watched with amazement as her mother crumpled in the face of Brigida's gentle rebuke.

"Once again you guide me to the light, Sister Brigida. My old ways are rutted and too familiar." Eleanor pressed her hand to her heart and bowed to the beguine.

Speechless, Kate turned to gaze out the window.

—◦◦◦—

When Brigida and Eleanor went down to the hall to pray, Kate wandered out into the summer afternoon. She found Lille and Ghent lying in the shade near Marie and Petra, who napped together in a hammock tied between the two lindens. They were both so precious to her. Kate would do anything to protect her girls from what Dina had suffered. Could Dina's mother really not have known what was happening under her own roof? How could she value her own safety above that of her daughter? Lille raised her head, sensing her distress. Kate knelt beside her, stroking her back, letting her nuzzle her neck.

Matt sat nearby, whittling. He was good with the children, thoughtfully sharing his favorite things from his own childhood.

He looked up now. "How is Sister Dina?"

"Resting."

He nodded. "You will want to talk to Jennet. She's in the kitchen."

"She has news?"

Matt was not smiling. "Let her tell you."

In the kitchen, Berend, the sleeves of his thin linen shirt rolled up above his elbows, chopped vegetables for a pottage as he listened to Jennet, who sat across from him shelling peas into a bowl in her lap. Kate's gaze lingered on the pale down of Berend's forearms. So strong, yet so gentle, so loving. None of the men in her household—she could not imagine them harming a child even to save their own lives.

"Did Matt tell you about Nan?" Jennet asked.

Kate shook herself, slipped down next to Jennet. "No. Tell me."

"I told Berend I would go to check her at her mother's, let him get on with his work. She's gone. The children—it was only the girls there when I went to warn her about Robin—said that a man came for Nan not long after Agnes left her. Told Nan that Robin was dying and he had asked for her. She must come quick."

Kate muttered a curse.

"I know. The children—they were so frightened. Their mother is in a bad way, clawing at her throat trying to breathe. I sent two of them to fetch Dame Jocasta. I managed to prop Goodwife Hawise up enough that she could breathe better by the time Dame Jocasta appeared, and shortly after a healer, who made a soothing drink and a paste for Hawise's chest and throat. She was much better when I left. Dame Jocasta will have the healer stay with them, and a man to watch."

"Bless her. And bless you for knowing what to do."

"The children had seen the man before, with Robin. The girls said they did not know his name. But Dame Hawise—I swear she whispered, 'Bran.'" Jennet scooped up more pea pods. "A woman who has so little breath does not waste it with nonsense. But I know no Brans."

Berend rubbed his neck, thinking. "No one comes to mind."

Nor could Kate think of anyone. But Agnes might know. What was the pattern here? The house, Hans, Nan? "It must be theft. Something the sisters brought. We must search for Nan. And I need to talk to Agnes." Kate rose.

"I have a few of the best trackers searching for her," said Jennet. "What of Sister Dina? Did she remember anything of use?"

All the sorrow welled up, and Kate needed to sit down for the telling. She wanted them to know all, that Dina must in no way ever feel blamed. When Kate was finished, Jennet sat silently, staring at her feet.

"May her father be thrown into the fires of hell and forgotten," Berend growled. He put a pitcher of ale and three small bowls on the table beside the vegetables and settled down across from Kate.

"As you see," she said, "her memory of the morning agrees with Kevin's, once he arrived, though it is incomplete."

"So Robin was searching the kitchen."

"Nan kept a key to the house there," Kate said.

"I should have gone to Nan earlier," said Jennet.

"There is no point to such self-recrimination," said Kate. *"None of this might have happened if* . . . We can always say that. What could Nan know? How can she be of help to Robin now? Might it be true—that he's dying and he's asked for her? They would not want to give away their hiding place."

"If she isn't part of the plan, what happens to her now?" Jennet's frown made it clear what she thought.

"I'll go to Toft Green this evening," said Berend. "We need to know the gossip in the camp."

Kate agreed. "I will accompany you."

"If I may advise, it would be best if I take Matt. This is a camp of soldiers, and you are a woman. Not only that, but there are those in the camp, many, I suspect, who think Lille and Ghent should be put to better use than guarding your interests here in York. You'll be noticed and I'll hear nothing."

Kate did not like it, but Berend was right. "I will talk to Agnes."

—◦◦◦◦—

The former mistress of the house was standing over the kitchen fire watching a pot of water, muttering to Eleanor's maidservant about her mistress's cursed insistence on boiling everything. She glanced up when Kate stepped into the kitchen, and began to apologize.

The steam in there was enough to make anyone testy. Kate held up a hand in peace. "I do not disagree. I never knew my mother to require boiled water. Some odd advice taken to heart?" A cure for some pain? A fear of poison? "Heaven knows. Agnes, might we have a word? Rose, would you watch the water?"

The maidservant gave a reluctant shrug.

Agnes wiped her brow and neck with her apron, tucking damp strands of her hair back into her plain white cap. Kate led her round to the back of the kitchen, an area of deep shade beneath the eaves and the plane tree, beside the tall hedge. She told her about the man coming for Nan.

"Dying? Poor Nan! Her heart will be breaking. She bragged that they were to marry and he promised her a house, pretty clothes, a cow, and a hen. I told her that a man will promise anything to get up a woman's skirts. But she would not hear me, she so wanted to believe him." Agnes muttered an apology as she drew off her veil and shook out her long braid. "God help us, there is so little breeze." Strands of wet hair now clung to her damp face.

As she could do nothing about the woman's discomfort, Kate ignored her complaints. "Do you know a man by the name of Bran?"

"Bran?" Agnes cocked her head. "I've heard it, but where? It will come to me."

"Do you have any idea where Robin might be?"

Agnes shook her head. "I never knew where he lived."

Nor had Nan. "What might Nan have seen in this house that was worth stealing? Some valuables she mentioned to Robin?"

"Nothing. There is nothing but the house itself. The sisters live so simply. The offerings on the altar are of no value but to them. I've no idea what Dame Eleanor has in her chests, but Nan had no reason to know either. Truly. The sisters have so lit—" Her voice trailed off as a man's voice rose in anger out in the garden.

Thomas Holme. And now Dame Eleanor's voice rose in injured retort. Kate caught Agnes's arm and stopped her from stepping out to look.

10

TENSIONS

———⚬⚭⚬———

"They walked off together," Thomas was saying. "Have you no control over your servants?"

"Griffin is not a servant," Eleanor snapped, "and Werner is now your responsibility. No doubt they have gone off to pray for the soul of their friend Hans. As should we all." A sniff.

"My gardener waited for him all afternoon, then did the heavy lifting himself and injured his back. He and Werner were set to finish clearing away the old stone shed down by the water."

"That old man should know better."

"*I* should have known better than to hire your servants."

"Werner will return and complete the work, I assure you. He is trustworthy."

"Is he? I would not know. And what about Hans's funeral? Have you made arrangements?"

"I assure you it is all in hand. Magistra Matilda's sisters have prepared his body for burial, and he will be buried at our parish church. *Your* parish church."

Thomas cleared his throat and spoke too softly for Kate to hear.

"Why are you so aggrieved?" said Eleanor. "It was Werner's friend who was murdered last night."

"And I am afraid I've lost two servants in one day. What monster have you brought into our midst? Why are you in York?"

When her mother called him a bilious old fool, Kate decided it was time to interfere.

"Go back to your work," she told Agnes as she moved out into the garden.

"I suppose I am a fool—for hiring your servants." Thomas stood with his hands balled into fists at his side, his face purple with rage. Kate had never seen her business partner in such a state. Her mother had a talent for drawing out extreme emotions in the most tranquil of souls.

"What is amiss, Thomas? Mother?"

"She is a snake in the garden, your mother. She's brought these troubles down on us."

Not entirely, thought Kate. There was the matter of Thomas and his friends supporting Duke Henry against their sovereign king. But she calmly said that she and her household were doing all they could to find out why Hans was murdered, and whether his death had any connection to the intruder.

"Of course it does," Thomas fairly shouted.

Kate quietly asked what the connection might be.

"Her!" The hand he thrust out, finger pointing toward Eleanor, shook with emotion.

"Might I be of assistance?" Berend came through the gate flanked by Lille and Ghent, who trotted over to Kate, sniffing her hands, then turning their gazes on Thomas.

"Find Werner," said Thomas, quieter now, though still angry. "And, for all our sakes, find out who murdered Hans before anyone else has their neck snapped." He bowed to Kate, to Berend, and, after a moment's hesitation, to Eleanor, and strode off through the gate in the hedge.

Lille and Ghent sat down at Kate's feet and peered up at her through their bushy brows.

"Forgive me for interrupting, but I heard shouting," said Berend.

"Oh, bless you, Berend, I am most grateful," said Eleanor, waving her hand as if to cool herself.

"Thomas is concerned Werner has disappeared. He has not returned since walking off with Griffin this afternoon," Kate explained to Berend.

"Mere hours," said Eleanor.

"After last night, I understand his concern," said Berend.

"You, too? I'd thought you were made of stouter stuff." Eleanor sniffed.

Kate gestured toward a bench at the edge of the garden. "Shall we sit, Mother? I would talk with you." She nodded to Berend. "Wait for me in the kitchen. I will not be long." She motioned to Lille and Ghent to follow Berend. Lille rose with a sigh, gazing back at Kate every few steps. Her concern warned Kate that her agitation was palpable.

"So, Mother, you have that look in your eyes. Where are Griffin and Werner? Did you send them on a mission?"

Eleanor would not meet her eyes but played with her sleeve and began to address the matter of Hans's burial.

"Do not play the feeble-minded popinjay with me right now, Mother, or I swear I will pluck your tail feathers. Where are they? Where are Griffin and Werner?"

Tears in her eyes, Eleanor shook her head. "How you speak to me—"

"People are dying, Mother. Do you understand? Look what Sister Dina has suffered. How much more will she suffer if she hears that Robin is dead?"

That caught her attention. "Is he?"

"Perhaps. And her rescuer is seriously, perhaps mortally, wounded. And Hans dead. How much more do you need before you take responsibility and tell me what is happening here?"

"You blame me? Oh, of course you do. It is ever your way." Eleanor's tone was whining, but her mouth trembled and the tears flowed.

Judging it time to change tactics, Kate took hold of her mother's hands, startled by how cold they felt on such a warm afternoon. "Mother, what is happening here? Help me protect you."

"Protect?" Eleanor withdrew her hands and clasped them in her lap. "Protect me? Why should I require protection? I am in no danger."

If Kate were not at once angry and frightened for her mother, she might have laughed. The tremor in Eleanor's voice, the fear in her wide green eyes, the way she clutched her hands on her lap as if forcing them to be still all betrayed her.

"I don't believe you," said Kate. "If you would begin at the beginning, tell me everything, you might provide some insight, some key that would lead us to the source of all that has happened. Tell me why you are here. How did Ulrich die? You returned so soon after his death—"

Lurching to her feet, Eleanor snapped, "Unnatural daughter!"

"Are Werner and Griffin in danger?" Kate asked.

"Do not pretend that you care," said Eleanor, stepping into the hall and shutting the door behind her.

Kate sat on the bench for a while, waiting for her heart to quiet, her thoughts to settle. Not even a gesture of concern and affection had moved her mother to speak. What did she so fear she might reveal?

—◦⊙◦—

There was an incongruous spring in Matt's steps as he and Berend headed over Ouse Bridge. Thinking it best to calm him before they reached the camp on Toft Green—such exuberance about going out into the city to investigate might be mistaken for a young man's aching for a fight— Berend asked him about the daggers that were his weapons, whether he had ever used them to defend himself or another, why he chose the two different blades. He kept asking questions until Matt was no longer grinning at everyone who passed.

To be sure, Matt's answers were reassuring. Though he'd never struck a mortal blow, he'd been in a fair number of fights and come away intact.

"Dame Katherine would not have hired me for the guesthouse watch otherwise," said Matt. "Although she did replace me with young Seth."

"You know he's a Fletcher—by name and training. Fletchers test their own arrows. Seth may not look strong, but he's an excellent bowman." Berend grinned and slapped the young man on the back. "A pleasure to meet you, Matt the Warrior."

A surprised snort. "I'm no warrior. Just a man who can hold my own in a fight."

"Plenty of men who consider themselves skilled in weaponry find themselves on the battlefield unprepared and unable to defend themselves, much less take the offensive. A quick way to lose the loyalty of your comrades. You're likely to get them killed along with you."

"Do you miss it? The fighting?"

"If you mean would I choose to return to that life—no. I've done with that. But the blood lust never fully leaves a man who fought as long as I did. Now and then—" Berend shook his head. "This is no time for such talk. Keep your ears pricked for trouble."

They heard the camp before they saw it, intermittent shouts punctuating the low rumble of men's voices, the scratch of blades being sharpened, the rattle of chain mail being tumbled.

As Toft Green came into sight, Matt whistled. "I would never recognize it if the friary weren't right there. It's all wrong." Men, tents, cook fires, stretching across the green and butting up against the friary walls. "And so crowded," he added.

"Not as crowded as when I last saw it," said Berend. He noticed signs of trouble here and there—fistfights; men guarding the perimeters of their campsites with knives drawn; men flashing daggers as they danced round each other, drawing blood when they struck. "And far less friendly." Most appeared to be preparing to move on—sharpening weapons, repairing harnesses, polishing pieces of armor, stuffing clothes into packs. "Looks as if the rumor has spread that Duke Henry's moved beyond York."

"Good news for us," said Matt.

"I would prefer to catch the murderer," said Berend. "And with everyone restive, we're likely to be attacked simply for being unfamiliar. Stay alert."

That sobered Matt. Berend grunted and led the way toward the target campsite up against the friary wall, skirting round the trouble, managing to avoid it.

The one-legged cook sat on a barrel picking through a pot of stew, a pile of used bowls at his feet. He watched their feet as they approached, shifting so that he could easily draw the dagger hanging on his left hip. When they stopped, he let his eyes travel up to their faces.

"I know you," he said, wiping his mouth on his sleeve. "The spicy recipe for pottage." The man was not smiling, but at least he had acknowledged they'd met.

Berend nodded. "Have you tried it?"

"I have indeed, and my comrades declared it the best they'd ever tasted. Any more secrets to share?"

"Plenty. For trade. I want to talk to your comrades."

A shake of the head. "Not here. Gone drinking. Don't expect them back till sunrise." He nodded toward two men wrestling nearby. "Camp's not the place to be tonight. Rumor is the soldiers've sat in this stink hole for naught. The king's men say someone in the camp sent word to the duke that York was so well defended he'd best move. And so he has, to Knaresborough. 'But we're *all* king's men,' they say, 'else why would we be here?'" A shrug. "Takes little to draw blood when you've been sitting in a hellhole with moldy rations and a city full of merchants refusing to sell them food. You cannot blame the anger when they're here to protect the greedy bastards. And all the while their captains live in comfort, drinking and carousing." He hawked and spat.

"Drinking." Berend nodded. Hearing the man talk—more than he'd said when they'd met at the market—he realized he was from the shire and spoke as if he did not consider himself one of the soldiers. It might mean nothing; the captain called up the men he could rally quickly. But that, paired with no livery . . . "Who's your captain?"

The man squinted. "Who are you? Who set you on us?"

Berend held up his hands. "I just want to talk to your comrades. Can you tell me where they'd be drinking?"

Another hawk and a spit, a drawn dagger.

"Steady now, we mean you no harm."

The cook began to toss the dagger from hand to hand, his eyes narrowing. Berend could crush him with a blow, but that would not further his purpose. He motioned to Matt to back away, then turned on his heels and strolled away. He reckoned that a one-legged man was not likely to pursue them in retreat—though he kept his ears pricked just in case. If he had not, he might not have heard the soft, low whistle as they passed a tent. He paused, crouching down as if fixing his shoe.

"You'll be wanting to ask about an injured man his lot left at the friary gate yesterday morning," said a voice from the tent. "Men were covered in blood, arguing about laying hold of him and letting the 'good Samaritan' get away."

That fit. "Bless you for this. Have you seen a Welshman with hair like copper wire and a stout, fair-haired companion?"

"They've been round the camp asking questions."

"Today?"

"They fled a while ago. Before the wind changed. Men did not like their questions."

"You did not happen to hear what they were asking."

"No."

"May God watch over you," said Berend.

"May he watch over us all."

Berend rose with effort, wincing at the ache in his knees. Too many years on horseback, too many injuries. He envied Matt the almost complete recovery from his leg injury earlier in the year.

"Who was that?" Matt whispered as they moved on out of the camp.

Berend shook his head.

"How do we know whether to believe him?"

"Feel it in my gut." Berend grinned at Matt's bewilderment. "Our bodies know. Thinking too hard can deafen us to that knowing."

Matt shook his head. "Still . . ."

"So what would you have us do?"

"Check the friary."

Berend nodded.

—◦⟨⟩◦—

Kate, Jennet, Petra, and Marie sat in the garden eating pottage and bread, a warm meal, soothing. They had assembled themselves on a blanket near the hedgerow gate, keeping watch on the Martha House until Griffin returned.

Kate lifted her face to the sweet breeze. Evening had brought with it a light wind and feathery clouds.

"We'll have rain tomorrow," said Petra. "Maybe as soon as tonight. Can you smell it?"

Kate nodded. The child was almost always right in her weather predictions, a gift she'd learned from Old Mapes, the woman who had raised her.

"I welcome a relief from this unrelenting sun," said Jennet. She shifted closer to Kate, whispered, "Marie is too quiet. She's been like that all day."

Indeed, the girl sat apart from them at the edge of the blanket, leaning back against Ghent's powerful body, her gaze fixed on the Martha House.

Putting aside her half-eaten pottage, Kate shook out her skirts and moved over to Marie, settling down beside her.

The girl glanced at her, then went back to staring at the hedge.

"Are you conjuring your true love?" Kate asked.

"My what?"

"When we were little, Geoff and I believed that if we stared at something long and hard enough with an image in our minds of what we most wished for, it would appear."

"Did it work?"

"Only once. But that was enough to make believers of us."

"What did you conjure?"

"Lille and Ghent's eldest brother, Macbeth."

"Macbeth?" Marie sat up, staring at Kate. "You named your noble hound for a Scots king? I thought you hated the Scots."

"A Scot who killed Scots," Kate noted.

"Did you conjure him from the dead?"

"No. He and Melisende had been chasing down a deer and disappeared into a wood where we dare not go. Melisende returned, but not Macbeth. Father could not call for him—if our enemies knew Macbeth was in their wood, they would hunt him down. So Geoff and I, we did what we could."

"And he came."

"Wolfhounds are smart. Maybe it helped that Melisende was sitting with us." Kate drew Marie close and kissed the top of her head. "So what shall we conjure?"

"Nan," Marie whispered.

Not what Kate had expected. "Why Nan?"

"They took her because of the golden baby Jesus. They want to know where it is."

Kate lifted Marie's chin. Her heart broke to read the fear in the child's eyes, see the quiver of her lips. She pulled her onto her lap. "What golden baby Jesus, my love?"

"That man told me I could have any ribbons I wanted if I told him where they kept it."

"What man? Tell me, Marie."

"In Hazel Frost's yard. I was waiting for Petra and Sister Brigida. I thought he was one of Master Frost's friends. He walked right through the street gate and knelt down to greet me most courteously." A little sob. "If I had told him, none of this might have happened. But I didn't know. I've never seen a golden baby Jesus."

The hackles on Kate's neck rose. "Where did he think you had seen it?"

"In the Martha House. He said the beguines had brought golden idols from Strasbourg."

"I have seen no golden idols, have you?"

Marie shook her head.

Is that what Robin sought? Fool's treasure? Geoff whispered in Kate's head.

"Did you tell Sister Brigida?"

Marie shook her head again, then buried her face in Kate's shoulder and sobbed.

God in heaven, all this because of a rumor? Was it possible? "There, there, my love, you are safe. I will not let anyone harm you." Meeting Jennet's eyes, Kate gestured for her to come take care of Marie.

"Thank you for telling me, Marie." Kate kissed her head, then lifted her chin, dabbing at her eyes. "When did this happen?"

Marie screwed up her face. "Petra had a tummy ache on Saturday, so we did not go to Hazel's, and we never go on the Lord's Day. Friday, it was."

Two days before the intruder. Kate nodded to Jennet as she approached. "My brave Marie. You have been most helpful." She kissed her forehead. "We will talk again, eh? For now, would you help Jennet take the bowls into the kitchen?"

"You are going away?"

"Just across to talk to the sisters. Stay with Jennet and the hounds. I will not be long away. I just need a word with them."

As Kate started toward the hedge, Ghent gave a little meep and rose to catch up. Marie followed, flinging her arms round him, asking him to stay with her. Bless the child. She could be so prickly, but a little attention at the right time, and she softened. Would that she were easier to understand.

As Kate crossed through the hedge a gust of wind blew her skirts about her.

—◦❦◦—

Eleanor glanced up from the prie-dieu as the opening of the door set the altar cloth and the Blessed Virgin's silk finery fluttering. Standing in the doorway, Kate cleared her throat to announce her presence. All three sisters—four if one counted Agnes—raised their heads from their prayerful bows and looked at her.

"Sister Brigida, Sister Agnes, I would speak with you."

Eleanor caught Brigida's arm as she began to rise. "When we are finished with our prayers, Katherine."

"I will go to her now," Brigida said, removing Eleanor's hand and pressing it firmly as one would a puppy, telling it to stay. She rose and crossed the room. Agnes followed. Kate paused, waiting for her mother's protest. But Eleanor simply returned to her prayers.

Plucking a bench from the kitchen, Kate placed it facing the small bench beneath the plane tree. She took a seat, inviting the two sisters to sit across from her. Without giving either time to speak, Kate repeated what Marie had just told her. At one point Brigida attempted to explain why Marie had been alone in the yard, but Kate held up a hand and continued. Brigida's negligence was another issue. When Kate mentioned the golden baby Jesus, Agnes gasped, Brigida frowned.

"Golden?" Brigida shook her head. "It is wood and cloth."

"So he was right that you have such a doll?"

"Many beguine houses have them. The Christ child in a manger, or a cradle. We place it on the altar during prayers and reflect on the great love God has for us that he allowed his only Son to be born as a human child so that he might live on this earth and suffer with us, show us the way. It is not a doll, and certainly not an idol. No more than the statue of the Virgin or Christ on the cross. But it has no monetary value."

"Why have I never seen it?" Kate asked. "Have you?" she asked Agnes.

Agnes bobbed her bowed head. "I have."

"Has Nan?"

"I believe she has," Agnes whispered.

"Why have I not seen it?" Kate repeated.

"We keep it hidden away when we are not reflecting upon it," said Brigida. "It has been misunderstood. Men of the Church have sneered at us, saying we play at mothering the Christ child. Some even say we pretend to nurse him. They ridicule us. For no reason. As I said, the purpose is the same as the images in churches—the statues, the crosses. I will gladly show you—there is no gold."

"Sister Agnes," Kate touched the woman's arm. "I think you know something you aren't telling us. Speak."

The woman shifted on the bench and raised her head. Her cap was damp. Overheated despite the chill in the air that was raising the down on Kate's neck. Agnes tucked her chin close, causing her multiple chins to line up beneath her, rather like a cat puffing up to intimidate its opponent.

"Well?" Kate said.

"There is a bit of gold thread in the baby's garments, and a little gilt crown circling his head. Nan might have asked me if it was of any value."

"She might have?"

An impatient sigh. "I do not recall all our conversations. She is my maidservant. *Was* mine. And her prattle is mostly silly. Baubles, men, how tedious she finds her work. I would slap her if I listened to it all. But you get little work out of a maidservant too often slapped."

Not so unlike her mistress. Kate just nodded.

"Do you think she told Robin that the Christ child was a golden idol?" asked Brigida.

Agnes shrugged.

"This incident took place before the night of the intruder," said Kate. "Friday. Why was Marie alone in my cousin's yard, Brigida?"

The sister frowned up through the crown of the plane tree as she thought back. "Petra had a bad tummy. I had escorted her to the privy."

As Marie had reminded her, Petra had spent Saturday and Sunday in bed. "So Nan told Robin at least a week ago."

"You are quick to blame Nan," Agnes snapped. "Poor thing is missing."

"Do you have a better explanation, Sister Agnes?" Kate asked sweetly. "Was it you who bragged of golden treasures in the Martha House?"

"No! No. Dame Eleanor explained to me why the Christ child is tucked away upstairs, and I told Nan."

Remembering Agnes's comments about Nan's chatter, Kate asked, "Did you tell Nan why it is kept hidden, or simply that it must be?"

Agnes's gaze slid sideways. "She wanted to see it up close and I refused. I said it was kept secret."

"Oh, Sister Agnes," Brigida whispered.

Yes.

Now Agnes's eyes began to shine with tears. "You do not think Hans died for this?"

"I don't know," Kate answered honestly. "If you would leave us now, Sister Agnes."

"Do not blame yourself overmuch," said Brigida. "Now is the time to open your heart to the Lord."

Much good that would do. "If you think of anything that might help us find Nan, come to me at once," Kate said.

Agnes bowed to both of them and walked slowly back to the house.

"You are thinking of Friar Adam and his questions about idols?" Brigida guessed.

Kate nodded. "My mother said you were taken aback by it at the time. So it is not a question one might expect a friar to put to you?"

"No. I thought he meant it as an insult. But why would he wish to steal it?"

"To bring it to light as proof that the city should shun beguines?" Kate shook her head. "Perhaps he might have encouraged the theft, but the murder I cannot see. For all that I dislike him, he is a man of God. What he might not have considered is that he has no control over the greed of thieves."

"They might have hoped to keep the golden idol for themselves." Brigida glanced up as a gust of wind shook the leaves, dropping several in their laps.

"Or they hoped that where there is a little treasure, there might be much more. So they questioned Hans, got angry . . . I admit I cannot make sense of it. Hans and Robin's trespass might not even be related." Each new fact seemed but to inspire more questions.

Brigida lifted one of the leaves and twirled it between her fingers. "I do not understand the yearning for others' possessions. They might fight for the king or the duke and earn their way honorably."

"You are a true innocent, Sister Brigida."

Brigida took it as an affront. "Not innocent," she said with some heat. "We have seen much in our work in the community. I believe most people strive to do good and avoid evil, yet evil is ever in our paths. Some have the strength to resist, others do not. If we might only teach them the benefit."

Kate disagreed. "You have no control over others. Friar Adam's belief that he might impose such control is an error for which many have suffered. Perhaps. I cannot yet prove he is behind this."

"For my part, I regret that I was not there to protect Marie."

"I do as well." It was not the time to placate the woman. "You will be more vigilant going forward. In any case, for the nonce you are tutoring the girls in my home, out of danger, so nothing can happen." As Kate rose, she told Brigida she would go to Dame Jocasta in the morning to speak with her about a more suitable confessor. "We do not want Friar Adam to return."

"No, Dame Katherine. He is not welcome in our Martha House."

As Kate rose so that Brigida might return her bench to the kitchen, her gaze wandered toward John Paris's property next door to the Martha House. It lay on the side with the alley in which Dina, Robin, and Kevin had struggled, and the soldiers had intervened. At her own gate, she called to Lille and Ghent. Jennet came to see why. When Kate told her that she meant to talk to John Paris, Jennet shook her head, not liking the idea.

"I have never trusted that man. Wait until one of us can accompany you."

"I will have Lille and Ghent with me—John fears them. And his wife, Beatrice, should be home at this hour. John fears her almost as much as he does the hounds. I will be safe."

～❦～

A workshop and several tumbledown sheds lay between the Martha House and John Paris's narrow, L-shaped dwelling. At one time all the property on this eastern side of Hertergate had been owned by one wealthy merchant, and Kate guessed that what was now the Martha House had been the primary residence. It had a more gracious façade than the house she approached, despite its added wing. Perhaps it was the lack of trees and the dark patches of damp and mold creeping up the plaster façade. So near the river, such a house required constant care, and this one did not receive it.

An olive-skinned manservant with dark eyes and a suspicious frown opened the door, courteously but pointedly asking her to state her name and her business. Kate had met him a few times but could not recall his name. And he clearly did not remember her.

A frail voice from somewhere behind him saved Kate. "Alonso, step aside so that I might see my visitor."

Alonso obliged, revealing the speaker to be Dame Beatrice, Mistress Paris, though so changed since the last time they met that Kate would not have recognized her had they passed on the street. Seated in a wheeled chair fashioned from parts of a garden cart, Beatrice reached out to take Kate's right hand in both of hers. Despite the house retaining the warmth of the day, the woman's hands were icy. And no wonder, her skin was stretched taut on her skeleton. A wasting sickness?

"May God bless you, Dame Katherine, it is a joy to see you so well. And your grand dogs. Lille and Ghent, if I am not mistaken. My memory is not what it was since my illness."

"I did not know you were ill," said Kate. "Perhaps one of the beguines next door—"

Beatrice gave what seemed an annoyed shake of her head. "I am well cared for by my husband and Alonso." She reached back to pat the hand of the manservant now standing behind her chair, ready to wheel it at her order. "You must forgive him for his caution."

"Of course. And I will not tire you. I came to speak with your husband."

"John? Ah." Beatrice's face registered disappointment.

"Do you ever venture out? Might Alonso bring you round to my house for dinner one day soon?"

A sad, slow shake of the head. "Alas, no, I have not stepped out into the light in a long while. I am told that you now have a niece living with you, as well as your mother just across the hedge in Agnes Dell's home."

"My niece, Petra, yes," said Kate.

Beatrice's eyes shone with tears—of delight or regret or illness, Kate could not guess. "Perhaps your niece might visit me some time. I should like that."

"We shall! And the beguines—"

Another, more pointed shaking of her head. "I will not have them on my property. I let Isabella Frost know that I disapprove of her hiring one of them as a tutor for her daughter. Fallen women. I will not have them here."

"Fallen women? I assure you—"

"Magistra Matilda tells me beguines invite such women into their houses, indeed welcome the return of those among them who have fallen from grace."

Kate was surprised Beatrice would listen to such gossip, but more surprised by the source—not Isabella but the sister. "Magistra Matilda welcomed the sisters into her house and knows they are virtuous women. I pray you misunderstood her." Was this Beatrice's bitterness regarding her husband's relationship with her neighbor? Or the illness? It did not matter. The woman was pinched and angry. "I will warn them not to stray near your home, Dame Beatrice."

"Alonso, show Dame Katherine to the master's parlor." Beatrice reached down to touch Lille, who was nearest, but, sensing the woman's mood, the hound backed out of her reach.

Alonso came round from the chair and led Kate and the dogs through the hall into the narrow wing of the house, pausing in front of a carved screen that acted as a partial wall. "Master John, Dame Katherine Clifford is here to see you. And her grand hounds."

A soft mutter, as if repeating Kate's name and puzzling over it, and then the sound of a chair being moved, footsteps. John Paris appeared, in tidy dress, if slightly worn at the elbows. Work clothes, Kate guessed.

"Dame Katherine. I pray nothing is amiss?"

"Faith, it is, John."

He thanked Alonso and sent him back to his mistress, inviting Kate to take a seat in his parlor, a comfortable room with a small brazier for winter, windows high in the south and north walls allowing the strengthening breeze to stir the air in the room and cool it. He kept his distance from Lille and Ghent. He was uneasy near all animals, including horses. It was said he had never learned to ride. A story behind that, no doubt. Perhaps a fall as a child. Or a nip. She motioned for Lille and Ghent to sit at her feet and proceeded to tell her tale, keeping it simple: an intruder, no doubt a thief, in the kitchen of her mother's new home, a frightened beguine, and, one morning later, a servant found in Thomas Holme's garden, beaten to death.

"God help us," John whispered, crossing himself. "Do you believe the thief returned, with deadly intent?"

She realized it might sound so, that in simplifying the tale she had not specified where her mother's servant now resided. But she did not take the time to correct it. "I come in the hope you might assist me with some information about someone you once employed who appears to be involved. A man named Robin. Agnes Dell says that you fired him for thieving?"

"Agnes? Oh, yes, she knew of the incident, of course." He looked uneasy, averting his eyes. Because of his liaison with Agnes, or something else? "Greedy cur, that Robin. He and his friends as well. I caught three of them in the warehouse one night, filling sacks with spices and animal hides."

Kate watched John closely as he spoke, observing how he repeatedly moved his left shoulder up and back as if to loosen a knot in his back, how his foot would start tapping, he'd realize what he was doing, stop it, begin again. He said he had noticed items missing from the inventory within a fortnight of Robin's switch from day laborer to night watchman, so he had set a trap, a second watchman who would already be in the warehouse, laying low to spy on Robin when he arrived. Unfortunately, the man John chose turned out to be one of Robin's comrades in crime. Or Robin had convinced him to join him. Either way, wares continued to disappear, so John took it upon himself to make surprise visits.

"Took four such to catch the louts. And a third they'd invited so they might carry more. I let them all go and set my own private guard round the warehouse."

Kate expressed confusion at John Paris's failure to call the sheriffs, who would have their sergeants take the men away and hold them for the next court session.

He gazed at the floor while he explained, "The quarter sessions were months away, their crime not so grave as to condemn them to the castle dungeon for so long. And hanging—for that would be their fate. I could not do that, even to them."

"Did you ask who had hired them?"

"Hired them? I don't understand. They are thieves."

No merchant would find that a puzzling question. "A man who has reasonable work is not likely to decide to risk more than the very occasional pilfering of small items. What you describe is far too bold for a man working alone. Robin must have known he would eventually be caught."

He shrugged. "I know nothing of how they work."

Incurious employer. Unless Paris himself had hired Robin to siphon goods from the merchants who leased space in his warehouses.

"I have not convinced you," said John. "Am I still welcome at your guesthouse?"

Interesting that should be his concern, considering he had no mistress at the moment. "Not with Agnes Dell. She has chosen to live as a beguine. Celibate, chaste. I advise you to disregard any rumors to the contrary. Have you a new mistress?"

"No. But—you saw Beatrice, how frail she is. A man has his needs."

Kate had often regretted including him on her list of clients, but she had considered him useful at the time. She had thought she might lease some space in his warehouse on the corner. And she thought it wise to befriend her neighbors. At the time she had been indifferent to Agnes Dell. "You will remain on my list as long as I do not discover you've lied to me."

John Paris shifted, uncomfortable in his chair. "I have not lied to you," he said. "You don't think I am somehow involved?"

She did. But she chose not to say so. Glancing down at his desk, she noticed that he was copying accounts from notes to a ledger much like some of Simon's, those recording his business partnerships with Thomas Graa. And the powerful, wealthy Graa had a particular interest in warehouses. "I believe you once told me you were factor to one of the aldermen." She lied. He had never admitted he was not his own man. "Was it Thomas Graa?"

"Why do you ask?"

"He might have some insight into Robin and his fellows."

"If you should ask him—"

"Graa?"

A nod. "He will—" A great sigh. "He does not know about Robin, Carter, and Bran. I made up the difference in money to hide my mistake. If he were to lose confidence in me, there are many who would gladly take over the managing of his warehouse."

Kate almost pitied him, but she sensed he still held something back. At least she had the names of the three men Paris had caught.

"What can you tell me of Bran and Carter?"

"Only that they were willing to do the work."

"Carter—was he a carter? That's surely not his Christian name?"

A shrug. "He went by Carter."

She let him stew in silence for a few moments, then said, "Might I ask, how did you come to own this property?"

"Own this property? Oh, no, no, I pay your brother-in-law Lionel Neville a sizable rent."

God help her. Of course he did. "And the warehouse belongs to Thomas Graa?"

A nod. "He sold the property with the two houses to Lionel when he and your late husband thought to live near each other. But then they had a falling out and Lionel leased the property to Leonard Dell and me."

"Do you also work for Lionel?"

A sharp shake of the head.

"If I find that you have lied to me . . ."

A cough. "I put aside fine items I know he would like."

"And price them low?"

A shrug. "A man does what he must to keep his landlord happy."

"What else?"

"An errand now and then."

"What sort of errand?"

"Delivering letters, for the most part. He does not like to travel through the Forest of Galtres, fears encountering robbers, so he sends me to his cousin's men at Sheriff Hutton."

More and more interesting. "In the past few weeks? Since the duke's landing?"

John started to rise, but when Lille sat up he thought better of it. "Not of late."

"Yes or no, John. I am not desperate for your patronage."

"Yes. One letter. A week ago. I do not read them, I swear. I cannot tell you what—"

"Lionel sent you out there within the week? And you handed the letter to whom?"

"Sir Elric."

"Did he seem eager for it?"

"I interrupted his dinner. He took it from my hands and waved me off to the kitchen for refreshment before my return."

"Did you deliver an answer?"

John shook his head. "Dame Katherine, I am trusted by this man."

"And so you shall remain. But the next time you have a letter, I want to know."

"I cannot."

Kate rose. "Have you any charges outstanding at my guesthouse? If so, make certain you have the money to hand. I will expect it within two days. Or I shall speak with Thomas Graa."

"Why do you want to know about the letters?"

He was angry now, feeling used.

Kate shrugged. "I am a Neville, and Nevilles spy on each other." She smiled. "Nothing dangerous. It is a game with us."

He was sweating now. But he nodded. "I will tell you when I've one to deliver. But you will not touch it."

"You are an honorable man, John Paris."

He bowed, oblivious to the insult.

She thanked him and took her leave. Robin, Carter, and Bran. Bran. The name Nan's mother had whispered to Jennet. It was he who had come for Nan. She shook her head as Alonso glanced up from where he was helping Beatrice eat. Kate called out a farewell and herded Lille and Ghent out the door. As she stepped out into the darkening evening she took a deep breath, relieved to depart that dreary house.

11

POISONOUS ROOTS
AND PENANCES

———⚬◦⚬———

Evening was settling in. Though the gathering clouds were still lit by the setting sun, down on the ground there was little light. Lille and Ghent flanked Kate as she moved down the alleyway between her mother's house and John Paris's. Though disturbing, the visit had been well worth it for many reasons—she had names for Robin's cohorts, and a connection between Lionel and Sir Elric through Paris. Much to consider, including warning the beguines about the rumors being spread about them. So much turmoil. It was as if the contest between the royal cousins had poisoned the land. Unholy alliances running underground like the roots of invasive weeds were sending up shoots everywhere. Lionel, Elric, Griffin, Werner, John Paris, Nan and her lover, Beatrice Paris—Isabella Gisburne Frost? Her uncle, the dean? Her mother? Could she trust any of them? When even the anointed king might be toppled by men's ambitions, where was the healthy heartwood?

"Who goes there?" a man's voice demanded.

For a second Kate's heart jumped, until she recognized Matt's voice. He must be watching the Martha House. "It's Dame Katherine." She reached the edge of the house and stepped into the light from his lantern.

"God go with you, Dame Katherine."

"By your presence I assume Griffin has not returned?"

"No. Jennet told us you were paying John Paris a visit. Was he of any help?"

"I have the names of two of Robin's cohorts—Bran and Carter. Do either of those names suggest anyone to you?"

Matt seemed about to speak, but hesitated. Then, "I wonder. Could Bran be Brandon, the lout Seth's father hired last Michaelmas? Was about to send him packing when he disappeared. With a few of Seth's father's best fletching tools."

"I hope so. And I hope Seth would be able to recognize him."

"Oh, I expect so."

"Any news of Nan?"

"No. Nothing." As Kate continued on into the garden, Matt added, "Sister Agnes wishes to speak with you."

Complain, more like. "Tell her to come to my house. I've been gone too long."

She pushed open the gate, allowing Lille and Ghent to precede her into her own garden and through the open door of the well-lit kitchen. For a moment she simply stood in the doorway, drinking in the looks of joy mixed with concern on the faces of her loved ones. Marie scrambled to her feet and poured Kate a bowl of ale. Petra shifted to the floor, offering Kate her seat. Berend sat back, his muscular arms folded over his chest, shaking his head; he'd been worried. Jennet poured a bowl of water for the hounds.

"Bless this house," Kate said as she settled and took a sip of ale. "Come, sit with me," she said to Marie, who hovered, asking if she wanted anything else. "This is all I need for now. Would it trouble you if I told the others what you told me?"

"Not if it might help us find Nan." Marie settled beside Kate and leaned against her with a sigh.

Kate kissed her forehead. "Bless you." By the time Kate was recounting her own conversation with Brigida and Agnes, the child was asleep, her head heavy in Kate's lap. She stroked the girl's soft curls, remembering her own relief when a worry had been handed on to her parents.

Berend was nodding. "Friar Adam might be a key to the puzzle." Kate listened with interest as Berend shared what he'd heard at the camp about the injured man left at the friary and the disagreement among the men who had taken him there. "What did John Paris have to say for himself?"

Kate started with Beatrice Paris and the impression Magistra Matilda had given her that beguines were to be shunned. While describing the unpleasant exchange, Kate noticed Agnes Dell peering in the doorway.

"Is there room for one more?" she asked.

"Come in, Agnes, do. No need to stand out in that chilly breeze," said Kate.

Jennet was quick to offer her chair, hoisting herself up on a corner of the table near the fire. Lille and Ghent lay on their sides in the doorway. Lifting her skirts, her expression one of mild fear, Agnes picked her way between them. The chair received her bulk with a creak. She blew up on the strands of hair escaping her cap and fanned herself. The woman certainly burned hot. Berend offered a bowl of ale, but she declined.

"I cannot stay long. I intend to keep vigil with Sister Dina tonight."

"Keep vigil?" Kate assured her that Matt was keeping the watch.

"Not that sort of vigil. Sister Dina is doing penance for all the troubles in our households and more. She intends to spend the night lying prostrate before the altar in prayer."

"But she did nothing," Petra protested.

Agnes agreed. "But she sees it otherwise. I'm here to offer my help in finding those responsible."

Kate thought she understood Dina's sense of guilt. "We see what she did as a courageous act, but she sees it as a breach of her dedication to God." She wondered how best she might test Agnes's sincerity. "Have you an idea where Nan might be? A friend who might give shelter to her and Robin?"

"I fear I have paid little attention to Nan's prattle. I know nothing about her friends or kin. I regret that."

She seemed sincere enough. "John Paris gave me the names of the two men he caught helping Robin steal from the warehouse," said Kate. "Bran and Carter."

"Bran. The name Goodwife Hawise whispered," said Jennet.

Noticing Agnes nodding her head, Kate asked if she knew Carter—she'd already denied knowing anyone named Bran.

"I do know a Carter," said Agnes, "and that he was part of it does not surprise me. Always complaining his work was not appreciated. And he had a temper. He once threatened my husband with a knife when Leonard caught him slacking on the job and reeking of ale. He was supposed to be loading a vessel down on the staithe. I heard about it for days. Leonard would not have him near the house after that, told John Paris he was not to load his shipments either."

"Did he have any trouble with him after that?"

Agnes shook her head. "Do you remember Leonard? How strong he was? Berend reminds me of him." Her eyes lingered on Berend's bare forearms.

Kate remembered Leonard Dell as a man with a temper, loud, red-faced when in his cups, which seemed to be whenever he was home. But in form, perhaps, a little like Berend, without the scars, with more hair. No, it was impossible to compare the two. She simply nodded. "What of Bran? Still no memory?"

Frowning, biting her bottom lip, Agnes shook her head. "I'm sorry."

"Were there any other troublemakers working for your husband or John Paris?"

"I knew only the ones who came for the midday meal. A dozen or more, and John Paris never shared enough of the expense. When I was told Leonard had been lost at sea, I put an end to feeding all those men, told John it was not seemly for a widow to have so many men in the house. I sent off the cook—he was none too pleased with being shown the door, but, truth be told, I was not easy having that one-legged letch sleeping in my kitchen."

"One-legged cook? Did you hear that?" Jennet asked Berend.

Kate looked from them to Agnes, who was shaking her head. "Is he here? In York?"

"Fair-haired, pale eyes?" Berend asked.

"That is him. He calls himself Thatcher. Would never give me a Christian name. Slippery, like Carter." Agnes looked round. "But what does he have to do with Robin's trespass? Or Hans? He surely could not be Hans's murderer. With one leg he's not likely to have gone down the gardens at night. And Nan surely knows not to trust him."

"What of the boarders?" Kate asked. "Who sent them to you?"

"John Paris arranged for the boarders, all respectable men, though not wealthy enough to rent a set of rooms in the city. I had no trouble with them. Nor did Nan. They watched her, but I made certain they understood I would have no such trouble in my house."

Jennet stretched. "Much to sleep on. Looks like I should tuck in the children."

Agnes rose. "And I must return to Sister Dina."

As Jennet made to follow her out, Kate caught her arm. "A moment."

Jennet settled back on the chair.

"We have a name, Thatcher, connected to the soldiers who plucked Robin away from Kevin," Kate noted.

Jennet nodded. "Perhaps Friar Adam hired a thief he knew to be familiar with Agnes's house, for the purpose of stealing the Christ child, but it all went wrong, so Robin's mates then went after Hans, to force him to help steal it?" She frowned at the silence that met her scenario. "I know, but it fits together." A shrug.

"Why did Friar Adam want the Christ child?" asked Berend. "If he wishes to spread rumors about the sisters, he need only join Magistra Matilda's effort." He shook his head. "Or was it Robin's rescuers, the soldiers who took him to the friary, who then went after Hans?"

"But why?" asked Petra, rubbing her eyes.

"And how would they know Hans had worked for Dame Eleanor?" Kate wondered.

"He talked in his cups?" Jennet suggested.

Seeing Petra's exhaustion, Kate thought better of more discussion. "It grows late. I think we will all be the better for some sleep."

Within moments Jennet had Marie and Petra in hand and led them out the door.

When Kate and Berend were alone, she slipped off her shoes and settled on the high-backed chair Jennet had abandoned, closing her eyes. The packed earth floor was cool on her feet, the sounds of Berend gathering ingredients to make bread dough for the morrow comforting.

Her thoughts drifted to Agnes Dell, how humbly she had offered her help. No imperious posturing, her voice soft, her tone beseeching. This night she had truly become *Sister* Agnes, inspired by Sister Dina's remorse.

Amends—her mother's homecoming with the beguines certainly seemed an act of penance. For what? She responded to any mention of Ulrich Smit by slamming the door on his memory—because she was wracked with guilt? She had embraced a work of penance—the beguines, perhaps coming home to be with Kate as well. Perhaps even her fatal interference in her son Walter's life had been meant as amends. What had she done? And how might Kate discover it without pushing her away?

"What happened between Mother and Ulrich?" She spoke into the silence that had stretched out too long. "And why is my uncle so keen to remind me that Mother is a Frost, but I am a Clifford? He is warning me about something, and I believe it has to do with Mother's silence on the subject of Ulrich Smit. How can I win her trust?"

"God knows you've tried. Stubborn woman," Berend muttered, but he did not look up, the table creaking as he kneaded the dough.

Was he angry with her for the risk she'd taken with John Paris? As her brothers would have been? "I am home, safe, unscathed," she said softly.

"God be thanked." Now he looked up, his scarred face dark with imagined grief. "I would kill anyone who harmed you."

"I can defend myself. I took Lille and Ghent, and was armed with a dagger and my axe."

A long silence. She could hear Berend breathing, a rhythm that matched her own heartbeat. Lille turned over with a shuddering sigh, causing Ghent to shift and thump his tail. It broke the tension. Berend returned to kneading the dough, Kate poured herself more ale.

"It is strange that Dean Richard considers Dame Eleanor a Frost," said Berend. "His brother's wife. And she took your father's name, she's kept it. It is as if he needs to remove all connection with her."

"I have never known my uncle to behave so. Could it just be the connection to the beguines? Has he heard about some incident in Strasbourg? Or is this not about Mother but about her nephew William Frost?" Kate drank down the rest of the ale, hoping it would stop her mind from spinning with questions. "If only Marie had come to me when the man asked about the Christ child. It was two days before Robin frightened Sister Dina. We would have been prepared, one of us watching the Martha House. I should have seen that Marie was troubled."

"She guards herself closely. How could you know? I noticed nothing out of the ordinary when she helped me in the kitchen, though now I look back and see that she has been too quiet, too courteous. *I* wonder whether the thieves moved when they did because Griffin was away, and they knew the house unguarded?"

"That might have been any time," said Kate. "Griffin had not planned to return to the Martha House. The sisters wanted no men on the property. But I see what you mean, Nan might have complained to Robin about not having a man around the house to see to the heavy chores. She inspired him to take the risk. Poor fool. I pray we find Nan attending Robin at the friary."

"I would not hold out hope. Would she not send word to her mother and the children if that were so?"

"That worries me as well." Kate reached down to stroke Ghent's ears. "Werner and Griffin—Mother knows something about their disappearance, I am certain."

"They've been seen at Toft Green. Asking questions. They were not well received. A dangerous time to be asking questions of strangers, especially armed strangers."

Lille whimpered in her sleep, waking herself, shifting so that she was reclining with her front paws crossed, watching the doorway. Not yet on alert, but watchful. Perhaps she'd heard someone passing the kitchen on their way to the privy behind it.

"What does Lionel have to do with any of this?" Kate wondered.

"Perhaps nothing but that he seems to ally himself with the underbelly of York." Berend wiped his brow, leaving a streak of flour. "Though no one seems to be behaving honorably at present. It was a bold move, for William Frost and the others to send money to Duke Henry. They are betting on Lancaster and want to be in his good graces."

"That is the prevailing wind. We never saw the number of soldiers we'd expected. And those who did answer the call are slipping away. It seems no one wishes to be remembered as having supported the king against Lancaster." Kate rubbed her temples, her head aching with all the threads she was trying to follow. "Damn the royal cousins. Where do our troubles end and theirs begin?"

Berend gave the dough a few more thumps, brushed off his hands, and covered the bowl with a cloth. He came round the table and drew her up onto her feet. "Time to rest. You will sleep better in your own bed tonight."

She touched Berend's flour-streaked cheek. "You never fail me. I can say that of no one else, at any time in my life."

"My life is yours."

She was blessed with her loyal household. "Good night, my dear friend." Calling softly to Lille and Ghent, she walked out into the night, heading to the main house, and sleep, if it would come.

A soft rain had begun, the air sharp with the smell that presaged a storm. Kate stepped out from beneath the overhanging trees and lifted her face to receive the cool drops.

He is the only one who has never failed you? You forget your twin.

No, Geoff. You took a risk that led to almost certain death, and you lost. I lost. Having you in my mind is not the same as having you beside me, to fight beside me in the flesh.

She felt the heat of her twin's emotion. It was an old argument, never resolved because it was true. Lille made a soft sound and headed toward the hedgerow gate, Ghent following. Someone stood there, reaching out a hand, tentative, shy, letting the hounds sniff it.

"Mother?" Kate stepped between the dogs. "Are you wakeful?"

"I heard the rain. Smelled it. I love this moment, when the rain returns after the heat. Like a benediction, God's grace lightly touching us."

A memory. Sensing her mother in the doorway of her tiny bedchamber. Eleanor had taken her hand and led her out into the fields. The trees rustling with the freshening breeze, the grasses swaying, clouds scudding across the night sky, making the stars wink out until the darkness was vast and terrifying. *Too big!* Kate had whispered. But her mother had laughed and told her that nothing had changed but the light, the sky was just as big in bright daylight as in a storm. But Kate could not stop shivering. *Dance with me, Daughter, dance with me!* Her mother had taken her hands and led them in a jig. Laughter rose up, and her fears were forgotten as Kate and her mother danced until they tumbled down in giggly exhaustion.

"Do you remember the night we danced in the rain?" Kate asked.

Eleanor reached out and touched Kate's cheek. "I do. The memory is precious to me. For once you found courage in dancing in joy rather than in weapons and war dogs. You were mine that night. For one sweet moment before it all fell apart."

Kate took her mother's hand and kissed it. "I am glad you are here." She meant it.

An intake of breath. Eleanor squeezed Kate's hand. "Bless you for saying that. I wish—I should have told you at once. I set Griffin and Werner the task of finding Hans's murderer. I believed they were better suited than you and your—household to do so. They know him far better."

At last, a slight opening. "Do you know where they are?" Kate asked, gently withdrawing her hand.

"No. I told them to return when they had news."

A very slight opening. Kate could not think what to say that would not dislodge the wedge in the doorway.

Eleanor leaned back as if to feel the rain on her face, a glimpse of the impetuous young woman her father once described as a forest sprite, never still, always flitting from place to place, never settling. Kate had laughed at the description, so opposite to her own experience with her mother, always sitting at her embroidery or the loom, urging her daughter to sit beside her and learn a woman's ways. Finding fault with everything and everyone.

"Sir Elric's men are watching from across the way," said Eleanor. "I invited them to come in out of the rain, but they said that was no way to stand watch. Shall I send Matt home? I see no need for him to stand watch in the kitchen tonight, with the men guarding on Hertergate."

For once Kate was glad that Sir Elric was still watchful. But it was not enough. "Their presence across the way merely shifts the trouble to the back gardens. Where Matt is."

Eleanor sighed. "As you wish."

"Sleep well, Mother." Kate turned into the rain, which was coming down harder now, and ran across the garden, in turns buoyant with hope—perhaps she and her mother might heal the rift—and ready to scream with frustration.

Up in the solar, as she stripped off her wet clothes, Kate questioned her purpose in searching for the reasons behind Robin's trespass and Hans's murder. If her mother preferred the help of Griffin and Werner, Kate was interfering.

Except for Marie's experience. And the men who had tried to take Lille and Ghent. But was the latter even connected to the incidents in her mother's household? Doubts—could she afford this when lives might be at stake?

Weary of heart, Kate worked her way into the crowded bed next to Petra, who was curled up against Jennet, who had an arm round Marie. Grateful for the warmth of her companions, she drifted into an exhausted sleep.

Sometime in the night Kate woke with Petra's head resting on her chest. Rain drummed overhead, wind rattled the shutters. She lay awake for a long while, imagining Berend lying near the kitchen fire, smelling of yeast and sweat and spices.

—◦◦◦—

In the morning, Dame Jocasta led Kate and Jennet down an alley off Colliergate to a tall, skinny house surrounded by a dirt yard and a noxious midden. Two young girls straddled a long bench set out of the rain beneath the eaves of the house, a pile of clothing between them. Wielding scissors meant for much larger hands, the children were cutting buttons and decorations off the clothing, dropping the trimming in a basket on the ground and tossing the stripped clothing in a pile that would be sorted into salvage and rags. They were tidy children, their gowns clean though much mended.

"Piece work," said Jocasta. "It brings in a little coin, along with what the two lads make sweeping out the shops on the Shambles."

"How long has their mother been ill?" Kate asked.

"Since the birth of the youngest—little Ann." Jocasta nodded to the smallest child. Kate guessed her age to be about five. "For a while Hawise's sister helped out, assisting with baby Ann and teaching the children how to do the chores. She expected Nan to give her notice and return to take care of the family. When Nan refused, her aunt left. Families." Dame Jocasta laughed as the two girls came rushing to her, asking if she had any sweets. "They live on the upper floor. Goodwife Ellen is there with Hawise now."

As Kate climbed the steep outer steps with Jennet, she imagined the children climbing them with buckets of water, food, coal, or peat if they were so fortunate. Exhausting work for a strong adult—she could not imagine how the children managed. Stepping through the open door, she paused to adjust to the dim interior. The chamber was loud with a painful wheezing in rhythm with a woman's chant, "Breathe in, breathe out, breathe out, breathe out. Breathe in, breathe out, breathe out, breathe out." Hawise was a pale, skeletal woman who sat on a cot against the far wall, propped up on cushions. A large woman sat at the edge of the cot, nodding in encouragement as she chanted. One small window let in a bit of air, but not nearly enough to freshen it. Other than that the house was tidy, the bedclothes washed. Bless Dame Jocasta, this was her work, Kate was sure of it.

The wheezing suddenly broke cadence as Hawise stirred and pointed toward Kate.

Breaking off her chant, the large woman turned to her.

Kate introduced herself.

A nod. "Goodwife Hawise wishes to speak with you."

Hawise's wheezing was more of a pant now as she reached out a hand, grasping Kate's.

"Bran. Nan's cousin."

"Yes, the one who came for her?"

Hawise shook her head. "No. It was not Bran who came. He must find her."

Jennet stepped forward. "Forgive me, Goodwife, I misunderstood."

"Who came for her?" Kate asked. "Did you know him?"

"No." Hawise held up a hand as she took a few labored breaths. "I'd never seen him."

"Forgive me for so many questions," said Kate. "Can you describe him?"

"Wore a hat." Her gesture described a hat pulled down to below the ears. "No beard." A shrug. "A man."

"Where might I find Bran?"

"Thursday Market. Or Ouse Bridge. Crowds." Hawise bit her lip and wheezed a few times, her breath catching at the edge of the inhale, as if trying for more. Kate found herself trying to breathe for the woman. "A cutpurse." Another few labored breaths. "Or with my boys. Sweeping out the butchers' stalls. In the Shambles. Blue eyes. Too pretty for a man. His bane." Still holding tight to Kate's hand, she shook it. "Do not tell him I told you. About the thieving. He thinks I don't know."

"Your secret is safe with me. You trust him?"

Hawise nodded. "Simple. Foolish. But loyal."

"I will look for him. We will do all we can to find Nan."

"Robin turned her head. Silly sot she is."

"If she has chosen to hide, where would she go?"

Hawise shook her head. "Holds her secrets close, Nan does."

Goodwife Ellen walked Kate and Jennet to the door. "I would not count on Bran. He's taken up with Robin and his lot, none of them meaning any good to anyone. Thieves for hire. Or worse. Bran is Hawise's kin. She will not believe he's gone over." A nod. "Best to look for Nan yourself. She'll be with a man, like as not."

"But who?"

Ellen paused, thinking. "She's friendly with the night watch. If any are unmarried, they might hide her."

"A bawd house?"

"No, never. Nan's determined to wed."

So were all the poor women left to their own devices, at least at the beginning, Kate thought. She thanked Ellen and hurried down the steps, Jennet right behind her.

Joining Jocasta, who was praising the girls for their work, Kate asked the children whether they knew the man who had come for Nan.

Both girls shook their heads.

She asked a few more questions, but they were of little help. They'd seen enough to know he was no one they recognized, but there had been nothing that stood out about him.

Dame Jocasta led Kate and Jennet away. "Children have poor recall of things they do not wish to remember, such as the man who took their sister away."

"Who will take care of them when Hawise dies?"

"Ellen and her husband, Jed, might, if the landlord will agree to their taking over the room. Or the children might go into service. It would not have been much different had their mother been healthy."

As they walked toward Colliergate, hoods up, the rain coming down more steadily now, Kate told Dame Jocasta enough about Sister Dina that she would understand her fragility, her need for a kind, compassionate, gentle confessor. Jocasta meant to pay a visit to the beguines so that she might describe their needs to her confessor.

"I cannot think how Friar Adam gained Isabella Frost's trust." Jocasta gave a little shiver. "A man devoid of heart. The sisters are best rid of him. I will ensure that their confessor is his opposite, one who listens through his heart. But may I say, Sister Dina could not have a better model for healing than she does in you, Katherine, the strength with which you protect yourself and your family, the wisdom with which you've chosen your household. At so young an age, you are remarkable."

Unaccustomed to such compliments, Kate could not at once think how to respond.

"Forgive me for presuming," said Jocasta, "but it is so."

"Your words are a gift. In truth, I do not think most see me so. I am all too often tormented by doubt. My mother disapproves. I fear the sisters do as well."

"Sister Dina would not have confided in you had she any doubt." Jocasta kissed Kate's cheek. "I am curious to meet Dame Eleanor." With an enigmatic smile, Jocasta set off down Colliergate.

"I am off to learn more of pretty Bran," said Jennet, "and I'll ask round the bawd houses. I will meet you at the deanery."

–◦◦◦–

Wise and strong. Kate smiled to herself as she blended into the crowd of folk moving toward Holy Trinity Church, the rain forcing them to move with heads down, watching for puddles. She kept one hand on the dagger hidden in her skirt, more aware than ever of the number of armed men on the streets. Without Lille and Ghent flanking her, Kate was jostled by passersby far more often than was comfortable. The crowd thinned as she passed round the church, crossing into Low Petergate. A passing group of vicars choral greeted her as they flowed toward the minster, merrily shaking the rain out of their hair into each others' faces. She followed in their wake, smiling at their casual banter, an argument about the best ale in the city, a complaint about the peculiarities of a particular canon, the strange echo in one of the chantry chapels in the minster. She parted from them in the minster yard—all but one, who strode along with her to the deanery. She tried to recall his name.

"I was summoned to assist the redoubtable Dame Helen in packing," he confided as Kate knocked on the door. "Can I satisfy her standards, I ask myself, or will she toss me out by my ear? But if there is any chance I might be rewarded with one of her custard tarts, or a meat pie, it is worth the risk."

"Packing?" Only now did Kate notice the carts, two of them off to the side of the deanery, one already sprouting her uncle's writing desk and several chests.

"Yes, they plan to leave two days hence." He doffed his hat and bowed as Helen flung open the door.

"There you are, Arnold. Two hours late, I note. Were you so wearied bringing the chests and packs up from the undercroft yesterday that you could not stir until now? Pitiful for a healthy young man such as yourself. Clovis has already begun. Shame on you. Go on, then, up the steps, you will find him up there."

"Sounds like no custards for my troubles," he whispered to Kate as he trotted past Helen and disappeared into the hall.

The dean's housekeeper shook her head as she turned to Kate. "Your uncle prefers these petted and pampered lads of the Church to ordinary hardworking servants. I will never understand how men's minds work. They are quite a mystery to me. Now, my dear Dame Katherine, you are wet through." Without bothering to ask permission she untied Kate's light hood and held it away from her, tsking at the damp skirts and sleeves. "You might have done better with a cloak."

"Too warm. And I like the dampness after all the heat."

"Oh, to be sure, you flaunt your northern upbringing. Well, I expect you are here to say your farewells to the dean, and just in time."

"No. I had no idea. I came to ask his advice about Prior Norbert. Where are you going?"

"The dean did not get word to you? He has been called back to Westminster. We leave Friday. Just two days hence. I do not know why we could not delay until Monday so we might have one more Sunday mass in the minster."

"Is he summoned by King Richard? Has the king returned?"

"No, called by his conscience. The dean says he is needed there. The work of the government rolls on, and clear heads are essential."

"But it is so sudden. What caused his abrupt attack of conscience?"

Helen shook her head. "Heaven knows."

"I don't want you to leave!" Kate felt tears starting.

"Oh, my dear, I will miss you, and all your household. I've grown so fond. Phillip was beside himself when I told him this morning."

"I believe it, poor child." Kate's ward, Marie's brother, was living with Hugh Grantham, a master mason overseeing the work on the east end of the minster. As an apprentice, Phillip worked in the minster yard just outside the deanery, where he had stayed during a difficult time the past winter. He found solace in Helen's kitchen.

"I daresay you will now see far more of him," Helen said. "He often tells me of the wonders of Berend's kitchen. He's another one I shall greatly miss, Berend, your rough giant. But I am keeping you from your mission. Your uncle is in his parlor."

"His temper?"

"Reflective."

"Is the archbishop still in the city?"

"He took leave of Dean Richard last evening. They shared a remarkable amount of brandywine. When His Grace departed, your uncle went to the minster and did not return until just before dawn, hollow-eyed and silent. Whatever His Grace shared with him, it was disturbing and secret. He has not said a word." A sigh. "Go to him, my dear. I will dry your hood by the fire and bring something to warm you."

12

SHIFTING LOYALTIES

———⚬⚭⚬———

While Richard Clifford was in residence, the deanery hall had been made bright and cozy with colored cushions and tapestries. Now the heavy wood furnishings were stripped bare, the whitewashed walls dingy. Kate's footsteps echoed down the hall.

The dean answered her knock with a sharp "Come in, come in."

"Uncle?" He was nowhere to be seen.

"Katherine?" He stepped out from behind the door, cradling a stack of rolled documents. "Good, good. I meant to send Alf with the news of our departure, but this is better." He moved past her, setting the rolls on a table already piled with documents, candlesticks, and lamps. The room was as gloomy and denuded as the hall.

"You would leave without seeing me?"

He turned toward her, brushing dust from his hands, the front of his gown. "I dislike farewells. We have enjoyed our time together, have we not? Let us remember those moments, not grim handshakes and promises of visits and letters that will never be. Though I hope to return to York, I cannot predict when it might be. I do have something for you. But first, what news have you for me?"

"News?"

"You have come to report what you have learned regarding the incidents at Dame Eleanor's beguinage, as agreed, have you not?" He turned away, sorting the documents into three piles. "I can deliver your report to Scrope when I join him at Bishopthorpe at the end of the week."

"I hoped you might advise me about how best to approach Prior Norbert."

"Oh, Norbert. Remind me what you wished from him." The dean brushed past her, returning to the cupboard for another armload of documents.

"That is part of my news." Kate told him about the wounded man left at the door of the blackfriars, possibly Robin the would-be thief. "If he is there, I wish to speak to him. Or send Berend to do so. And if he is not—"

"You become more and more involved in this despite knowing that Dame Eleanor will not thank you for your help." Richard Clifford spoke to the table, not to Kate. "Has she told you anything about Ulrich Smit's death? Why she fled to York?" Now he turned to face her, brushing his hands. "Why do you persist in this? God knows you've had no peace since she returned."

"With armed men hungering for battle camped inside our gates I cannot be certain that Mother has brought her troubles on herself. How can you? Do *you* know something about his death that would cause her to flee?"

"What could I possibly know?" He shook his head as he crossed the room to fetch several large books. This was no temporary move. Despite what he'd said, he did not expect to return. At least not as dean of the chapter of York Minster.

"Have you any idea what the thief wanted?" he asked as he crouched down at an open chest.

Apparently he did not intend to answer her question. Perhaps if she gave him the news he wanted . . . While he loaded the books into the chest, Kate told him about Marie's encounter, and what she had learned from the sisters about the Christ child. All the while the dean continued his task, pausing now and then to rub his lower back—the chest was deep, the books heavy—never once glancing her way.

"Are you listening, Uncle?"

He nodded as he rose with a grunt. "I heard, I heard. Mothering an image of the infant Christ child—they bring it on themselves, these silly women."

"It is the vicars choral who are silly. Brigida, Dina, and Clara are pious and dedicated to being of service to the community."

A shrug. "Perhaps I am mistaken. If they are so, more's the pity they tethered themselves to Dame Eleanor. Look what she's done—she takes in a stranger—"

"That is not fair. It was Agnes's house—"

"It was a poor choice."

"In your opinion."

"I cannot believe my ears. You, defending your mother?" He shook his head as he turned back to the table. "Have a care, Katherine. Do not hold onto hope that her spiritual endeavor is a sign of change. She will disappoint you."

As he had disappointed her of late? "I merely noted that you are placing the blame before the facts."

The dean shrugged. "As for Prior Norbert, he should be favorably disposed toward assisting your inquiry. He and Friar Adam are not the best of friends."

"I should simply ask after Robin and request that he tell Friar Adam that Dame Eleanor and the sisters are not in need of him?"

"You might tell him first about Friar Adam, then ask after the wounded man. On second thought, better the other way. A mission of mercy."

"I am grateful for your guidance in this." She stepped over to the table, glancing at the rolls. Many bore royal seals. "I see you've been doing the king's work while here in the city. Perhaps I should not have been surprised to hear that both you and the archbishop are abandoning the souls in your care to see to your more temporal duties. But why the haste?"

He moved the documents away from her. "The worthies of York have withdrawn their support from King Richard despite the charter he granted the city, and His Grace and I have been subtly advised to do likewise. But as men of the Church, we strive to remain neutral in this quarrel. We will be of more use in Westminster, where our voices might be heard, than we are here, where our voices cannot."

"Not by the wealthy and powerful, perhaps, but what of all the others? Both of you are abandoning your spiritual community the moment you are challenged by the aldermen and their cronies—it seems a cowardly retreat."

"Courage has nothing to do with it. It is about duty."

"Your temporal duties, but your spiritual responsibilities? How can you disparage the beguines when every breath they breathe is dedicated to God?"

"Personal piety cannot be measured."

"Yet you claim to measure theirs."

"When did you become so concerned about matters of faith?"

"When you and the rest of the hypocrites in York set yourselves up as judges of others' faith." They stared at each other for a long moment, the dean's eyes pained, Kate's own filling with angry tears. She felt lost, hated herself for attacking him. He had been one of her staunchest supporters. "Just months ago you and Scrope hosted Lady Kirkby on her mission to gain support for her husband's peace efforts," Kate reminded him. "What of that?"

When the tensions had escalated between the two cousins on the death of John of Gaunt, Henry of Lancaster's father, Sir Thomas Kirkby had gone to the Continent to discuss with the duke a road to reconciliation. His wife, Margery Kirkby, had traveled to wealthy cities, raising money for her husband's efforts. As a favor to her uncle, Kate had hosted Lady Kirkby in her guesthouse.

"In winter we held out hope that all might be peacefully resolved. But the royal cousins were not interested."

"What of Sir Thomas Kirkby? Has he returned from the Continent?"

"I think he would be wise to stay away until all is settled."

"As you intend to do?" Kate wanted to kick something. "King Richard entrusted you with the Privy Seal, the Wardrobe—indeed you were once his chaplain. And surely you have heard the rumors that a bishop's miter and crozier are in your future. Will you not stand by him?"

"Will he stand by me? That is the question all ask themselves. The king's temper flashes at the subtlest suspected insult. What is meant in praise might be received as blame or disrespect."

"And Duke Henry? Have you faith that he will be of a more appropriate temperament if crowned?"

"He seems a straightforward man. But if he surrounds himself with counselors who fear every twitch signals rebellion—" The dean pressed his hands over his eyes for a moment, then suddenly drew her into his arms, holding her tightly. She could feel his heart pounding. "Such a fierce pride. I shall miss you, Katherine." A glimmer of hope. This was the uncle she knew. "As I said, I have something for you. I was going to have Alf deliver it, but now I see the error in that." He released her and stepped back toward the table, plucking a scroll from a small pile to one side. "I've signed over to you my property on Low Petergate—the large house a door down from Stonegate. You've only to add your signature and seal. Thomas Graa and Archbishop Scrope have witnessed it. I've also included two horses."

Dizzy with the sudden shift, Kate sank down on a chair. "What is this? You are not ill?"

"No. No, not at all." Richard tapped his palm with the parchment as he looked aside, as if searching for what to say. "Forgive my harsh words about your mother and the beguines. I worry that you are attaching yourself to a woman who is viewed with distrust. If Duke Henry takes the throne, he will never rest easy. The subtle divides we see now will become far more obvious. If King Richard manages to keep his crown, the unease and distrust that have set him on this destructive path will deepen. In either case, you need to ally yourself with the powers in York in order to survive. I know you can do this. You have the heart of a warrior and the head of a merchant prince. With this gift and whatever comes to you from your late father's estate, you will thrive. Lionel Neville has no claim to it. You will be free to wed whom you will, and all your children will have a good future."

A heady proposition. "Why me? And why arrange it without consulting me?"

"I have grown fond of you and your household—Phillip, Marie, Petra, even Berend and Jennet. I watched you pick yourself up from the shock of your late husband's will, embrace the children in whom you might have seen a betrayal. I admire you. Even the guesthouse. Indeed, I believe you would be better able to see to your guesthouse—more important to you than ever for the power it gives you over the city leaders—if you move your household to the house on Petergate. You can run the dogs in the fields beyond the walls. With the horses you can ride out to the manor west of Galtres, the dower property that you've slyly hidden from your creditors."

He knew her so well. Too well. It felt as if he had studied what she would most desire and offered it to her—in exchange for what? "And you ask for nothing in return?"

"Prayers? A welcome when I return? I am leaving in much more haste than I had expected." His expression was earnest, encouraging. "I have handled this awkwardly." He held out the roll. "Will you sign it?"

"It must be done in your presence?"

"That is what I promised His Grace and Thomas Graa."

"I will sign it in Thomas Graa's chambers. Is that acceptable?"

"You do not trust me?"

"Your offer is generous, but I never sign anything before I've had time for careful consideration, Uncle. I pray you understand."

The dean bowed to the wisdom of that. "And if you refuse, how am I to know?"

She did not mean to refuse, but it was not the moment to reassure him. "Thomas Graa has the means to send a messenger to Westminster. I must think, Uncle." *I must discuss this with Berend*, she thought. "But I am moved and grateful. You honor me."

He shook his head, frowning, but there was no anger in his voice. "I should have guessed you would be cautious. But I agree." He handed her the roll.

"May God watch over you in your journey." She kissed his cheek. "I pray you are able to stay peaceably above the fray, Uncle."

"And you as well. God go with you, Katherine."

She withdrew from the room in a daze, her mind unable to quiet.

In the corridor, Arnold, the vicar choral, shuffled by with a large box out of which peeked one of the pelts that cushioned her uncle's bare feet when he rose from sleep. A man who loved his comfort. She had a nagging feeling that she had missed something with her uncle, but what? Perhaps she should return. Or invite him to dine at her home before he left? Resolved, she continued on to the kitchen, pausing just outside, listening to Helen and Jennet laughing at the antics of the household cat, Claws. How wonderfully ordinary. Stepping into the room, Kate sought a chair, settling with a sigh.

"Might I have some brandywine?"

"Oh! In all this fuss I forgot to fetch you something to warm you. Forgive me. Did the dean not offer you anything?" Helen tsked as she went for the flask and found a goblet not yet packed. Italian glass, a vibrant blue. "I see he upset you, as he has done us all with this murderous haste." Helen sighed. "I shall miss both of you so. As will the dean."

"I cannot bear to lose either of you. I don't know what to think—I called him a coward and he offered me a great gift. I'm not so much upset with him as confused. Come dine with us tomorrow. Berend would enjoy the opportunity to make some special dishes, and you can say farewell to the girls."

"Oh, I should like that. I will pose it to your uncle." Helen kissed Kate's cheek, but as she resettled, her expression clouded. "Though I fear he will decline. He has not been himself."

"Shall I go back and ask him myself?"

"No, no, it's better coming from me. I can be quite persuasive." A secret smile.

Kate drank down the brandywine much more quickly than was wise, bringing tears to her eyes.

Jennet pressed her hand, apparently misinterpreting the tears. "What urgent work awaits the dean in Westminster?" she asked Helen, giving Kate time to recover.

"Keeping the king's peace, collecting taxes to fill his coffers, executing his treaties—all this must continue despite the cousins' conflict," said Helen.

"But is it Richard's peace, or Henry's?" asked Jennet.

Helen sniffed. "Do not think I hesitated to point that out to the dean. 'Would it not be wise to wait here until the matter is settled? You might not even be in the new government. King Richard might purge all his officers in spite. And Henry would most certainly wish to choose his own men.' But he is determined to depart by week's end."

"Yes, he sounded resolved." Kate rose. "And I must be on my way. If I linger much longer, we shall cry on each other's shoulders and the friars will be at their dinner when I arrive." She plucked her hood from a chair near the fire, winning a growl from Claws, who had been guarding it. "I forget. Is Claws the deanery cat, or will she travel with you?"

"With me, my dear. A kitchen is a hellhole without a good mouser." Helen rose to embrace Kate, kissing her cheek. "May God watch over you, and may you find joy in all your days."

"And you, Helen. May God watch over you both."

—⟨∞⟩—

Stepping out of the deanery, Jennet told Kate of her morning's work, observing Bran among the merchant stalls on Ouse Bridge. Winding round the shoppers, waiting until they were caught up in negotiations with a merchant or in heated conversations. Snip, snip and the purse slipped into his tunic. "He does not look to me like a man who believes he is about to make his fortune by returning to the Martha House to steal a golden idol." But she had failed to speak to him. One of his intended victims got to him before she had the chance, drawing a knife on him, discreetly, hidden from the crowd, and threatening to castrate him if he ever saw his face again. "I can outpace most runners, but not a man desperate to save his cock."

They were laughing as they approached the stonemasons' lodge and spied Phillip standing over a grinding stone.

"I want a moment with him," Kate said.

He had already caught sight of them, waving. His face, apron, and hair were white with the fine dust from sharpening a pile of chisels. He set the tools aside, wiping his hands on his apron. It did little good—he left a streak of white across his brow as he raked back his hair. "Did you hear? Helen and the dean are going south?"

"Just now, yes. Had you known they were going?"

He shook his head. "I will miss them. Helen fears it will be a long while before they return."

"I will not be so comfortable about your biding with the Granthams now. You say they are stingy with food."

"That was my story for Helen." Phillip grinned, wiped his nose on his sleeve, leaving more streaks. Like the storied Scottish warriors who painted themselves before battle. "Is Dame Eleanor's Welshman escorting them?" he asked.

"Why would you think that?"

"I saw him there yesterday. Early. And then again last night. Well, I think it was him, red hair in the lamplight."

Kate glanced at Jennet, who shook her head. She'd not managed to track Griffin. The man's talent lay in disappearing, it seemed. "Tell me all that you noticed, Phillip."

He looked at the two of them. "What's wrong?"

"Much is wrong, else why would we have so many soldiers crowding inside the gates?" said Jennet.

Phillip shrugged. "They say many of them are leaving. That knight at your house on High Petergate—Sir Alan? Griselde says he is there all alone now, and she expects him to be gone any day."

Kate shook her head in wonder. "You have your finger on the pulse of the city, living at Hugh Grantham's."

"You might as well if you moved to the High Petergate house when Sir Alan leaves. Then I could see you and Marie and Petra every day."

Or if she moved to a larger house just past Stonegate.

"When you saw Griffin, was he alone?" Jennet asked.

"The redheaded Welshman?"

Jennet nodded.

"Yes. He has always been alone when I have seen him. But last night he was with Dean Richard. In the minster. I was taking some food to Master Hugh. He was working out a problem with one of the stonemasons up above the chapter house. I noticed the dean kneeling in one of the chantry chapels as I passed. When I came back through, Griffin was speaking to the dean. As I said, copper hair in the lamplight."

"Kneeling with him?"

Phillip shook his head. "No, standing, though Dean Richard was still kneeling. The dean bowed his head and crossed himself while Griffin was talking."

"Could you hear what they said?" Kate asked.

Phillip looked askance. "That would be spying."

"Did you?"

"No. Should I have?"

"Did either of them look angry?"

"Both of them. Though I would say the dean was also sad. Bothered. Something like that."

"You've seen Griffin often? Near the deanery?"

A shrug. "Now and then."

"And always alone except for last night?" Jennet asked again.

A nod. "Is he trouble?"

Kate looked at Jennet, who grinned at Phillip. "Not if he's an honest man, eh? Come to dinner tomorrow. Dame Katherine has invited Helen and the dean. Berend will make something special."

"And then you'll tell me what is wrong?"

"By then I pray it will all be right," said Kate.

"So does King Richard, I'd wager," Phillip said with a shrug, then took Kate's hand and kissed it. "I will pray that you move the household to High Petergate." With an impish smile he kissed Jennet on the cheek and shuffled back to take up his work at the grinding wheel. Several times he glanced back over his shoulder, lifting his hand in answer to Kate's wave.

"Wrong direction," said Jennet as Kate turned back toward the deanery.

"I need to know what business Uncle has with Griffin."

⚬⟨⊙⟩⚬

Hands clasped behind his back, Dean Richard was pacing the length of the hall when Kate opened the door, not bothering to knock.

"We need to talk, Uncle."

He paused. "You have made your decision?"

She waved that away. "I understand you and Mother's Welsh retainer have had several meetings. One last night in the minster. Late last night. What is your business with him?"

He brushed dust off the sleeve of his dark robe. "Ah. Griffin. Yes." Head down, he took a few more steps, nodding to himself.

199

Fashioning a good lie?

"He seems determined to extract from me a promise to protect Dame Eleanor. I have explained that I have no armed retainers to offer her, and I leave the city in a few days, but still he persists."

"She *is* your brother's widow."

"More recently Ulrich Smit's widow."

"Is that it? Is the enmity between you and Mother about her remarrying before my father was cold in his grave?"

A hesitation, his eyes sad, and then he gave a little shrug. "Perhaps a little. I do not think David was much mourned by Eleanor."

Kate would be a hypocrite to defend her mother when she, too, resented her hasty marriage. She returned to the matter at hand. "Does Griffin always come alone? Werner is never with him?"

"Who is Werner?" The dean's voice caught slightly. Lying? Worried?

"One of Ulrich's servants. She chose two menservants and Griffin to escort her here with the sisters."

"Werner and Hans." The dean nodded. "I see."

Kate watched how her uncle avoided her eyes. "What do you know?"

"What could I possibly know? Katherine, look to the children and depend on the strong alliances you've made in the city. Move to the house I've deeded you. A large house, large enough for your household . . ."

"And far from Dame Eleanor."

"And near Phillip. He misses you. Perhaps I speak out of my own guilt in abandoning the lad. He has found comfort in Helen's kitchen, and I've enjoyed evenings with him over a chessboard. He has a subtle mind and a quick wit. If he ever wearies of working with stone, I would not hesitate to sponsor him for the Church."

She could not imagine Phillip setting aside his hammer and chisels for the Church. "Tell me about your meeting with Griffin in the minster last night. You argued."

She smiled at his confusion, the high, noble brow furrowing. "We were observed?"

"You were. It seemed an argument, Griffin standing over you as you knelt. What did he want?"

"His message does not vary."

"So he came to you late at night, seeking you out in the minster—how did he know you would be there?"

"I wondered that as well." A flicker of something, so quick that Kate had only a vague impression. "Perhaps he is not what he seems? But his message is always about Dame Eleanor." There was a hesitance in his answer, as if he warred with himself.

"Come dine with us tomorrow, Uncle. Berend would enjoy the challenge of impressing Helen."

The dean bowed his head. "If all is ready for the journey, I would enjoy that. We can discuss my offer in more depth. I will send word to you in the morning, in good time."

They embraced, kissed each other's cheeks, and parted.

"So?" Jennet asked as they turned up High Petergate.

"His story is that Griffin wants his word that he will protect Mother. He will not accept a no, no matter how many times my uncle says it."

"Dame Eleanor has set him to that? That might be what has so irritated the dean."

"That is just the thing. I do not believe she sent Griffin. Nor did Uncle suggest that."

"Would Griffin take it upon himself?"

"God help us. Instead of answers we find more to question." Kate did not choose to tell Jennet about the deed tucked in the slit in the lining of her sleeveless overdress.

The prior's apartments were more simply furnished than Abbot Thomas's, yet the prior himself commanded respect with his aquiline nose, arched brows, and low, resonant voice. His smile was welcoming as he invited Kate to sit. Jennet had chosen to stay out in the yard, listening, watching.

"I am grieved to tell you that the man you seek was injured beyond our ability to save him. He had been stabbed many times and badly beaten," said Prior Norbert. "He died last night, with his friends round his bed."

"His friends?"

"Bran and Carter, two ne'er-do-wells, I must say, yet they were loyal to the end," said the prior. "Robin asked for a woman. Ann? But his friends said she had disappeared. He also asked for his brother Fitch but was told the man had been forbidden to come. By his master."

"Fitch? Lionel Neville's manservant?" Kate wondered aloud.

"Oh?" the prior brightened. "Is Neville Fitch's master? I did not know."

Kate had had no idea that Lionel's manservant was Robin's brother. "Had he any other visitors? Anyone else asking after him? A woman, perhaps?"

"No, no woman, and no one else that I know of, though his friends were keen to discover who brought him to us." At Kate's questioning look, he shook his head. "By the time someone answered the bell, there was only poor Robin. Shall I send for Friar William, the infirmarian? He might tell you more."

Kate declined the offer. Lionel Neville's manservant Fitch was Robin's brother. That was an unpleasant twist. Before she departed she mentioned Friar Adam's visit to her mother's Martha House and asked Prior Norbert to inform Adam that Dame Eleanor had made other arrangements for a confessor. She would not require his services.

A pained smile. "His companion Friar Walter knows better than to encourage such visits. Rest easy, Dame Katherine. You need not fear his return. Adam does not have permission to offer such services. He is old, infirm, and, God forgive me, but he is much confused of late, believing that he has been given a mandate to purge the world of all sin."

"But I understood that he is confessor to Isabella Frost."

"Ah. She visits him often, it is true, but I had not known that he fashioned himself her confessor. I will speak with him, and with Dame Isabella." He bowed to Kate, thanking her for the warning.

"About Friar Adam's confusion. Would he go so far as to tell Robin and his friends to steal something from the beguines Dame Eleanor brought to York in order to hold it up as a pagan idol—to defame them?"

Norbert muttered something under his breath as he glanced away. "He did know something of the three rascals. We employed Carter for a short time."

Another connection. "You did? Is he here?" she asked, her voice crackling with excitement.

"No, alas, he did not work out. Some items went missing." A shrug. "I thank you for reminding me of my duty concerning Friar Adam. And I shall send word to Lionel Neville, requesting his advice on the burial of his servant's brother."

Kate bit back a smile, imagining Lionel's response.

—◦⊙◦—

A sudden squall forced Kate to wait in the prior's doorway, watching black-robed friars bustle past with their hoods up, hands tucked up their sleeves, feet squishing in their waterlogged sandals. As soon as the rain ceased, the sun burst out of the clouds and she needed to shield her eyes against the blinding glare on the puddles and the rain-heavy shrubs lining the walkway as she hurried toward the church, hoping Jennet had taken refuge within. She found her just stepping out from the church porch.

"So. Did you speak to Robin?"

"He died last night."

Jennet crossed herself.

"Bran and Carter were by his side, but not Nan. I don't understand—she loves Robin so. She would have been at his bedside if she could."

"I have not given up the search," said Jennet.

"Perhaps she does not wish to be found?"

A shrug. "Even so."

"Nor was Robin's brother, Fitch, at his deathbed."

"Lionel's Fitch?" Jennet shook her head. "That's a nasty bit of news. Along with Robin's death and the dean's odd behavior, a difficult morning for you."

"Yes, I believe he meant Lionel's manservant. The prior hopes so. He now expects Lionel will take responsibility for the burial."

Jennet snorted. "He might as well ask the Devil for alms."

Kate agreed. "I think it's time I paid a call on my brother-in-law."

They headed out onto Micklegate, passing William Frost's grand house.

"Your cousin will be happy to see the last of the campfires doused," said Jennet.

"It is a wonder that Isabella has not found a way to evict them," Kate chuckled, but her spark of amusement flickered and went out. "I wish I could keep the news of Robin's death a secret. Sister Dina—"

Jennet pressed her heart, shook her head.

They walked through an eerie, rainbow-sprinkled mist as the hot sun sucked the moisture from the street and the houses round them. The Ouse Bridge, with its buildings climbing up to the crest, shimmered in the weird fog, rooftops sparkling. The sun also teased out the stench of the fish sellers' carts, by midday always ripe, but even worse now.

"It's a wonder we can stomach to eat fish," Jennet muttered.

"It's Berend's skill that makes it palatable."

As they passed the council chambers on the bridge, Kate called out greetings to acquaintances but kept most of her attention on the crowd milling round her. And then she caught a flash of movement, a disturbance in the crowd as someone pushed through. "Jennet, look. Over there." Jennet looked where Kate pointed. "Bran?"

He turned for a moment, and when Jennet saw his pretty face, she nodded. "That's him."

Kate followed Jennet as best she could, but Jennet blended skillfully into the crowd, weaving among the folk who were strolling, talking to shopkeepers, greeting neighbors, trying to push their way through, hurrying to make their next appointment, or home. Kate stepped on feet as often as hers were stepped on, trying to stay in Jennet's wake. The odor of bodies first soaked then heated almost gagged her so soon after the spoiling fish, and she stumbled, but Jennet plunged on. Ah-hah! Bran was forced to pause as he cut a strap. Long enough for Jennet to step behind him and lock him in a deadly embrace, pressing a knife against his throat, while with her other hand she twisted the wrist of his beweaponed hand until the knife dropped with a clatter, along with the cut purse. Bran was so poorly trained that he hardly struggled. Jennet easily yanked his right hand behind his back. She whispered something in his ear. He groaned, but moved with her as she inched them off the bridge and down beneath the pilings on the bank. Muddy, but quiet.

As Kate joined them, Bran tried to kick out at her. She kneed him in the groin. He doubled over, Jennet not quick enough moving her knife from his throat. Kate saw the blood on her hand and hoped it was not a deep cut, else he'd be of no use to them.

"I'm bleeding! You've killed me," he gasped.

"Clearly not." Kate pulled him up by his hair, looked at the wound. "It is nothing. Tell me, Bran, why did your friend Robin risk his life to rob Dame Eleanor and her sisters?"

He coughed, spit to one side, cleared his throat.

Jennet grinned at Kate over the thief's shoulder.

"So, Bran?" Kate demanded.

"How do you know about that?"

"Never mind. Who hired you and what were you after?"

"You're Mistress Clifford." He strained to see behind her, into the shadows.

"Ah, you fear the hounds," Jennet said, controlling him with the arm she held behind his back. One strong jerk and he would collapse with the pain of his shoulder popping out of its socket.

Kate took firm hold of his chin, forcing him to meet her gaze, preventing him from looking round to see what was near. "So you fear my hounds? My great war dogs?"

"It was not me who robbed you, mistress. It was Robin, as you said, may he rest in peace." He crossed himself with his left hand.

Bad luck, that.

"Yes, poor Robin. Now, if you tell me what I want to know, I will not set the hounds on you."

"But I—"

"A generous offer," Jennet said in his ear, startling him. "I advise you to take it."

He began to squirm.

"Is there someone you fear more than you fear Lille and Ghent?" Kate gestured as if the dogs were right behind her and she was holding them back.

Bran suddenly eased his squirming. Thinking he might be going limp to slip down, Kate reached out. Noticing, Jennet squeezed him tighter. Kate smelled piss. The fool had wet himself.

"Just tell my mistress what she needs to know and I'll release you," said Jennet.

"Our mate Thatcher offered us the job."

"The one-legged cook," said Jennet.

"That's him. He said we was to be richly rewarded for the books—holy books—and a golden Christ child, from the chests up in the solar. Agnes Dell's solar. We would receive more than we ever made at the staithes or the warehouses."

"He cooked for her," Jennet said.

"She turned him out without warning. And him a cripple."

"Who has done quite well for himself," said Kate. "How did he hear about the items in the chest?"

"That was Robin bragging of his Nan to the soldiers, hoping to join them. The soldiers Thatcher was cooking for."

"So why was Robin sneaking into the kitchen?" asked Kate.

"For the key to the house. Nan had said—Is she all right?"

"I don't know. And then, once he had the key?"

"All he wanted that night was the key. In the morning, when the household went to mass, we would slip in, take the books and the golden doll, and slip away, tossing the key in the grass. Nothing simpler, said Thatcher."

"What happened when you did not succeed?" Kate asked.

"Thatcher warned us to stay away. There were far worse things about to happen there. 'You don't want to be caught,' he said. So we stayed away. Nan is not with you?"

"No," said Kate. "We are worried about her. You do not know where she is?"

"No. God help her."

"What did they mean, 'far worse things'?"

"I don't know. I swear!"

"Who was Thatcher working for?"

Bran shook his head. "He wouldn't say."

"The soldiers he cooks for, they wear no livery. Whose men are they?"

"Don't know. Thatcher never said."

"Was he thieving for a friar named Adam?" Kate asked.

"Where would a friar get such coin to pay us?"

"How did you know you'd be thieving for someone with the money to pay?" Jennet asked.

"He's done well by Thatcher. Fitted him up with a better peg leg." A shrug.

"Not too sure about that, are you, Bran?" Jennet taunted.

"One more thing." Kate stepped closer. "Do not tell Thatcher that we talked. I will know if you do. I've a man in the camps."

"Could not tell him if I wanted to." A shiver went through Bran. "I went to see him just now, to ask about Nan. But he wasn't there. And the soldiers, they pretended they never saw a one-legged cook. Laughed at me. Bastards."

He kicked out instinctively, but Kate caught his leg and knocked him off his feet.

Jennet grinned as she pulled him back up, supporting him until he found his footing. "Wouldn't want the hounds thinking you were dinner, eh?"

"I've told you all I know!" Bran whined.

"Where's Carter?" Kate asked.

"Waiting for me on the other side of the bridge, behind the fishmongers."

Where no one cared to linger. Good choice. Jennet nodded at Kate's look, let him go so suddenly that he collapsed in the mud. She kicked him. "Tell your mates to stay away," Jennet warned. "The hounds will attack anyone who threatens the sisters. They feed them bits from the table. They are their favorite people." She did not look at Kate as she lied.

Bran rose from the mud, fists clenched. "I won't be thrown in the muck by a wee lass like you." The punch never came. He was on the ground with Kate's boot on his chest, Jennet's on a thigh. "I swear, I swear we'll stay away."

"A pity you pulled Nan into your trouble," said Kate. "How did you persuade her to help you?"

"She'd do anything for Robin. Thought he was special, been places, knew things. Promised to take her away." Bran was craning his neck again.

"Goodwife Hawise believes you will do all you can to find Nan and bring her home," said Kate. "She trusts you. Shall I tell her what vermin you really are?"

"I don't know where to look."

"Useless." Kate lifted her boot, brushed off her hands.

Jennet gave his legs a kick before following after Kate, who was whistling as if calling the hounds. Bran scrambled to his feet and ran off over the staithe. Jennet nodded to several men taking a break, sitting on barrels they were unloading from a barge.

"Routed the cutpurse maggot, eh?" one of them called out.

"That's me Jennet," called another.

"Never yours, Cam, never yours. But I'll take credit for the other," Jennet grinned as she hurried to catch up with Kate as she climbed back up to Ousegate.

13

UNEASY ALLIANCES

Kate interrupted Jennet's laughter about Bran's hasty departure with a reminder that telling tales about the hounds was dangerous at the moment, that she could be playing into the hands of the soldiers who thought wolfhounds wasted in the city. But she waved off Jennet's apology. "It worked with the pretty cutpurse, I admit."

As they headed toward home, Jennet asked why Kate had taken such a circuitous route. "Why didn't we just turn up Hertergate from the staithes?"

"That way we would pass the Martha House. I am not ready to face Dina with the news."

"Oh. Of course."

Kate was trying to sort all she had learned, not liking where it led. Worst of all would be delivering the news of Robin's death to Dina, who would take full responsibility, no matter that Prior Norbert had said he'd also been badly beaten. And how to approach her mother about Griffin's meetings with her uncle the dean?

Berend greeted them as they reached the garden. "Muddy hems and damp clothes. Fishing in the rain?" He grinned.

"Pour us ales and we'll tell you a tale," Kate said, calling to Lille and Ghent as she passed the open door of the hall. "They deserve a treat as well, though they were part of it only in spirit." She ruffled the rough fur on their heads, leaning to whisper their praises, then settled on the bench tucked up beneath the eaves of the kitchen. Jennet offered to find a treat for the dogs.

"The bone on the table," said Berend.

Jennet saw to them, then pulled up a stool in the kitchen doorway.

Kate made short work of the first bowl of ale, recounting her conversation with Prior Norbert and their confrontation with Bran in between long drinks.

Berend raked his three fingers through imaginary hair as he listened, straddling the bench beside her. "I agree. It feels as if there is more to this than the theft of holy books and golden idols—Hans's death, Nan's disappearance, petty thieves hired by soldiers. Robin was Fitch's brother, you say? Might Lionel be involved?"

"I mean to pay him a visit. But this does not smell like one of his schemes. Especially with the murder. Lionel is too much a coward for that. How are the sisters?"

"Pleased with the Franciscan. You will find them smiling about their new confessor, Friar Gerald. At least Sister Brigida was when she came to give the girls their lessons. She said Gerald is a scholar, and holds Meister Eckhart in high esteem."

"Bless Jocasta. She listens and provides. Will you return to Toft Green after I've seen Lionel? Perhaps someone will have seen Thatcher. Or Griffin. I don't like it that Griffin and Werner have separated." She told him what Phillip had observed about Griffin and Dean Richard.

"Which one do you distrust?" asked Berend. "Griffin or Werner?"

"I don't know. I'm worried about Nan. Bran had no news of her and no idea where to look. Surely he would know if she were involved in the attempted theft. And now Thatcher's disappeared."

"He might intend to break away from his thieving friends."

"Because they failed at the Martha House?" Kate wondered. "They did bungle it badly."

Berend nodded. "Yes, I want to hear it for myself from the men at the green. But we'll dine before I go to the camps."

Kate nodded. "I've invited the dean and Helen to dine with us tomorrow. He will send word in the morning. I pray he comes. Serve our strongest wine. I want him talking." She rose. "I'll spare the sisters the news of Robin's death until after they've had their meal. First I'll see Lionel."

"Shall I accompany you?" Jennet asked.

"No. I'll take Lille and Ghent."

⚬⚬⚬

Walking up Coppergate to Fossgate, Kate encountered Dame Jocasta and took the opportunity to ask her to spread the word that she was worried for Nan and would be grateful for any news of her. Thatcher as well.

"Fair hair, peg leg?" Jocasta nodded. "I will do so." In turn, she told Kate more about Friar Gerald—he had studied in Paris with several teachers who had known Meister Eckhart. "He was as excited to meet the sisters as they were to meet him." Dame Jocasta stroked Lille's back.

"Thank you for bringing them together."

"I take much joy in it. In truth, I predict that in time all will thank Dame Eleanor for her generosity in bringing the beguines to York. Learned women eager to teach the girls, a gifted sempster with—I sense a depth of spiritual awakening in Sister Dina unlike anything I have encountered before, Katherine. Have you noticed it?"

"I sense a good woman in much pain. My gifts do not extend to loftier realizations."

As they paused in front of Dame Jocasta's house, she asked where Kate was headed.

"Lionel Neville's, to tell his man Fitch of his brother Robin's death."

"Brothers? I never would have guessed. May Robin rest in the peace of God's grace." Jocasta crossed herself. "Then I will not keep you. It is best to arrive before he sits down to dinner." As Jocasta was turning, she paused. "Your mother carries a terrible burden. I cannot guess what causes her suffering, but I pray that Friar Gerald will draw her out. I do not believe she is called to a life of service among the sisters, but for now they are a comfort to her." She patted Kate's arm. "Be patient with Dame Eleanor. You are everything to her."

"You gleaned this in one brief encounter?"

"Some I have gleaned from you. God go with you, my friend."

As Kate continued down Fossgate she puzzled over the sting she had felt in Jocasta's comments regarding her mother. *Be patient.* She tried, but with lives in the balance she found it difficult to accept her mother's secrecy. *You are everything to her.* Kate *was* all that survived of her mother's marriage to David Clifford. But how much of that was her mother's doing? She paused on the bridge, startled by that question. Is that what she thought? Did she blame her mother for her family's troubles? Her brothers' deaths? Walter's death, yes, but Roland's? Geoff's? Of course not.

Father challenged Mother about everything, Geoff said in her mind. *He taught us to doubt her.*

Kate had forgotten. *We were to check with him before doing what she asked. Is that why she took Ulrich as a lover?*

You would be a better judge of that, Kate.

Kate stared out over the Foss, the brown waters calmly flowing down to join the Ouse. Dame Jocasta had given her much to ponder. She shook herself, remembering her mission. Once across the bridge, she must set her mind to how to give her brother-in-law the impression that her sole purpose in visiting was to bring the news of Robin's death to his brother, when of course that was but a small part of her mission. Her mother's landlord. She must tread softly.

Maud Neville, Lionel's eldest daughter, answered her knock and surprised Kate with an enthusiastic embrace. When Simon was alive, Kate had spent many happy hours with Winifrith Neville and her children. She was fond of them all, save Lionel. "You never come! And you never, ever bring Lille and Ghent! Welcome! Mother would like to see them. She is abed. The babe is coming any day now. They can climb stairs, can't they?"

"Yes, of course. But are you certain she will welcome them in her lying-in chamber?"

"She talks of the countryside, you know how much she misses it. A horse would be even better, but lacking that, dogs are the best I can imagine. They will cheer her."

Of course Winifrith would need cheering. She had borne so many children, the house was bursting, and she'd come close to death bearing the last baby. *Blessed Mother, bring Winifrith through this birth with grace.*

Without giving Kate a chance to state the reason for her visit, Maud escorted her and the hounds up the outer stairway to the solar. Lille and Ghent hesitated on the threshold of Winifrith's chamber, the room hushed and stifling, the windows shuttered and a smoky brazier adding to the misery. But seeing them in the doorway, Winifrith called out in delight, urging Kate to bring the hounds to her. Their training overruled their unease.

The expectant mother's usually bony face was swollen and damp, as were the hands that reached out to stroke Lille and Ghent. Kate wanted to fling open the shutters and put out the fire, but it was not her place.

"I would so much rather be lying in somewhere far from the city, in the peace of the countryside, with my own hounds lying at my feet. Bless you for this moment, Katherine, the pleasure of stroking them, remembering my own. Though I suppose you are here to see my husband?"

"His manservant." Kate told her about Fitch's brother and the heavy news she bore for him.

Winifrith waved a swollen hand. "Half brothers, or so they believed. I doubt their mother, the strumpet, knew who had fathered them. But that is no matter. My discomfort makes me spiteful. I am sorry for him. Maud, help me sit up." Winifrith reached out to the dogs.

Kate motioned for Lille and Ghent to put their front paws on the bed so that Winifrith might scratch their necks.

The woman cooed to them as she worked their necks and their ears, taking her time with them, drinking them in. At last, visibly weary, she nodded to her daughter that she'd had enough. "You will find Lionel in the hall. I will make sure he sees to the burial for Fitch's brother. It is the least we can do for his long service in this challenging household."

"Bless you," said Kate, calling Lille and Ghent to her. "Have you a midwife you trust, Winifrith?" Sister Clara was an experienced midwife, though she had not put herself forward as such in the city, fearful lest she antagonize those already caring for the women of York.

"Are you offering one of your mother's beguines? To irk Lionel?" Winifrith sighed. "I weary of his constant battle with all and sundry. The man lost all humor when Simon died. His adored elder brother. He blames you, though in truth I should think it was that whore in Calais who exhausted him. So many unnecessary journeys."

Kate tried to ignore the prick, but it was difficult. "Would you prefer to tell Fitch?"

"No, no. And thank you, but no beguines in this house. I would never be at peace with that man." With a great sigh Winifrith closed her eyes.

Kate could not escape from the stifling chamber fast enough. At the bottom of the stairs she paused, indecisive—find a servant to announce her, or simply enter the hall? She decided on the latter when, through the slightly opened door, she heard Sir Elric's ringing tones. Elric and Lionel. How convenient.

Pushing the door wide, she startled Fitch, who was hovering at the edge of the hall, ready to jump at his master's command.

"Just the man I came to see," Kate said quietly.

The man squirmed in his master's old clothes, always slightly too large for him and absurdly fussy for a servant. He backed away from Lille and Ghent, having experienced their strength once in an unfortunate encounter. "Me? Who is telling tales on me?"

Kate caught both hounds' collars, keeping them by her side. "No one, Fitch. I saw Prior Norbert this morning, and I thought you should know that your brother Robin has died."

A hand to the heart and his pained look were all Kate needed to see. He had heard.

"May he rest in peace," she said, and began to step past him toward Sir Elric and Lionel, who were talking quietly now, their backs to Kate and Fitch. But she paused. "Might I ask who told you about your brother?"

"His friend Carter called this morning. Said Robin had passed at the priory, shriven. I was grateful."

"Had you known he was there, that he'd been injured?"

Fitch glanced toward the hounds. "I might have heard it in the wind, mistress. Not much happens in the city doesn't become gossip."

"Of course. Your mistress assures me that she and Master Lionel will see to your brother's burial."

A frown, sharp shake of the head. "I would not ask for that."

"You need not. Dame Winifrith wishes to do it in respect for your long service. Fitch, your brother had a sweetheart. Nan. Did you know her?"

He shook his head. "I knew little about his life."

By now they had been noticed.

"Dame Katherine!" Sir Elric's voice rang out across the room. "I was just speaking of you. Come. Join us."

She bit back a smile at Lionel's sour reaction, wrinkling his nose and waving toward Lille and Ghent. "If you would permit Fitch to watch them by the door."

The poor manservant looked to Kate for help. She gestured for Lille and Ghent to stay, whispering to Fitch that he would be fine so long as he ignored them.

"We have just been to see Dame Winifrith," said Kate as she approached the two men. "She is so fond of animals, is she not?"

Lionel grunted.

"As the two of you are here, I would like to ask what you think of my neighbor John Paris. Is he trustworthy?"

Lionel's long face tightened with suspicion, an expression that brought his close-set eyes even closer, making him seem cross-eyed. Sir Elric merely tucked his hands behind his back and fixed his gaze on the floor.

"Why ask me?" Lionel inquired.

"You are his landlord, are you not? And employ him as a courier from time to time?"

Lionel squirmed. "Of course. Of course. I've no complaints about the man."

She glanced at Sir Elric, but he continued to study the floor. It was enough that he knew she knew John Paris had a connection with him. "He was mentioned in connection with Fitch's brother, Robin, and who might see to his burial."

Lionel straightened, glancing toward Fitch. "Your brother is dead?"

"He died of injuries suffered in a brawl with soldiers," said Kate. She saw no need to make Fitch tell the tale. "They did him the kindness of taking him to the Dominican friary. Prior Norbert asked me who might see to his burial. John Paris employed Robin at one time. But then I learned of the connection." She glanced back at Fitch with an encouraging nod.

"And Winifrith has assured me you will see to his burial. After all, you were so good to recommend him to John Paris." It was a wild reach, but if she had learned anything from her mother, it was that speaking quickly and making connections that challenged the listener to keep up often resulted in responses of refreshing honesty—spoken in haste to silence her, regretted at leisure long after the damage was done.

"Yes, yes, well, I thought it best to set Robin an honest task, and Paris was happy to oblige. Winifrith promised, did she? Well," a glance at Sir Elric, who now seemed quite interested in the conversation, "of course. Anything to keep the peace, eh?"

It was far more than Kate had hoped. "So. Trustworthy?"

Again Lionel glanced at Sir Elric. "Well, if you have spoken to John Paris, you will know that I did him no favor recommending Fitch's half brother. He's a thief. Was." He crossed himself. "But Paris is a satisfactory tenant."

"Why do you ask?" asked Sir Elric. "Are you considering some trade with him, Dame Katherine? Or using him as a courier?"

"I have from time to time considered some arrangement about his warehouse."

"Business is good?" Lionel asked with interest.

"Not at present, with the soldiers on the roads, the king's men on our ships, but when the royal cousins resolve their differences . . ." She shrugged. "I plan for better times."

"So do we all." Lionel tried to smile, a disturbing business.

Clearing his throat, Elric said he must take his leave. "Remember what I have told you," he said to Lionel, who sniffed as if insulted but nodded, nevertheless.

Kate had noticed that Elric was dressed for hot weather travel, a linen shirt beneath a short, sleeveless leather jacket and leather riding breeches. He might have dressed so to ride into the city, but it was possible the earl had summoned him, and, if so, this might be her last chance to find out what he knew about the troubles at the Martha House. She declared herself ready to depart as well, telling Lionel she wished Winifrith a safe delivery.

As they stepped out into the warmth of midday, Elric said, "Why have you taken such an interest in John Paris?"

"I'm more interested in Fitch's late brother, Robin."

"Ah. And why is that?"

She gave a little laugh, glancing at him to see whether he was aware of what a ridiculous question that was. But he feigned confusion. Glancing round, gauging they were far enough away from the windows and there was no one about who might overhear, she said, "You ask why I am interested in the man who stabbed your man Kevin? The man whom Sister Dina surprised in the kitchen? You insult my intelligence."

As they approached a stone archway into the main yard, Kate signaled the hounds to block Elric's way. When he stepped toward them, Lille growled.

"What is this?" Elric looked at Kate. "You do not want to challenge me."

"Oh, but I do. I want to know why you lied to me the morning after Kevin's wounding."

"I did—"

"You said you'd not yet talked to your men, yet you went straight to St. Mary's Abbey, where your man Kevin lay in the infirmary."

He took a step toward her. "Who—?"

Ghent growled as Lille blocked Elric with her body.

"A man is dead and a maidservant is missing, neither of which might have happened had you told me what you knew that morning. I've wasted precious time gaining the abbot's trust, access to the infirmary—"

"And what have you held back from me?" Elric said. "Frost and Holme and their fellow members of the council sending money to Duke Henry—news I would have expected you to report to me. For the earl."

"When we spoke, I only guessed they had some communication with the duke in Knaresborough. I knew no more than that. And then I hear you've gone to the abbey infirmary, and I find your men guarding Sister Dina at the *maison dieu*. By the time I learned about the funds for Henry I did not think I could trust you." In truth, she had never yet felt she could trust him.

Elric bowed his head. "I see I was in error. I am sorry if—"

Kate shook her head to silence him as the door behind him opened, Maud Neville stepping out, a basket on her arm, a maidservant following on her heels.

"Oh, Sir Elric, did you annoy Dame Katherine? Mind the hounds!" Maud Neville giggled as she swept past.

Elric muttered a curse, but when Maud was gone he apologized for doubting Kate and any harm that might have come from it.

Kate nodded but did not call off the hounds.

"Do you believe the murder of your mother's manservant is connected to the attempted theft?"

"I don't know."

"Perhaps this Robin had thought the man bided in the kitchen of the Martha House."

That was a possibility she had not considered. And she quickly discarded it. Robin seemed to have been acting on information either willingly or unwittingly shared by Nan, who knew there were no men biding on the premises at the time. But Kate pretended to consider it. "Perhaps. In truth I have not yet found the link between the two." Judging that she had made her point, Kate signaled Lille and Ghent to release Elric, and, as they walked out of Lionel's yard, she told him what she knew of Nan's disappearance.

"And your redoubtable Jennet has found no trace of her?" he asked.

She shook her head. "A favor. Could you ask your men to help search for her?"

"I will tell them to come to you with any information." He proffered his arm.

"I cannot—I have two leashes to hold." But she thanked him, and they proceeded toward the Foss Bridge. "You are dressed for travel. Are you going away?"

"Soon, yes."

Halfway across the bridge, they both began to speak at once. He laughed, his usually chilly blue eyes warm, his chiseled features softer. Dangerously appealing. Kate looked away.

"Do you think Lionel put Fitch's brother up to the theft? Is that what you hoped to learn?" Elric asked.

"I am not inclined to suspect Lionel of the deed. I was more interested in how much of what John Paris told me was the truth."

"Are you satisfied?" he asked.

"For the most part. I was curious to find you in my brother-in-law's hall."

"The earl bid me warn Lionel that if he should stir up trouble in York during my absence, he will pay, and pay dearly. It seems the powerful men of the city have offered their support to Lancaster—now is the time for peaceful cooperation. As you know, Lionel has on occasion interfered with the earl's"—a shrug—"spy work in the city. I was also to advise you to send a messenger to the earl at Raby if Lionel should transgress. It seems my lord still hopes to make you an ally."

"You might have thought of that before lying to me."

"Surely you cannot fault me for expecting either your partner Holme or your cousin Frost to inform you of their support for Duke Henry?"

He's right, Geoff whispered in her mind. *Even you were surprised. You cannot fault him there.*

No, I cannot.

She sighed. "I should think I have proved I am your lord's ally."

"In matters you deem safe for your friends." Elric raised a brow. "Am I wrong?"

Kate smiled.

They were back to their familiar sword dance. Soon he would ask about the letters he still suspected she held, incriminating the earl. But Kate was not entirely averse to his request to keep an eye on Lionel. It was in her own interest to keep him in line.

"Of course I will inform the earl if Lionel should transgress. And I am glad of the chance to thank you for keeping watch on the Martha House."

He glanced at her. "It was Kevin's doing. At first. And after that—I did not know whether you would find it annoying or helpful, but I'd heard about Hans, and that Griffin and Werner had disappeared, and thought you could use some additional eyes."

My, he knew much about her affairs.

"I still hope to make amends for my part in your troubles this past winter," Elric added. "And—"

Kate grinned. "Your lord would like his letters."

The skin round Elric's eyes crinkled in his tanned face when he laughed, and his eyes, his broad shoulders . . . Kate was glad of the crowd round them, forcing her to pay attention to where she was walking. She had been far too long without a man in her bed.

"What word of your man Kevin?" she asked.

"I am aware that Berend has talked to him."

Kate nodded. "But have you more recent news?"

"He is healing well. In time, he may recover his strength and faculties. But Brother Martin warns his will be a long healing. I wondered. Might he find a temporary place in your household? So that he might be near the abbey infirmary? Sheriff Hutton is too far. Not at once. He is still confined to bed. But by Martinmas at the latest . . ."

"Of course. He has done much for the sisters. If not mine, I will find him a place in a good household."

Elric thanked her. "And the letters?"

She laughed. "If I were in possession of them, I might be quite disposed to hand them over to you. But as it stands . . ."

"They are of no use to you."

"Then all the better I do not have them."

They had reached Coppergate. Sir Elric paused, turning to her, his eyes warmer than she had expected after that exchange. "My plan is to depart tomorrow. I will leave two men here in the city. Should Lionel cause trouble for you—"

"Where do I find your men?"

She was interested to learn that they were lodged but five houses from her guesthouse, on Stonegate, in the home of a goldsmith. Very near the property her uncle was deeding to her.

"They take their midday meal at the York Tavern, so you might always leave word there as well. And I will not forget to tell them about Nan."

How he smiles at you. And you, him, Geoff whispered in Kate's mind. *Be quiet.*

Elric had begun to take his leave. "Before you go," she said, "what can you tell me of Sir Alan Bennet and his fellows?"

"Ah. A puzzle that intrigues me. No livery. Even those he hosted in your home on Petergate were circumspect, saying only that he had the ear of barons close to King Richard, that he had been sent by them to see that those arriving to hold York for the king were welcomed and honored. Have you any more?"

"No. My uncle sent him to me, yet now vaguely claims he was recommended by friends."

"Richard Clifford, the noble dean of York Minster." Sir Elric clasped his hands behind his back and gazed down at the cobbles for a moment. "He is a slippery one. My lord would give much to know where his loyalties lie."

"I would say with the king, whoever he might be, and with the Church." Kate smiled at Elric's expression, how pleased he seemed. "Yes. Cliffords, Nevilles, Frosts—Northerners all, seeing to family first. Why risk land and status when one royal cousin is much the same as another?"

"They disappoint you?" Elric asked.

"I agree with them, more's the pity. Lives will be lost. And for what?" Bidding Elric good day, Kate clucked to Lille and Ghent and moved on, hoping she did not show her dismay. She had shared too much, let him see her too clearly.

Do you believe that about all such struggles? Do you think we died for nothing? Geoff whispered in her mind.

I wonder, Geoff. I do wonder. And I hate that it might be so.

―⁂―

Dinner sat heavy in Kate's stomach as she took a seat near where Sister Dina sat, examining the swirling pattern on a deep blue brocade. Quietly, Kate told her that Kevin, her rescuer, was on the mend, but that Robin, her attacker, had died. The brocade slithered off Dina's lap as she covered her mouth. She stopped breathing, her eyes registering the enormity of her deed. Kate touched her shoulder, spoke about the rough handling by the soldiers, by Kevin, how there was every reason to believe he would have recovered had he suffered only the wound she inflicted. Kate sensed the other sisters crowding behind her as she spoke, recognized her mother's hand on her shoulder.

Brigida and Clara flowed round Kate and knelt to their friend, touching her, offering her soft words. Kate rose, genuflected at the lady altar, saying a prayer for Dina, Robin, Kevin, and all who were suffering, and then walked out into the sunny afternoon.

"What was the purpose of the intruders?" her mother asked.

Kate had not noticed her following. Turning, she was taken aback by the fear in her mother's beautiful green eyes. "I do not believe they will be back." She shared Bran's account of their scheme, as well as Prior Norbert's promise to see to Friar Adam. "Even Lionel Neville should be on his best behavior for the nonce. Rest easy, Mother."

But Eleanor shook her head. "Someone wishes to discredit us."

"Mother, I've just told you—"

"Of course Robin and his fellows would think it was a simple theft—why would those seeking to discredit me bother to explain that to such simpletons?"

Her mother seemed quite certain it was not over. "How would they discredit you? What is in the books?"

"Nothing but God's word, Christ's teaching. But the Church twists the lessons so that the people are humbled, fearful, so that we crawl on hands and knees to the priests begging for absolution and offer them all our wealth."

What could Kate say? It was no more than what others thought but dared not say aloud. "Are you a Lollard, Mother? Do you renounce the authority of the pope and his priests?" She had heard sermons against the followers of the English theologian John Wycliffe, as well as much quiet agreement among her acquaintances.

"Lollards. Pah. I am merely a Christian who has heard Christ's message of love. But what of Hans? And Nan's disappearance? What did they have to do with the books and the Christ child?"

Good questions, all. Kate had been so busy trying to calm her mother she had forgotten how much remained unresolved. Particularly the murder of Hans. It was possible she was blinded by her insistence on seeking connections. These were troubled times, violence ever close to the surface. But so much coincidence? "I know you do not wish me to ask why you fled Strasbourg after Ulrich's death, but—"

"I did not *flee*, Katherine. You make me sound like a criminal."

Patience, Kate schooled herself. She touched her mother's arm, gently, affectionately. "Forgive me, I did not mean it in that way. What I was suggesting is that you might share all that I have just told you with Griffin and Werner. It might help them in their investigation."

Her mother said nothing.

"I trust that you have the items—the books, the Christ child—safely hidden? No longer in the chests that Nan told Robin about?" Kate asked.

"Do not worry. They are safe."

Kate did not believe her. But challenging her would do no good. So she changed the subject. "Dean Richard is leaving the city. He believes he best serves the realm from Westminster during this—until the royal cousins resolve their differences. Did Griffin tell you? Dean Richard says he explained that to him."

Now her mother turned. "What are you saying? Griffin met with Richard Clifford?"

"Did you not send him to my uncle to request his support?"

"No. What—" She shook her head, looked away. "Griffin seeks to protect me. But from whom?"

"If you would confide in me, I might help you."

"No. No, I do not want this to touch you."

For a moment Kate's breath caught in her throat. An admission, however small and vague, that something was afoot. Gently she asked, "Is that why you will not tell me about Ulrich's death—you fear for my safety?"

"Why do you think this is about his death?"

Because I see it in your eyes, Kate thought. She was certain of it now. But to say that would only push her mother away. "If it is not about what happened in Strasbourg, then what is it that you fear? What task have you set Griffin and Werner?"

Whispering to herself—a prayer? a vow?—Eleanor sat down on the bench outside the garden door and covered her face with her hands.

"Mother?" Kate sat down beside her. "Please, I could help if I knew what troubled you."

With a sharp intake of breath, Eleanor straightened and patted Kate's arm. "I see why you like Jocasta Sharp. She is so kind, so helpful. Friar Gerald will serve very well for us. Bless you, Katherine."

⁘

Kate spent the time after dinner lazing in the river gardens, letting Lille and Ghent explore with Petra and Marie while she sat beneath a linden with Sister Clara. They began in silence, Kate listening to the life of the garden—the birds, a persistent woodpecker providing the rhythm beneath the songbirds' melodies, with insects buzzing about in a wild counter-tempo. Her companion fingered beads, murmuring prayers. Petra and Marie addressed Lille and Ghent in French, dissolving into giggles whenever the hounds regarded them with their soulful eyes, as if asking for translation.

"Children, dogs, a garden, a river. God's gifts for troubled hearts," Sister Clara said, pausing in her prayer. Peering into Kate's face, her own shadowed by her veil, the beguine whispered, "But not comforting enough for you, I see. Is it Hans's death?"

"All that has happened weighs on me, but it is my mother's silence that darkens this sweet moment."

"Silence? Dame Eleanor?" Clara gave a little laugh, but quickly sobered. "I have noticed that she uses speech as if it weaves a protective shell round her. One cannot break through to what is truly in her heart."

Well said. "She hides something that causes her pain. But it is that pain I *must* plumb to understand what is happening here—the murder, the intruder. I need to know what happened in Strasbourg so that I might prevent another death—perhaps hers."

Clara placed a hand over Kate's, pressing it gently. "I will pray for her heart to open to you. You are everything to her."

"You are the second person who has told me that today. But we have ever been at war with each other."

"Not war. I sense nothing but love. It is life that has come between you. If you put all that has happened aside when you come together, you will see only the love, the godhead, heart to heart, soul to soul."

"Beautiful words. I have tried patience, stepping away, waiting—but I see no crack in the shell. She gives no hint of what happened." Kate turned on the bench and took Clara's hands, looking into the eyes that radiated such warmth. She could not imagine how someone could be so unguarded. "Would you speak to her as you just did to me?"

Clara blinked. "I would if I might speak so to her. With Dame Eleanor one must be less direct. I will think what readings might inspire her."

Readings. Well, it had worked with Dina. Kate thanked her, and they resumed their former occupations, Clara praying, Kate worrying, both of them watching the girls, who were down by the water, picking flowers to adorn each other's hair.

Petra and Marie still fought, yet it was clear that they also cared deeply for each other, Kate thought. Perhaps she should spend more time with them, discovering how they managed to have such peaceful moments.

As the afternoon lengthened, Sister Clara rose to go about her duties, and Kate gathered the wanderers and led them home. Too much sitting. In late afternoon, the two great oaks in Thomas Holme's yard cast long shadows across Kate's garden—the perfect time to practice at the butt without being blinded by the sun's glare. The archery might help Kate collect and order her thoughts. Petra and Marie wandered over as she was stringing her bow, fingering the arrows, asking whether it was Seth's father who had fletched them.

"Many of them," said Kate. "Would you like Seth to show you how to do it? I could take you to the guesthouse one afternoon." After guests had departed and before they arrived for their evenings.

"I would prefer to learn how to shoot the arrows," said Petra. "How old were you when you learned?"

"My father had a bow made for me when I was ten, so a little older than you. But my brother Walter—your father—let me play with his old bow long before that. Out in the fields, where Mother would not see. She wanted my hands soft and smooth for embroidery and weaving."

"But you weave."

"I do. And I did with Mother."

"But your needlework is sloppy," said Marie.

"Thank you, yes, it is, and ever will be," said Kate. "So you disapprove of archery?"

"No! If Petra learns, so do I."

"And your soft hands?"

"Matt's cousin Bella has lotions that will keep even a gardener's hands soft and smooth, she says. And you wear those hand and arm guards." Marie plucked at the leather.

"Ah." Kate smiled. Marie's affection for Petra seemed to inspire more curiosity. A blessing. "Your first lesson, then, is stillness. Sit down and be as still as you can be."

The girls, giggling, sank down in the grass just behind her.

Kate paused a moment, eyes closed, quieting her mind. It took longer than usual, but at last she felt the calm spreading out to surround her. She had just reached for an arrow from her quiver when the gate in the hedge swung wide and Eleanor swept through, bearing a bowl.

"Sugared almonds, my dears. Would you care for some?"

Marie and Petra rushed to claim their share, inviting Eleanor to join them on the grass. To Kate's surprise, her mother accepted, settling beside them.

"Are you comfortable there?" Kate asked.

"I am quite content," said Eleanor, patting the girls' hands.

But Kate was not. Her calm was already fraying at the edges with her mother's presence. Eleanor had been furious when Kate's father gave her a bow, a quiver of arrows, and lessons at the butt for her tenth birthday, and she had never changed her attitude. Kate felt her mother's eyes on her now, but there was no courteous way to coax her away, and it was possible that her mother meant this as a gesture of peace. So she proceeded to notch the arrow, draw back the string, aim.

This one is for all the pain between us. She let fly the arrow. Centered. Perfect.

She reached for another, notched it, drew back the string, aimed. *For Hans's murderer.* It landed just to the left of the first.

Your best form despite Mother's presence, Geoff whispered in her head.

Kate ignored him, always worried her mother would sense him. She notched another arrow, aimed. *For whoever put Robin and his fellows up to the theft.* She let fly the arrow, knocking the other two out as it hit the center.

Another arrow notched. Her mother's arrival in York had unsettled Kate's life and that of those she most loved, even her uncle. But Kate loved her. She was her mother, all she had left of her family. Perhaps it was her own reaction to Eleanor that had kept her in the dark about what drove her here. Whom could her mother trust? Had she been betrayed like Kate, who had believed all Simon's words of love, only to hear his cruel will and discover that he had a family in Calais? Had Eleanor discovered that Ulrich was not the man she had thought? Had his death dealt a blow to her love?

She drew the string, aimed. The arrow hit wide of center.

Dame Eleanor rose, brushing off her skirts. "A sugared almond?" She held the bowl out to Kate.

Setting the bow atop the butt, Kate accepted one of the treats as she searched for something to say, something that might bridge the divide, begin to build trust. Eleanor, too, seemed to be searching for words.

Petra and Marie chose that moment to hop up and retrieve the arrows for Kate.

"Tell us more stories about your brothers," said Marie.

"Would you teach me to shoot?" asked Petra.

"Us, teach us," said Marie.

"You are so young and slight," Eleanor said to her.

"My da taught Aunt Katherine when she was just a mite," said Petra. "Tell me more stories about my da. I want to know him."

"Walter," Eleanor whispered, her expression pained. "I—I have work to do," she said, shoving the bowl into Kate's hands and retreating to the gate.

It clattered loudly as it shut behind her.

Kate closed her eyes, taking some deep breaths. The girls were not at fault, and she did not want to snap at them.

"Should I not have mentioned my da to her?" asked Petra. "Is she angry with him?"

"No, not at all. She is grieving her son. Her eldest. You must never doubt our love for him. And you."

"How did he teach you?" Petra asked.

"Please, Dame Katherine?" said Marie, taking her hand. "Show us!"

Such a gesture from Marie was a rare event, not to be wasted. "It takes strength," Kate said, forcing a smile. "You must practice every day to build your strength. Are you ready for that?"

Marie nodded. "I want to be strong like you. Then nothing will frighten me."

"Old Mapes said only a fool fears nothing," said Petra.

Marie rolled her eyes and danced away toward where Lille and Ghent lounged beneath the kitchen eaves. The hounds glanced up at her approach. "With a bow and a quiver of arrows and two war dogs I will fear nothing!"

"You never want to excite them, Marie." Kate grasped the opportunity to give both girls a lesson in the sort of discipline required to train as an archer. Working with the girls usually lifted her spirits, but not at the moment. Her mother's pain and her own part in it weighed heavily.

—⁌~⊙⊙~⌐—

The houses along Micklegate cast long shadows as Berend and Matt approached Toft Green, the elder instructing the younger in demeanor—walk with purpose, not too curious, skirt the clusters of tents, avoid any visible reaction to things overheard.

"Well, what have we here?" Berend said as they passed the first cluster of tents. He nudged Matt, nodding toward the priory wall, the camp circle that was their destination. "Sir Alan Bennet—the knight leasing Dame Katherine's tenement beside the guesthouse."

The knight was kicking a pile of blankets with his foot, then toeing the cold coals of an extinguished fire.

"At the camp where Thatcher was cooking? The men who came for Robin?" Matt gave a low whistle.

"Aye. The soldiers appear to have broken camp. Now what did Sir Alan want with them?"

"Wondering where they've gone? Shall we rush him?"

"And reveal our interest?" Berend shook his head.

He asked a few men about the one-legged cook as they picked their way through what was left of the campsites. Only four clusters of tents left. No one had seen the cook for at least a day, maybe longer. The stragglers were friendly enough until he pointed to Sir Alan.

"The king's man? Who's asking, eh?"

"Who're you spying for?"

Berend asked no more.

"Sir Alan's gone," Matt muttered as they moved away from the last campsite.

"We know where to find him. Nothing to see here." Though Berend did search the abandoned campsite, dreading to find Thatcher's peg leg, evidence that the petty thief had been used by them and then cast aside. Or worse. But there was no sign of any of the men, nary a sharpening stone, a pot, or a jar of spices. As if they had never been there.

They caught sight of Sir Alan on Micklegate and followed him as he walked with seeming purpose, pausing only once, to talk to Severen.

"Now that's an interesting acquaintance," Berend said. "Nan's night-watch friend, the one injured by Hans's assailants." He motioned to Matt to slip closer, see whether he might overhear. He was smaller than Berend, less noticeable. He'd almost reached the two, standing just beyond the fishmongers, when Severen bobbed his head and continued on in Berend's direction. He had just enough time to slip into a crowd clustered round a street musician playing a hurdy-gurdy while his monkey hopped from shoulder to shoulder. As soon as Severen passed, Berend whispered to the woman beside him that the monkey had stolen her earring, then strode on to join Matt, grinning as the hurdy-gurdy stopped amid angry shouts. Bloody fool of a thief to weigh himself down with a costly instrument. Made him hesitate just long enough upon discovery to get jumped on by his victims.

"Could you hear anything?" he asked Matt.

"Too little. Something about all being quiet and departing soon. Nothing telling."

"But that they know each other."

They hurried after Sir Alan as he headed over Ouse Bridge. He turned into the alleyway on Petergate that led to the door to his lodgings. Berend heard him greet Griselde, who was sweeping the entrance to the guest-house. When the knight had firmly shut the door behind him, Berend and Matt strolled up to the housekeeper.

"Bonny afternoon after all that rain," she said, setting aside her broom. "And far fewer armed strangers on the streets. Once that lot goes," she nodded toward the door through which Sir Alan had gone, "I'll breathe easy. Some are already doing so. Master Frost and the widow Seaton will be our guests tonight. Dame Katherine will be pleased."

Berend agreed.

"You two look thirsty. Come to the kitchen and tell me all the news."

Clement nodded to them as they stepped into the kitchen. "Matt, my lad, it is good to see you."

Berend left them to talk while he asked Griselde about Sir Alan's visitors. She had set Seth Fletcher to watching for visitors in the evening, which was when they tended to arrive. But they all wore dark clothing, hats covering their hair and sometimes parts of their faces. Berend told Griselde about the meeting on the bridge between Sir Alan and Severen.

Her round, placid face registered no surprise. "The night watch, yes. They all seem to stop by sometime during their rounds. Seth thinks they are treated to food and brandywine. As they are elsewhere. How they all stay awake till dawn I will never understand."

⚬◦⚬

Laughing as they were caught in a downpour, Kate, Jennet, and Berend hurried into the kitchen, watched with interest by Lille and Ghent, who'd had the good sense to seek shelter with the first drop. The three had lingered out on the bench beneath the eaves, talking quietly while listening for signs of trouble. That was Kate's doing. Or Geoff's. He was strangely present in Kate's mind this evening, worrying, wondering about Eleanor's behavior, itchy with foreboding.

Earlier, Kate had found her mother in the Martha House garden and tried to make peace. "I have invited Dean Richard and Helen to dinner tomorrow. Will you join us?"

Instead of a surprised smile, Eleanor shook her head, a tight shake, more a shiver. "How well do you know your uncle?"

Kate thought about his surprising gift. "Not as well as I might like. He has been helpful." Until Eleanor arrived, she thought. "But we have argued of late."

"You are strong, Katherine. I am proud of you, of the life you have made here despite Simon's regrettable behavior."

"Thank you," Kate said, surprised and moved by her mother's praise, though uncertain what that had to do with her invitation.

"But the girls, the weaponry," Eleanor added. "They are not being brought up on the border as you were, they are city girls. Such knowledge—it will only hurt them when it comes to marriage. Or the religious life."

"They have both suffered much loss," said Kate, "and the indifference of their parents. They both know how unreliable others can be. How important it is to know how to care for oneself."

Eleanor covered Kate's hand with hers. "They have you, my dear. Your task is to prove that to them. That you are always there."

As Mother was not? She was so busy blaming Father for our troubles when we were small she could not be bothered protecting us. How would she? She disdained anything resembling a weapon. Geoff's words were so loud in her head that she braced herself for her mother's reaction.

But Eleanor was patting Kate's hand and talking about Marie's delicate frame, how Petra might benefit from more time with the sisters, learning to be quiet and still.

"Petra is skilled in the art of stillness," said Kate. *Be quiet, Geoff. I do not want her to know you are here.* "Will you come to dinner with the dean tomorrow?"

That tight shake of the head again, the unease in her mother's eyes. "No. No, I think not." Eleanor rose, shaking out her skirts. "It is time for prayer."

She trembles, Kate. What frightens her?

"Did the dean offend you, refusing to be the sisters' confessor?" Kate asked.

Eleanor touched Kate's cheek. "He is *your* family, not mine. I feel about the Cliffords"—she seemed to search for words—"much as you feel about the Nevilles. It is said we marry the families, not the individuals, but that is not true. We are tolerated by the families while there is the possibility of an heir, a son who will bring renown to the name. I lost my sons, you were denied them." A shrug. "I have no quarrel with your *uncle*." She emphasized the last word. "He is nothing to me."

Not true. He is something, and it terrifies her, Geoff noted.

Kate saw it as well. *He is a Clifford. This is about the Cliffords.* Before she could ask her mother if that was so—she might not respond, but her reaction to the question might be telling—Eleanor had changed the subject.

"You should know, Thomas Holme says the sheriffs are making no effort to find Hans's murderer. They presume it was one of many brawls among the soldiers and the men of York that begins in taverns and ale-houses and spills out onto the streets, that he might have been as much to blame as the man who unwittingly killed him. I have never heard such nonsense. Thomas says they care naught because Hans was but a servant, not even a man of the realm, and therefore not worth the bother. He thought, hearing that, I would tell him where Werner is. He said Werner was his servant, his responsibility. But I cannot help Thomas. I've no idea where Werner might be."

"Is that true? You do not know where he and Griffin are?"

"That part is true, Daughter. I deemed it best I knew nothing of their plan, how they intended to find out who murdered Hans, and why."

"You said *that* part. What knowledge did you keep from Thomas?"

Eleanor waved away the question. "I misspoke. A storm is coming—can you smell it? My head is pounding. Of course I misspoke. You must have patience with me, Daughter. I am not so young as I was."

"Werner is with Griffin, and they have a plan?"

A hesitation. "Of course they have a plan. They walked off together, did they not? They must have some plan. We would be lost without a path, an intention, a guide—that is what the beguines have given me, a guide for living." She waved a hand and began to walk away.

There was cunning in her mother's feigned confusion. "Werner has not been seen with Griffin."

A shrug. "They are being cautious. That is all to the good."

Frosts and Cliffords. Her uncle, her mother, both pointed to a rift in the bond of Kate's two families.

Three. The Nevilles.

For once, that lot are not troubling me, Geoff.

Another feud. Will it prove as deadly as ours with the Cavertons? Or the king's with his cousin?

Ever since Kate's conversation with their mother, Geoff had whispered of feuds and imminent danger.

I will wish you gone if you persist, Geoff, she'd threatened at last.

He had been silent since that thought, his absence simply adding to Kate's unease. Lille and Ghent had caught her mood, eyeing anything that moved, peering into the shadows.

Now, Kate tried to shrug off her concerns about that conversation as she rushed into the kitchen, forcing herself to laugh with Jennet and Berend. Laughter cleared the mind. She blinked in the light. The kitchen was bright with lamps and the fire that would keep the bread dough rising through the night. The three moved close to the fire, drying their clothes, grinning at themselves for biding there as the fat drops began. They'd all known that was prelude to a downpour.

"Aimed at us where we sat!" Jennet said with a laugh.

Berend nodded, but he eyed Kate with concern. "All the while we sat out there, you were listening for something. For what?"

How well he knew her. She told them about her conversation with Eleanor, all her pauses, the care with which she chose her words, words that denied the fear so evident in her cold hands, her shakiness. All so tangible that Kate could not even now, in the warmth and comfort of the kitchen, escape the sense that danger was near. She held up her cup for more ale. "And she will not dine with us tomorrow. My uncle distrusts the Frosts, Mother distrusts the Cliffords." She paused there, glancing at her companions, waiting for them to say it.

Berend tilted his head, considering. "A feud between your families?" A slow nod as he left the fire and checked the large bowl in which dough was rising. Standing there examining it, he seemed at peace, as ever he did when going about his tasks. He once called his work in her household his redemption. "But you know nothing of a feud." As he glanced up at her, she saw the lines of care return. Would there ever come a time when there were no cares?

She shook her head. "My uncle never approved of his brother's marriage, and Mother's hasty remarriage further soured his feelings for her. But it is a passing discomfort, surely. I believe this has more to do with the beguines. Heretics, in his mind. Their house founded by a woman who carries the Clifford name."

"And why the theft?" asked Jennet. "What might the Christ child and religious texts mean to the Clifford family? They belong to the beguines, not Dame Eleanor."

"By association?" Kate rubbed her eyes. "I do not see the whys or the wherefores yet, but one thing has occurred to me. My uncle was cordial to Mother at first, almost welcoming, remember? Yet recently, I think quite recently, he must have learned something, received a warning—whatever it was, he resolved to keep his distance from her. And to warn me away."

"He warns you but will not tell you the cause," said Jennet. "He cannot think to win you over with no explanation. Surely if it were merely the beguines, he would say."

"Nor does it explain his gift." Kate told them about the house in Petergate.

"A generous gift," said Berend, giving a little whistle. "It's a fine house."

Jennet softly cursed. "It smells of blood money. What has Dean Richard done?"

"Families do this all the time," said Kate. "It keeps the property in the family."

"Will you sign the deed?" Berend asked.

"It is a clear deed, no conditions. I think I would be a fool to let it slip through my hands. What do you say?"

Jennet shrugged.

"It would be a fine addition to your holdings," said Berend.

"But as for living there . . ." Kate shrugged.

"If you live there, so shall we, eh, Berend?" said Jennet with a conciliatory grin. "But it is not empty."

"Who lives there now?" asked Berend.

"Knights," said Jennet. "Only not so well behaved as Sir Alan's lot. They have spent a great deal at the bawd houses at the edge of the Bedern, paying more than the vicars choral can afford. Poor laddies, they have felt the pinch. They will be glad to see the back of the knights." She rose, stretched her arms, rotated her freckled wrists. "With Matt in the kitchen next door I should be in the house with the girls and allow Brigida to go to her evening prayers. Should I be wary of Griffin? Or Werner?"

"For the nonce, I am wary of everyone but my own household," said Kate.

"Then I shall be likewise." Swinging wide the door, Jennet apologized as a gust of wind sent rain into the kitchen, showering Lille and Ghent before she'd closed the door behind her. The hounds stood to shake off the spray.

"The girls will not like being alone up in the solar," said Kate. But instead of rising, she asked for more ale, then settled back to tell Berend about Geoff and her own conflicted feelings about her uncle.

Berend put a cloth over the dough and stretched out beside her, stroking Ghent's head. "You've plenty cause to wonder at Richard Clifford's behavior. And Dame Eleanor's, Werner's, Griffin's. Even Hans, stealing away to the taverns—something changed him. I wonder whether Werner might explain that. Do you believe Dame Eleanor, that she did not send Griffin to your uncle?"

"I don't know what to believe where Mother is concerned. And Griffin— I think you trust him more than I do."

"I did, but he's given me cause to question my judgment, wandering off as he did. If she did not send him to the dean, what is his game?" Berend sat up and plucked a leaf from her hair, tossed it into the fire. "We need to find him. And Werner."

Kate stared into the flames a moment. "Agreed. Tomorrow morning, you, Jennet, and I will go out in search of them—Griffin might hide his hair with a hat, but he cannot hide his west country speech. Or his brows—bushy, copper-colored. Someone will have marked him. And Werner—his size, *his* speech." Kate set aside her bowl as the wind rattled the shutters. "The girls will be wanting me."

Berend held out his hand to help her up. His was warm, his grip strong.

"Bless you," she whispered, and hurried out into the night.

14

THE STORM

━━─◦⦿◦─━━

A thunderclap and a flash of lightning shook the house, waking Kate. A second flash revealed Petra lying on her back, her eyes wide open, her fingers bending one by one. Counting the distance.

"Close," she whispered to Kate. Another clap. She counted slowly on her fingers. A flash. "Closer."

Do you remember counting our heartbeats? Geoff asked.

He was still with her.

How could I forget? That summer the thunderstorms came rolling in day after day. The Trevors' house burned down. Our great oak.

Marie mumbled something in her sleep, tucked up so tightly against Kate that she could feel the girl's heartbeat.

A sound. Out in the storm. A man crying out?

I heard it, too, Geoff.

"The kelpies are riding the storm," Petra whispered.

Kate kissed her on the forehead. "I will go down and ask Lille and Ghent whether we heard a kelpie or a drunk soldier." Crawling out from beneath the covers, kissing Marie and assuring her that she would be back in a moment, Kate slipped on a pair of shoes, wrapped herself in a woolen mantle, and stole down the steps.

The soft glow from the hearth revealed Lille and Ghent standing by the garden door, their ears moving to catch sounds. Beside them, the loom cast a great shadow on the wall. A movement near the steps. Jennet was sitting up on her pallet, raking a hand through her hair.

"They woke a few moments ago, suddenly, as if they heard something," she said. "How can they hear anything over the storm?"

"You were lying awake?" Kate asked.

"Thunder and lightning. I never liked it. My mates said it was simply God up above tapping flint. That was no comfort to me."

"Petra is staring up at the roof listening for kelpies. None of us feel at ease in such a storm. I'll put Lille and Ghent on their leads and go out, walk round the house."

"I should go with you."

"If you wish. Bring the lantern. All but one side shuttered." She fetched her heavy cloak off the peg by the door and slipped into Geoff's old boots. Only then did she remember her weapons, up in the solar. She was more disturbed by the storm—or the cry—than she'd realized. "I will depend on you," she whispered to the hounds as she attached their leads.

Jennet shrugged into a jacket, tucked a dagger in her belt, picked up the lantern. Hand on the door latch she asked, "Ready?" At Kate's nod Jennet pulled open the door and stood back to allow her out first, with the hounds.

Lille and Ghent trotted out into the garden, Kate following, pulling her cloak close as she bent into the driving rain, chill on her skin. Berend stood in the kitchen doorway, backlit by the hearth light. So he'd heard something as well. Jennet hurried forward to light her way. They proceeded once round the house, Kate's boots squishing in the soaked grass, the dogs shaking off the rain, halting to listen, then trotting on. They crossed to the kitchen.

Berend's clothes were soaked, though he stood beneath the eaves. "I could not tell where it came from," he said. "So I went over to the Martha

House kitchen and woke Matt. We walked round the house, the kitchen. Nothing. He's wakeful now, on the alert."

"Good. We've seen nothing."

"Jennet could have done this."

"I needed to see for myself." She nodded to him and called to the dogs. They strained on their leads, wanting to track behind the kitchen. Already soaked, Kate did not begrudge one more circuit. They sniffed at the fence in the back corner, John Paris's fence. His midden was on the other side. "Rats," she said to Jennet, who nodded.

They sloshed back to the house.

Jennet stoked the fire. "I doubt I'll sleep more tonight."

Kate shook out her cloak, spread it out on a bench near the fire, put her boots near the hearth. Lille and Ghent shook themselves out, then settled where the fire would dry them.

"You honestly think it was rats?" Jennet asked.

"Not the cry. But Lille and Ghent's interest, maybe." Kate yawned. "I will try to sleep a while longer." She climbed wearily up the steps.

Petra was sitting up, Marie's head in her lap. "Was it kelpies?"

"Rats, I think. And drunken soldiers finding their way home in the storm. We checked round our house and the Martha House. All is quiet."

⎯⎯∞⎯⎯

"Murder! Murder!"

Kate opened her eyes. Petra and Marie bolted upright, holding each other. It was just dawn, pale light coming through the chinks in the shutters. Her heart pounding, Kate slipped from the bed, fetched her clothes. "Stay put," she commanded the girls as she dressed hurriedly, collecting both dagger and axe after such an awakening, tucking them in the slits Jennet had sewn into her skirt.

Someone pounded on the door just as she made it down the stairs to the fire, where Lille and Ghent awaited her. Kate held the hounds by their collars as Jennet opened the door. It was Sister Agnes, her face red, her eyes bulging, her white nightcap askew.

"Dame Eleanor says come at once, the sheriff's man is at the house and John Paris is threatening the beguines."

"Stay here with the girls, Jennet." Kate slipped the leashes through the hounds' collars and followed Agnes. God bless, at least the rain had stopped and much of the standing water was already soaking into the ground.

Berend met them in the yard. "I heard what she said. Matt's already gone to see what this is about."

In the Martha House garden Clara and Brigida hovered round Dina, who was sobbing out a prayer of contrition for bringing all this trouble down upon the house. One of the sheriffs' sergeants was trying to coax John Paris away down the alleyway toward Hertergate. Kate was about to follow when her mother stepped out of the hall, hugging herself, weeping. Nodding to Berend to go on, Kate approached the cluster of sisters, asking Clara, who seemed the calmest, what had happened.

"Our neighbor rushed into the hall while we were at prayers, demanding that we remove our devil work from his property."

"Devil work? Benighted dullard. That is his wife, Beatrice, poisoning his mind." She noticed her mother heading down the alleyway. "I will see for myself. Stay here," she told Clara. "Comfort Dina and Brigida. Assure them that no one will believe you've done anything to cause whatever has upset John Paris." Calling to Lille and Ghent, Kate went after Eleanor, catching up to her as she stepped through John Paris's gate. "What happened, Mother?"

Eleanor turned to Kate, grasping her arm. "He is mad. His man Alonso discovered a body lying by the midden. Paris raised the hue and cry. He says it is Werner. Dear God, I pray he is wrong. How would he know him? It cannot be him. No, John Paris—the man is quite mad. The day we moved into the house he complained about the wagon blocking Hertergate. I sent Werner to threaten him. Oh dear, I suppose he would recognize Werner. Dear God."

She was babbling, but the pieces were helpful. "What did the sergeant want?"

"To take John Paris back to his house. He is blaming us for this, when it is clearly not our fault. He says we do the devil's work. The man is quite, quite mad."

Kate put her arm round her mother. "Perhaps you should stay at the Martha House with the sisters. I will see to this."

"If it is Werner, I will claim the body, Katherine. He watched over us on our journey with never a complaint." Eleanor shook her head and crossed herself. "And Griffin as well. I pray he is safe."

Kate could see her mother needed to see for herself. She steered her toward a small crowd hovering round the midden, Berend among them.

"Oh, God help us," her mother muttered, pulling a scented cloth from her sleeve.

Berend came to them. "Perhaps it is better you do not see him so, Dame Eleanor."

"She needs to," said Kate. "To be certain it is him."

Eleanor strained to see past Berend to the figure on the ground. "Is it Werner?" When Berend bowed his head, Eleanor struggled free of Kate and hurried forward.

Lille and Ghent danced on either side of Kate, restive. "You knew, my angels, you knew." Lille looked at Kate, her large brown eyes sad, knowing. Ghent nudged her hand. She stroked them.

With a moan, her mother fell to her knees in the mud and bowed over the body, keening her grief.

Matt, who had been exploring along the back fence, started toward her, but Berend was there first, helping Eleanor rise.

The hounds flanking her, Kate approached the corpse, whispering a prayer to steady herself so that Lille and Ghent might remain calm as she moved close enough to see Werner's injuries. His throat was slit, his head thrown back so that the gaping wound looked like a mouth opened wide in a silent, eternal scream. He was unshaven, his hair wild, his clothes muddy. With the tip of her boot Kate lifted Werner's shoulder. It looked like dried blood mixed in the muck on which he lay. So he had likely been here, in the yard, when attacked. The noise that woke her in the night. His attacker perhaps crept up from behind, one stroke of a sharp knife, then eased Werner down onto his back. Someone strong. The murderer's clothes would be stained with blood. They might look for that. But clothes could be changed, disposed of.

"You, madam," John Paris jabbed a finger at Eleanor, "you have brought this on us!" Red in the face, his tunic askew, his hair matted on one side from sleep, Paris looked like the madman Eleanor had said he was. "God help me. What will Thomas Graa think?" he whined more quietly.

"Thomas Graa will commend you for raising the hue and cry," said Kate. "But not for calling down curses on a widow and the poor sisters."

One of the sergeant's men restraining Paris gently suggested that Eleanor withdraw to her home. "My men will bring the body to you when the coroner has recorded the death and the circumstances of discovery."

"One of the men has gone for Friar Gerald," Berend told Eleanor. "You will wish to be in the hall when he arrives." To Kate he suggested that he take Lille and Ghent and walk them along the fence.

To Kate's relief, her mother agreed to return to the house. Handing Lille's and Ghent's leads to Berend, Kate put her arm round Eleanor's shoulder. "Come, Mother."

Eleanor leaned into Kate.

⁓⊙⊙⁓

"It was just as Ulrich looked when they pulled him from the river. Whoever did this—" Eleanor sank down onto her bed.

A memory of Ulrich's death? Drowned? An accident, or . . . ? Kate felt sick to think they might have prevented this if only . . . Damnable woman! She wanted to shake her mother and demand answers. But this was not the moment to press her. "Let us remove your wet clothes before you settle, Mother." Kate helped her back up, unlacing her gown, trying not to touch the stains—they stank of the midden.

"I told David the border country was no place to raise children." Eleanor's voice was but a whisper, as if speaking to herself. Kate leaned close to catch what she said. "All would have been so different had we come south."

One moment of clarity and then this. Kate felt the familiar tightness in her stomach from her mother's seemingly random explanations. *She will come to the point,* she told herself as Eleanor grasped her shoulder for support, then stepped out of the gown and pushed it toward the door with her stockinged foot. *Patience.* Padding over to a large chest, Eleanor drew out another gray gown, of fine wool, and held it out to Kate for her help. As Eleanor worked her arms into the sleeves, Kate heard Berend down below, then footsteps on the landing, a knock. She called to whoever it was to come in.

Her mother's maidservant looked askance. "You had only to call me." Kate assured Rose that she was capable of helping her own mother dress.

"Is Friar Gerald here?" Eleanor asked.

"Yes, mistress. He awaits you down below. Dame Jocasta is here as well."

"Have they brought Werner to the hall?"

"Not yet, mistress." Rose bobbed and departed, carefully closing the door behind her.

"Leaving him lying in that stench—it is not right, it is not—" Eleanor covered her face with her hands. "So like Ulrich." She began to sob.

In life Werner looked nothing like Ulrich Smit, but clearly he did so in death. Was this the murderer's intent? To remind her of Ulrich's . . . murder? Kate hurriedly finished lacing the front of her mother's gown, her fingers fumbling as she searched for what she might say to encourage her mother to confide her grief. "How cruel to remind you of your sorrow," she murmured as she began to help Eleanor to a chair.

But Eleanor pushed her away. "I will go down and pray with Friar Gerald and the sisters."

No! "What did you mean, that Werner looked so like Ulrich, Mother?" Kate blurted out. "Was your late husband murdered? His throat cut?"

"Of course that is what I meant. And then they threw him in the river." Kate felt ill. "Who?"

"We will discuss this anon. Now come. We do not want to keep them waiting."

Biting back a curse—John Paris's lunacy was nothing to her mother's— Kate forced her voice low. "Let them wait. This is important, Mother. Ulrich was murdered? Why? Do you know who killed him? Were you in danger as well? Is that why you fled Strasbourg?"

"You and your incessant questioning. The rest will wait, Katherine. Do not be so selfish!"

Kate watched with despair as her mother swept out the door. Ulrich Smit had been murdered. That changed everything.

15

REQUIEM

———⟨∘⊙∘⟩———

Candles and oil lamps lit the altar and circled down round the corpse laid out on the floor before it. Eleanor and Jocasta knelt on prie-dieux, praying, while the gray-robed Friar Gerald knelt on the floor beside the body, within the circle of light. The sisters stood behind the prie-dieux, heads bowed, chanting a litany, their voices soft.

Kate and Berend stood just within the garden door. He'd already told Kate that Lille and Ghent had found nothing, the storm having washed away the scent, though the hounds seemed keen to continue on to the staithe. Matt had offered to go search for a boat on the far bank. An aunt lived near there, and he knew the folk who lived near the bank. If someone had noticed anything in the night, they would tell him. Berend had thanked him and sent him off, for which Kate was grateful.

Outside the circle of light, the shadows lengthened as the clouds darkened the day. Another storm—Kate had sensed it coming, the heaviness of the air, the stillness. She closed her eyes, hoping the ritual might quiet her thoughts. This moment was for grief, for prayers for Werner's soul,

nothing else. But her mind continued to spin with the questions and possibilities stirred up by her mother's revelations. Above Kate, heavy drops
began to hit the roof. Pat. Pit pat. Pit pat pat patter. Quickly growing to
a loud drumming. Out on the street, a man loudly cursed.

Friar Gerald's voice rose in prayer and the novice assisting him, just a
youth, he seemed, stepped out of the shadows beside Berend and moved
forward, adding his high voice to those of the women as he entered the
circle of lamps. Friar Gerald rose, took a cup of oil from his assistant,
and sprinkled it over Werner. He had died unshriven, but perhaps his
spirit lingered. Kate stepped away from Berend as Gerald and the novice
approached. Friar Gerald made the sign of the cross over Kate and Berend,
and then he and the novice took a seat on a bench near the door.

The service over, Eleanor directed Rose to open the shutters so that the
sisters could see to clean Werner and then sew him into the shroud. The
flames danced wildly in the draft from the storm.

Jocasta rose to greet Kate. "I came to see whether they were happy with
Friar Gerald, and found my answer in that they had already sent for him
in their need. Dear God, such a need. What more must they endure?" She
crossed herself. "I feel blessed to be given this opportunity to help these
gentle sisters, to support them in their grief, to join their beautiful voices
lifted in prayer. And especially to comfort Sister Dina, to assure her that
the murders are not the result of her courageous act. I will assist them in
preparing his body after you have seen what you need to see."

"And Friar Gerald?"

"He awaits the wishes of Dame Eleanor."

As do we all, Kate thought.

The maidservants were snuffing the candles not needed by the sisters
and setting them on a table to trim. The lamps flickered on the altar.

"If we might move him closer to the light from that window before
you sew him into the shroud," said Kate. She turned to the younger friar.
"Would you help Berend do so?"

Both Gerald and his novice rose to assist Berend. The men worked in
silence, moving Werner, then tenderly unwrapping him. A cry of pain from
Kate's mother shattered the quiet moment. Sister Dina was the first to go
to her, cradling Eleanor's head against her breast and whispering to her.

Kate crouched down to examine the blood-encrusted slash in Werner's neck.

Berend knelt opposite, watching her.

She nodded to him that she was able to do this. With care she straightened Werner's jacket, noting the bloodstains and the mud and muck from where he had lain. Following down the sleeves to his wrists, she found no sign of ligatures. Opening his jacket, she noted to Berend that his shirt was filthy. Whatever he had been doing, he had not considered it necessary to wash and tidy himself. He wore thick hose, warm for summer. Sleeping outside?

"He's been in the water." Berend pointed to the discoloration that rose halfway up his thighs, and the sad condition of his shoes.

There was some bruising on one ankle, bad bruising. It would have been painful to walk. He might have limped. What had this man suffered before his death? Had he known he was next? For clearly this was a pattern—Ulrich, then his servants. Was Griffin next? Where *was* Griffin?

Sister Clara joined them, holding out a pair of scissors. "To cut away his clothes so we might wash him. Shall I?"

Berend held out his hand. "I will do it."

Clara bowed and handed him the scissors. But she did not withdraw. Kate touched her arm. "He was your friend?"

"On our long journey he saw to our safety, and I am grateful."

Both turned to watch as the long, slender blades cut through the rough fabric of Werner's clothes, revealing a well-muscled body riddled with sores. Kate reached out to touch them, then looked more closely at the undergarment he wore beneath his shirt. "A hair shirt. Penance," she whispered.

Sister Clara crossed herself, and, as she bowed her head, a sob escaped her. "Such a good man."

Kate wondered. A good man? Or had he donned the shirt when he feared for his own soul—perhaps his own life? Many turn to piety in fear, including her mother.

A gust sent the lamps sputtering as someone opened the garden door. Kate turned and, seeing Sir Elric with Phillip, hurried to greet the newcomers. That they were together made her heart race. More trouble. She embraced Phillip, then anxiously looked him over. His workaday tunic and breeches were soaked from the downpour. To be out in the storm, and after such a murder.

"We must get you out of those wet clothes," she began.

Phillip shrugged out of her grasp. "Not now."

Sir Elric was shaking his head as he looked toward the sisters kneeling over the corpse. "Another death."

"Werner, the other servant," said Berend. "Murdered. His throat slit."

Taking off his hat, the knight crossed himself. "By the rood, this is an evil business. I was on my way with news of my own when I caught sight of young Phillip hastening in the same direction." He nodded to the boy. "Tell them."

Phillip shifted on his feet, water seeping onto the floor from his wet shoes. Tempted to suggest he remove them, Kate bit her tongue.

"I wanted to tell you before I began work—Griffin met with Dean Richard again last night, and this morning, when I went to the mason's lodge, the dean's carts were gone. The men said Dean Richard and Dame Helen left just after sunrise."

Werner was murdered and her uncle fled. Is that how it was? But why? "Uncle Richard met with Griffin in the minster?"

Phillip nodded. "Again, it was late. Master Hugh is worried about a settling in a corner of the east end, so he is up late every night with the other master masons working on a solution. Dame Martha wanted him to have a cloak and a flask of brandywine to warm him—the stones of the minster keep it cool, and drafty at night. As I passed through the nave I saw Dean Richard and Griffin sitting in one of the chantry chapels again, talking softly. The dean seemed upset."

"And Griffin?" Kate asked.

Her mother glanced up from her prayers, watching them.

"He looked weary," said Phillip, "rubbing his face as if to keep himself awake." The boy's attention kept straying toward the sisters cleaning Werner. "Do you think Griffin knew? Was he telling the dean of the murder?"

"I would have expected Griffin to tell Dame Eleanor rather than Dean Richard," said Kate. Her mother rose. "How late was this?" Kate asked.

"Before midnight," said Phillip.

"Then they met before Werner was attacked," said Kate, assuming that what had wakened her and the hounds in the night had been the moment Werner was murdered. Had Griffin and her uncle met to plan it? An unwelcome suspicion. Kate thanked Phillip for bringing the news. "Go to the kitchen where it's warm. Dry yourself—"

"I'm not a child," he grumbled.

Reluctantly, Kate desisted, instead turning to Phillip's companion. "And you, Sir Elric? What is your news?" From the corner of her eye she observed her mother approaching, her head tilted as if straining to overhear their conversation.

"My men report that Sir Alan left your tenement early this morning, his esquire and manservant with him, carrying their packs. Moving with stealth. At Toft Green he met up with the men Thatcher had been cooking for—though Thatcher himself was not in the party. They headed out the gates just ahead of your uncle's carts. Or with them. My men say they all seemed to know one another."

Sir Alan? Is that why he wore no badge; he did not wish her to know that he was a Clifford retainer? She glanced at Berend, who was staring down at the ground, shaking his head. Eleanor stood directly behind him, craning her head forward. Why would her uncle wish to hide Sir Alan's affinity from her?

"I am surprised to learn that my uncle might be traveling with Sir Alan," said Kate.

"So much early morning activity after a murder in the night." Elric shook his head. "Though I cannot yet see the connection, I cannot help but think one led to the other."

Eleanor finally spoke up. "Ever since I saw Sir Alan in High Peter-gate I have been certain it was not the first time we met, but I could not remember where it might have been. Now I do. He was one of the retainers escorting your father's cousin Thomas, Baron Clifford, to our hall years ago, on one of his last visits before his death. Sir Alan was clean-shaven then, a rather handsome young man." Eleanor touched Sir Elric's arm. "When your men saw the travelers by Micklegate Bar, did they have a woman in their company? Nan?"

"My men said nothing of a woman. It is possible she was in one of the carts."

Kate wished her mother had shared her suspicions about Sir Alan earlier. Why wait until now? "What else do you suspect, Mother?"

"I fear Griffin has uncovered a Clifford plot against Ulrich's men and he is in danger. Help him!"

"A Clifford plot against Ulrich's men? Did you suspect this all along? But what had my uncle to do with your late husband?"

"Not necessarily your uncle the dean, but the family. I—I have feared this."

Most infuriating of women. All this time she had feared—what? "Precisely what do you think happened?"

Eleanor shook her head but said nothing.

"Why did you not—" Kate bit her tongue. Not now. She looked to Elric and Berend. "We must follow them. I want to know what they are about. Or what they have done."

"Katherine, is that wise?" Eleanor asked. "Let Sir Elric and his men go after them."

Kate could not look into her mother's eyes. She would spit at her. "Wise or no, I am going, Mother."

Elric bowed to Kate. "If you mean to catch up to them, we must make haste. I can have horses awaiting you outside Micklegate Bar within the hour. Provided I ride with you. And Berend?"

Kate nodded. "Berend as well."

"What about me?" Phillip asked.

Kate wanted to tell him to stay here, get out of his wet clothes, but she did need him. *My Lord, watch over him.* "Return to the minster yard," she said. "Watch the deanery. If you see any sign of Griffin—" She looked to Elric.

"My men are searching the house Sir Alan vacated."

"You took it upon yourself to search the house? Why all this interest?" Kate demanded.

"Forgive me, but it seemed wise to make certain the missing maidservant was not tied up, left there to starve. The earl charged me with keeping peace in the city."

"And to make note of the knights' alliances, no doubt," said Kate.

"That as well." Elric turned to Phillip. "I have men standing watch at St. Mary's Abbey—in case someone wants to silence my man Kevin. Go to them with any news."

Phillip nodded. "I will."

"Who will see to us?" asked Eleanor.

"Jennet will be next door, guarding Marie and Petra," said Kate. "Shelter in my house if you feel unsafe."

"And the hounds?" asked Eleanor.

"They will come with me," said Kate.

"I suggest you keep Friar Gerald here, Dame Eleanor," said Elric. "The threat of a curse will scare off the likes of Bran and Carter. All the others are leaving—the knights and soldiers are clearly on their way to wreak havoc elsewhere."

Dame Eleanor sniffed at his reassurance, but prayed aloud that God would watch over them, and then withdrew.

As Kate, Berend, Elric, and Phillip moved out into the garden, they were hailed by a breathless Matt rushing round the corner of the house from the alleyway, limping slightly. He rested a hand on Berend as he bent forward to catch his breath.

"You found something?" Berend asked.

A weak nod. "A small boat belonging to my aunt Alice." He took a few more deep breaths before straightening. "She has been in a fury since the soldiers crowded onto Toft Green. On recent mornings she has been finding her boat left far from its usual spot, and sometimes it's not there at all, but on the far bank. A cousin who works on the staithe rows it back. So my aunt and her sweetheart set up a watch, and last night, during the storm, they recognized one of the men who pushed off into the river with it. He is, of late, lodging nearby. They saw him a few days hence with a buxom woman who was loudly arguing with him as he pulled her up the stairs to his room. He has red hair, with the speech of the Welsh archers, my aunt says."

"*Raro breves humiles vidi ruffosque fideles,*" Sir Elric whispered.

Elric knew Latin. Kate would never have guessed. She looked to Phillip to translate.

"It is an old Latin saying. 'Proud are the short, and untrustworthy the red-haired.'" Phillip ducked his head at Elric's surprised nod.

"You've suffered that taunt?" she asked her ward. In the gloom of the day his hair looked brown, but sunlight fired the coppery strands. And he was short and slight, like his sister. Not at all like his Neville father.

Phillip shrugged. "The older boys think I know no Latin."

She must think of a good retort for him. Perhaps she should confer with Elric.

"So you think the red-haired scoundrel is Griffin?" Kate asked Matt.

"Who else?"

"Can you take us to his room?"

"I can. Hugo, my aunt's intended, is watching. He's a big man and he does not mind a scuffle. Works with my cousin on the staithes."

"What do you want to do?" Elric asked Kate.

Get to Griffin before you do, she thought. Aloud she was more diplomatic. "Prepare the horses. Berend and I will accompany Matt with the hounds to Griffin's lodging, then meet you outside Micklegate Bar."

"And if you find the Welshman?" Elric looked as if he'd heard her thought.

"I will ensure that he cannot follow."

The knight understood. "I will await you outside the walls. *Bonne chance.*"

⌖

Built so close to the edge of the tidal flat that when the river swelled with runoff from the high moors it stood in saturated mud, the house leaned into its neighbor, the base of the steps rotting.

A short, stocky man emerged from the shadow of the house beside it, nodding to Matt, who introduced him as Hugo, his aunt Alice's intended. He eyed something on Kate's chest, and she realized that she had folded back one side of her summer cloak, revealing the bow and quiver beneath.

Covering the weapons as best she could—there was no need to flaunt the fact that she was armed, not with the city so tense—she thanked him for watching the house and asked if he had seen the Welshman this morning.

"I have. He returned early but left again almost at once, looking round as he walked off, as if he felt me watching him. I kept well to the shadows."

"Did he use the boat last night?"

"Aye. In the storm, can you believe it? I almost did not watch, thinking no one would take such risk."

"You did not confront him?"

"Didn't like the looks of him. I've seen what happens to those who take on the armed men from the camp. Now we have a description of him, we were going to report it. Let the sheriffs deal with him."

Kate described Werner and asked whether Hugo had ever seen him at the house, or in Griffin's company.

"The first time, when he talked to the landlady about the room, he did have another with him. It might have been this man. Henna—the landlady—said he did not speak, and the Welshman said it would be just himself staying there, with his woman."

Griffin—and Nan? So where had Werner been staying? Kate recalled the signs that he'd not washed, perhaps slept rough. But why? What was their scheme? Was Griffin now on the run for his life? And what did Nan, if it was her, have to do with it?

Hugo offered to help search the chamber. Kate said they needed him to stand watch down below, with Matt. If trouble approached, he was to start up the steps—calmly, without raising an alarm. The hounds would hear his approach and warn Kate and Berend.

Berend took the steps slowly, minimizing the telltale creaks, Lille right behind him, then Kate, then Ghent, who would snap at anyone trying to sneak up behind. At the top, the door was barred from the outside, secured with a padlock. Berend put his good ear to the door, shook his head. No sounds. He motioned for Kate to let Lille come forward. Lille sniffed, then pawed at the door. No laid-back ears, but she whimpered, which meant she sensed no immediate trouble, but something was not right. Kate let Ghent come up beside Lille, holding them ready to enter the chamber. Berend crouched down, picked the lock with a wire, then eased the bar out, setting it aside. He pressed his ear to the door again, listening, then, nodding to Kate, he rose and eased it open.

A thump and a woman's muffled cry.

The room was dark. No windows. Kate cursed herself for not thinking to bring a lantern. Berend identified himself and his companions. Kate released the hounds' leads so that they might move into the windowless room, guiding Berend to the source of the sound. Ghent made a soft sound of recognition.

"I'm removing the rag over your mouth now." Berend spoke in a soft, calming tone. "Quiet, I pray you. I know you will want to scream out all your anger, but I do not advise it. We want to take you away from here without raising an alarm, eh?"

"Bless you," Nan's voice cracked.

"I'll cut the ropes now and carry you out," said Berend. "You will want to rub your wrists and ankles when they are free, but wait if you can until we clean any abrasions and bandage them."

"Who did this to you?" Kate asked.

"The Welsh traitor," Nan croaked. "Griffin." Nan's voice was weak, though not her spirit.

"Traitor? Traitor to whom?"

"Dame Eleanor, and all of us. Can't talk. So dry."

"You will have water soon. And food," Kate assured her.

Berend scooped Nan up. "Put your arms round my neck if you can."

"Only take me from this place," Nan whimpered.

Kate withdrew to the landing with the hounds. As Berend brought Nan out into the light, Kate saw that she was filthy, her clothes muddied and torn, her hair sprouting a spider's web and who knew what else. She touched the woman's back, assuring her that she was safe now. To be trussed up and locked in that windowless room, not knowing if she would die there, alone, unshriven—Kate silently cursed Griffin as she followed Berend down the steps. Ghent descended alongside, as if to support her. She rested her hand on his back, appreciating the bond. "Some things are worse than murder," she whispered, as if he could understand.

Down on the street, Matt cursed softly. "What has he done?"

"Might your aunt care for Nan until we return?" Kate asked.

He assured her she would. "Poor Nan," he whispered.

"We'll do whatever you require, Mistress Clifford," said Hugo, offering to take Nan from Berend.

"No need," said Berend. "Lead the way."

Two doors down and up a short flight of steps, he led them into a large room with a stone fire circle in the center and pallets piled in a corner. Five children rose from their play to stare at the newcomers.

"Alice, we have the care of this poor woman until Mistress Clifford returns for her." Hugo gave a little bow toward Kate, who introduced herself and Berend. "She needs water," she said from the doorway, still holding Lille's and Ghent's leads. "Her name is Nan. My mother's maidservant."

Alice was a small, slender woman, her face beginning to line with age, her dark hair caught up in a kerchief. With a nod, she called, "Kit, water!" One of the children went running to a pail in the corner. "You may entrust her to us, Mistress Clifford." Alice took the cup from the girl and directed an older boy to drag one of the pallets toward the fire circle. Eyeing Nan as Hugo helped Berend settle her, Alice muttered, "God help us, is that what he was at? Are you injured?" She bent to Nan, helping her sip some of the water.

Three younger children, two boys and a girl, rushed toward Lille and Ghent. Kate knelt to intercept them, explaining that they must keep their distance at first, let the dogs become accustomed to them. "They are here to protect me. Think how you feel after a fight. Still ready to pounce. So do they."

Round-eyed, the three backed away. Though the cloth of their clothes was old and worn in places, they were clean, healthy, and courteous. She promised each of them a sweet when this was all over.

"Just now we must find the man who hurt Nan."

Three fair heads nodded.

"My wrists and ankles burn," Nan whimpered, tears running down her cheeks as she squirmed and scratched her head, crying out when she felt the knots and spiderweb.

Alice snapped her fingers at the youngest boy. "Comb!" She stroked Nan's forehead. "We will see to your sores and get the debris out of your hair. You are safe now. Kit, put some broth in a bowl, move sharp, child."

The girl, about Marie's age, busied herself by the pot hanging to one side of the fire.

CANDACE ROBB

Leaving her bow and quiver by the door and handing the hounds' leads to Matt, Kate carried a small stool over to sit near Nan, taking the bowl of broth from Kit with thanks. As she helped Nan take a sip, Kate asked her when Griffin had last left her.

"This morning. Still dark." Nan took another sip. "He said sorry for leaving me there to die. But he locked me in." Her bottom lip trembled.

Alice clucked softly to her, smoothing her hair, as Kate helped her to another sip.

"And Werner?" Kate asked.

"I haven't seen him." Her breath was a painful wheeze.

"Have you had any water, any food?" Kate asked.

"A little water, but I tried to scream and bit him, hard. Then he gave me nothing. It's been a day? More?"

Griffin was injured. That might be of use. "Where did you bite him?"

"His forearm. I think his right."

"Can you tell us anything more? Why did he take you?"

"He told me he'd brought Robin there, and I was to nurse him back to health. But he was never there, was he?"

"No, Nan." Kate stroked her hair, offered her another sip of the broth. But Nan looked away. "He is dead?"

"Robin received the best of care at the priory, but he died of his wounds."

"Dead," Nan whispered, her breath catching.

"I am sorry to tell you when you have already suffered so much. His friends Bran and Carter were with him. They are worried about you. Can you answer a few more questions?"

"Anything to help you catch the bastard."

"Why did he want you silent? What did you know?"

"I do not know! Maybe—I saw Griffin in the city when he said he was away in the country visiting an uncle. He was in High Petergate, coming from the house you lease to Sir Alan Bennet. In the early morning hours. Severen, the watchman, he said he often saw Griffin drinking with Sir Alan there."

"How did you recognize him? Surely he hid his red hair?"

254

Nan looked away, and Kate thought she might be too weary to say more, but then she began to speak. "He wore a hat pulled low over his hair. But he is a man a woman notices."

"Did Griffin see you?"

"I didn't think so—And I told no one. Except Severen."

Severen. Kate glanced back at Berend, who nodded. He had heard.

Nan began to cry and rub her forehead. "I trusted Severen. He said he cared for me."

"Best to lie back now, rest," Alice said, nodding to Hugo to ease Nan down. "Let us wash your wrists and ankles and bandage them."

Kate rose to take Matt aside, commanding Lille and Ghent to sit quietly in the doorway. "Go back to the house, Matt. Let them all know that we have found Nan and she is safe, being cared for, but we've not found Griffin. Then go to the minster yard. Tell Phillip we've found Nan, and ask the stonemasons to keep a watch over him, quietly, so he does not suspect. Tell them where they might find Sir Elric's men. Then go to Nan's house—you know where Goodwife Hawise lives?" He nodded. "Tell her that her daughter is safe. Then return to the Martha House. I cannot predict what they might need."

"If Griffin comes there?"

"You and Jennet will know what to do. I trust you, Matt."

No charming smile now. He nodded, took leave of his aunt, who had Hugo supporting Nan to sit while she combed through her hair.

"She will be safe here," said Alice. "Now go on with you."

Kate thanked Alice and Hugo, then assured Nan once more that she would be cared for. The children hovered near Berend, who stood at the door, waiting, with Lille and Ghent. The dogs were quiet now, watching the children calmly. Kate promised that she would return later, with the promised treats.

"And them?" the youngest asked.

"Lille and Ghent as well."

The three dark-haired sprites nodded solemnly.

As Berend handed Kate the bow and quiver, she noticed that he'd tucked the stained ropes that had bound Nan's arms and legs in his belt. "For Griffin?" A nod. As she followed him out the door, she asked, "Search for Griffin? Or go straight to Micklegate to meet Elric?"

"To Micklegate," said Berend. "Griffin told Nan he was leaving her. He has accomplished what he set out to do. He will follow Sir Alan and the dean." His tone was flat. He would have made decisions like this in his former life.

Kate did not often ask about his assassin days. Nor did she know in any detail what event had caused him to leave it behind. If ever he wished to tell her, it would be his decision. All she knew was that there were times like this when he became quiet and drew a wall round himself. But she needed him now. "What do you think might be Griffin's purpose? Nan called him a traitor to Mother and all of us."

"The timing suggests that he, Sir Alan, and your uncle are all involved. A Clifford mission? Your mother hinted at that. Did she do something to call down their wrath?"

"Would that I knew," said Kate. "I cannot think what would warrant the murders of Ulrich and two of his servants. Nor can I imagine for whom Sir Alan is working—my cousin John, the current Baron Clifford, is but ten, younger than Phillip. Neither Dean Richard nor his brother have the means to support a knight as a retainer."

As they'd followed Matt to the house on the riverbank, Kate had told Berend of her mother's cryptic comments.

"But Griffin was also Ulrich's man," she said now.

"For how long?" Berend wondered.

Good. He was engaged. "Let us say it *was* a Clifford plot. How would a powerful family like the Cliffords plot revenge?"

"You are thinking Griffin is an assassin."

"I begin to think so, yes."

Berend clenched his jaw, looked away. "They take their time, ensuring that it plays out as they wish it. I would guess the plan was to murder them all in Strasbourg, but your mother foiled them by taking flight. Griffin played along."

"A cuckoo in the nest. Someone played Ulrich for a fool, someone he trusted. As my uncle played me. But why would he wait all this time?"

"That is the question. Dame Eleanor has not said how long Griffin served Ulrich?"

"You know she's told me nothing of her life with Smit."

That was the rub. Who was at fault in her mother's reluctance to confide in Kate, she could not say. But now she dreaded the story. It could not help but be painful, a tale of betrayal, involving her family.

Crossing over Ouse Bridge, Lille and Ghent were on high alert while Kate and Berend scoured the crowd for a shock of red hair. The need to concentrate helped Kate push back the unpleasant surprises of the day that clamored for her attention—Severen's apparent betrayal of Nan, Sir Alan's betrayal of Kate, Griffin's betrayal of Dame Eleanor and all of them, including Werner and Hans, who had thought him one of them. Worst of all was that her uncle had betrayed her, that all this might be the doing of the Cliffords. A movement caught her attention, and she turned just in time to notice the cutpurse Bran moving through the crowd. Whistling, she caught his eye and motioned for him to meet her at the far side of the bridge.

"You have broken his cover, he'll not help you," said Berend.

Kate thought he might if he were sufficiently worried about his cousin Nan. And there he came, though he halted when he saw Lille and Ghent flanking her. She lifted her hand in peace.

"Nan is safe and sound," she said.

His wry face crumpled in tearful relief. "God have mercy, that is a blessing, mistress."

"Griffin, the red-haired Welshman who accompanied Dame Eleanor and the sisters to York, do you know him?"

A wary nod.

"Have you seen him this day?"

Bran frowned down at his feet, peering surreptitiously at Lille, who watched him with an unwavering gaze he might interpret as hunger.

"If I help you, will you call off the hounds? For good?"

"If you help me *and* trespass no more on my properties or those of my kin, yes, Bran, I will."

"He wears a soft hat pulled down over that bright hair and sneaks about. He crossed the bridge early this morning. While the merchants were still setting up. Pack slung over his shoulder. Just beyond the bridge he gave a low whistle, and out hobbled Thatcher. I could not believe my eyes. We've fretted and searched and he's been in hiding. He hobbled off up Micklegate with that Griffin fellow with nary a glance back." An injured sniff.

"That is helpful," said Berend. "Did you notice any other folk moving along toward Micklegate Bar earlier than their custom?"

"Dean of the minster and his comely housekeeper came trundling along with two ox-drawn carts this morning. A priest with his whore on a donkey came slowly past—she's about to give birth, that one, on their way to a midwife, I reckon. And that knight Sir Alan with his men. All the knights and their companies are deserting the king, that is what folk are saying. Even the earl's man, Sir Elric, came by with a small company not too long ago. They all came to hold York for good King Richard, but now Lancastrian gold has turned their heads round to their asses." He winced. "Forgive my tongue, mistress."

"You have been helpful, Bran. Your aunt Hawise will hear of this," said Kate.

A bobbed thanks, and Bran disappeared back into the crowd on the bridge.

"My uncle took advantage of my trust," Kate muttered as they headed on up Micklegate. "Did he think to make amends with the house and horses?"

"I never took him for a dishonest man," said Berend. "He may not have known what was intended."

"But I doubt he was unaware that Sir Alan's livery would have shown the blue and gold of the Clifford arms, had he and his men worn it. My uncle hid that from me. A small matter of family business. To what purpose? To prevent me from warning Mother? That is betrayal to my mind." Kate kicked a pebble on the street, then was forced to plant a false smile on her face as an acquaintance approached. The woman merely nodded as she passed, not attempting to start up a conversation, which was fortunate, for Kate had no patience for courtesy at the moment.

The bells of Micklegate Priory began ringing terce as they passed.

"Midmorning," Kate noted. "I feared it was later than that." Though the rain had ceased, the sky remained overcast, lending a gloom to the day.

"Helen said they were to rest the night at Bishopthorpe," said Berend. "Perhaps they all mean to gather there. If we do not catch them before they reach the palace, will we confront them in the presence of the archbishop?"

Kate had not thought that far. "Do you think they would dare reveal their connections to Archbishop Scrope? If he became curious, asked questions . . . He, too, is from an old, established family, but is it so common for families to hire an assassin?"

"More common than you would care to know. But that Sir Alan Bennet is a Clifford retainer is all your uncle need say. And perhaps Griffin—well, Archbishop Scrope would not realize he was not in Sir Alan's party." He stopped, looking Kate in the eyes. "So. Will we confront them at the palace?"

"We will do what we must."

A curt nod. "So be it."

Kate bent to rub the hounds' ears and whisper a prayer for their protection before continuing on through Micklegate Bar. As they moved through, she listened and watched for signs of trouble or anything that might inform their search. But she heard nothing of use and noticed only one soldier, directly behind them, expounding on the waste of such fine war dogs on the streets of York. Berend silenced him with little more than a growl. Yet Kate felt the rub—she was taking Lille and Ghent into danger.

They love it. They were trained to it, Geoff reminded her.

But they have not been run of late. Might they misjudge how quickly they can move?

"There he is," said Berend. Sir Elric and four of his men waited for them just past the barbican. "Those are fine horses we'll be riding."

"I am grateful that someone is true to their word," said Kate.

For once, she was glad of her Neville connections.

16

THE CHASE

Kate listened to Elric's report with interest. He, too, was aware of Griffin's departure with Thatcher. He'd sent several of his men ahead, tracking both parties; Sir Alan and the dean had departed on horse, Griffin and Thatcher on foot.

"Taking the peg leg." Elric shook his head. "He will only slow him down."

"Unless he means to dispose of him outside the city walls," said Berend. "He knows too much."

Elric nodded. "And what of the missing maidservant? Has she played a part in this? I saw no sign of her."

"We found her," said Kate.

"Did you?" Head bowed, Elric rubbed his mount's mane as Kate recounted what they had learned from Nan. The possibility that the Cliffords were taking their revenge on Ulrich and his household had him studying her with his cool blue eyes. "They have departed without troubling Dame Eleanor. Revenge on all but his widow? Why is that? Because she is a Clifford widow?"

"My mother has not been left unscathed. She will suffer long, I assure you."

"Of course she will. Forgive me." He pressed his hand to his heart and bowed to her.

She acknowledged the apology.

"If you are right about their purpose, I am surprised the *Clifford*s have permitted any of the deaths within the walls of York," said Elric. "They'll want nothing to connect them—as well you know." He said the last with a nod to Berend. "And why not Thatcher as well?"

"He has nothing to do with Ulrich Smit," said Berend. "If Dame Eleanor is right, the deaths of Hans and Werner are a point of honor. If members of the Clifford affinity are brought to law for them, they will defend themselves with a tale of betrayal—of family and the realm. No matter how personal in truth. Isn't that what the Nevilles would do?" Elric glanced away with a wince of discomfort, signaling his reluctant agreement. "But Thatcher—he was a means to an end who now knows too much and so is a danger."

Kate stepped between them. "We waste time. I want to catch up to Griffin before we confront my uncle."

Elric looked to Berend, who nodded his agreement. "I thought that might be the case," said the knight. "My man Arne returned shortly before you arrived with word that they have gone off the road not too far from here. Toward the river. They are moving slowly. The Welshman is staying off tracks, paths, which makes it difficult for Thatcher."

"Then let us be off," said Kate.

"The hounds will keep up with the horses if we are caught in a chase?" asked Elric.

"They will, I assure you. They were trained to chase large prey and bring them down." Though they had not done so for a long while.

Elric motioned to his squire, who brought forward one of the horses. "I chose one for you that has some experience with hounds." She was impressed that he'd considered Lille and Ghent. But then he would be accustomed to hunting with hounds for sport, and was also perhaps accustomed to working with war dogs. "But you'll need to ride astride," he said. "He's not trained to a lady's saddle."

"Astride is preferable," she said. "Thank you for your care in choosing a mount for me. Are all the horses accustomed to dogs?"

"I cannot vouch for three of them."

"They should take up the rear. I don't want them to take fright."

He ordered three of his men to the rear.

Kate accepted the assistance of Harry, Elric's squire, in mounting. Once astride, she gazed round with a sense of coming home. It had been a long time since she'd sat astride such a fine horse. It felt good. She signaled to Lille and Ghent to stay with her, clear of the other horses, and nodded to Berend to ride close. He said nothing, merely seeing to his own mount. Elric had managed to worsen his already dark mood.

⁓ঔৄ⁓

"It is long past time you confided in your daughter," said Dame Jocasta. "Now she rides out to confront them without an understanding of the gravity of Ulrich's betrayal. I pray God watches over her."

Eleanor had stood in the window, her back to Jocasta, all through the telling. She'd sought the woman's advice but now dreaded to see the judgment on her expressive face. "How do I mend the rift between us? How do I win back my daughter's trust and her love?" That is what she had asked. She was disappointed in Jocasta's response. Should not have, should have—all in the past, and unhelpful. Katherine was riding out to challenge her uncle and Sir Alan, and she would learn all. From them. From the family Ulrich had betrayed. Jocasta was right, it would have been far better coming from Eleanor. "How will she ever forgive me?" It burst from Eleanor as a sob. She covered her face and wept.

Soundlessly, Jocasta rose and embraced her, whispering of God's compassion, his limitless love and forgiveness.

All very sweet, but Eleanor already had faith in *God's* forgiveness; it was *Katherine's* of which she despaired.

⁓ঔৄ⁓

A light drizzle did nothing to freshen the air, which felt heavy with moisture as they rode through fields toward the trees lining the bank of the Ouse. Kate fretted about her bowstring wicking up moisture and sagging. She had remembered to bring a spare, but it would take time to restring. She must plan accordingly.

You intend to shoot Griffin on sight? Geoff asked.

She had not consciously planned it. *No. I want him to talk, to tell me all Mother should have told me.*

He's not likely to oblige.

When he refuses to say more, then *I'll shoot him.* She expected laughter.

Instead, Geoff warned her, *Do nothing that will endanger your plans for yourself and the children. Do not risk all to avenge Mother's loss.*

Would it be for her mother that she shot Griffin? Or would it be for Nan and Sister Dina? Hans, Werner, and, likely, Thatcher?

What does Dina have to do with this? Geoff asked.

I cannot believe the attempted theft was not part of this plan. Look how the rumors about the beguines have spread. Mother's attempt at good works discredited, rendered suspect.

Geoff was quiet.

Kate watched as Lille and Ghent explored beside her, pausing now and then to gaze round them, then catching up. Her heart eased. They had been bred and trained for this. Her uncle's horses would encourage her to run them more often. Blood money or not, she was grateful for the gift. The house would enable her to lease out her present home, adding more regular income. Considerably more. And, as her uncle had reminded her, Lionel could not touch it—a gift in her name, made in her widowhood.

She glanced up as Elric rode back to tell her that they were close to where his man Arne had last tracked Griffin and Thatcher.

"Dismount and approach on foot?" he asked. When she agreed, he called to his squire Harry to help Kate dismount and take her reins.

The fields beyond Clementhorpe Nunnery were more bogs than meadows in all seasons but summer. Now the grass grew so high that Kate lost sight of the hounds once she was on foot. It took but one call and they were suddenly beside her, their fur a mess of seeds and burrs, their ears flicking at the insects buzzing round them. Walking through the high grass was unpleasant, Kate's skirts already damp, the insects noisy, and she could not imagine how she might use her bow, nor how they would spot the two men they tracked. Glancing back, she saw that she was not alone in regretting the decision to dismount, Elric swatting at the insects, Harry sneezing. Only Berend stoically waited for her to proceed.

A rustle in the grass. Lille and Ghent stood at attention, and Kate fingered the axe hidden in her skirt. But it was Arne, his freckled face seeming to glide over the grass. "Found this." He raised high a length of wood from which dangled leather straps. Thatcher's peg leg, or what was left of it. "Found it just ahead, where the grass ends at the edge of the trees. Only one set of footprints moves on, and they are deep. I would say the Welshman carried the cripple to the river."

"Lead the way," said Kate, relieved that she would soon break out from the grass. Within a few moments she stepped onto dry soil beneath the trees, shaking out her skirts as Arne pointed to where he'd found the peg leg and the footprints. Berend and Elric moved on to the river, but Kate was in no hurry. Griffin had reached the bank a while ago. Already the footprints were powdered with debris. He would be downriver. Alone. She stayed with Lille and Ghent while they inspected the area, gathering scents. Suddenly they halted, glancing back to her. She praised them for discovering a patch of grass smeared with blood, bloody fingerprints on a fallen limb. Thatcher had not gone willingly. When had he realized he'd been betrayed? she wondered.

"Look! There, in the branches," Berend called out from somewhere farther on.

Signaling the dogs to follow, Kate moved toward Berend's voice as he directed the men, the sound of the river growing louder as she walked.

The peat-darkened waters of the Ouse flowed sluggishly under the wide gray sky. Near the bank, Thatcher floated face up, bobbing with the current, his hair and clothing snagged on the branches of a fallen tree whose roots still anchored it to the bank. He had a gaping wound on his forehead, washed clean by the river. Two of Elric's men sat on the bank, removing their boots and rolling up their breeches, preparing to wade in and pull him out of the Ouse.

Elric paced the bank, listening to Berend and Arne arguing about whether marks in the soil were that of a coracle or a more substantial boat.

Kate saw no purpose to the argument. "What matters is that Griffin has moved on by water. Downriver, toward Bishopthorpe. To meet up with Sir Alan and his men."

"To Bishopthorpe Palace then," Elric said. He ordered two of his men to follow with Thatcher's body.

⁓◦◦◦⁓

The guard at the gate of Bishopthorpe Palace bowed to Sir Elric and sent his fellow running to inform the archbishop of their presence. The power of the Earl of Westmoreland. Or the Neville name. Elric had taken care to introduce Kate as well, lingering on the surname.

"Are you part of the Clifford party visiting His Grace?" the guard asked her as they waited.

"The Dean of York Minster is my uncle," said Kate. "We have cause to believe a murderer will seek refuge here with his party. We found his victim upriver. I have come to warn Dean Richard and His Grace."

"Two of my men are following with the body. The murderer will come by boat and is unlikely to tell them of his crime," said Elric. "Do you guard the river approach to the palace as well as the road?"

"We do."

"Is it possible to land elsewhere on the property?" asked Elric.

"A small boat? Yes. Lawns down to the river, and a woodland farther downriver. In times of threat we have sentries throughout the grounds."

"But not now?"

"We were not aware of a need." He glanced behind them, on the road. "Are those your men with the body?"

Elric glanced back. "Yes. If they might stand watch over it someplace private in the grounds?"

The guard nodded as the second retainer came hurrying from the palace, gesturing for his comrade to open the gate. He was followed by a tall, elegant, elderly man in clerical robes, who bowed to Kate's company and introduced himself as Don Vincent, His Grace's secretary, welcoming them and inviting them to follow him to the palace. He ordered the second guard to assist Elric's men with the horses.

"They will be well stabled, I assure you." Don Vincent stood a moment, considering Lille and Ghent. "It is customary to take hounds to the stables as well."

"My uncle, Dean Richard Clifford, can vouch for them. They are well trained and will stay with me," said Kate.

"I pray that is so." He looked past them. "And the body?"

Elric repeated his request.

"Of course. I will have someone come out to assist your men." Don Vincent swept round and led them through the gate and on to the palace.

His Grace the archbishop stood just within the grand entrance, Richard Clifford beside him.

"You are most welcome, Dame Katherine, Sir Elric, Berend, I believe?" said Archbishop Scrope. "But I am at a loss as to your mission."

Kate and Elric repeated what they had told the guard. While they were talking, Sir Alan Bennet appeared in the doorway of a small room off to the side of the hall entrance. As soon as he saw Kate, he began to retreat, but His Grace addressed him, repeating what Kate and Elric had just told him. Sir Alan frowned, shaking his head as if to counter their claim. And, indeed, he proceeded to sputter as soon as the archbishop was finished.

His Grace raised his hand for silence. "There can be no argument against fact. Sir Elric, you are welcome to set your men to searching the grounds. Anyone who takes it upon himself to interfere with their task will answer to me."

Richard Scrope rose several choirs of angels higher in Kate's esteem. Clearly His Grace's acceptance of Kate's earlier request for help had been in character. Sir Elric bowed and went out to the stables to instruct his men.

Sir Alan made to follow, but Scrope called him to heel.

Alan was not the only person looking glum. Her uncle watched her with an unease she had only before glimpsed in their most recent conversation.

"If I might have a quiet word with my uncle?" she said.

Scrope nodded to his secretary, who showed her into the room from which Sir Alan had emerged. High-ceilinged, with several high-backed chairs surrounding a long table piled with documents, a tiled floor, and a window opening onto the garden, it was an inviting chamber. Looking back, Kate signaled to Lille and Ghent to wait just outside the door.

"Katherine," the dean bowed to her as he entered the room.

"You left betimes, Uncle. We expected you to dine with us today."

"I had said perhaps, that I would send word."

She inclined her head. "So you did. And, in the event Griffin finished his task earlier than expected?"

"Griffin? Task?" His expression was almost convincing. Almost.

"The murders of Ulrich Smit's servants. Dame Eleanor and the beguines are preparing Werner's body for burial. And he added another victim, Thatcher, a man of York who had assisted him and was of no more use. We found him drowned in the Ouse, with a great wound to his forehead—Griffin made sure that he would not survive despite the sluggish summer current."

Her uncle blanched and turned away from her, clearly struggling with how to respond. He was saved by a sharp knock on the door and the entrance of His Grace.

"The gardener's boy observed a red-haired man pulling a coracle into the woodland downriver. Sir Elric's men are spreading out in search. I thought you would wish to know, Dame Katherine. I would think this a task well suited to your wolfhounds. The boy awaits you by the door."

She thanked him and hurried out, calling to Lille and Ghent. Berend followed.

The lad grinned at the sight of the hounds, bobbing his head at Kate and Berend. "This way, mistress," he said, turning about and leading them off into the gardens. Lush and peaceful, the landscape seemed an unlikely place for a murderer to hide. But as they moved beyond the graveled paths into the trees, the grounds grew wilder. She saw Elric's men ahead, signaling to each other to spread out as they moved with practiced stealth into an area with underbrush. One glanced back toward them—Elric's squire, Harry. She motioned to him to push Griffin toward the river. He nodded and disappeared.

If Griffin had thought to hide in the gardens, the men would flush him out. Realizing he was hunted, he would know the palace was not safe. "Take us first to where he landed," she told the boy.

A wind came off the river, damp, heavy. No more rain today. The heat was settling in again. As the coracle came into view, Lille and Ghent began to slow, sniffing the ground, looking up, listening. Nan said she had bitten Griffin. How deeply? Might the scent of his blood be on the coracle? Kate led the dogs to the boat. It interested them, and they circled round it, taking in the scents, then took off in a direction farther downriver.

"Did he go this way?" she asked the lad, who had been watching the hounds with fascination.

He nodded. "I saw him head into that brush, and then I hurried back to tell my da. This is Church land, not for poachers."

Kate thanked him and told him to return to his father. She would not want him injured if Griffin were cornered. Disappointed, the lad turned with reluctance, glancing back several times as he retraced his steps. Kate removed her short cloak, dropped it into the coracle, unhooked her bow, and checked the string. Dry. Good. Pulling an arrow from her quiver, she looked to Berend. "Ready?"

At last he graced her with a smile as he patted the soiled rope tucked in his belt. "Let us be the ones to truss him and carry him to His Grace."

They set off after the hounds, moving into the wilder part of the woods, where fallen limbs, old stumps, and mounds of fallen leaves slowed them. They had not gone far when the dogs paused, heads up. Kate nocked the arrow and moved forward to stand beside Lille and Ghent at the edge of a clearing. Holding her breath, she listened. Lille turned slightly to the right as Kate registered the snap of a twig. With care, she took a step out into the clearing and caught a movement, a man rising up from the shrubbery, still shadowed by the trees. As she watched, he raised a bow with the arrow ready, drawing the string back—the arrow pointing toward Lille. Kate called to her hound to drop as she let her arrow fly, aiming for the archer's shoulder. Lille's reflexes proved as quick as ever. She just missed the arrow meant to kill her. The archer dropped down.

"Careful," Berend whispered.

A rustling. The man rose up, and, to Kate's puzzlement, seemed unharmed. She had missed? *Damn you.* He took a step toward the clearing, dappled light revealing his coppery hair.

"Drop the bow and come out with empty hands, Griffin."

He nocked an arrow.

She let hers fly. This time she saw him fall back with the impact.

Berend rushed him. Silence.

Kate walked across the clearing to join him.

If he's dead, he deserved it, Geoff whispered in her mind. *His arrow would have killed Lille had she not obeyed your command. Well done.*

Berend rose from beside the still body. "Your arrow pierced his heart. A clean kill."

A kill was not her plan. "I would have preferred that he surrender, and talk. Tell me who had hired him, why, how he was to carry out their orders."

Berend shook his head. "Assassins never talk." He called out to Elric's men to come collect the body. "Go back to the palace, Dame Katherine. I will assist them." He avoided her eyes, though he did crouch down to Lille and Ghent to rub their ears and praise their tracking.

"Berend?"

He shook his head as he rose, looking out to the river. "Too many unwelcome memories." He pulled the soiled ropes from his belt. "I'll bind him."

Kate called the hounds to her side, slung her bow over her shoulder, and headed for the palace.

17

A TALE OF BETRAYAL

──── ❧❧ ────

Kate returned to Bishopthorpe Palace silent, exhausted, and annoyed by Geoff's accolades buzzing in her head. It had been necessary to stop Griffin, but he was no prize kill, his death nothing to celebrate. He would have been far more useful alive.

Helen, the dean's housekeeper, rushed out past the dean and archbishop to embrace Kate. "We heard Berend's shout and feared the worst. God be thanked. And Berend? Is he injured?"

"No. Only Griffin." Kate rested her head for a moment on Helen's warm shoulder. "He tried to take Lille down with him. I was forced to kill him before I could learn anything."

"My dear Katherine, I doubt he would have told you anything. He gave the dean no ground in his arguments against violence. He was deeply committed to completing the bloody deed as Baron Roos, in his fury, had commanded him."

Kate pushed out of the embrace, shocked. "Roos?" The light dawned. The young Baron Clifford's mother was Elizabeth Roos; her brother William, Baron Roos, acted as John's guardian. "So you knew about it?"

"Not until today. Your uncle told me everything after you went out to hunt Griffin. Something about family honor avenged. Ulrich Smit and the servants who had accompanied him to Northumberland were executed for crimes against the family and the realm—treason."

"Treason? What was the deed?"

"He did not say." Helen closed her eyes. "I do not know what to think now, that he would hide such a thing from me. He lied to me about Griffin's purpose, implying it was your mother who connived and deceived."

Kate fought to slow her spinning thoughts. Ulrich accused of treason. Griffin carrying out the orders of William Roos, a powerful man, a member of the Privy Council and one of the men who had negotiated King Richard's peace with Scotland. Her home in Northumberland on the border with Scotland. The late Baron Clifford, Thomas, John's father, had been Warden of the West Marches, responsible for keeping peace of that border. *God help us. Did we harbor a traitor? Was Ulrich in league with the Scots?*

Did Mother know? Geoff whispered in her mind.

No, Geoff, no. Think of all she lost to the Cavertons. All three sons. No.

Helen touched Kate's arm. "What can I do for you, my dear?"

Kate shook her head.

"A quiet place and a flask of brandywine?" Elric suggested, joining them. "His Grace's servants await your commands."

"Yes," Kate breathed, crouching down to give Lille and Ghent each a hug while she collected herself. When she was composed, she signaled to the hounds to accompany Helen to the kitchen. "Please see that they are properly rewarded, Helen. Thank you. I will join you in a little while."

"Of course." Helen took the leads in hand.

"Here they come." Elric looked toward the gardens.

Out of the brush stepped two of Elric's men carrying Griffin in an improvised sling. Berend and Elric's squire Harry followed. A manservant hurried out of a small stone outbuilding, gesturing them inside. Harry broke away and headed toward Kate and Elric, but Berend continued on with the body.

"A sorry ending to a sorry deed," Elric said softly, nodding to his man.

"I could use that brandywine now," said Kate, turning toward the hall. Elric walked with her.

And here is the go-between, Kate thought, glaring at Sir Alan, who strode out from the palace as if to attend Griffin.

His Grace stopped him with a stern shake of his head. "Don Vincent will see to it."

"Your Grace, he was—"

"Say no more of this in my presence, Sir Alan," said the archbishop. When the man began to protest, Scrope thundered, "No more!"

Tight-lipped, the knight withdrew.

And then Harry was with them, congratulating Kate on her remarkable aim. "I've seen where he fell. Still in the cover of the trees and yet you found his heart. I've never witnessed such shooting."

"Nor did you witness it this day, or you would know that I missed the first time. The first arrow wounded a tree. A birch, I believe. But it is such a waste." She shook her head at him as the young man, startled, began to apologize. "I am tired and filthy, Harry. You must excuse me." She turned to the archbishop.

He bowed to her. "You will stay the night, Dame Katherine. I will see that Sir Alan and his men keep well away from your company. I am sending a messenger to inform Dame Eleanor and your household that you are safe and the danger past."

Kate considered protesting the delay in returning to York, but thought better of it. "Once I have had a wash and a cup of brandywine, I would have you hear my confession, Your Grace." No matter how deserved the killing, it was still a sin requiring absolution.

"Of course."

A servant escorted Kate to a bedchamber, bringing a basin of warm water, lotions and cloths, a goblet, and a flagon of brandywine. Kate poured herself a measure more than she usually considered wise and sank down onto a chair near a window, pushing open the shutter just in time to see Berend exit the stone outbuilding. Glancing toward the palace, he turned and headed toward the river. *No, not away from me.* She wanted him near. There was no one else with whom she could share the turmoil inside. But she knew this mood, and that there was nothing for it but to let him be.

Drinking down the brandywine, she closed her eyes and felt the heat in her face, her throat, her chest. Rising for more, she caught a glimpse of herself in a small mirror beside the basin of water, her hair wild, face smudged. She set down the goblet and had just begun to scrub at her face when someone knocked on the door behind her.

"Might I serve as your lady's maid?" asked Helen, peeking in.

"Bless you, yes."

⬥

Kate spent a long while with His Grace, confessing that she could not be certain she had not aimed for Griffin's heart—she had been so angry, though she was unsure whether it was because he had dared to threaten Lille, or, worse, because she had missed the first time, when she'd aimed for his shoulder.

Scrope was of the opinion that she was misguided in seeking reasons to chastise herself when she had ample cause to consider Griffin a deadly threat. "He had murdered three men, abducted a woman and left her to die, and those are only the sins he committed in York. He also murdered your mother's husband, Ulrich Smit. In truth, you did him a favor. I am sure Griffin knew that he would have been hanged or beheaded and much preferred being shot right there. He may even have coaxed you to it, knowing your bond with Lille."

"I would agree but that it seems Ulrich was accused by Baron Roos of treason. If this is true, Griffin acted as an agent of the baron in defense of the realm."

The archbishop sat back with a sigh, rubbing his temples. "Yes, I see why you question your actions. I absolve you, and I am certain King Richard would absolve you of any sin regarding this deed. Smit, if indeed guilty of treason, should have been handed over to the law for trial. Your uncle the dean agrees. It was not Baron Roos's place to mete out punishment for crimes against the state. Or the Clifford family. Yes, one might argue that the man who paid with his life was merely carrying out orders, but so, too, were Smit's servants." He leaned forward, forearms on the table, looking Kate in the eyes. "I absolve you of any stain of sin in this deed. Take comfort in knowing that you have ended your mother's ordeal. You are a courageous and loving daughter."

A courageous and loving daughter. She could imagine her mother shaking her head and launching into a litany contradicting such praise.

※

Richard Clifford threw the document he'd been holding onto the table. It skittered a distance, knocking other parchments to the floor. He pressed a hand to his brow, as if that might clear his head. "God help me, Katherine, had I known what Sir Alan had planned I never would have set him up in your house. Never. But why should you believe me? Even as I say it I know that I suspected something. His explanation for not wearing the Roos livery—that the family did not want to be noted as supporting King Richard against Duke Henry . . . But it was the secrecy about who he was, his request that I say nothing of our connection, of his being in John's guardian's household . . ." He cursed. "I did not *want* to know. That is the sad truth of it."

Kate stood with hands pressed to the long table, pained to feel enmity toward this man she had held so dear. "I care nothing for your excuses, Uncle, you with your secret meetings with Griffin. I want to understand why this happened. What did Griffin tell you? What drove Baron Roos to command these deaths?"

"Sir Alan would be better able to tell you, but even he knows little more than his orders."

"I do not trust myself to speak to him. Not yet." It was difficult enough to stand here listening to her uncle squirm under a belatedly active conscience; the uncle she had loved, trusted, entrusted with her wards when she'd feared they were in danger. She stood alone, betrayed by her own family. "I will hear it from you!" She slammed her hand down on the table, startling him. "Tell me what you know. Then I will hear my mother's side of it."

"I pray I have not turned you against your mother."

"It is a little late for that, Uncle."

He bowed his head. "When I understood the severity of Ulrich's betrayal of the family and the realm, and the extent of the vengeance planned by my brother Robert—for our brother David, blood for blood, and our cousin Thomas's widow—for besmirching our good name and risking the realm . . ." He went for the brandywine on a small table near the window, poured generous amounts in two goblets, handed one to her, and drank half of his in one gulp. A pause as the liquor took effect. "Now that I know, I regret what I said about your mother and the Frosts, calling them selfish, and worse. I cannot believe Eleanor knowingly betrayed David in such wise. Surely she was ignorant of Ulrich's part in the feud with the Cavertons. I cannot believe she could love him had she known that he had set into motion the feud that destroyed her sons and her husband."

The Cavertons. God help her. Kate fortified herself with several sips of brandywine before she asked, "How did Ulrich betray my father? What had he to do with the Cavertons?"

"He was an agent of the French, working for the Scots-French alliance—in secret, of course. The Cavertons were part of the link through which he fed to the Scots all he learned from your father and his neighbors on the English side. He was also passing money and documents back and forth, but your family's unwitting contribution was the information about border activities. Ulrich had been particularly well paid by the French when John's father, Thomas Clifford, was Warden of the West Marches. You would have been but a child then."

"My memory of Ulrich goes back to early youth." Kate sank down onto the chair she had earlier refused. "God help me." The Scots and the French had used her family, used up her family.

Damn him to hell. Geoff's fury felt like the blood rushing in her head.

Quiet, I pray you, Geoff. Let me hear what our duplicitous uncle has to say.

As the dean continued, she came to learn that even her father's death was suspect—her uncle believed he had not died of a fever but rather of a slow poison, a gift from Ulrich to the Cavertons for their service. He had also assisted that family when possible with information about Kate's family, their comings and goings, strength and weaknesses.

Kate's heart hurt with the enormity of Ulrich's betrayal.

"And Mother learned of this?" she whispered, breaking a long silence. The dean nodded. "In Strasbourg, already wed to Smit."

"How in heaven's name—Why—*why* would Ulrich wed her? How could he look her in the eyes, knowing the pain he had caused her?"

"Protection? God knows. They had been lovers for years. Perhaps he did not think of her as part of the family he destroyed."

"Did Griffin kill Smit?" she asked.

"He did." Dean Richard crossed the room and knelt to her, taking her hands. "No, do not think it. You were right to execute him. Smit deserved to die, but the others? And what of Nan and Thatcher?"

The concern in his gray eyes, this was the uncle she loved. But she was not ready to forgive him. She withdrew her hands and turned her back to him.

"Griffin had another mandate," he said. "To find Ulrich's gold. The French paid him well."

"Did he find it?"

"No. I tell you this so that you do not make the mistake of trusting your cousin Baron Clifford or the Roos family in future," said the dean. "Nor should Dame Eleanor."

"So the robberies were an attempt to find the gold, with Robin and his fellows taking the risk? Why wait so long?"

"Sir Alan knows only that he was sent to hurry Griffin along."

"How much gold?"

"More than your mother would dare carry from Strasbourg to York in such a small company."

"Mother has been spared because she might still lead them to the gold?"

"Yes. And because she is a Clifford, if only by marriage."

"I need air. I need to walk with the hounds."

"Of course."

⁓◦◉◦⁓

In the early morning, as the sun woke the countryside, Kate rode back to York deafened by the storm in her mind, Berend silently leading, the hounds flanking her. Her uncle had been unable to answer all her questions, and Sir Alan had not bothered to learn much about his mission. He served William—Baron Roos—and obeyed his commands. Why would he question them? He had used the Duke of York's call to arms as the perfect cover in which to complete the task of revenge against Ulrich and the retainers and servants who had assisted him in his spying.

Sir Alan had ridden out before Kate and Berend had broken their fast. He and his men would join the companies supporting Duke Henry, riding westward to confront King Richard. Archbishop Scrope saw no point in charging him. The man with blood on his hands was already dead. Griffin, the instrument, would be buried in an unmarked grave.

"An assassin knows his fate," Berend had said. "Rage all you wish, Dame Katherine, I understand, but Griffin himself would tell you that you waste your breath. God will judge Sir Alan, his men, the Cliffords, the Rooses, in his own time, his own way. The law sees only the murderer."

"And what of me?"

"You were the law in this instance. The archbishop of York sent you out with his blessing."

Kate wished she might have drunk until she was so numb she fell into a blessed forgetfulness. But she had work to do. Questions that must be answered. She had talked to Sir Alan after her long walk with the hounds, wanting to hear his version. He confirmed that Griffin's primary reason for pursuing Eleanor to York was to recover the gold. It was not enough to have murdered Ulrich and all his retainers; the Cliffords wanted the gold with which he had been rewarded by the French for his spying. Not finding it in Strasbourg, he believed Eleanor had it and would lead him to it. Hans and Werner might have knowledge of it. When they proved ignorant, Griffin had no more use of them and carried out their sentences.

Where was the gold? Was her mother still in danger?

Both the archbishop and her uncle assured Kate that Baron Roos would be exposed and ruined should any harm come to her or Dame Eleanor. But with such uncertainty in the land, Kate did not see how they could be so certain of their own future power.

At the sign of an alewife, a bushel basket on a pole in the yard of a small farm close to York, she and Berend paused to water Lille and Ghent and their mounts, and to refresh themselves.

"It is good to be free of Sir Elric and his men, eh?"

Kate was moved by how Berend had put aside his mood to engage her, draw her out of her dark study. But he had chosen an unwelcome topic. She was not ready to tell Berend of her arrangement with Elric. How after meeting with her uncle and the archbishop she had sought out Elric in the stables and invited him for a twilight walk in the gardens. As soon as they were far enough that no one might overhear them, she asked how much he knew about Griffin's mission. He was hesitant at first to admit how much he had managed to learn while at the palace, but she persisted in her questioning until he confessed that he knew all of it. At another time she would have cursed him, but at present she was relieved.

"My mother will not be safe until Baron Roos possesses Ulrich Smit's gold."

"And you have a plan."

"I agree to be the earl's eyes and ears in York if your men in the city are my eyes and ears regarding anyone too curious about my mother, her Martha House, or my household. And, if I have need of them, your men will summon support from Sheriff Hutton Castle."

"And the letters?"

"I will see what I might discover about them."

He had smiled. "Agreed. I look forward to a long and interesting partnership."

They would see about that. If Lancaster prevailed, Westmoreland might have need of Sir Elric elsewhere. He might never return to his post at Sheriff Hutton. And if King Richard prevailed, there was no predicting Westmoreland's fate and that of his properties.

This morning, while Berend had prepared their horses, Kate had bid farewell to Sir Elric in the palace yard. He and his men were off to the northwest, to Raby. He had kissed her hand, and again expressed his delight in their partnership.

"We have an agreement, Sir Elric, not a partnership."

He'd bowed. "As you wish. But I can hope."

She had not told Berend. Not in his present mood.

Now, in answer to his question about her relief in being free of Elric, she said, "I am grateful for all his help. But it is good to be heading home, just you, me, Lille, and Ghent." She emptied her cup, called the alewife's son over to refill it.

"Steady now, we are not yet within the gates of the city," he warned.

She hardly felt the effects of the ale, though it tasted strong.

"What are you stewing over?" he asked.

"How could we all be so fooled by Ulrich Smit? He was an honored guest in our house. I named Lille and Ghent for the cities he told us about. Mother loved Ulrich. She took him as her lover long before Father's death. Father's murder," she whispered those last words.

"Clearly the man excelled in his work. Which is why the French paid him so well."

"The gold. Where is the gold?"

"Dame Eleanor is resourceful."

"She is indeed. That is what worries me."

Berend rubbed his shoulder, stretched. "We should continue."

"Wait." Kate put her hand on his and looked into his eyes. "I am sorry, Berend. I would not have you suffer the pain this has stirred for you."

"I could not let you deal with this alone."

They studied each other for a long while, then withdrew their hands and split the rest of the tankard.

⁓

"Katherine! You stayed the night at the archbishop's palace! You must tell me all about it." Eleanor reached out to embrace her, but Kate slipped out of her reach. She had something she must do before she spoke to her mother.

Ignoring the questions, the protests, Kate stormed up the steps and into the bedchamber of the beguines, startling Sister Dina, who had been resting with a cloth over her eyes.

Kate stepped back, remembering herself. "Forgive me. I was so intent on my mission, I did not think to knock." A gray gown with as yet a solitary sleeve lay on a table by the window. The dimensions were for someone wide and short. "Are you making this for Agnes?"

Removing the cloth from her eyes, Sister Dina sat up. "I do this for her, yes. Did you know—her mother was a—how is it—a midwife? She knows plants, physic—no, medicines." She nodded, whispering the last word again. Her accent was still thick, but her vocabulary much improved. "We learn much about what we might find here, in city and out in country. We are grateful."

"And Dame Eleanor?"

Dina made a little face. "She struggles to accept her, but I have hope? Faith." She nodded. "She will see. Agnes will prove to her. And Nan."

"Nan has been welcomed back into the household?"

Dina nodded. "Rose is happy."

Much had transpired since Kate was away. A day and a night. Was that all?

"What do you seek, Dame Katherine? Griffin—The messenger said—"

"Griffin is dead. I made sure of that. Judge me as you will—" Kate closed her eyes. Perhaps she had drunk too much, to barge in here and then say that to Dina. "Forgive me."

Dina reached out to touch Kate's hand. "Me? Judge you?" She put Kate's hand on her heart. "Nothing to forgive. How do I help?"

"The golden Christ child. I need to see it. Just guide me to where I might find it."

"I help you." Dina went to the closest of three chests tucked in the corner where the roof slanted to the floor. As she knelt down and lifted the lid, Kate knelt beside her. "Small casket. Under cloak."

Kate felt for it, lifted it out. It took some effort.

Dina nodded as Kate sat back with the casket on her lap.

"It is heavy. The casket, the carving of the Christ child, oak. Here." She took Kate's hand, turned it over, placed a key in her palm. "Open it."

Within the small casket was a carved wooden Christ child painted gold. It lay on a bed of gold damask hemmed in gold thread. "The golden idol."

"No idol. Not gold." Dina smiled. "We use it to feel in our prayers the love a mother feels for her child. But for us, all God's children."

Kate lifted it, admiring the delicacy of the carving, the face with a sweetness that gave it life. But though the heft of the carved child was substantial, it did not explain the heft of the small casket. She handed the child in its golden bed to Dina, who took it with puzzlement. Returning her attention to the wooden casket, Kate compared the depth of the inside to that of the outside. So simple. She felt around and found something like a small pin in the corner. A slight tug lifted the false bottom. Beneath it lay a leather pouch. Drawing it out, she untied the leather cord and teased open the pouch, letting several gold coins drop into her lap. A mere sampling of what was hidden within. Ulrich's gold.

"What is this?" Dina gasped. "How did we not see?"

"We see what we expect to see."

"For this Griffin killed Hans and Werner?"

"It is why he let them live as long as he did, hoping they would lead him to it."

"For this, Robin died."

"Your part in his death was accidental." Kate slipped the pieces of gold back in the pouch. "Forgive me for intruding. I will take this and leave you to your prayers."

Dina touched her face. "You are in pain as well. When you are ready, come. We will talk. Pray together."

⁓◦∾⁓

"Do you have some brandywine up here?" Kate asked her mother. They were closed in her bedchamber.

Eleanor waved toward a shelf near the window. Kate sniffed the contents of the elegant Italian glass bottle. Costly and strong. She poured only a little in the matching glass cup. Bringing a chair to face her mother's, Kate sat down and handed Eleanor the cup. She was glad she had poured but a little, for her mother downed it in one gulp.

"Now tell me all of it, and do not think to deceive me, for I learned much from Sir Alan and Dean Richard."

"All of it, you say." Eleanor turned her gaze to the window. The skin sagged beneath her clear green eyes, remnants of her grief. Kate steeled her heart to it. "Where does it begin?" Eleanor whispered. "I wish I knew where to begin. *Where* it all began, *when*. Your birth? With David's fury when I presented him with twins?"

"I asked about Ulrich, and you want to talk about my birth?" But down she went, caught in her mother's web. "What are you saying? Father was angry about my birth? And Geoff's?"

"That is when David pushed me away. 'Twins,' he roared. 'I am cuckolded. You have shamed me.' How could he, a Clifford, be so ignorant? Twins have nothing to do with how many men a woman has slept with. You were so clearly both our children—by his first birthday Geoff had my green eyes, you had your father's nose and his wild hair."

Kate played along; she could not help herself. She had heard this about twins. Many folk believed it. But her father? He had never said anything like that, not in her presence. "He loved us."

"Oh, that he did. He loved you and you him. Never me. I was cast aside. You and Geoffrey adored him, and, seeing how he shunned me, you learned to please him by disobeying me. You wished nothing to do with me."

"Not true, Mother." But was it? "Our hours at the loom—"

"Yes. We had that." Eleanor patted Kate's hand, her eyes glistening with tears. "But you and Geoffrey were so different from your brothers Walter and Roland, so *as one* that I began to fear it *did* mean something. You knew each other's minds, as if you shared a soul. A manservant called the two of you abominations. I sent him packing. And then, years later, the hounds. The four of you bonded so tightly. The master of hounds said he had never seen the like, how the two of you took to training them."

Kate had taken such pride in the master's admiration.

Eleanor held out the cup. Kate poured a little more. Her mother drank it down, her cheeks on fire. "Ghent paced and paced the morning Geoffrey went missing, and then he set up a howling. Long before Geoffrey's body was borne home, Ghent howled. Lille joined in."

"I remember," Kate whispered. As her mother spoke, Kate poured herself some brandywine. Drank it down. Such heartbreaking howls. She had known . . .

"And the pain of your births—the suffering. I would bear no more bairns for David—though that was as nothing to him, he never again came to my bed. Perhaps you were a test. *And I failed.* But he loved you. He shunned me, but loved you so."

What had she ever known of her parents? Steady. That was a conversation for another time. "Ulrich, Mother. Was he murdered in the same way as Werner, his throat slit?"

Eleanor turned her gaze to the window, looking out. "Yes. He looked just like Werner when they fished his body out of the river. That horrible wound in his neck." A hand to her mouth. "The worst of it—I received a letter, unsigned, a fortnight before Ulrich went missing, telling me that he had betrayed David—that all the while Ulrich enjoyed our hospitality he was sending messages to the Scots, everything he learned from David— foolish, trusting David. I went through Ulrich's things, found nothing. I confronted him. At first he denied it. Said the letter must be from someone who resented his happiness. Sweet words, sweet promises. But I refused to believe him. Memories were speaking to me. All the strangeness since we crossed the channel—the need for secrecy in Calais, the French escort to Strasbourg, how welcomed we were in the finest homes on our journey. French homes—they are the Scots' allies, why had I not questioned him then? He finally admitted his betrayal, but he swore that his love for me was real, unplanned. It had tormented him. Oh, Katherine, I've been such a fool."

Kate fought the urge for another gulp of strong drink. Geoff was growling in her head as he had done since learning of the betrayal from her uncle. *Silence, Geoff, I beg you.*

The quiet was so sudden she shivered.

"Katherine? What is it? Someone walked on your grave?"

Still no sound from Geoff, no sense of his presence. "The brandywine is strong," said Kate as she fought to compose herself. "Tell me. You saw Ulrich's body?"

"I was meant to. I am sure of it. Some of Ulrich's men found him. They had been searching for days. I quietly buried him with the assistance of a priest who had befriended me when I went to him for help after learning how Ulrich had betrayed me, how I had betrayed David, taking his enemy for my lover. I did not know how I might ever forgive myself . . . The priest was kind, arranging everything."

"You believe Ulrich was executed by someone who knew of his betrayal, who had written to you?"

"Of course. They followed me, murdering his servants, discrediting me with rumors about golden idols and heretical writings. They mean for me to suffer all this and survive to remember. Monsters. Cowards."

"Ulrich's murderer was hired by young Baron Clifford's guardian, William Roos."

"Roos?" A gasp, and then a long silence as Eleanor took it in, her eyes moving back and forth as she made connections. "Oh, yes, I can see Elizabeth Roos behind all this, proud, overweening woman. A curse on her and all her family!"

"When did Griffin enter Ulrich's service?" Kate asked, drawing her mother back to the point.

"What?" Eleanor blinked at Kate, as if she'd forgotten her presence. "Oh, yes, I'd . . ." A sigh. "In Strasbourg. We had lost a man on our journey. Oh, dear heaven, Griffin showed up as if summoned. Ulrich asked round about him. He seemed satisfied by what he heard. Griffin." Eleanor crossed herself. "God forgive me, I sent Werner to his death. I sent him with Griffin in search of Hans's murderer. I told them to disappear, then watch. I sent him to his death. But I never dreamed . . . He seemed so kind."

Kate's uncle's meetings with Griffin, always without Werner. She did not know if she would ever forgive him. "Why did they not just take Ulrich's life, his wealth, and let you be?"

Eleanor shifted uneasily, avoiding Kate's eyes. "They could not find his gold. I am certain they questioned Hans, then Werner, before killing them. But neither of them knew anything about it."

Kate forced herself to sound surprised in asking, "His gold?"

"The French paid him well for spying. Griffin did not find it. Not even the guardians of the gold know where it is."

Enough of this. Kate could not keep up the pretense. "By guardians you mean the beguines?" She drew the pouch from her skirt, took her mother's hand, crossed her palm with gold.

Eleanor stared down at it. "You toyed with me. How did you know?"

Kate told her Richard Clifford's version of the story. And Sir Alan's.

"Baron Roos and his sister Elizabeth." Eleanor spat the words, though her mouth trembled and her eyes mirrored Kate's own pain. "I am not at all surprised that they were behind this. Black hearts, the pair of them, I have always said so. But why ask me, when you knew all this?"

"I am angry. Angry that you did not tell me what had happened when you arrived. We might have prevented much of this had we worked together. You endangered all of us with your silence."

"Oh." Eleanor looked down at her hands. "I—I was so ashamed," she whispered, then closed her eyes, going silent.

Kate helped herself to a gulp of brandywine and waited. The skin of her mother's face sagged, her hands were spotted with age, the joints of her forefinger and thumb swollen. Kate fought the urge to apologize for her harsh words.

Eleanor reached up to fuss with her veil, as if aware of Kate's close study. "How did you guess where the gold was?"

"When I heard of it, I remembered the man who approached Marie. And you did little to quiet the fuss about a golden idol. You go on about everything—but not that. You are clever, Mother. The sisters saw only the gold thread and so dismissed it."

An enigmatic smile. "There is even more gold. Much more. Before he was murdered, Ulrich sent it on to my elderly uncle in Hull. A peace offering to me. He told me to hasten home if anything should happen to him. Apparently while busy eliminating his fellow retainers in Strasbourg, Griffin missed Ulrich's final sleight of hand. I've recently had word through your cousin William that his great-uncle awaits my visit."

"Were all Ulrich's retainers murdered in Strasbourg?"

Eleanor crossed herself. "All who had accompanied him to England. Some died before Ulrich. Why do you think Hans and Werner agreed to escort me? They had been in the party. They were frightened for their lives. Griffin suggested to them that they would be safe with me."

"And you agreed, knowing the part they played in Ulrich's betrayal?"

"They were servants, Katherine, not spies. Good men." Eleanor's breath caught. Softly, she said, "Perhaps Ulrich as well. His first wife was French, as was his mother. He and his wife fostered two Scots boys orphaned in an English raid."

"You knew all this?"

"Only later, when he confessed. He said that by the time he grew to care for David, me, all our family, he could not—He had gone too far." A sob. Eleanor fumbled for the glass. "I loved them both—David, Ulrich. I loved them both."

Kate took the glass from her mother and poured her a generous amount, which Eleanor dispatched with alarming speed.

Kate's own heart ached with doubt. How could anyone judge who was at fault, who was in the right? There were no winners in a feud. How could there be?

"What will become of me?" Eleanor moaned. "When people hear . . . And what of the Cliffords? Surely the archbishop will demand justice?"

Kate was relieved by the practical questions, ones she could answer. "His Grace is a reasonable man. He convinced me that it is in my best interest, and yours, that we allow the healing to begin. We have revised the story to make Griffin a solitary predator. Sir Elric and Dean Richard have agreed to it. Griffin preyed on you, a wealthy widow, doing his best to damage your reputation so that you would be dependent on him, and then he would slowly relieve you of your wealth. Your faithful servants saw through his scheme and fought to defend you, but Griffin was more than a match for them. The dean and the archbishop have seen to his punishment."

Her mother's eyes shone with tears. "I—Bless you. Bless you all. But how will people hear of this?"

"I will see to that." Eleanor winced as if Kate had slapped her. Her tone had been sharper than she had intended. "I speak of healing, but there is still the gold. If you are determined to keep it—"

"Not for selfish ends. I want to use the blood money to help others."

"The Martha House."

Eleanor nodded. "If any Clifford—or Roos—believes they deserve that money, that it should feed their greed, I will fight them."

"*We* will outwit them."

"We? You and I, Daughter?" Eleanor looked wary. "How?"

Kate did not feel inclined to tell her mother of her deal with Elric. "We will speak another time. Do nothing until we speak, eh? Will you promise me that?" Kate held her mother's gaze.

"I do." A slight flicker, there and gone again.

Kate placed the pouch of gold in her mother's hands. "Hide this well." Rising, she thanked Eleanor for finally telling her all she wished to know.

As Kate was closing the door, her mother whispered, "'The fall is so deep, she is so rightly fallen, that the soul cannot fill herself from such an abyss.'" Kate must have made a sound. Eleanor looked up at her. "Marguerite Porete. She knew the pain of losing one's way."

Kate shook her head. "Fallen? No. You tripped, Mother, and already you are back on your feet."

18

PEACE?

—⚬⚭⚬—

Throughout the following week, Kate called on the clients of her guest-house. Those who had appointments that week saw her there, others received invitations to dine, after which a stroll in Thomas Holme's gardens provided the necessary privacy for a confidential discussion. Each was told the sad tale of her mother's betrayal by her late husband's trusted retainer. When they balked, as some astute observers did, Kate reminded them of the delicacy of their business relationship. All went away agreeing to spread the tale. Indeed, by week's end, Jennet reported hearing it throughout the city.

Kate's cousin William Frost was by far the most difficult one to convince. "Isabella will never believe it."

"Why? Because the tales she has concocted are so much more satisfying to her and her fellow gossips?"

"Katherine!"

But he agreed in the end, for he owed her a great debt. In winter, his lapse in judgment had threatened a scandal that would have ruined her, sneaking a man into her guesthouse, where he was murdered. The very man who'd carried the letters the Earl of Westmoreland was desperate to recover.

"This will go some way to redeeming your debt," Kate assured him.

"I should think we are even now."

"No, I do not consider us even."

Though she wondered. There was talk he had already received assurances of being called to Duke Henry's first Parliament. Perhaps she would be wise to make peace with him.

At least she could hold out an olive branch. His daughter, his only child, was most precious to him. "If you wish, Sister Brigida can bring Marie and Petra to your home tomorrow, resuming lessons with Hazel."

A small smile. "Bless you. Hazel has missed the lessons."

"And see to it that Severen is removed from the night watch."

"Severen?"

"See to it."

-⦿-

On a gray, airless morning a fortnight after her return from Bishopthorpe, Kate walked with Lille and Ghent in the river gardens, considering a request from a potential new guesthouse client. A widow who wished to entertain a distant relative who regularly traveled to York for guild meetings. Kate had set Jennet to finding out more about this relative, his contacts, his kinship ties, his marital situation. So far he seemed unlikely to cause trouble, but she wanted more information.

Uneven footsteps on the path above her warned her of company a heartbeat before Lille turned her head and gave a little bark, a greeting. Ghent wagged his tail.

"So this is where you come to hide from me," said Eleanor, slightly out of breath. To Kate's knowledge, this was her mother's first venture down through the gardens to the river.

"I have been next door all along, Mother. Hardly hiding."

"You said we would talk."

"I wanted to be sure of some things before we spoke again."

"I am your mother, Katherine, not a business acquaintance with whom you set appointments."

"Ah. But it is a business proposition I wish to discuss."

"Oh?" Eleanor fanned herself with a scented cloth, her face flushed.

"Come, let us sit over here and talk." Kate led her mother to a bench between two apple trees.

Before Eleanor sat down, she wiped the wooden seat with her cloth.

"Thomas Holme's gardeners clean the seats each morning, Mother."

"Never trust a man to clean anything with care."

Kate settled on one end of the bench, Lille and Ghent coming over to sniff her hands, then loping off to gambol near the riverbank.

After one final wipe, Eleanor perched beside her. "So? What is your proposal?"

"Instead of the house on Hertergate, lease mine for your Martha House."

"The one in which you are living?"

"Not for long. The sisters might use the small house that fronts it on Castlegate as workrooms, perhaps even a small school. And you would not be tarnishing your wealth by giving it to Lionel Neville."

A long silence. "It is a generous offer, Katherine. But what of you?"

"I have a house on Petergate."

"Is there sufficient room for your household?"

Kate did not explain that she did not speak of the one beside the guest-house. She had not yet told her mother of the dean's gift. "That was what I was making sure of. We will be quite comfortable."

"And far from me."

Kate gave a little laugh. "I confess there is a certain appeal to that. But I will also be closer to Phillip and the guesthouse, and the Castlegate house will afford me additional income."

"You will charge me good money for the lease, no doubt."

"Of course I will. But you will have the satisfaction of helping ensure good futures for your granddaughter and Marie and Phillip."

A chuckle. "You are clever."

"So are you, Mother. So. What say you?"

Eleanor reached for Kate's hand. "How could I refuse? Thank you."

"I know I am not who you hoped I'd be, Mother. I never will be. Could not be. But I am satisfied with the life I have carved out here."

"We are perhaps both of us better off at the moment not complicating our lives with husbands. Though Sir Elric has behaved most honorably."

"Yes, he has."

"Nan tells me that his men called on you. Did he send a message?"

"They came to tell me of Kevin. He will likely remain in the abbey infirmary for a while yet. He is healing slowly." They had also come for the letters. She had put them off for a few days—she was having them, including their seals, copied at the Franciscan friary, in case she should ever need to protect herself against the Earl of Westmoreland. Her mother's confessor was proving useful, and resourceful.

"We will pray for Kevin."

"Berend will tell him—he visits him quite often."

"Berend has been so quiet . . ." Eleanor glanced at Kate.

"Yes, he has." He had not sought out her company since Bishopthorpe. Always busy, or too exhausted to stay up and talk. Kate missed him.

"Berend—you care deeply for him . . ." Eleanor said, then shook her head. "Forgive me. It is not my place."

"No, it is not, Mother."

A moment of silence. "I am sorry Simon Neville turned out to be a fraud. I did not know."

"Simon. He could not be farther from my mind at this moment. I am not sorry I married him. He loved me, in his way. Set me up in business, in a fashion. And he gave me Marie and Phillip."

"But they are not yours."

"No matter. I love them fiercely. As I do Petra. And you." Kate patted her mother's hand.

Eleanor shook her head. "You are such a mystery to me."

They sat quietly for a while, until Lille and Ghent came trotting up the path and settled at Kate's feet.

"Did Sir Elric's men say whether Westmoreland has remained at Raby?" asked Eleanor.

"He has not. He is with Duke Henry."

"Ah. There are rumors King Richard has returned from Ireland. That he is somewhere in Wales?"

"I have heard them as well. And that his uncle the Duke of York is unable to be of much use—unable or unwilling, depending on the rumor." Most of his army had fled to the duke's side.

"By Christmas we may know more than rumors," Eleanor said.

Kate thought it might be much sooner.

A rustle of silk as Eleanor turned to Kate. "Will I ever see you once you are established in Petergate?"

"I will be your landlord. And Lille and Ghent love this garden."

"Good," Eleanor said softly. "When will we shift houses?"

"The week before Michaelmas? Would that suit? Your lease with Lionel would need to be renewed then, am I right?"

"You have seen a copy of the deed?"

"I have."

"Cunning. You are cunning." Eleanor rose, smoothing her silk skirt, her silk veil. "That will suit me very well." She bent forward to pet Lille and Ghent, her movement stiff.

Her age—Kate so easily forgot how much life her mother had seen. How much she might learn from her.

Straightening, Eleanor touched Kate's cheek. "I am moved by your faith in the good my sisters and I will do in York. Bless you, Daughter."

Faith had no part in her offer. Kate simply hoped the sisters continued to be a calming influence on her mother, and that the Martha House kept her too busy to seek out more troublesome schemes.

"Time to head for home." Kate rose and proffered her mother her arm. "It is quite a climb back up to Castlegate."

Eleanor gazed up, up. "Mother in heaven, so it is."

AUTHOR'S NOTE

—◦◦◦—

Had someone in the editorial department of *The Economist* corrected an error in a headline back in 2013, I might never had created the character Eleanor Clifford. I read "the world's last Beguine" headlining the obituary of Marcella Pattyn and wondered.* My question led me to historian Jennifer Kolpacoff Deane, who has researched and written about medieval religious movements and is presently writing a book about the beguines.** As it turns out, Marcella might have been the last beguine living in *Belgium*, but she was not the last beguine: in Germany the movement has enjoyed a revival in this century.***

But the article rekindled my interest in the beguines. Who were they? They were part of a lay religious women's movement that swept medieval Europe between the thirteenth and sixteenth centuries. It created an

---

* April 27, 2013.

** Working title, *Sisters Among: Beguines and Lay Religious Women's Communities in Medieval Germany*; also by JK Deane, *A History of Medieval Heresy and Inquisition* (Rowman and Littlefield 2011), and "Pious Domesticities," in *The Oxford Handbook of Women and Gender in Medieval Europe* (OUP 2013, chapter 17).

*** Cornelia Schäfer, "Sisterhoods Make a Comeback in Germany," *Deutsche Welle*, DW.com, September 22, 2005.

opportunity for women to lead lives dedicated to spiritual practice while still remaining in their lay communities. For some it was an alternative to marriage; for others it was a chance to test whether they truly had a vocation or were simply not yet ready to wed—the beguines took no formal vows and were free to leave; for many it was the only affordable entrance into a religious community, as established orders required a dowry.

Though many people associate them with the Low Countries, hundreds of beguine-like gatherings independently cropped up across what is today France, Germany, Italy, England, Sweden, the Czech Republic, and Spain. As Jennifer wrote for my blog: ". . . beguines were single women of any life stage enacting visibly pious and chaste lives of Christian service and community; they took simple oaths of chastity and obedience, lived according to a specific but local house rule, and were under the supervision of a house mother, elder sisters in the community, and an array of parish and civic authorities; and finally, beguines received charitable donations in exchange for prayers, memorial services, and other caritative services."

In York there are records of houses of poor sisters, often *maison dieux* (hospitals), but it's not clear which were beguine communities—they went by many names throughout Europe—and which were much more closely associated with the major religious orders, often referred to as third orders, or tertiaries, whose rules might be stricter. I use that tension between more traditional orders and beguines in this book.

The sisters and their devotion are a rich example of the medieval mind. It was a quietly private piety, available to those women who had no dowry to offer to a convent in an established religious order. In the early years of the movement, women might remain at home; but the Church in Rome distrusted any group or spiritual teacher who might encourage people to commune with God without the middleman, i.e., a priest, and it was increasingly alarmed by the lay religious movements. After the thirteenth century the Church required beguines to be part of a community, a house of such women headed by a woman of good repute and guided by a male cleric. Hence Eleanor's search for a cleric to serve as guiding teacher and confessor for her Martha House.

Women mystics were another source of discomfort for the Church. Marguerite Porete, mentioned in this book, was tried and condemned by the Church in Paris in the early 14th century, and burned at the stake. According to her inquisitors, in her book *The Mirror of Simple Souls* Marguerite claimed that a soul could become one with God, and that in such a state a person might ignore all the moral rules and sacraments of the Church and do what she pleased. But that was not her message. What she *actually* said was that in such state a person would wish to do only good. Perhaps her two greatest sins in their eyes were that she was a woman who deigned to teach through her writing, and that she refused to retract her work. Her writings inspired another great mystic of the period whom I mention in the book, Meister Eckhart, a Dominican who was also eventually condemned as a heretic. You may not have heard of Marguerite, but it's quite likely you've heard of Meister Eckhart, who is widely respected today.

Despite the Church, the beguine movement, with its message of a life of the spirit combined with charitable work in the community, prevailed.

For the situation in and around York as Henry of Lancaster returned from exile, I depended on the work of Douglas Biggs and Chris Given-Wilson.[*] I found the role of Edmund of Langley, Duke of York, of particular interest. He was custodian of the realm while his nephew King Richard II was on campaign in Ireland, but Henry of Lancaster was also his nephew. From itineraries, calendars, rolls, and other official government and household records, Douglas Biggs gleaned sufficient detail for the reader to observe Edmund's gradual shift from fully supporting King Richard to backing Duke Henry in his rebellion. Edmund went about his duties through the end of June as if unaware that his nephew Henry was planning to return to England to claim his inheritance. And then Lancastrian Sir John Pelham seized Pevensey Castle and held it for Duke Henry. Edmund moved quickly to ensure that Pelham would be contained within the county of Kent, unable to spread the insurrection. Practically, in point of fact,

---

[*] Douglas Biggs, *Three Armies in Britain: the Irish Campaign of Richard II and the Usurpation of Henry IV, 1397-99* (Brill 2006); Chris Given-Wilson, *Henry IV* (Yale 2016).

Edmund was hobbled by King Richard's Irish campaign. The king had taken the most effective and experienced military personnel with him, and much of the available transport such as horses and wagons. And Edmund soon discovered that Pelham's seizure of Pevensey Castle was but the tip of the iceberg—he soon discovered that most of John of Gaunt's estates and more important castles were being held by Lancastrian retainers for Duke Henry. This was the situation when Edmund ordered the city of York to hold against Henry. He'd managed to secure a strategic line of castles in the southeast, and was ready to move north to St. Alban's. Messengers were sent to the king in Ireland to alert him to the situation so that he might return to defend his crown.

At St. Albans, Edmund, Duke of York, proclaimed that he had no desire to hinder Henry's efforts to reclaim his inheritance. Still, he and the council were mustering an army to ride west and join up with the king on his return from Ireland. Henry, now claiming his inheritance as Duke of Lancaster, was also riding west, with a rapidly growing army. The most powerful northern nobles joined him. By the time Henry reached Pontefract Castle, he was making promises to his supporters that made it clear he now set his sights even higher, on claiming the throne.

Whether it was rumors of the Duke of York's confusing partial support of Duke Henry or the news of so many barons joining him, we can never know. But soldiers paid by Edmund, Duke of York, began to desert and hie to Henry's camp. Once it was clear he was heading west, not south to York, the soldiers mustered in preparation for a siege began to leave; it appears that most of them joined Henry.

And a group of York merchants that included William Frost and Thomas Holme, seeing which way the wind blew, sent a messenger to Duke Henry offering monetary support. The duke was promising to end royal taxation, and the merchants liked the sound of that. King Richard had leaned heavily on them for loans which they knew would never be repaid, and they hoped for better treatment from his cousin.

Time would tell.

ACKNOWLEDGMENTS

———◦⟨∞⟩◦———

My books would not be possible without the generosity of historians working in the field. Special thanks to Jennifer Kolpacoff Deane and Tanya Stabler Miller, whose work on the beguine movement sparked my imagination, to Susan Signe Morrison for a small detail about beguines that inspired a plot point, and to Louise Hampson for help in sorting out locations in medieval York.

I am grateful to Laura Hodges, Joyce Gibb, Mary Morse, Chris Nickson, my agent Jennifer Weltz, and my editor Maia Larson for reading the manuscript and offering insightful comments and suggestions; and to my husband, Charlie, for creating a coherent family tree out of what looked like the web of a psychotic spider, for designing and updating the maps of York, for figuring out what was unclear in a troublesome scene, and, most of all, for being there for me no matter what.